THREE MEANT TO BE

THREE MEANT TO BE

BRANCHES *of* PAST *and* FUTURE

BOOK ONE

MN BENNET

Copyright © 2023 MN Bennet

All rights reserved. No part of this book may be reproduced or transmitted in any form or by any means, electronic or mechanical, including photocopying, recording, or by an information storage and retrieval system - except by a reviewer who may quote brief passages in a review to be printed in a magazine or newspaper - without permission in writing from the publisher.

Names, characters, businesses, places, events, and incidents are either products of the author's imagination or used in a fictitious manner. Any resemblances to actual persons, living or dead, or actual events is purely coincidental.

Paperback ISBN: 979-8-9872532-3-6
Ebook ISBN: 979-8-9872532-2-9

Edited by Charlie Knight (CKnightWrites.com)
Cover art by Miblart (miblart.com)

www.mnbennet.com/

Dedication

To my mom, who has supported me on every path I've followed.

To Bev, who tricked me into thinking I'd be a good teacher. I'll always cherish our walks and the insightful conversations.

Author's Note

READERS BE ADVISED

Thank you so much for considering Three Meant To Be. I've included a list of content warnings on the following page for those interested. I absolutely love Dorian's journey and think there is so much humor and joy in this story; however, there is grief and pain in his beautiful growth.

There is also fun in this story, especially with the teenage students and all the wild, humorous banter they add to the novel. It's important to remember, though, that this is an adult novel with adult themes. Many of the notes below are in reference to adult characters but is not limited to them.

This book contains the following elements:

Foul language
Smoking and alcohol use
Blood and violence
Scenes of graphic sex between adults
Character deaths (off page)
Strong themes of grief and guilt
Depression, anxiety, and self-hatred (both mild and overwhelming)
Mental and physical assault
Bullying
Mild torture

I believe in HEA and HFN in all my works, something I strive to bring no matter how long winding the journey is. I hope you'll enjoy Dorian's story as much as I did.

REJUVENATION
PRIMAL
PSYCHIC
HEX
ENCHANTMENT
AUGMENTATION
BESTIAL
COSMIC
ENTROPY
ALTERATION
ARCANE
TELEKINESIS
SENSORY
BANISHMENT
LEVITATION

Chapter One

I sank into the stiff auditorium seat, wishing I had a few more days of summer vacation since I'd wasted too much time off floundering about instead of preparing for the school year. It was obvious the administration hadn't used their summers productively either. Our admin team fumbled with setting up the projector, computer, sound system, and whatever else they'd waited until the last minute to arrange. Massaging my temples helped silence the pressing inner thoughts of staff members but didn't remove the growing headache as they babbled on about their summers aloud.

Oh, joy. They were all thrilled to be back in the building. I seconded that mentality only because when summer hit and I lacked a rigorous schedule, I lost all momentum and often slipped into distracting habits. That said, I couldn't muster an ounce of enthusiasm for the week of professional learning they'd planned for us before the first day of classes.

The fact that admin remained tightlipped on the agenda meant one of two things. First, and highly likely, they were still figuring out the new state laws which affected the curriculum of magic at our academy. In which case, this entire week would be dedicated to teachers breaking into groups so we could brainstorm 'fun and inventive' ideas that tied into the academy motto or some shit. I groaned at the thought. The second—and quite possibly worse outcome—was they'd understood the new measures and created their own plan. A plan they knew we'd despise, so their hope was to unload it on us at the last minute, leaving us too stunned and ill-prepared to protest. I clenched my teeth, annoyed and justifiably curious. Fixating on the stage and administrators, I carefully peered into their surface thoughts.

"It's not that one. Come on. What does this thing plug into?"

For Christ's sake, they were more unprepared than our students. Well, some of our students. Nothing about the agenda bubbled along their surface thoughts as each one of them was wrapped up in the moment of fixing the technical issues.

I took a deep breath, channeling my magic, and inched further into the administrators' minds. Tiptoeing around memories, inner thoughts, and the psyche, careful not to disturb anything or leave a trail. Diving deep into minds wasn't my favorite thing in the world, but it was my magic, so taking advantage allowed me to avoid my least favorite thing—surprises.

A hand slapped my shoulder. The jolt reeled my attention back. Chanelle stood in the aisle next to my row, hand on her hip and eyes locked on the seat next to mine.

"You look like you're in a mood, Dorian."

I'd intentionally sat further back to avoid others, intentionally taken the edge seat, and intentionally spread my legs out so my knees grazed the empty back of the seat in front of me. Chanelle pushed her way past my outstretched legs, not allowing my posture to deter her. Her bag swatted my face. So annoying.

"Just thinking how much I could get done this week if they actually allowed us to work in our rooms," I sighed.

"Oh, come on." Chanelle leaned close, her fruity fragrance overpowering the stale cigarettes in my jacket pocket. "You're going to spend all year alone on that island, might as well make the most of this week."

That was what teaching was—isolated in your room on an island with children and little time to breathe until the end of the day. Well, metaphorical island. The classroom really was its own world most days. Kids were annoying, but honestly, adults were equally irritating without the excuse of being young.

I could also be making calls or sending emails to guilds I'd reached out to over the summer, which I should've fully confirmed before the first day of classes. I'd rather do something beneficial with this PL training time to ensure my upcoming third-years had their internships lined up. If I left it in the hands of some of my homeroom coven, they'd end up applying to second-rate guilds because they slacked on deadlines or did shitty research. Not that I cared what my homeroom coven chose after leaving the academy, but I'd make certain they landed with the most compatible witches to fine-tune their last year of magical training.

Admin huddled, whispering at the front of the auditorium near the podium. Wasting more time. I checked my phone, ignoring the texts from a certain someone I'd semi-avoided since the end of summer because I'd already spent too much of it rolling in bed with him.

Milo.

I couldn't tell which annoyed me more, the fact we were easily fifteen minutes behind schedule or how my heart thumped with excitement from each buzz of my phone. Milo had that nauseating effect. I didn't want to want him, didn't want him to care about me, yet even our most casual encounters sent euphoric waves of memories and feelings and sensations I never could fully quit. No matter how much I needed to, for his sake more than mine. But he did paint a lovely picture. Always did when thinking about the future. Mine. His. Everyone else's.

Dammit. Milo's effervescent enthusiasm had a way of rooting its way deep into my hollow heart. Even miles away, unable to feel his mind, his thoughts, his delight, I still had these ridiculous blossoming ideas.

> Milo: How's day 1 treating you? Lots of learning about learning? Maybe you can tell me all about those 100% useful not at all a waste of time trainings after work?! ☺

"Geez, I could've had another smoke break at this rate," I said, switching my phone to silent because I refused to allow my mind to wander elsewhere.

"You should quit smoking. It's bad for you."

I kept my gaze fixed on the admin team making their final preparations but felt Chanelle's side-eyed glare and heard the bubbling thoughts.

"*And others, and the environment, and baby seals, and...*"

"Aren't they part of the environment so it's basically the same thing?" I asked with a yawn so she'd know I'd eavesdropped.

"**Dorian.**"

I cringed at Chanelle's thought. People screaming their thoughts was the worst kind of piercing pain. Like nails along a chalkboard scraping the inside of my skull and rattling my ribcage.

"Save the PSA." I stretched, arching to crack my back in the stiff seat.

"Fine. I'll save the PSA and replace it with curiosity." Chanelle sat forward, arm pressed to the back of the seat in front of us, invading my space.

Great. I should've stuck with the lecture.

"What'd you do this summer?" She was the most invasive woman I knew, which I enjoyed, but I glared nonetheless to feign annoyance. Another thing I enjoyed. Life was easy when you could read people's intentions, but I preferred they knew nothing of mine. "You spent the entire time dodging me."

I shrugged.

"What'd you do? What'd you do? What'd you—you realize I can do this all day?"

I blinked, unwilling to let her know I'd dipped into her surface thoughts. Honestly, the thoughts that bubbled to the top of someone's mind were the most difficult to quell. It took extreme focus to keep others out of my head, which years of experience had helped with. Unfortunately, the more time I spent with someone, the more I understood them, the easier their minds attached to my magic, like pairing two wireless devices. So irritating.

"Meet a new guy? Have blissful, mind-blowing sex? Experiment with drugs and orgies?"

I snorted. "Christ, seriously?"

"Well?" She leaned closer, the sleeve of her bright yellow dress slipping lower and exposing the brown skin of her bare shoulder. "You're such a closed book, and I'm an avid reader."

She batted her eyes as if that'd somehow work. No. It was a distraction. I ground my teeth as she screamed my name internally on a loop.

"Fine," I said, burying her thoughts with a calming breath. "I worked on a few house projects, watched television, and read. Oh, and listened to one cat complain that I didn't spend enough time with him because of renovating, while my other cat simultaneously complained I spent too much time at home. They're both exhausting."

"Wait. Your cats?" Chanelle raised a thin brow. "I thought only witches with certain bestial magic could communicate with animals. See, this is what I mean. A closed frickin book. If I knew I had a telepathic pet whisperer, I would've made you tell me why my dogs are—"

"We don't communicate," I interjected because she had the look of someone about to go on a tangent. I closed my eyes, rubbing the edges to wash away the stirring headache. "Per se. It's more that I've mastered their expressions and the tones of their meows."

"Oh. That's nothing special." Chanelle leaned back, waving a dismissive hand. "You're just another cat lady."

"You say that like it's a bad thing."

Breathy static hit the mic, silencing Chanelle before her opportunity to comment, and I stifled my magic so she couldn't send the message my way.

"Welcome back, everyone," Evans said with anxious enthusiasm.

Not sure anyone could see the trepidation in her light brown eyes, but it radiated this way in waves. That wasn't my magic at work, just an acute understanding of expressions after thousands of registered thoughts over the years. The crease in her forehead, the slightest tremble in her dimpled cheeks, and the shaky but firmly trained stance.

Ah, great. We were definitely getting bad news.

Evans looked a moment away from hurling the guilt that consumed her.

"I hope everyone had a wonderful summer. I know many of you followed the new mandates Illinois issued on casting proficiency." Evans chuckled into the mic, causing an erratic and nervous boom throughout the auditorium, almost as annoying as the bubbling thoughts of concern. "I did read your emails but wanted to wait until we were all here as a group to address the changes."

I liked that the academy hired someone with so many inclusive ideas about expanding the number of kids properly licensed in casting before graduation. The fact that the state finally agreed with this seemed too ideal. The mandate in question allowed all students across the state access to licensing before graduation, with a goal of eighty percent proficiency. Pursuing magic had always been a luxury, never a core at the curriculum level in high schools. More like a bonus class for kids with the drive and the privilege, which was why I taught at an academy, hoping to prepare as many children as possible for the rest of their lives whether they pursued a career in casting or simply had the fundamentals in their back pocket for whatever path they chose.

"This ten-year plan will affect how most of the academies are run," Evans said.

I scoffed. When in the history of education had a ten-year plan lasted more than five years?

"But before we jump into business, how about some shoutouts?" Evans pressed a button on her laptop, brightening the screen behind her with the first slide on today's agenda. Then she clapped her hands together like some eager child.

> Staff Summer Success Shoutouts!

The only thing worse than unnecessary professional learning was unwanted team-building exercises. If I wanted to know these people better, I'd jump into their minds and learn exactly how much more annoying they were.

Evans strolled to the edge of the stage, passing the mic to our headmaster, who shared a story on her flowers or vegetable garden or something I effectively tuned out.

"I wish she'd just get this over with." I dropped further into my seat and raised my knees to block my view of Evans, the headmaster, and the screen on stage.

"Get what over with?" Chanelle asked.

"Screwing us. Whatever they've sat on all summer is obviously going to greatly affect magic academies, so I wish she'd just bend us over already and be done with it."

"Hmm. No, thanks. I like a little sweet talking first. Are you telling me you really prefer just having it rammed in?" Chanelle winked, twirling a finger in my direction, which cast a slight telekinetic burst to brush my long brown bangs out of my face. With precision and a delicate touch, she swept the hairs behind my ears.

"With metaphorical screwing, absolutely." I shook my head, undoing her magical efforts and covering my eyes. Hiding behind my hair was a preference, a tiny distancing tool like many others I'd mastered.

"Sounds like some amazing summers." Evans's heels clicked along the hardwood floor of the stage as she positioned herself back at the podium with her computer. "Moving forward into this year, we're planning on making some significant changes to the scheduling here at Gemini Academy. We've been afforded the opportunity to increase our roster thanks to some wonderful funding from the state. Since the academies in Chicago have better success rates with producing licensed witches, we'll be doing our part to help decrease this generation's rate of active warlocks."

Warlocks. Such an absurd term. It suggested they were somehow different from the rest of the witches in America, but they weren't. Well, there was one distinct difference. We were all witches born with the capability of casting magic. Many elected not to train their abilities in favor of living their daily lives without it.

Elected. Okay. They came to the realization that licensing was overpriced and selective, and a career in magic was highly competitive, so why bother paying all those fees when you couldn't cast for a living? Yeah, that sounded accurate. Every single person in the world had magic to some degree, but so few had the finances or privilege to freely cast it.

Warlocks were nothing more than factions of witches who opposed government oversight. They used their magic without proper licenses, ignoring laws and endangering others and themselves by recklessly casting. Couldn't say I agreed with their tactics, but the fact so many were detained and labeled a warlock for simply utilizing their magic without proper permission left an unsavory taste in my mouth. The public's too. Hence the new strategy of ensuring every young person had the opportunity and access. Great in theory, but I was certain the politicians dictating our curriculum would find new and more profound ways to fuck it up.

"We're still working on finalizing some schedules, which is why we've held off on releasing them." Surface thoughts of rage festered in the audience, and based on the swelling dread inside Evans, even from the back of the auditorium, I knew every teacher shot her daggers. "Many academies within the state have optioned to utilize the new voucher system in place, which will increase our student body this year and years moving forward. Our first-years at Gemini will eclipse our second and third-years twice over."

I raised a hand, one Evans ignored as she continued her rehearsed speech. *If the first-years are going to increase that much, what does that mean for class sizes and homeroom covens?* The question popped into everyone's head.

I stood up, clearing my throat. "Are we merging homeroom covens?" I asked, unconcerned with how large my actual class sizes became. I could handle those, but homeroom covens were specifically designed to have twelve students—an old lore to the effect that twelve represented a full coven. But in today's modern society at the academies, it allowed us to develop deeper relationships with the students, follow them all three years at the academy, and make certain they were given the best training and attention we could provide.

If they planned on merging covens, making them larger, I could lose a few of my students in the shuffle. I glared, imagining some of the half-assed instructors who wouldn't know the first thing to do with the more complex magics my kids possessed.

"Homeroom covens will remain the same in size, as it's fundamental to ensure each of our students receive that one-on-one time with instructors. It's part of why the state reached out to so many academies. Unlike public schools, we have more flexibility in scheduling and can cap our roster size at a particular number."

I wanted to release a sigh of relief, yet the festering blocked thoughts from Evans gave me pause.

"But?" I balled my fists.

"Those teaching third-year homeroom covens will be returning to the first-years instead of following along for the final year." Her face scrunched as she forced the words out with a tight smile. "It was a discussion many admin teams throughout the state had with each other over the summer since third-year homeroom instructors are mostly a check-in during that last year."

"We're more than a check-in." By their third year, we'd followed these kids for two years, working closely with them to understand their control of magic and which avenues they should pursue for internships, all to prepare them for the real world. Many of them needed that final year of encouragement and assistance to find the right path. "And even if we were just checking in with them, how are they supposed to be evaluated without a homeroom instructor?"

"They'll still have an evaluation. Third-year covens spend the majority of their time at internships. Honestly, they only utilize their homeroom for check-ins and evaluations. For them, this is a dry run in the real world."

Yes, a dry run where we still held their hand and walked them through the process. One where, if they fell flat on their face, which so many of them did, we'd be there to pick them up, dust them off, and push them forward.

Rage seethed out of me. If I weren't the only telepath on campus, the palpable fury fuming from me would bombard another psychic.

"You can't seriously expect them to handle their final year independently? They still need—" I gritted my teeth. *Us.*

"Given their off-campus schedules, it's necessary we prioritize staff where they're most needed. We admin will be relieving you of the burden of handling third-year evaluations. We'll handle that while instructors rotate with first- and second-year homeroom covens. This plan will help ensure the state of Illinois reaches the projected proficiency rate."

Evans said it like they'd done those of us with third-year covens some grand favor right after slapping us in the face by saying our last year was too easy, so why not burden us by changing our schedules at the last possible minute?

"This sucks," I muttered, plopping into my chair.

"You said it," Chanelle whispered. "Third-year homerooms are such a cakewalk. I am not mentally prepared for first-years. Ugh. So many lesson plans I'm going to have to change."

So much wasted preparation during the summer. What a drag.

My leg bounced furiously. Now, I really needed a fucking cigarette.

Chapter Two

I exhaled smoke that blended with the cloudy gray sky. After a full day of professional learning meetings to assist teaching staff in the social and emotional well-being of our incoming students, I slipped out early, skipping the closing discussion on shoutouts to successes we'd had during our collaborative brainstorming and the building blocks of strengthening our academy. Such a wasted effort to pat each other on the back for doing a training we didn't need because we actually spent time in the classroom every day. Besides, these trainings were designed by folks who'd never taught a second of their lives.

    Damp air created a thick wall of humidity, choking me as I walked to my car. I checked my phone, finding twelve unread messages. I'd used the excuse of work to dodge Milo's texts all day. I scrolled to the most recent.

> Milo: The gloomy doomy weather got me thinking about you. XD

I huffed. Was that his idea of flirting? Insufferable. I left the message on read and stuffed the phone back into my pocket.

Cheery thoughts blossomed inside me. My palms turned clammy. The last time I'd spent with Milo swirled in my head, making my face heat and skin tingle. Did I miss him? This sensation and longing for someone was something I usually did a better job of burying.

The way Milo full-heartedly believed I could find happiness again gave me anxiety because I knew all too well I deserved nothing—especially not his devotion.

Still, the joy festering inside me didn't fit with my other mixed emotions. Like shoving a jigsaw puzzle piece into the wrong spot. The wrong picture. I took a deep inhale from my cigarette, ignoring the internal itch.

This wasn't my excitement. I clenched my jaw. Someone else's overjoyed happiness for the impending rain crept into my mind because I'd let my magic wander.

Chanelle. She shuffled along behind me, calling my name out loud and thinking it even louder. I kept moving, hopeful of reaching my car before she caught up.

She looped her arm around mine, interlocking them and tugging me closer as she walked alongside me. I narrowed my eyes, rubbing the back of my neck with my free hand to lessen the growing tension. I should've grabbed my cigarette, which now remained trapped in the hand of the arm she'd locked in hers.

Seriously? She was enjoyable in small doses, but I'd had my fill by the end of our morning meeting. I blew smoke in her direction.

"You know the policy, Mr. Frost. No smoking on campus." She used her free arm to wave the smoke away with a slight telekinetic burst, sending slender gray waves cascading across the parking lot. Then she slipped her fingers above mine, pinching the filter, and snatching it away in one quick motion. It lingered between her index and middle finger momentarily.

A glint of her college years rolled out because of our physical contact. Thoughts came as words when the person was distant. Images when touching. Memories when delving deep. A party with cocktails and laughter and the taste of tobacco on her lips. She danced on a bar. Cat called anyone and everyone. Kissed them all, too. It was a feeling she buried most days—the cigarettes, not the kisses. This overlooked desire struck her in the moment, sparking a wave of secret yearning. Hesitantly, she dropped the cigarette to the ground and snuffed out the glimmering ember with the tip of her heel.

I sighed, defeated. Not a second of peace between her and Milo.

"Please release me." I tugged loose from her grasp and adjusted my rumpled sleeve.

"You know, a few of us are going out tonight." Chanelle tightened her grip on my nearly freed arm.

I resisted the tremble of fright that came from too much contact, the desire to push her off, and tried to convey with a disapproving expression that I wanted her to let go. It didn't work.

"I have plans."

"Do you?" Her grip didn't relent. "What if I said it's a very select group?"

Breaking loose would involve a more hostile tactic. I paused, taking a deep breath, quelling her mind and her whispering childhood. Fuck, I hated touching people.

"Let me guess. A bunch of teachers with third-year covens pissed for being blindsided?"

"Oh my God, you mind reader, you." Chanelle winked, then released my arm. "Come on. Join us to vent."

"I didn't read your mind, and I don't need to vent," I said, walking to my car. "Besides, I told you, I have plans. Important unchangeable plans. Ones that can in no way be altered. If I'd known about this earlier, I could've considered, but unfortunately..."

My phone buzzed. Milo, undoubtedly.

"Unfortunately? Is that it?" Chanelle stood with crossed arms of judgment.

I couldn't stand her sometimes.

"Unfortunately, nothing. I have stuff, things." I reached for my phone. "Leave me alone."

Sliding into my car, I gulped, checking Milo's next intolerable text.

> Milo: So, you don't wanna text. We can talk in person. I'm actually wrapping up a case near your place.

My heart thumped. Liar. There was no way an enchanter of his caliber had work in my neighborhood.

> Milo: Care if I pop over and say howdy?
>
> Not sure if it's a romcom move or stalkerish
> Is it *still* a surprise if I text you? lol

Nope, nope, nope.

If he was heading to my house, that meant he wanted to talk, have an adult conversation, which theoretically, I could handle.

I ran my hands through my hair. The problem was, after over twenty years of skimming Milo's thoughts, his intentions, his everything, I should've been better at predicting his little not-so-romantic gestures. I could always dodge conversation by redirecting our interests to something more sensual, which was how I skirted around discussions best left unsaid when he hung out over the summer. Milo was lovely in that way, always ready to talk, willing to listen, insufferably considerate, and patiently waiting for when I was ready.

I found it impossible to avoid Milo during the summer. I had too much time on my hands, and he was a beautiful distraction. But if I went home right now and saw Milo, I'd lose myself in him, in my longing, my desires, and all the wonderful memories that stirred inside him. And with those memories came…someone who meant so much to us both, someone who cared so deeply for us, someone who deserved better than—

No.

I squeezed my steering wheel tightly, keeping the past locked away. One look at Milo and our entire history would flood my mind, leaving me paralyzed with guilt. It wasn't the summer anymore, where I could lie in bed all day dwelling on Finn's death and how I'd failed him. I needed to be functional for work, for these new mandates, and a roster of a bunch of untrained, likely incompetent first-year witches.

I leaned out of my driver's window, taking advantage of the uneasy out that'd already presented itself. "Where exactly are you guys heading tonight?"

Chanelle clapped like an obnoxious seal. Suddenly, smoking didn't feel all that terrible.

"Do you want me to drive?"

"No," I said, slinking back into my car. "Clearly, I'm capable of following."

She shrugged, then stepped into her vehicle and whipped out of the parking lot. It took some effort, but I managed to follow her wild lane shifts and swift turns.

An easy twenty-minute drive outside my comfort zone, and we'd arrived at a bar. Correction—we'd arrived at an overpriced parking garage on a busy strip with too many bars.

Such a mistake.

I walked down the sidewalk, reaching Chanelle, who gripped my arm and dragged me inside. She was so touchy. All the time!

"The biggest complaint I have for admin is how mentally unprepared I am for the lack of maturity from first-years." She strolled quickly, guiding us through the crowded sidewalk. "Honestly, there's such a difference between fifteen-year-olds and seventeen- and eighteen-year-olds."

Thankfully, the small bar was mostly dead. They'd propped the backdoor open with a bucket filled with dirt and cigarette butts. Stale smoke wafted inside, a comforting sensation reminiscent of the South Side.

"Drinks?" Chanelle asked like I had a say as she raced off before I responded.

"Nothing with gin," I shouted, scanning for other teachers.

No one noticeable popped out. Were we early? I could properly examine the area, but that'd involve a type of effort I didn't want to utilize. At least not for a so-called outing. The point of tonight meant avoiding my problems, magic, and anything involving Milo. Just teachers bitching about being teachers.

"Sucks, doesn't it, Frost?" A hand slapped my shoulder and pulled me into a half-hug embrace. I cringed at his deep, baritone voice booming in my ear. "Not in the way you like. But, you know, not all sucking is the good kind. Wink wink."

Seriously, who said 'wink wink'?

Peterson gripped my shoulder, holding me in place while joyfully sloshing his plastic cup of blue booze. I clenched my fists, desperate for an escape and knowing nothing would do. His heart called out for conversation, oozing from his every immediate emotion, which clung to my mind like a sludge. It didn't help his mind slipped to playful homophobic jokes he truly believed I'd get a laugh out of because he wanted to break the ice with friendly conversation.

"I have to piss." I skirted loose from Peterson and made my way to the urinals.

I debated whether to leave or not since Milo had likely taken the hint when he showed up at an empty house.

I sighed. All I wanted was to drink in peace and drown the frustration from today's professional learning. When I returned to the bar, Chanelle sat across from Peterson and four others from our school with an empty seat next to her. I took the seat. She smiled and slid a screwdriver in front of me. The orange juice had reddish drops in it, creating a blobby smear of colors.

"Cute, right?" She beamed. "Sort of like a tequila sunset without the tequila."

I gulped my drink until every ounce of licorice-flavored red garnish was gone, and all that remained was icy orange juice and vodka. "How much do I owe you?"

"No worries. I got this round." Chanelle waved a hand.

"The only thing I'm worried about tonight is those mandates Gemini is embracing," Peterson scoffed.

"A certain admin whose name I won't use hinted our class sizes will be doubled this year," Thompson said.

She was a stout redheaded woman who always remained "in the know," as she so often put it. An eloquent way of saying she was a busybody who never minded her damn business and spread idle gossip without ever confirming it. I realized cliquey educators didn't embody us as a whole, but with the handful determined to relive their high school years as the authority figures in the room, it was nauseating.

"That's ridiculous." Peterson took a swig of his drink, muttering something crude and thinking far more callous things.

"Well, it all comes down to"—Chanelle rubbed her fingers together, indicating money—"because the voucher system is going to cover most of these kids' tuition. Plus, I think the academies participating in the state's experiment are also getting tax credits if they reach a certain percentage. Saw that on the news when they were talking about California's rollout. It's all bureaucratic bullshit to account for funding, but I'll make it work."

Our state was among a dozen or so attempting this new model, while many resisted the shift in order to keep things traditional.

"You think you'll make it work," Peterson said. "The problem with opening the floodgates like this is now they're allowing kids who have no business at an academy simply because it's 'fair' for everyone."

"So, you don't think poor witches should practice magic?" I sipped my drink.

"That's not what I said." Peterson pointed an accusatory finger, his thoughts swirling in agitation that I'd somehow intentionally misinterpreted him. "We have a scholarship program for a reason. But this state mandate to lower the bar so everyone can reach it will produce more licensed witches, sure, which is what they want—" geez, he said it with such an ugly, superior tone, like someone evil actually intended on destroying society—"but at the cost of our society's overall comprehension."

"I even heard the participating academies waved the entrance exams this year," Thompson added because of course she fucking did. "Basically opening the doors to a first come, first serve standard with some exceptions. Or so I've heard."

"Total travesty." Peterson had an expression of utter defeat like he stood upon the battlements of a war in which proper education had finally been defeated. What a tool.

"Wow," I said with no real enthusiasm for the word. "Waved the entrance exams?"

"I know," Peterson interjected, face burning red. "Might as well just hand the incoming students a diploma and license now and thank them for participating."

"**Participation trophy**," roared in his mind on a loop. I ground my teeth. This elitist wannabe truly considered himself closer to the wealthy families he taught than the average person he sat side-by-side with daily.

"Absolutely right," I said, rubbing my fingers along my chin to playfully muse over the conversation. "You know, it sort of reminds me of how they give entrance waivers to kids who get in on recommendation or come from alumni."

Chanelle snickered, watching everyone's eyes lock onto me.

"No." I waved a hand to dismiss my own words. "That doesn't make any sense. It's clearly these new teen witches cheating our previously infallible system."

Chanelle's small laughter burst into an unhinged cackle, which drowned out opposing thoughts from staff members who greatly disagreed with my comment.

"Can we all agree the system's royally fucked, and we should throw the whole thing out?" Chanelle raised her glass to pull everyone into a cheer for solidarity.

"Absolutely." I swallowed the last of my screwdriver and shuffled to the bar.

"What can I get you?" the bartender asked.

"Another screwdriver, please." I shook my glass, clinking the ice inside.

She hurried off to make my drink along with three others, nodding to customers hurling their orders at her before she'd finished the four in front of her. I smirked at her thought process to keep up with the onslaught. *Another whiskey sour for Limp Dick. An extra spritz of cola, hold the rum, for Ms. Tipless. A round of shots for Mr. Always Lost in My Tits.*

"That'll be eight fifty." The bartender slid the drink toward me. "Got an open tab?"

I reached my hand into my back pocket and paused. "As a matter of fact, I think I do. Should be under Peterson."

She went to the computer and punched buttons along the screen. Sipping the bitter orange juice, I strolled away from the bar and past the table of teachers. I gave Peterson a friendly grin, raised my glass, and nodded.

"Where are you going?" Chanelle asked.

"Outside for some fresh air."

"You realize all that smoke you're inhaling is just counteracting the fresh air you're getting."

"Good."

I stood outside, under an awning with several others. Slurred, unfocused thoughts bounced about, unable to fully form. They were hammered. Rain drizzled but not so hard that I needed to stand among these chatty drunks. I exhaled and slipped between them, cutting around the side of the nearby alley with an unguarded entrance to another building and an empty awning to protect from the rain.

I'd finish this cigarette and my drink, maybe have another, and then head home.

"I knew booze would win over books," Milo said.

I jolted at his voice and turned to find him at the end of the alley where the city lights illuminated his smile. The rain did nothing to dampen his spiky, chaotic blond hair. It always looked like he'd just rolled out of bed but was perfectly gelled in place.

"Books?" Ugh. I could've totally avoided him and everyone else by hiding out at a bookstore.

"But your wallet just can't afford you adding to that massive stack of unread stories." Milo raised a finger, tapping his skull and pretending to read my thoughts. His dress shoes splashed against the puddles. Each heavy step closed the distance between us, making my skin warm. "Plus, no booze with bookstores."

He'd played me through probability. Damn clairvoyants.

Nearly every witch had a branch connected to one of twelve unique magic types that witches were born with. Milo and I both had psychic branches. But while I heard thoughts through telepathy, he played guessing games with a weighted scale on future events.

I inhaled and contemplated going back inside, but if anyone from work spotted us together, I'd never hear the end of it.

"Never." He slipped under the awning, faking a shiver from the rain.

Please. The humidity made the late August afternoon feel like a sauna. I blew smoke at Milo, forcing him to backstep and wave a hand to clear the haze. His eyes watered at the harsh exhale.

"If you knew that text would get me here versus home, why bother telling me you were going to my place?" I avoided his gaze. "Could've saved us both the hassle of getting caught in the rain."

"You know predictions are never a certainty." He huddled closer, bumping my hand with his broad bicep and knocking the cigarette loose. "Oops."

I stared at my fallen cigarette, snuffed out by the wet concrete.

"Can I finish one smoke in peace today?"

Milo raised his left arm, exposing an eight-ball tattoo he'd gotten after receiving his first magic practicing license. My chest swelled at the memory of his goofy smile the morning he walked up to me, flashing his tiny tattoo. The one-and-done effort to be edgy.

Milo shook his arm and blinked at his tattooed wrist. "Says outcome unlikely."

"Ha. How very unfunny."

"Please, that was witty." Milo adjusted his tie, and the guild enchanter emblem pinned to his jacket glimmered.

"Did you even have a case?"

"Hmm, yes and no." Milo grinned. "I did have a case—literally just finished it, in fact—but it was sort of on this side of town, opposite your place. Figured I'd save myself the drive and meet you here. Hence part of why I suggested you come."

Suggested. More like manipulated the situation. I hated his magic. Hated it so much. It made him impossible to gauge, predict, or plan for. Fuck, he was exhausting.

"You're the most irritating person I know, you know that?" My cheeks twitched, resisting a smile because whenever Milo looked at me, the weight of the world faded away.

"You like it." Milo pressed his chest close to mine, backing me against the metal door.

I held my breath as his cologne hit my nose, sending a blissful reminder of lust indulged over the summer. I did like his persistence, his unyielding care. Everything about Milo was perfection, from his sweet smile to his eternal understanding, all the way to his puppy dog eyes. Whereas I was a mess of unbridled anger, constant regrets, and looming guilt that reminded me every minute of every day that I wasn't worth his compassion. Wasn't worth his love, time, or kindness.

"If you want me to leave, I will," Milo said, backing away from the protection of the awning. "It's just…we had fun over the summer. And then Finn's birthday rolled around, and you ghosted me—which I allowed because it's Dorian fashion—but I missed you. I miss us. Sometimes I think you work up how much—"

Fuck it.

I'd already made a thousand mistakes opening the box of emotions between us. What was one more?

I yanked his tie, pulling him into a kiss.

His soft lips met mine, and his tongue eased its way into my mouth. I found myself lost in his embrace, excited and eager but reminded this happiness wasn't meant to be.

I dropped my drink, the glass clinking and cracking against the concrete. I couldn't even feign care for the lost screwdriver. I knew I shouldn't be kissing him. This would only further complicate things—for him, for me—but I didn't care. Right then, all I wanted was the sweet taste of his mouth and the firm press of his muscles as I pulled him closer.

He ran his hand through my hair, tilting my head in a passionate, all-consuming kiss. The sort of thing I couldn't handle. Surrendering myself to another person, their desires, their dreams, their life—I wasn't made for it. I wasn't meant to co-exist with another person. It involved a type of effort I'd never quite fathomed.

Yet I lost myself in the smack of his lips, the grind of his hips against mine, the lust oozing from every pore of his body filling my mind with infinite flashes of every time we'd spent together.

Milo's lips broke away from mine, and I craved their supple touch again. A breathy chuckle escaped his mouth, and he smiled. A coy smile that curled into a minxy grin. "You know, I really did come here to talk."

"What could you possibly want to talk to me about?" I asked, unable to quell the arousal filling each of our minds.

"Figured today was rough for you, back to work and all."

"It was nothing." Even the break in physical contact didn't sever my magic linking his mind to mine, and he knew it, too. Years of connection made Milo's mind the easiest to latch onto in a sea of thoughts. "And since when do you care how teaching's going?"

"To be clear, I've always cared." Milo trailed his fingertips down my arm, sending goosebumps from his sensual touch. "But I figured the big changes they're throwing your way… Maybe you weren't too happy."

"You speaking as a guild member who was informed about academy policies before the actual teachers were or as a clairvoyant who caught a sneak peek of admins' plans?"

Milo grabbed my wrist, ignoring my question. The touch strengthened the bond of our thoughts. His thoughts. I skirted through his mind toward his current passing notions, attempting to understand where this fascination or curiosity for my workday came from, yet I stood in front of him, lost in his sparkling blue eyes.

I kissed him again, this time leading with my tongue. He released my wrist and wrapped his arms around my waist. I focused on the now, keeping my mind locked here, but it didn't matter how much I tried—I became entranced with images Milo held close to the surface of his mind, flashes through his perspective from our last encounter. His hand pressed to the small of my back, arching it further and pushing my knees deeper into the mattress. His other hand wrapped around my shoulder, fingers outstretched and lightly gripping my throat. A primal urge to pull my shaggy brown hair. Then or now? Perhaps both.

I attempted to shake it off, but the sensation of his memories spiraled in the now, turning the world into a foggy mix of the rainy alley and my bedroom. His body had pulsed with ecstasy the moment he tugged my hair, and he replayed the moan I released on a loop until he silenced me by shoving his tongue into my mouth. Fiery kisses as his hips thrust harder and faster, and electricity surged into my body.

Even now, my legs trembled, my body eager for him to take me here behind this bar the same way he had the last time we'd spoken. Images sprang to life, clouding my vision of the now. Milo had slid his tongue along my ear…

"*I love you.*"

I shoved him away, breaking contact in the alleyway and burning his memories of us screwing out of my mind as swiftly as they'd invaded it. Droplets fell harder, and Milo stood exposed to the downpour, his smile unwavering.

He'd uttered those words like they were still so easy. Perhaps he'd only said them because of the heat of the moment. And I couldn't decide if that made it easier or more difficult to avoid him. Or whether I wanted them to be true or a lustful lie. Milo confused me too much. Not only in sex but in personality and thoughts. He was a Jack-in-the-box I didn't want to open. Ever.

Chapter Three

Milo stepped under the awning again. Rain dripped down his face, and a single drop ran along his chiseled jaw, accentuating it. He brushed a hand through his hair, adjusting the single bang that drooped onto his forehead. His smile pushed his cheeks up, revealing only the slightest lines along his eyes. Lines that held a history of joy. Nothing like mine. I had deep bags because of my constant invasive magic since I was eight years old. Guyliner became a friend at a young age, and the raccoon look kept people asking more about my questionable makeup choices as opposed to the black rings under my eyes. My hair hid the deep creases along my forehead.

I wasn't unattractive. I had a slight muscular form that'd gotten too scrawny over the years with a belly pudge I'd given up removing since hitting my thirties. Pale in the ghostliest sense. And, of course, the face.

Milo and I sat in different leagues of beauty, though. Everything about him had an element of perfection to it. His naturally stunning features. Bright eyes. A firm body that filled every outfit in all the right places. Flawless skin with adorably discreet tan lines below the waist. It wasn't like one could expect any less from a professional enchanter in a guild. So many factors played a role in their success—unique and flashy magics, good looks, charm, and an ability to balance and build a strong social platform.

I missed the days when casting for guilds was about helping people instead of impressing them with your presence. I missed a lot of days before now.

"You're honestly cuter than you give yourself credit for." Milo winked with a boyish grin, which only made him more kissable.

I hated his kissable face.

"Now who's mind reading?" I glared.

"We've had this conversation like a thousand times." Milo inched closer. His confident strides closed the distance between us again, but I skirted away from his touch. Keeping my mind clear of him meant no contact. He lifted his hand to his chin, posing thoughtfully. "Well, we've had it a few times, but we've preemptively had it a lot more. I'm really good at setting you straight before the feels set in. Straight was not a pun, by the way. Just a poor choice of words."

"There aren't feels." I ducked past him.

"We don't have to talk about it," Milo said, backstepping to follow me as I walked through the alley back to the bar. "It's not a necessary conversation for our immediate future."

"We don't have a future, Milo." I paused. "I know you're hung up on what could be, but I assure you, nothing that might happen is worth this effort."

"Can't give up on a soulmate."

"I'm not your soulmate." I stopped, staring up at the final glimmers of sunlight piercing through rain clouds. What an ugly sight, sunshine pathetically attempting to brighten those dreary clouds which carried melancholy throughout the city. "If soulmates were real, which they aren't because I refuse to buy into some archaic one-and-done belief system—"

"So snappy."

"If it were real," I said, ignoring his commentary, "surely, you'd envision someone better. Someone who wanted you."

"I'd say you want me." Even keeping my magic quelled and gaze ahead, I could feel the chipper, cocky wink.

"All of you."

"You do want all of me." Milo ran his hands along his firm abdomen, strutting as he waltzed backward beside me. "Just not now. I can wait. I'm patient. Well, not perfectly patient. I mean, a boy's got needs, right?"

That was our biggest problem—his patience for what could be. His biggest problem.

I lingered at the end of the alleyway, reaching for my pack of smokes, relishing the lessening rain. The clouds separated. It was like the earth itself knew I needed a cigarette to carry on with this conversation.

Milo's clairvoyant magic allowed him to envision the future. A powerful skill when handling danger throughout the city. Yet, he fixated on deluding himself with futures he wanted to happen instead of the ones that actually happened. Concrete, fractured realities of sorrow. Since we were eighteen, he'd believed we were meant to be. It used to be three meant to be; that proved untrue.

And there it was. The worst part about Milo—how much he made my mind wander back to Finn. The two of them together used to be such powerful pillars of positivity in my life, keeping me afloat in a world where everyone's thoughts sought to suffocate me. He and Finn had always found my reluctant nature and brash behavior intriguing when together. The pair never tired of whittling away the rough edges of my thorny personality. But without Finn, my negativity, my weakness, would drag Milo down.

He'd flourished for years as a professional enchanter, not requiring the anchor of my presence. I just wished he'd get the idea of the two of us finding our way back to each other out of his head—and out of mine, too. If I'd accepted I didn't belong with Milo and Finn back then, Finn might still be alive.

I sparked a cigarette, inhaling a little death but trapped among the living another day. Our futures weren't written in the stars or foretold by magic. It was a lie. One he refused to accept. Our past held too much pain and death for a future of joy.

Milo traced his fingers along my neck, etching them along the tattoo behind my ear, spelling the name I'd lost the will to speak aloud. Milo's name sat tucked behind my other ear, a permanent reminder of a life I'd foolishly envisioned, too.

"You should choose a future that'll make you happy and stop seeking one that's haunted."

"I've seen my potential future a million times over." His fingers tickled my ear, delicate and affectionate and painful. "What can I say? I'm after the happiest ever after. The one that'll eclipse all the others that ever were or will be."

"You're an idiot." I sucked a deep inhale of smoke, allowing it to waft from my lips as I spoke. "Nothing about me screams happy."

"Happy is subjective like everything else." Milo's fingertips tiptoed to the nape of my neck, muting all stirring thoughts. The gentle touch left only his mind and mine, offering a calm I so rarely achieved, given the constant hum of nearby thoughts.

I went to kiss him, allowing my magic to rage and consume his mind and preparing myself for a million unspoken words, but as our lips reached, everything turned black. Telepathy superseded what I saw in the moment. Usually, I maintained a balance between what I'd see in my mind versus what I'd see in reality, like a very annoying dual-screen monitor. Or watching anime and reading subtitles.

This hit differently. Darkness swept across my vision, and silence echoed. No drips of water. No traffic. No drunken fools. Not even the nearby mental mutterings of a thousand random people, soft surface thoughts that whispered at the lowest frequency constantly, thoughts I'd grown accustomed to ignoring. Even my dreams were plagued with the rumbling whispers of people in the area since I couldn't quell my magic when sleeping. I hadn't had this type of complete silence in my head since I was a child. I'd forgotten how peacefully silent the world could be, and it was beautiful.

A white dot emerged in the distance. As it grew, a human form came into sight. That dot belonged to a teen boy, no more than fourteen or fifteen. Sweat coated his face as he sprinted closer through the shadowy ground with silent steps. He had curly white hair with brown roots like muddy snow. Vibrant green eyes shone in the darkness, illuminating the terror on his face. His clothes were ragged and torn and soaked in blood.

My chest tightened. I wanted to extend a hand, call out to the frightened kid, but here in this blacked-out space, my body ignored commands. He collapsed in front of me. No thud. No attempt to brace his fall. Just a swift tumble forward, revealing a silver-hilted blade buried in his back.

What was this? My magic couldn't do this. Unless it was a memory, but memories carried some kind of world around them. At the very least, what the person envisioned or recalled from that day. The mind did wonders at filling in the gaps to blank spaces, but this was all blank space aside from the dying boy who lay before me.

I ground my teeth. Finally. Something. My knees buckled, and in that instant, I reached forward to help him. My hands hit the wet, gravelly ground as reality surrounded me again. I stood, spinning in circles, attempting to listen to any nearby panic and find this frightened kid.

"If she says one more thing about my relationship, I'm gonna reach across the table…"

"I need another shot."   *"Prick."*

"What an ugly dress."

"How long does it take to make a long island iced tea?"

"What'd she say? Nod and smile."

"Why can't I meet someone decent?"

"This motherfucker probably went to smoke and left."

The onslaught of the usual bombarded my brain.

"You all right, Dorian?" Milo patted my back, easing my need to quell the useless drivel. "Looks like maybe you've had one too many drinks."

"No. What…what was that? Something's not right." I continued searching, tearing through the nonsense thoughts.

Nothing.

Nothing.

Nothing.

"There's a boy somewhere here," I said as my breathing tightened. "I think he's in trouble or—"

"Or will be? Yeah, I saw that, too."

"You what?"

"I think you might've delved into my mind right as I was having a vision. Guess it was bound to happen, eventually." Milo spoke so nonchalantly. Not at all the way someone who witnessed a death should react. I pressed a palm to my chest, easing my quick and shallow breaths. Maybe he made more sense of the vision and had a plan in place.

"Are you going to contact your guild?" I asked.

"For what?"

"The kid."

"You catch a name in that vision? Spot anything remarkable in the area? All I saw was a void this time. They happen. Not much I can do when voids pop up. No timeframe or location. Those one notes hit more often than I like. Could be someone I'll meet, someone you'll meet, someone I brushed by today, or someone they'll encounter in the near future. Honestly, clairvoyance is all about rooting through the rubble of constantly shifting futures, and void visions are just useless snapshots."

"You're going to do nothing?"

"What's there to do? If I tried to make sense of every vision, it'd be maddening. So, unfortunately, I have to tune a lot of the mysteries out. Plus, let's be real. I don't get to do an instant replay."

"You need to replay that vision? His face is locked in my mind." The sweat, blood, tears, and terror stretched across his entire expression.

"Yeah, because you had one glimpse into one future of one vision. I've had somewhere between thirty to fifty today. Some dire. Some nonsense. Heck, one of a lady eating a sandwich and regretting she asked for extra mayo. Should I find her and warn her it'll ruin her lunch?"

"This is a life, not lunch." I stepped close to Milo, closing our distance and gripping his tie. Partly because I wanted to strangle him with it and partly because I hoped the physical contact would spark a second vision. A helpful one, so he'd take this seriously. Nothing.

"Hey, the lady's an accountant. Maybe that crap lunch soured her mood. Maybe she'll be distracted at work, yearning for the sandwich that could've been. Maybe it'll make her overlook someone's money.

Maybe a family will go without because of that damn extra mayo. Who really knows? Besides, the future's an ever-changing wheel. Just seeing the vision might alter the course of events. Clairvoyance is some wacky shit."

"Just shut up and…I don't know, think about the future," I said, running my fingers along his neck, hoping the skin-to-skin contact would heighten our channeled magic.

"Oh, I'm always thinking about our future." Milo leaned closer, his lips almost touching mine. "I get you want me to do something, and I'd move mountains for you. But I can't move said mountain if I don't know when, where, or how the mountain mounted."

"A cigarette doesn't take this long." Chanelle's boots splashed puddles as she traipsed around the corner, a scowl on her face. Her eyes darted between Milo and me, then fixated on my palm pressed firmly to Milo's neck, hand clutching his tie, and our lips a single breath apart. "Oh, did I walk in on a little back-alley fun? Oops."

"It's not… It wasn't." My face burned from a mix of embarrassment and resentment toward Milo's cavalier attitude. I released him, backstepping.

"You don't need to be a mind reader to see all the sexual tension." Her face lit up, eyes wide in awe when she reached Milo. "Enchanter Evergreen, such a pleasure."

She extended a hand to shake his, and Milo, ever the flirtatious showman, took her hand, kissed it, and nodded with a slight bow. "Please, call me Milo."

"Of course, Milo." Chanelle let out a girlish giggle like she was one of his fans. *"Mmmmm. I need all the details on how you bagged this hottie. All the dirty details. He's the whole damn package and then some."*

Chanelle locked eyes with mine to ascertain that I'd, in fact, eavesdropped on her ridiculous comment. I rolled my eyes.

As one of the highest-ranked enchanters belonging to the most renowned guild in Chicago, Milo was basically a local celebrity. Guild witches were flashy heroes, working as independent contractors to assist in many different tasks.

Chanelle backed up, pretending to use the wall as protection from the tiniest of drizzles. Her gaze fixed on Milo's butt in the least subtle manner. His tight dress slacks did well to accentuate his form. *"Honestly, how do you handle all that ass?"*

Milo smirked, having already resigned to forget his vision. His eyes searched my face, and the coy grin meant he knew I was using my telepathy and had heard something about him. He was the only person in the world who could read my mind by studying my expressions. I hated how he knew me. It was annoying. Everything about this day had been.

"I'm leaving." I stuffed my hands into my pockets and stormed down the alley toward the main street.

"Oh. Guess I'll see you tomorrow," Chanelle shouted before bursting into laughter at something playful and perfectly timed Milo had undoubtedly said. I had no time to figure it out. All I wanted was to escape.

I replayed that vision the entire drive home. That mystery boy's terrified expression haunted me as I went through my evening checklist of to-dos. Feed the cats. Pet the neediest little boy Charlie until he begged for belly rubs which ended in play biting. Cook my own dinner—thankfully, microwaveable. Listen to the rudest fat girl Carlie naggingly meow because she wanted my meal.

"You've already eaten."

"Meow." She hopped onto the couch.

"You don't like red sauce." I lifted the tray.

"Meow." Her paw stretched, desperate for the flavor.

I held out my tray, sulking, allowing her to sniff it, turn up her nose, and trot off, enraged I cooked myself something unworthy of stealing. Their antics were comforting most evenings. Not tonight. Not with a dying boy's face stuck in my head.

Unable to remove the image, I made a drink, then another, and one more for good measure. I couldn't sleep, not yet, so I went to my guest room closet, rummaging through the back in search of an old sketchbook. Afterward, I hid in my room from curious tabbies and traced the anguished mystery boy's face.

I hadn't drawn anything in years. My passion for art had faded like most things. People had critical and subjective comments vocalized, but you'd be amazed at how much more ruthless they could be when holding back what they were actually thinking of saying. I suppose they could be kinder, too, but I rarely recalled the joyful comments. It was the disgust that remained.

Memories of those harsh words lingered on every line I drew. Six attempts in, they all looked like trash. More sad-eyed caricature than personal portrait.

Surrendering to recreating the vision, I slept. Or tried.

I woke up dehydrated from too much booze and a dry mouth from smoking, quelling buzzing thoughts of people desperate to remain locked in their dreams and comfy blankets, fumbling for the snooze button.

I pushed Charlie, who'd nestled into a tight little ball, off my neck and slid out of bed, beginning my morning ritual. Morning cigarette and the first cup of black coffee while contemplating the worth of going to work versus staying home. That existential debate had the added bonus of the vision I had no way to make sense of. I fed the cats and made a quick microwave breakfast biscuit. Turning the TV on helped provide an auditory distraction to morning minds, so I could focus on getting ready instead of quelling channeled magic.

The news was perfect. It kept me informed yet unattached. If I turned on something I liked, chances were I'd get sucked into the plot and end up later than usual. I washed back the flakey crumbs caught between my gums with a second cup of coffee and used the restroom twice because my teacher's bladder had spent ten years training itself for early morning and afternoon relief.

"In other news, Donna Langley had a sit down with Cerberus Guild's very own Enchanter Milo Evergreen."

A sharp slicing sound indicated a cutaway.

"You're assisting local Chicago PD with investigations on the recent surge of warlocks. How have things been?"

"It's always a wonderful experience working alongside these professionals when we're invited," Milo said, enthusiasm oozing out of each word. "I won't lie; there are always hiccups when guilds work with local law enforcement. We're structured differently, and some people still resent the loose authority we possess, but I'm honored by how forthcoming and inviting everyone I've worked with has been."

I ground my teeth while throwing on a clean shirt and pair of jeans. Something baggy and comfortable. Hiccups—what an understatement. Guilds were established as a way to protect casting rights and keep the government from overseeing every aspect of magic in civilian lives. When magic returned to our world in the eighteen twenties, it created quite the kerfuffle as every country worked to adapt and structure new laws surrounding but not condemning magic. More than two centuries later, they continued struggling with these rules.

"What are your thoughts on Illinois' new educational policies? Do you believe this will help lessen the increase of warlock activity?"

I took swift steps back into the living room and snatched the controller.

"It's fantastic to see the improvements they're making, but the spike in illegal casting happening now needs experienced guild support." Milo smiled. The camera zoomed close to his face. I gulped, staring at his perfect face filling the screen that took up half my living room wall. "In the long term, for sure. And that's because teachers rallied together for years demanding academies with the resources do their part. I'm honored to know some of the academy educators who helped in this effort. Some who helped prepare me for this position when I was still a student, and some who studied alongside me. All of them—"

"Oh, shut the fuck up, Milo." I jabbed the off button and tossed the controller onto the coffee table.

Charlie darted out from under the couch, frantic because of the crash from the controller. I grabbed my satchel and keys and filled a thermos with enough steaming black coffee to get me through the morning. The drive to work was quick.

"So?" Chanelle practically tackled me when I entered the building. "I told you, I want all the details. Feel free to be as explicitly inappropriate as possible."

"Not happening."

"Oh, come on. Milo was so sweet but more tightlipped than you." She nudged my ribs. "I knew you two used to work together, but I didn't know you two worked together."

"We don't. Aren't. Whatever." I picked up my pace.

I could feed into her nonsense. Answer all her nosy questions about my sex life with Milo, our dating history, the death that divided us, and the guild life I wasn't cut out for anymore. Then again, rehashing old horrors probably wasn't the best strategy for dodging new ones. I went into the auditorium, where they'd posted a screen with the agenda for our training. Maybe diving into whatever planned professional learning admin had in store would help. Unfortunately, I doubted anything would distract from the gnawing guilt of abandoning that boy.

Admin Evans led the professional learning on creating student connections because we seriously needed to spend all morning learning how to develop relationships with students so we could improve in assisting their success. I hated these repetitive lessons from facilitators outside the classroom, teaching me how to be a better instructor in the classroom.

Ignoring the discussion, I dove into my all-consuming fears and scoured missing reports, news articles, assaults, fatalities, and everything else I could Google. So many kids I put out of my mind every day posted with a blurb on the tragedies they endured. None of them the boy I feared stumbling onto. And what had I done before this moment? Reminded myself there was only so much I could do, this sort of thing wasn't my job, and their story belonged to someone else to solve. But not this boy. I wouldn't abandon the vision even if Milo believed nothing vital presented itself.

It didn't help that Milo had a point. Everything I searched came up short. None of it helped. Not to find leads. Not to assuage my guilt. Not to silence the chipper voices of admin. Or to shut Peterson and Thompson up. Thompson had "just one more" question during the session. And Peterson had so much condescending commentary screaming in his head. I pressed my fingers against my temples, drowning out their words and thoughts, rubbing away the migraine of irritating voices. These fucking people.

The week of training blurred together. Each day, I spent time looking for anything I could, replaying that vision, and always coming up empty. Ignoring Milo's daily texting check-in, I dwelled on how this type of thing contributed to why I'd left the guild enchanter career behind. Many aspects of that career hurt but failing to save a life cut deeply into me every single time. That alone should've made the decision clear.

Maybe that was why Milo maintained such an aloof attitude. He stayed. Pushed through his regrets, doubt, and weakness to become the ideal enchanter defending our city. He knew how to make the public swoon and criminals cringe. Still, I couldn't squash the lingering doubt of indecision.

I swallowed hard, silencing the shame of abandoning this mystery boy. I went through my rosters of students. Since I couldn't help this kid, at least I'd prepare for the others, assist them even in the most useless of ways. Admin made it clear we weren't getting any time in our classrooms to prepare lessons for incoming students because we needed to spend time in the auditorium planning through state-mandated professional learning on preparing for the kids.

Skimming Chanelle's mind allowed me to answer the surveys we received for every "engaging lesson" we'd worked on. I couldn't totally hate the accountability for surveys proving we'd paid attention during the trainings since they were instilled because of people like me who actively ignored them, but also screw them for not trusting us in the classroom.

This was the only career where they trained us on a new strategy at the beginning of the year only to clear the board a year later and say, "Everything you knew before is wrong, and we'll prove it while teaching how to actually do things right in this new and amazing way."

My phone buzzed again. Milo had returned to pestering me with a swarm of many short, supposedly charming messages. Another thing that muddled this week.

> Milo: Back to ignoring me. Le sigh.
> Is it because you can't handle all this dick, or you think I'm being one? 😉
> Void visions are no joke. Which we could discuss if you, you know, responded.

I stuffed the phone back into my pocket, using the final day of professional learning to study Individualized Education Programs and create a spreadsheet of modifications from my rosters, along with personal techniques I'd had effective results with over the years. Techniques that were certainly outdated as they were a whole five years old. I swear, iPhones had more longevity than educational strategies. The spreadsheet was only a temporary go-to resource until I gained better insight into each of the students, memorized their accommodations, and took their actual levels and pacing needs into account.

IEPs were written in highly complex language. Like most things in education, no one could simply say what they meant. Nope. They had to word it in the most pretentiously eloquently complicated manner, so it sounded elevated and would trick onlookers into believing that it created more care for the individual. Instead, it made each kid's plan a not-so-fun little game of deciphering the meaning behind this word versus that word. Also, reading a lot of bullshit that couldn't cut to the point.

I sank into my seat, tuning out the continuous and boring reminders of information I already knew through new and inventive hypothetical scenarios.

"Finally," Chanelle said.

I glanced at her screen, reading the email a counselor had sent to everyone informing us homeroom covens had officially been finalized and our rosters should reflect those changes. Yes! This would help in tweaking my lesson for the start of the year. Especially since until a few days ago, I'd intended to use the plans to work with third-year witches, not first-year kids. I opened my gradebook and clicked on student profiles.

One by one, I checked over the students, glossing past their messy freshmen picture day photos in the system, scanning the extensive list of personal information, and noting their magical capabilities and levels—or the levels the state had records on.

I noted a Whitlock joining my roster. That was quite shocking, despite my resting don't-give-a-fuck expression I wore almost exclusively. I should brace myself for a long year considering the Whitlocks were the wealthiest, most esteemed witch family in Chicago, pulling the strings of guilds and pushing strong legislation against the so-called warlock problem. Whatever. I'd deal with it when I dealt with it.

I clicked the next profile and froze.

My chest caved in. My knees trembled, rocking the laptop pressed against them. It fell, but Chanelle swooped in, catching it before it hit the floor with surprise on her face—nothing like the shock rattling my core.

"You all right, Dorian?" Chanelle smiled, shaking away any sign of anxiety. "You look like you've seen a ghost."

"I'm…" My throat tightened, poorly trying to imitate her swift transition to calm.

Chanelle's expression softened, and she placed a hand on my shoulder. "What's wrong?"

"Nothing," I said, resisting the swelling tears in my eyes. "I'm fine."

I hadn't seen a ghost. Not yet, anyway. The mystery boy had a name and a connection to me—Caleb Huxley, one of the kids assigned to my first-year homeroom coven.

This meant I could pursue the vision to save his life.

Chapter Four

Caleb. He had curly brown hair. There was no obvious snow-white hair dye job, which was probably a good sign indicating he was far from death's door. Then again, while he didn't have the same frantic and bloody expression in the vision, he didn't look much different. Either he wouldn't have an ounce of a growth spurt this year, or the attack was imminent.

The anguished face from the vision was replaced by this picture with an awkward smile. A slight quirk in his lip, like he couldn't decide between teeth or closed mouth, and in the end had bright eyes with a confused expression. I fought a chuckle. Been there. Which was why I preferred not smiling.

This one kid shouldn't have rattled me so much. People always died. It was the way of the world. Yet, all week, he was the first thing that rang inside my head when I woke and the final thought before bed.

I'd known Milo for over half my life and glimpsed his mind more times than I cared to count, but not once had any of his visions struck me, syncing perfectly to my magic. This meant something. It meant I could help.

I had to help. The swift relief that came from finding out the mystery kid in the void vision was quickly replaced by fear and doubt and knowledge that, like so much in my life, I'd fuck this up and somehow make it worse.

I needed Milo. Sinking lower in my seat, I pulled out my phone and texted him.

> Milo: So you're not butt hurt anymore? Or wishing you were? 🍆 😼
> Wait. That sounded sexier in my head.
> You still wanna meet, right?

Before I could respond, three floating bubbles started. Stopped. Started. Stopped. Jesus fucking Christ, Milo.

> Me: Yes. I'll meet you after work.

> Milo: I get done around 8. My place or yours?

Probably should've specified meeting him to talk, not, well—oh well.

> Me: Your guild.

> Milo: Kinky.

Chanelle's thick curls draped along my shoulder as she snuck a peek at my phone. I stuffed it back into my pocket, ignoring the buzz which undoubtedly signified a flurry of sexting emojis.

"Wow," Chanelle whispered. "You got a branchless kid?"

Yeah, she was totally staring at the computer screen, not the texts I sent. I read over Caleb Huxley's data.

"I knew they were opening the doors to everyone at academies, but someone without an ounce of unique magic… Hmm. I wonder if there are any others."

"Unlikely." I tapped the screen. "Check out his proficiency scores."

"Oh, a 4.0 freshmen year. Like anyone can't get that at a South Side public school."

"No, you dick." I pointed to his state exams.

All his English and Math scores were well above average. Even his magical comprehension scores—which were totally biased against students who didn't have a curriculum on the subject—were higher than most of the private school kids who got accepted at Gemini Academy. Caleb might've lacked in a branch magic, but one glance at these results showed he had massive determination.

"Well, hopefully he's decent with his root magics since he doesn't have a branch."

"Please. He's an incoming first-year student." I scoffed. "Their fundamentals always suck."

Now that I knew who he was, where he was going to be five days a week, I found it difficult to accomplish anything productive. I could be tweaking lessons for my homeroom coven, planning something to work on understanding where each of them leveled in their root magics since every witch possessed the same four fundamental magics. I could also research each of the branch magics these incoming students inherited, preparing ways to help them excel. The ones who had gained a branch magic, unlike Caleb Huxley.

Instead, my wandering mind created a thousand scenarios of how my inadequate teaching somehow led to the unfolding events in the vision. Or the academy not taking the mandate seriously, shrugging him off because of his lack of a branch magic. If I hadn't seen his death, would I have doubted his place at Gemini, too?

I shook my head. No. No. Definitely not. I bit my lip. Right?

I needed to talk with Milo before my mind drifted through a million other crevices of 'but, maybe…' or 'what if…' because none of that helped anyone. I'd read enough minds to know overthinking created self-doubt, which in turn stunted potential successes before they ever manifested into effort.

"With that," Evans' voice crackled into the mic, snapping me back to the meeting I'd ignored. She lowered it away from her face, giggling. "Whoops. Guess I'm a little excited, too. Anyways, on that note, I hope you all have a lovely weekend. I can't wait to see everyone Monday morning."

"We're done?" I asked.

"About time," Chanelle said, clutching her packed belongings. "I'm starting to think Thompson's branch magic is pissing me the fuck off with how many useless questions she can ask to extend meetings."

I checked the time on my laptop. Twelve minutes after three. I furrowed my brow. Seriously? Twelve extra minutes' worth of questions on a Friday meeting? Screw you, Thompson. I put my laptop in my satchel bag and walked outside, lighting a cigarette in the parking lot.

Chanelle rushed beside me, faking a cough.

"Not right now. I don't need a lecture." I took a deep inhale.

"Practicing your sucking skills?"

I choked on the puff, coughing gray spurts of smoke.

"Told you they were bad for you." She winked. This woman was a devil. "A few of us are heading out, blowing off steam. Care to join?"

"Can't." I reached my car, unlocking it and gripping the handle. "Got plans."

"I see. Or saw. Blowing me off to blow Milo?"

My ears burned.

"I'm teasing." Her heels clicked along the pavement, and she stepped in close, her breath hitting my already hot ear. "Like I'm sure he'll be doing to you tonight."

"You've concocted your own reality, haven't you?" I shrugged her off and slid into my car.

"So much tantalizing teasing tonight," she said, waving a hand as she strutted away. "*Mmmm.*"

I slammed my car door shut. Ugh, I hated her sometimes.

Traffic was thick, and Milo's guild was on the other side of the city. Honestly, it'd be quicker to find a parking garage and take the subway. At least the stall in traffic gave me a chance to think on how to address this with Milo, make him realize the importance of the void vision, and force him to get off his nonchalant ass.

Cerberus Guild had expanded since I'd worked here. They'd always done well in Chicago, but once Enchanter Evergreen became a sensation, their offices moved to a twenty-story sleek building housing more enchanters on a single floor than most guilds had overall. This overpriced building with positions holding outrageously high salaries was part of what fed into the problems with licensing and why so many aspired to be at the top or settled for remaining at the complete and total bottom of the system.

Then again, it wasn't like I should talk. After all, I worked at Gemini Academy cranking prospective professional witches out onto the world on a little conveyor belt. I sighed. Fuck me, I hated dwelling on what a cog in the machine I was.

I stepped into the building where acolytes monitored the front lobby, greeting and checking in those of us entering.

"Hello, sir," a young woman said. "Do you have an appointment?"

"No, I'm—"

"Oh, if you're here to make an inquiry about our services, much of that information can be found online." She typed on a tablet. "Let me show you the website. There, you'll be able to input the type of magical services you require, pricing estimates you're comfortable with, and we'll generate matches for you with suitable enchanters on the task. This way, you can schedule an appointment because many of the enchanters are booked weeks, sometimes months, in advance. Unfortunately, we don't have time to accommodate walk-ins."

"I know how the system works. I'm—"

"Dorian Frost!" a high-pitched voice bellowed throughout the lobby.

I balled my fists. Would anyone at Cerberus let me get a word in edgewise?

Enchanter Campbell waved, and I resisted a frown. Her vibrant rose-red lips pursed into a graceful smile as she shook hands with a client, bidding them farewell.

"Are you here to provide me with more excellent referrals?" she asked, sauntering across the marble lobby floor. "Your young witches seem to get better every year."

"I'm actually not handling third-year students this year." I tucked a hand behind my head, massaging the impending headache she'd likely give me with her prodding curiosity.

"Boo. Why aren't you teaching them this year?"

"Some internal shifts," I replied. "That said, I know the kids I recommended would make excellent matches with your agency. And each of them is eager to work alongside your enchanters to gain more insight into how the industry works."

"Internal shifts? So are you not teaching at all then?"

"Still teaching. I'm back to working with first-year witches. It should be exciting to focus on the fundamentals again." I faked a smile because my gruff, unenthused voice gave her internal doubt, which bubbled into many questions I wanted to squash before she blurted them.

"I don't know how you handle that. I'd climb the walls trapped in a room with children all day." She shivered like she'd envisioned the reality of education in one tiny glance. She had no idea.

"You get used to it. And it's pretty rewarding."

"I bet it is." Enchanter Campbell's smile didn't hide the venom behind her words. *"Rewarding getting to go home early, having your weekends and holidays off, not to mention the entire summer. Must be nice."*

I smiled back, my cheeks twitching along with my fingers as I resisted a deep-seated urge to flip her off. She had some points, but most of them were off. I didn't have the time, energy, or desire to convey how exhausting teaching a room full of children all day could get or the massive burnout from everyone's outside opinions on how things should be done because we had it too easy.

A hand slapped my back. "Oh, wonderful that you made it, Mr. Frost."

Enchanter Campbell's opinions were so loud, I didn't even notice Milo sneak up until he stood beside me.

"Shall we discuss that business we'd planned on discussing today at this time now?"

Really subtle, Milo. "Sounds good."

"Have a lovely day, Dorian. Try not to work too hard." Enchanter Campbell swayed away, practically floating on her internal judgment. *"Not that he does."*

If she weren't such a competent pro witch, I'd seriously consider taking her off my shortlist, but these internships weren't about what enchanters thought of me or my position. The networking involved provided the student's opportunities. Every time I attended guild events, set up lunches, or put myself out there during academy galas, I reminded myself that.

"Uh, Enchanter Evergreen." The young acolyte strolled alongside Milo as he ushered me toward the elevator. "Your four thirty should be arriving soon. He can't just walk in and—"

"I've already emailed and rescheduled. They were very willing."

"Rescheduled?" She blinked, scrambling to scroll through her tablet. "The update isn't on your calendar."

The elevator doors dinged open. Milo shoved me in, waltzed inside, and pressed the button rapidly. "Oh, yeah. I totally forgot to update that. I'll be sure to do that after my very important meeting right now."

"Enchanter Evergreen, it's important you always have your schedule—"

"Uh huh, totally." Milo smirked as the doors sealed. He exhaled a calming breath and leaned against the wall. "Everyone wants a piece of me today."

"Must be hard."

"It has its moments." Milo moved closer. "You know what else is hard?"

I crossed my arms. The doors opened, and I stepped out onto the floor before Milo's breath reached the back of my ear. He walked out, nodding to others on the floor, and escorted me to his office.

His office was twice the size of my living room, filled with furniture for lounging, a wet bar, overpriced and unimaginative portraits, and a very disorganized desk.

I eyed the stack of papers covering his workspace. He blushed, bashfully averting his gaze.

"I get so preoccupied with fieldwork, I tend to fall behind on the actual paperwork. It's so much sign here, check there, wait, not there, then here, and make sure we've amended this line, now initial. I don't know."

"Uh-huh. I'm not here to discuss your contracts."

"Oh, I know what you're here for." Milo undid his tie. "That said, I seriously can't reschedule my five o'clock. They've got some type of demonic haunting, and the city has been dragging their feet for weeks on the issue, so this will have to be quick. No cuddles, which I'm sure you're heartbroken over."

Milo winked, sliding his jacket off slowly, seductively. He folded it over his arm, placing it delicately on a chair. He puffed his chest, bragging, and locked eyes with me as he unbuttoned his shirt one at a time, teasing me with whispers of what he planned on doing.

"Milo, I came to talk—"

"You can talk dirty all you want." He hovered toward me, channeling his levitation root magic, legs dangling, and tips of his dress shoes touching the carpeting. "I've always found your voice in my ears quite sexy."

He continued to levitate, which meant Milo wanted a real magical fuck right now. Quicky my ass. Or in this case, his, because he only ever floated in that graceful pose when he wanted me to snatch him out of the air with an assertive grasp. His exposed abs flexed with stirring magic, keeping him afloat.

My stomach tightened, magic instinctively channeling to my core so I could levitate into the air, meet him, grip him in a strong embrace, kiss him, and have my way with—

NO.

I settled the building magic and ignored my body's desires.

"I'm here about the vision."

"Wait. You actually came to talk?" Milo descended to the floor, buttoning his shirt. "Consider me shocked. I mean, it's not what we do. We just bang."

"That's not true." I gulped, averting my eyes because his bare chest still called.

"Let's see." Milo strutted to the other side of the office, plopping onto a couch. "Last time we screwed, it was because I asked you a question and you wanted to avoid answering, I distinctly recall you dropping to your knees and ripping my belt off. Not even a little foreplay."

He spread his legs, his tight slacks barely containing his thick thighs. God, Milo had no subtlety for the life of him. When he wanted to tease, he made certain his body timed everything perfectly. His bright blue eyes followed the shifting wrinkles in my face, each line probably revealing my desperate thirst.

"It's cool. It's how we work. You blow me, I blow you. Lots of kissing. One of us pounds the hell out of the other until splooge, and then you immediately regret every life choice that turned you into this commitment-phobe with abandonment issues."

I scowled. "That's an oversimplification."

"Is it, though?" Milo tilted his head, practicing his Hemsworth judgment expression since he lived for imitating or quoting memes, something the public loved for whatever ridiculous reason. His gaze shifted, eyes staring at the ceiling in a thoughtful daze. *"What would you even call that? Cobandonment phissues or abammitment issobe?"*

His face perked up, dimples deep with a minxy grin, as he caught me eavesdropping. I huffed and rolled my eyes.

"Maybe I'll make a Twitter poll on it. Bitches love that stuff." He hid his lips behind his phone, giggling. "Okay, it's me. I'm bitches."

"Can we discuss the vision?" I stood behind a chair, uncertain I trusted myself to join him on the couch and certain if I sat, he might very well leap onto my lap.

"This again? I told you, void visions can't be prevented. Let me explain. The universe just likes to mock clairvoyants with them." He extended his arms, gesturing. His voice dropped, deeper and almost as rough as mine. "You see this, dear psychic. Here is something super life-altering I wanted to alert you about, but I also wanted to make sure there's not a damn thing you can do about it. LOL—have fun with the horror."

"The universe uses lol?" I raised a brow.

"But of course. They're hip with the times, my man."

"Well, the universe isn't screwing with you on this one," I said, clearing my throat. "I found out who the mystery kid is."

"How?" He chuckled. "Impossible. I searched and searched, and there's absolutely nothing distinctive from that snapshot."

My face burned. That liar. "You did replay it."

"Yeah, for you, maybe. For me, too, because I like to occasionally dwell on the things I can't fix. What can I say? I'm masochistic that way."

"His name is Caleb Huxley, and he's a new student at Gemini Academy."

"Oh, and now we know why the void vision hit. Makes sense. Someone you're going to encounter, so when I touched you, the premonition triggered, and our magics just sort of got tangled at the wrong time." Milo nodded with affirmed satisfaction. "Sucks for the kid. Maybe cut him some slack on his classwork and try not to get too attached when he…you know."

Milo rolled his eyes back, sticking his tongue out and playing the crudest imitation of a dying person. My blood boiled.

"You can't be serious? What the actual fuck, Milo?"

He sighed, pressing his hands against his knees and forcing himself to stand. Unlike his typical broad-statured pose with a puffed chest, raised shoulders, and arched back, Milo hunched almost in defeat. He slinked toward the wet bar and made two drinks.

"I've had enough void visions over the years to know they're utterly impossible to alter. It's not the universe laughing at me. They're spitting in my face and cackling." Milo gulped his drink down, quickly making a second one for himself before I'd walked over and grabbed my first. "I've tried, you know. Some I never learned the name of the person in question. Some I just couldn't be at the right place in the right time. A few times, I thought I'd done everything right—perfectly, in fact—but those bastards still died. Void visions are simply impossible."

He raised his glass, saluting the outside world from his window view of the city.

"So, you're just going to give up?" I asked, unable to mask my rage, which swirled alongside disbelief.

"I am, and you should consider putting it out of your mind. It's not a reflection of you or your commitment to the kid. Fact is, sometimes interfering with the future can make everything so much worse."

"Maybe you're just too jaded to try." I swallowed my drink and slammed the glass against the bar, releasing a slight telekinetic burst to crack the glossy glass surface.

I avoided using my root magics carelessly, but in this moment, Milo infuriated me to the point all my channeled magic funneled away from telepathy toward the root of telekinesis.

"That's rich coming from you," Milo laughed, pouring himself a third drink. "After all, jaded is just another word for burnt out, right? Weren't you so burnt out, you quit this industry? Or was it because you couldn't save Finn? Oh, wait. No. It's because in failing to save him, you also—"

"Shut your fucking mouth." My heart pounded, raging and ready to rip through my ribcage. "Don't you dare throw his name at me like that."

A name that haunted me twelve years later. Finn's beautiful, soft face and unrelenting smile filled my mind. His ruffled chestnut brown hair always looked like he'd found the perfect breeze. His lost life cast a heavy shadow between Milo and me. A best friend to each of us, a lover, one who dreamt of becoming the greatest professional enchanter the world had ever seen. He dragged Milo and me into his life, leading us onto a path to joining Cerberus Guild.

"We're the three meant to be running this place. Just you wait. With our magics together, we'll be an unstoppable trio." Milo's eyes watered as Finn's light voice rang in his head.

My jaw clenched. I'd forgotten—forced myself to forget—how he sounded. My time with Finn, the romantic relationship the three of us created, was possibly the happiest of my life, even if I never showed it.

"I'll be okay, Dorian. You'll see." Even as darkness swept over him that last day, his smile never wavered.

Milo buried his thoughts, rolled his eyes up until the teary eyes faded, and his entire expression changed into a full-formed professional showman smile.

It was difficult finding joy again, knowing I spent so much time resisting it when I lost the chance to be happy with Finn and Milo. I couldn't imagine ever finding happiness again.

"If you're serious about picking up your old career, dusting off that enchanter license, and using your magic for something good"—Milo leaned against the bar, flicking a piece of stray glass I'd cracked—"I can think of a thousand better things your magic would be suited for. But saving that kid isn't one of them."

I choked back a scream at his comment, his reminder of Finn, and the ever-present regret that consumed me daily. Unable to look at Milo any longer, I stormed out of his office. On the drive home, my nostrils flared. I squeezed my steering wheel, whipping between other drivers who couldn't keep up with the flow of traffic. Enraged minds flurried and horns honked, but my music blared, mostly silencing them as I zipped past.

Chapter Five

I used the weekend to disappear into my despair. Huddled beneath a blanket, I hid in my room, drinking enough tequila to sleep through the festering thoughts of nearby neighbors. While I preferred vodka, it burned too much going down straight from the bottle, and I was too miserable for cocktails, so I thought I might as well enjoy the light citrusy burn of the tequila as opposed to gasoline that tasted best with orange juice.

Whether or not Milo planned on helping make sense of *his* vision, I'd see this through. This wasn't because of Finn. Even if it was—why would that be a bad thing? After what I did, what I didn't do, I owed him that much.

I took a swig from the bottle. I ruined everything. Every fucking thing in my life. Milo was right. I'd probably hurt this kid more than help.

Meows came from the other side of my door as Charlie wedged his claws under the sill, whining for affection.

"Sorry, buddy." I chugged the last quarter of the bottle, easing back onto the bed. I didn't have the energy for love right now. All I wanted was to blackout and vanish from the world.

And I did. My head was so heavy and blurred it couldn't make sense of the constant mental mutterings of those nearby. I sank deeper into the mattress until everything faded. Not a comfortable slumber but a temporary reprieve from the world.

I woke up groggy, preparing for school. I could hear Mom in the kitchen, thoughts buzzing about how I never took anything seriously and was screwing off during another semester. How the hell did she get into my house?

I rolled out of the twin bed, stepping onto dirty clothes, and... Oh, great. This wasn't my room. This was my childhood home, and I was fucking dreaming.

I hated dreaming. Possibly the worst rollercoaster ride ever. Whether it was because of my telepathy or just really shitty luck, I rarely dreamt, but when I did, they were lucid dreams. Not the kind I controlled or interacted with, more like I remained consciously aware of the dream that trapped me. And whenever I dreamt, two things happened.

The first was a horrible need for my subconscious to continuously stab me with memories I'd long since buried, hopeful of forgetting. These unaltered memories never deviated, playing out a script to the past I couldn't escape.

The second...

My childhood bedroom door swung open. Mr. Hammonds from the apartment complex down the street from my actual home strutted into the room wearing a powder-pink unicorn onesie. The big burly old man tiptoed next to me, bowing and twirling like a ballerina.

The second thing that happened when I dreamt was my memories mixed with other people's current dreams. Whatever oddities their mind played tended to merge with the unfolding events of my horrible past. It often felt like being forced to sit through a really screwed-up movie where the director took acid.

Staring in the bathroom mirror, I applied heavy doses of eyeliner and eyeshadow. Not for the bags under my eyes. Nope. This was my goth phase. If I could control my expression at this moment, I'd cringe. Instead, I glared at my reflection, sending some badassery vibes I'd practiced every morning to ensure others stayed away. Ugh, this was painful. Okay, truthfully, if I had control over my actions in this moment, I'd slap the frown off my teen self and give that angry prick something to be pissed about. It wasn't assaulting a child if you were hitting yourself.

Was I seriously reliving freshman year again? God, I'd forgotten how scrawny and pale I was. Not that my pasty skin ever adapted to sunlight. Still, with the black and purple hair and Slipknot T-shirt, I wasn't doing my ghostly self any favors.

"Off to school." I darted out of the house, skipping breakfast because my mother had spent that entire morning contemplating finally having *the talk* with me.

I'd learned more about sex from her confused surface thoughts buzzing with reactions on all the research she'd done than I had from actual porn at that point. Dear God, if I endured "the talk" with my mother and those damn Barbie dolls she'd bought again, I'd kill myself.

I zipped out the door and blinked at the morning sun's glare.

"You're free to work in groups or independently for this project. I leave it entirely up to you," Mrs. Jacobson said.

I stood by a desk, hand blocking the harsh fluorescent lights of the classroom that had replaced my front yard. Another thing to hate about dreams. A quick blink and the setting shifted beneath my feet in an instant.

"Oh, my flipping goodness, this lady." Finn shook his head, and chestnut locks bounced back. "I mean, why does she always do that?"

Ugh. Not this day. I'd argued with Milo, so my subconscious decided to throw this day at me in the most annoying way possible.

"Pick your own groups or work independently?" Finn asked, imitating her voice. "She knows people are just gonna work with their friends and ignore others. Like, is she even trying?"

He snapped his fingers, not-so-politely requesting I read her mind to determine her efforts. Reluctantly, I skimmed her semi-efforts in the lesson she'd prepared.

"Yeah, whatever. She's trying-ish." I shrugged. Finn was the only person at school I'd talked about my branch with. He thought it was the most amazing thing ever, something he actually thought often and told me regularly. Back then, it seemed like the worst magic to gain. Still did most days.

"Trying-ish? That sounds like sugarcoating if I've ever heard." Finn glared, full-on judgment, at Mrs. Jacobson because he never hid his disapproval. Or his approval. Something I fondly recalled when the memories of him didn't break me. "Seriously, her lack of confrontation is frustrating."

"Your lack of chill is frustrating," I said, desperately wishing I could scream or run or escape this memory. Or change how it actually played out and tell him how I'd really felt that day. How I'd felt every day. "Why do you always get so worked up over everything?"

"It's just her *everything* is so irritating. She just lets everyone do whatever they want all the time." Finn stood at his desk, rolling his eyes at the class already talking over Mrs. Jacobson about things in no way related to the project. "I can't wait until I leave this school."

I remember wanting to touch his arm that day, a small sign that showed I cared. A desire to hear his thoughts over everyone else's. Urges bubbled in my chest as I stared at Finn. He was so much taller and more muscular at fourteen than I was. It created an insecurity in my teenage mind, resentful of how everyone fawned over him, mistaking him for an upperclassman. It also caused confusion in how alluring his Adam's apple was, how everything down to the overpowering Axe spray had drawn me in.

This was agonizing, reliving this memory of us. Suffering those confused sensations I had for Finn when I was still figuring out my own sexuality.

"Okay. I'm inviting him into our group." Finn slapped a hand on my desk. My fingers inched closer to his, my pinky almost touching his, before he strolled across the classroom.

Back then, it was more difficult to comprehend any thoughts beyond the surface ones without contact. They'd get too muddled to fully understand. Yet I desperately wanted to know everything Finn thought. I still did.

"Whatever, like I care," I said, resting my head on my other hand propped with my elbow on the desk. Not whatever. I wanted to leave. Wake up.

Finn brought back a tiny boy, smaller than me, with hunched shoulders retreating into himself. He wore an oversized hoodie that covered his curly, dirty blond hair. Even then, Milo's blue eyes shimmered. Only at fourteen, they didn't hold the same confident joy.

My heart raced. Not because of the fight current Milo and I had had. No. A spike of jealousy over how Finn nudged Milo's shoulder with his as they walked to the back of the room.

My neighbor Megan unicycled into the classroom, past the pair, frantically pedaling between the aisles as coyotes chased her. I ignored her nightmare, content with only enduring my own.

"You're sure you want to work together?" Milo asked.

"Of course. I wouldn't have asked otherwise." Finn grinned. "Besides, we're gonna spend less time on this project and more time practicing our casting."

"Oh." Milo tugged his fingers, keeping his head low. "Shouldn't we do the assignment, though?"

"Please. Dorian says she doesn't even bother reading them all the way through."

"Shut up," I snapped, embarrassed he'd brought my magic up to this kid I knew nothing about. A kid who was about to enter my life and never leave. Even when Finn did. When he…died.

"I've seen you casting during gym. Your root magics are pretty solid, dude."

"Really?" Milo smiled; his braces gleamed under the fluorescent lights. He lowered his head as quickly as it lifted. "Maybe, but my branch magic isn't good at all."

Milo still hadn't learned much about interrupting his visions. Clearly, I was reliving this day as a reminder of how utterly useless his branch magic was when it mattered.

"That's why we're practicing, duh." Finn plopped into a desk and dragged another between me and himself. He patted the top, inviting Milo to sit. "So, tell me. What's your branch magic?"

"Clairvoyance," Milo muttered.

"What's that?" Finn cocked his head, bangs resting against his forehead, almost brushing his beautiful long lashes.

"It means he can see the future, idiot." I hated myself for being such a little dick all the time back then. "God, do you even bother reading those practice exams I loan you?"

"The future? Holy flipping flippers," Finn squealed.

The classroom had gotten so chaotic not a single person stared at the outburst. I scanned Mrs. Jacobson's mind, worried she'd notice.

Nothing. Looking back on things, she really wanted nothing to do with education.

"Why are you so fucking loud all the time?" I asked.

Finn had an aversion to swearing, which fueled my own desire to add more profanity to my vernacular as a way of freaking him out so he'd stop talking to me. It never worked. He'd just thank me for swearing on both our behalves. He was simply sweet that way. It was the worst. And it made my insides ache. Then and now.

Finn gripped my arm, squeezing it tightly and shaking me. "You know what this means, right? Right?"

"I could read your mind to find out, but honestly, everything about you is a serious headache." That was a lie. I scanned his mind the moment we touched, searching for anything and everything he thought about me, utterly confused and frustrated when all that popped into his head were images of Milo between the two of us. My feelings were all kinds of wonky in ninth grade.

"This means we're the perfect psychic trio. Milo can be the future, you can be the present, and I, the most important role, can be the past." Finn pointed his thumbs to his chest. "We're sure to impress the academies with an intro like that."

"How is the past the most important part?" I asked with a snarl. "It already happened. Done. Pointless. Retrocognition makes you nothing more than a glorified historian."

"You can't achieve anything if you don't learn from the past," Milo sheepishly answered.

"I didn't ask you," I snapped, baring my teeth at him.

Milo tugged his hoodie further over his bright blue eyes, hiding his face.

"I'm stealing your answer. That's some wise shiitake you've got going." Finn grabbed the hoodie and pulled it up some, revealing Milo's worried face. "But try not to hide your face so much, man. It's a pretty cute one."

"*Cute?*" The thought ran through both mine and Milo's minds on what felt like an infinite loop.

It'd be months before I fully understood Finn's sexuality. Milo's. Mine. Not long after that, the three of us would end up in the most bizarrely comforting friendship, which would evolve over the years into lust and romance, an exploration of our bodies, and a so-called relationship I resisted every step of the way because I was such an insufferable asshole who couldn't accept happiness until it was gone.

"Totally," Finn answered, posing. "But not as cute as mine. I mean, look at all this sexy."

My face burned. I hadn't stopped looking for the entire class.

Finn nodded to the textbooks in the corner of the room. "You can use your telekinesis root, right?"

Milo nodded, then frowned because he was a ball of anxiety back then. It took years for Finn to break away that introverted shell, but once he had, Milo never looked back. I hated him for that. Finn, I mean. If he'd kept Milo small and frightened, maybe he wouldn't continue chasing me to this day.

"But it's just, are we even allowed to practice magic in here?"

"Technically, no, but Dorian's gonna play lookout to see if she notices us." Finn beamed, always smiling all the time like an unyielding sun illuminating the shadows of my soul—that was the actual thought running through my fourteen-year-old brain to one of the twisted gothic poems I'd been working on. If I ever found that poetry journal, I'd burn it. "She can only write us up for casting in class if she catches us."

"We're not playing around," I said, glaring at 'this kid' because that day and for several weeks later, I'd refused to learn Milo's name. "This is serious training."

"Yeah. Dorian's got his heart set on joining Gemini Academy." Finn winked at me.

"No, I don't." I sank into my seat because I read and misread and overanalyzed every single potentially flirtatious thing he did that year a million times. "They don't even take public school kids. Not really. I'm just trying not to get stuck with some boring ass stupid job hating my life."

I gestured a hand at Mrs. Jacobson because so many of the teachers I'd eavesdropped on seemed to hate their choices. *Ironic, I know.* So many of the adults, in general, hated their lives and jobs and choices. And from a very young age, I knew I wouldn't end up like any of them. I'd love my life and hate everyone else in it. As a kid, I had it all figured out. Except, I never had any of it figured out. Not really.

"Best way to do that is to get a license and work as an enchanter. And I can do that anywhere, not just some snooty rich kid academy like basic ass Gemini Academy," I said, desperate for Gemini to accept me but knowing that dreaming and desiring something meant nothing.

People craved what they'd never have every day, and I'd heard their internal devastation for years, which weighed on my every waking moment as I tried to make sense of my magic. It was always confusing. No matter how raw and honest a person was about their failure aloud, it always rang tenfold louder in their minds. Tiny little words thrown at themselves, slicing their souls and willpower to pieces.

Finn released a telekinetic burst, easing a few textbooks off a dusty stack in the corner of the room. We'd hardly touched textbooks anymore, but the school wouldn't throw them out and lacked proper storage, so they just sat in classrooms, unused. Except by us.

"Try with one at first," Finn said, keeping a steady flow of magic to hover three above the class. "It looks easy, but it's super tiring. This is a really good way to practice precision control and weight training."

Darkness swept across the room. I wanted to scan the surroundings, wondering whose awful nightmare brought all this creeping horror. Shadows stretched wide, shattering the ceiling lights and drowning classmates in black sludge. It didn't matter. My body continued replaying the events exactly how they'd occurred that day, practicing discreetly with Finn and Milo, so with my current vantage point, I only saw it out of the corner of my eye.

I blinked.

Once I'd opened my eyes, I stood in the middle of a street. My legs trembling, clothes ripped, and body mostly numb at this point. This wasn't someone else's dream invading mine. No. Not this memory. Not this day. Anything but this one. Take me back to any other failure.

Buildings were on fire, debris everywhere. People all around, dead or dying or terrified they'd end up swept into the chaos.

Half a block away, Finn stood tall, taking tired breaths, face caked in dried blood and a shaky smile he refused to surrender. *"Contain the situation. I've got this."*

By twenty-two, he'd believed he could handle anything and everything. It didn't help that the guild masters bought into his charm, assigning us missions we had no business taking on.

A black portal opened with magic ready to transport Finn out of reach. I raced down the street, wincing from the pain in my body, quelling the frantic minds of civilians screaming for help, all so I could reach Finn. I stumbled forward, bracing myself and refusing to stop moving. Crawling, I ignored the deep cuts and blood loss, sucked in what breaths I could through the thick soot in the air.

"I'll be okay, Dorian. You'll see." And with that, the portal enveloped him, and I never saw Finn alive again.

"Give him back!" I gasped.

"You got this, Dorian. Don't let your regret for what happened

stop you from helping that kid. Show Milo he can fix the future. With you at his side, I truly believe you'll both do amazing things."

Even long gone, transported far away, his light laughter rang in my ears. The sweet chuckle he released whenever he thought about how great his future, our futures, would be.

That didn't happen. His future or this moment. *That doesn't happen.* My dreams never wavered off script. They were exact reproductions of memories I'd rather keep buried. What did this mean? How was this happening? Why did I always come back to the biggest failure of my life?

Chapter Six

I woke, unable to breathe like the smoke from that day actually embedded itself into my throat. I sprang up, pushing Charlie off my neck. Sweat drenched my face, and I panted, trying to compose myself and make sense of the nightmare. Charlie chirped at the end of the bed, ready for food and affection. My bedroom door was swung wide open.

I side-eyed Carlie. "How the hell do you always do that?"

She yawned and stretched long, arching her back, and laid back down.

"Must be nice." I carefully slipped around the pair of tabbies so as not to disturb them and went to the bathroom to wash away the memories and prepare for work.

Hot water sprayed against my back, somewhat soothing, as I tried to make sense of Finn's message. The one that shouldn't exist. Maybe my dreams were changing. Maybe my subconscious wanted me to pursue this void vision and used the worst memory possible to motivate me. Maybe allowing my magic to merge with Milo's temporarily scrambled my brain. Maybe I simply read too deeply into things that didn't matter. Yep, the maybes had taken root, and I spent extra time in the shower, dwelling on everything, including my insignificant place in the universe.

After my existential crisis, I fed the cats and myself, smoked, and packed for work. I didn't have time to sort any of this out because I had to prepare for the first day of classes, which really sucked since I spent the entire weekend hating myself and life, so I hadn't finished my lessons. I loved how so much of this career involved preparing for work at home because I was always too busy at work with other work to work on necessary work. I should've finished those plans before I drank myself into a weekend coma.

I went to the academy, pulled out my laptop, fine-tuned my plans for the week, and checked emails. A message sent from the headmaster at 7:28 PM was flagged as important. I rolled my eyes. Nice of her to send this update the night before the first day.

> Dear Staff,
> I hope everyone's weekend was restful and rejuvenating. Please read over the agenda below, and see the attachments based on grade levels. I included a few friendly reminders as we embark on a new year.

I skimmed through the overly detailed bullet points and formal, flowery bullshit. A reminder on the student orientations. A reminder of upcoming staff meetings. A reminder to set up department and grade level meetings. A reminder to complete our self-evaluations and set teaching goals for the year. A reminder of the student safety training videos we needed to watch on our own time, along with completing the yearly certifications that proved we kept our academy safe for everyone. A reminder to make our rooms as inviting as possible.

I sipped coffee, scanning the bare walls of my classroom. No tacky posters or motivational quotes. Six rows with seven desks each. Sleek and simple. Nothing fancy. Further into the semester, I'd rearrange for collaboration and group work. For now, this was their invitation.

Finally, my favorite friendly reminder in Headmaster Dower's email:

> Remember to take time for yourself, meditate, and self-reflect. We are in this together.

Oh, go fuck yourself.

I read through the attached agenda for Headmaster Dower's insightful orientation on better understanding our incoming students. How would listening to her ramble about the rules for three hours help with that exactly? No thanks.

I highlighted and copied the attached text. Noting the need-to-know topics to circle back and discuss with my homeroom coven later. The rest they could read and forget for all I cared. Honestly, most meetings could be emails. I had zero intention of wasting my first day, or my homerooms, listening to the headmaster drone on.

I'd review the extensive student handbook in smaller, more digestible mini-lessons over the first two weeks of classes. It astounded me she actually believed first-year students would retain all that information in one long sitting.

As seven o'clock rolled around, I finished tweaking my intended lesson for the first day, gulped the last of my coffee, and made my way into the hallway. The bell rang, and the silence ended.

A swarm of children walked in mass. First-year students held out their phones to read their schedules or carried a crinkled piece of paper with the same information. Paper they'd already ruined with grubby hands. I'd forgotten how messy and disorganized first-years were. I'd have to make lessons on self-management and organization because nothing was quite so annoying as scattered fifteen-year-old kids scrambling to keep up with their expectations.

"Good morning." My first student arrived, giving me a friendly wave, oozing kindness and excitement. "Hope your morning is going great."

"It's going," I said. "Sit where you like."

"Cool deal." His spiky bleach-blond hair shook. A hairstyle either meant to match Milo's, the beloved Enchanter Evergreen, or compliment the literal spikes from his magic. He wore the short-sleeved uniform without the academy jacket, revealing the white bone-like spikes along his forearms, and dress shorts which allowed the spikes on his legs room to breathe.

Quite the unique branch magic. I checked over my notes where I kept names, branch magics, and other comments about those on my roster. It helped me quickly put names to faces, not only for my twelve homeroom students but the hundred-plus kids in my history courses.

```
Name: Gael Martinez
Branch: Augmentation (Spike) (Spikes)
```

Of course, the school records were filed incorrectly. He didn't possess a single spike but a multitude. This type of distinction was important for licensing and something no school, public or private, took seriously enough.

Another boy brushed past him, bumping Gael's shoulder. He hit a spike and winced. "Move it."

"Oh, I'm so sorry." Gael smiled, flashing his pointed sharklike teeth. He ran a finger along his sharpened spikes, glancing at the other boy before lowering his head and averting his gaze from the glare. *"Espero no haberlo lastimado."*

Gael was bilingual, so I'd only understand the English surface thoughts if he had any. He might be the type who bounced between the two languages depending on his conversation or someone who thought exclusively in a preferred language.

I didn't need to understand the words to feel the longing in his mind.

"Whatever." The other boy stormed into the classroom. "**Annoying motherfucking porcupine-looking witch.**"

I shuddered. For fuck's sake. How could someone be that angry this early in the morning? He scowled as he sat in the front row, rubbing his arm.

A few other students in my homeroom walked by the door. Gael scooted out of the way, extending an arm and smiling, letting them know to go ahead of him. He was too polite.

Kids continued shuffling through the hallway, some talking, others searching doors for room numbers or attempting to make sense of the all-too-confusing building map. A few more students walked into the room. A tall blonde girl with hair draped over her shoulder slinked through the doorway, walking directly to the back and sitting in the furthest corner.

"I don't belong here. I wish they'd have just rejected me." Sorrow. It ran along my spine, one chilling column at a time. *"Theo would've... Theo would've done well at an academy. But me? What can I do?"*

Not all thoughts hit with the sharpest inflections of emotion, but like rage, true depression—the type that lingered within a head every single day—struck my mind harder. It came across like a faint cry smothered by the depths of a well dug deep within the earth.

She was one to keep an eye on. It was only the first day, and her doubt was intense, casting waves across the classroom. Even without telepathy, the signs were clear. Sure, she wore her uniform with elegance, applied perfect makeup, and finely styled her hair. Still, her expression was vacant of emotion, resisting the default frown beneath her somber blue eyes holding back tears. If she faked a smile, her composure might shatter.

A kid whistled to the tune of music playing loudly on his phone as he strutted down the hallway carrying a small cage draped with a cloth. Peterson said something, but the carefree student ignored him. Peterson's internalized offense was quite entertaining until the kid moved closer to my class. Ugh. My student. Great.

"Good morning, Mr. Teacher." He had a mischievous grin. The type of smirk that had irritating written all over it.

"Frost."

"No, it's not that chilly. Pretty nice out, in fact." He giggled, rubbing a burr away, waiting for me to elaborate that my last name was, in fact, Frost.

"Uh, huh." I squinted as he entered.

"Um, do you know where room one forty-eight is?" a girl asked, recoiling inwardly like a shy turtle.

I nodded, trying my best not to exude my usual stern expression, but too tired to smile. It didn't work. She trembled the entire time I explained where to go, leaving more frightened than when she'd arrived.

"Who wants to touch my cock?"

What? My face contorted in shock, and I turned back to my classroom. The mischievous boy held a rooster above his head, an open cage on the floor. It took him all of fifteen seconds to stir up chaos in the room without someone watching. I sighed, checking my notes.

This must be him.

```
Name: Gael Rios-Vega
Branch: Bestial (Familiar)
```

Why couldn't he have had a cat or something simple? His dark orange and black feathered rooster clucked. A short, stubby bird with plumy feet and a bright red comb atop its head that matched Gael's black faux hawk. Some light delving into surface thoughts revealed the smaller rooster as a breed from Belgium, Barbu d'Uccle Bantam, and a real fucking mouthful. Familiars traveled far to find their witch, but crossing nations, that was a new one.

"Can I pet him?" Gael Martinez raised a hand.

Gael Rios-Vega pursed his lips. "Normally, I prefer girls touching my cock, but so long as you're careful with those spiky thingys, sure."

"Always." Gael leapt out of his desk to pet the clucking rooster.

I squeezed the bridge of my nose. What a headache. "Please put your familiar back in his cage."

"You want me to put my cock away?" Gael tilted his head, delight in his dark brown eyes. "But I have a waiver that allows me to have my cock out during class. Do you want to see it? My waiver, not my cock." He held the rooster proudly against his bronze cheeks. "You can already see him."

I'd read his waiver and the others from my rosters. He was goading me into a game of tug-of-war for the class's attention. I kept my expression blank, refusing to shift even the slightest. Definitely a class clown, and the literal second he registered his playful antagonizing got a rise, it'd escalate. If I told him to call it a rooster, he'd just ask, *"Why can't I call my familiar a cock? Is there something wrong with that terminology?"* The prepped comment, along with a dozen others, danced on his surface thoughts, eager for engagement and an audience.

I stared, not speaking, moving, or blinking, while other students sat silently waiting.

"*So scary.*" The thought crept to the top of many students' minds.

It helped, reading their expressions or thoughts to gauge when intimidation would neutralize classroom disruptions versus further fueling them. Antagonizing a kid never worked as a catch-all solution to handling behavioral issues. That said, rightly timed stern-faced judgment could keep chaos from spreading.

Gael's grin faded, and he lowered the rooster. "I'm just playing. I'll put him away."

I turned back to the hallway, shifting my position so the corner of my eye remained fixed on the inside of the class and outer halls in case Gael performed an encore. His rooster clucked furiously as he placed him back in the cage. I sighed. As if my mornings weren't already rough enough. I clutched my clipboard, keeping my hands steady.

At the end of the hallway, Caleb Huxley rushed past others, smiling and apologizing profusely when he spun around them. His hair was still curly and brown.

"No running in the hallways," Peterson snapped, half inside his classroom. "I'm not sure how they did things at your last school."

"Oh. So sorry, sir." Caleb froze, then nodded apologetically.

"This is a prestigious academy, not some playground."

Caleb's jacket was a bit wrinkled and stitched with an older version of the academy logo, meaning he'd received the donated uniforms. Peterson immediately went to work sniffing out the voucher kids. I fought a snarl.

"Of course. Again, I'm very sorry." Caleb turned, biting his lower lip, and walked down the hall, scanning each room number until he reached mine. "Morning. Is this room one thirty-one?"

My jaw tightened, unable to speak because there were a thousand things I wanted to tell him. Warn him. Ask him. Help him. None of that would solve the void vision, and if Milo's anti-assistance was any indicator, informing Caleb might make things worse. Or make things happen. Or not happen. My teeth ground harder because who fucking knew?

"So intimidating."

I released my jaw. "First days can be confusing. This is the room."

"Phew. Overthinking things. Chill out, Caleb." Half smiling, he entered the classroom. *"Something about him looks familiar. Was he a guild enchanter?"*

We were all former guild enchanters. One of the major requirements for teaching at academies came with not only gaining an enchanter license but having some experience in the industry. Still, how'd Caleb recognize me? I had a pretty low profile compared to Milo and… My heart pinched. But that was more than twelve years ago.

I fixated on his mind, knowing nothing would present itself on his death this soon. Hoping, at least. It spun with thoughts on dozens of current and former guild enchanters. A literal encyclopedia of everything he researched his entire life, unfolding as a mountain of data. Talk about dedication to his studies.

Caleb's face burned bright red, and he let out an internal yelp. *"Kenny's in my homeroom coven? He's gonna kill me."*

What? Kill him? Clearly, hyperbole. Yet, Caleb trembled; green eyes locked on the angry kid. I didn't have any Kenny's, which meant it was probably a nickname but not a preferred name. Those were already documented in the academy database.

```
Name: Kenzo Ito
Branch: Hex (Disruption)
```

He glared at Caleb as the boy walked to the front of the class and sat in a front seat several rows from Kenzo.

"*They really let this branchless loser in? Gemini is supposed to be the best in the state. What fucking ever.*"

I pressed my fingertips against a temple, silencing the rage pouring out of Kenzo. I'd need to keep an eye on him because enraged thoughts usually came and went with most people, but not as a constant flow. It'd been a while since I'd dealt with someone fueled by anger coursing through their every surface thought. They were difficult, almost paralyzing if I dwelled on them for too long.

The bell rang, and I entered the classroom, standing at the front of the room. Shifting from summer mode to structure was tiresome for me and the students. Most of them were still thinking about their lost summers, a few fixated on the excitement of the academy, and two remained laser-focused on goals they wanted to achieve this school year—Caleb Huxley and Kenzo Ito.

"I'm Mr. Frost. I'll be your homeroom instructor while you're attending Gemini Academy. Some of you may also have me during general studies history courses. Let's start with attendance. If I pronounce your name incorrectly, let me know. If you have a preferred nickname, let me know," I said, reading off the list. "Melanie Dawson, Katherine Harris…"

A spike of anxiety hit as I reached the next name. I froze, panicking with tight breaths, and almost to Caleb's name. I confused this nervousness for my own, but when I peered up from the roster, Carter had a tightened smile. His cheeks trembled, and his foot bounced. Sweat pooled on his forehead, mixing with the gel seeping from his hair. That fear came from a name he knew was placed on the roster. One he'd hoped to pull me aside about at the start of class and prayed someone else had made a note of already. He regretted spending the morning in awe of the campus and chatting with other students.

```
Name: Carter Howe
Branch: Rejuvenation (Vitality)
```

"Carter Howe," I said, having already crossed off the other name Gemini Academy had to include due to state legality on records. I'd make certain, alongside our school counselor, that each of his teachers did the same thing. Carter shouldn't have to stress about a birth name that belonged to a person he never was.

With all the policies Gemini flipped and changed and improved or ruined over the years, I'd hoped they'd have figured out how not to include the birth names of our trans students for official documentation. But that was a headache for them that only affected a small percentage, so they passed that bureaucratic mess onto the families to handle.

"Howdy." Carter waved. His tension eased, and his smile remained. Somehow, he'd passed all that dread over to me as I moved on to the next name.

I immediately recognized each of them from their student profiles, yet…

"Caleb Huxley." I did my best not to look in his direction until he raised a hand, a foolish attempt not to indicate I knew him, knew him from a vision, a vision where he'd die. It wasn't like I had a plan, idea, or an inkling of what my next step should be. So, I did the only thing I was half-decent at: focused on my classroom while mulling this vision over. And making a plan. Soon. Before he died. Zero pressure.

So what if this vision came from a guy I kind of sort of didn't hate being around most of the time? Or that the person I felt closest to before he'd been killed literally spoke to me in a dream changing the script of my past and flipping it over?

Nope. Just another day in the classroom.

"Kenzo Ito." I paused, waiting for him to mention his nickname, but he simply raised a hand and glared. I continued down the list. "Gael—"

"Here." Both boys raised their hands. "Wait, really?"

Ugh. They spoke in unison and then laughed. So annoying. "Gael Martinez."

"Oh, that's me, sir," Gael said, turning to Gael. "Cool name, bro."

"Best name, except I do have a nickname, and you said to let you know if we—"

"No," I said, smothering his ridiculous nickname.

"But I haven't even asked yet."

"I'm not calling you Sir-Cocks-A-Lot," I said, completely deadpanned, feeding absolutely zero emotion into my response. Even if the name was a little funny, he didn't need to know that. Especially since I couldn't discern if my entertainment came from my own joy of crude humor or the bubbling giggles festering within half the class infecting me with bad taste.

"W-what?" He snickered with wide eyes. "How'd you know I was going to ask that?"

"Does Mr. Frost have telepathy?" Caleb flipped through his notebook, mind swirling with mutterings of names belonging to guilds, enchanters, and branch magics. He slammed a fist against his palm. *"Dorian Frost. That's it. The Ubiquitous Present."*

I froze. No one had called me that in years. Not even Milo. Oh, how I hated enchanter stage names and the way some witches used them to stand out while working within a guild. How many witches did this kid research, and how far back did he go? I shook it away and read through the rest of the roster, pausing at the last name. Only the blonde who'd hidden herself in the back remained.

"Tara Whitlock."

"Here." She raised her hand.

When they assigned me a Whitlock, especially one with her magics, I expected someone with more attitude. Tobias Whitlock, her father, owned and oversaw several of the best guilds in the state, along with a multitude of companies, so I figured I'd get arrogance radiating from Tara the second she arrived. Instead, I had a somber girl questioning her place in Gemini, questioning more than I could hear from the surface. I recalled rumors about the Whitlocks; their family heir Theodore Whitlock lacked a branch, much like Caleb, and due to some unfortunate and highly debated circumstances, Theodore lost his life during an encounter with warlocks. Hence the Whitlock's stance on keeping branchless witches out of guilds and warlocks off the streets.

I ground my teeth to bury my thoughts and everyone else's, practically snarling at my homeroom in the process.

It'd been five minutes, and I already found myself concerned for a girl lost in her despair, a boy with a massive chip on his shoulder, and a half-dozen others struggling to find their place here at Gemini Academy. All the while, I was compelled to keep a determined branchless witch alive even if the universe predicted his days were numbered.

"This is your first day at an academy, so I don't expect you to know, but I'm curious," I said, wandering around the room to bury my doubt or perhaps outrun it. "Does anyone understand the purpose of academies, truly understand our functions?"

They all stared, some with absolutely no idea, a few with an inkling, and one—Tara Whitlock—with complete certainty in the answer but unable to respond. I quelled my magic. Reading so many minds at once often agitated me until I'd established rapport, which I normally knew to avoid. I glanced at Caleb, who had a hand up. Nothing about this year was normal.

"Go ahead..." I glanced at my roster, pretending to review it,

"Caleb, right?"

"They're the only way we'll get our licenses."

"Yes and no. They're the easiest way to obtain a license, but not the only way. After all, anyone's eligible to apply for a license through the state. All you need is an understanding of your magic and—"

"Money," Gael Rios-Vega blurted, nodding with satisfaction at cutting me off. "That's what you were gonna say, right? I figured, so I thought I'd help you out."

"Yes, the fees are exorbitant," I said, watching his brow furrow with the effort to piece together the word based on context. "Truthfully, though, any witch could obtain a license by joining a casting club. Who here has trained at a casting club?"

Hands shot up. Anyone aspiring to gain a license would attend one. These sanctioned places allowed unlicensed witches free rein to cast without penalty or fines since casting clubs were designed to handle all forms of magic. Basically glorified, overpriced gyms.

Kenzo's arrogant disdain for casting clubs clawed at my magic. Not sure if it had to do with our equal disgust for their profiteering or his overbearing rage.

"And how many of you paid for those casting club memberships?" I asked. Since no hands dropped, I elaborated. "Out of pocket. I don't mean through your school program or your parents' pockets."

Every hand dropped except for Caleb. Curiosity captured me.

"It might be expensive, but I'd work a thousand side jobs to prove I belonged in a guild."

I cracked my neck, silencing his determination, the kind of bold belief that rang loudly like the dead, one dead soul in particular, which became unsettling because if I failed him—he'd join them.

"The main thing that distinguishes an academy like Gemini from your schools or those casting clubs is we're sanctioned for training."

Expressions shifted to wide-eyed confusion.

"Let me clarify," I said. "Through your homeroom coven, you'll be issued a fledgling permit. Once you get the permit, you'll be able to practice your magic freely on or off campus without regulations, fines, or penalties. Just free casting."

"What about those of us who can already cast off campus?" Gael Martinez asked with a raised hand.

"There's a difference between having a waiver that exempts your flow of magic versus a permit that allows you to train your magic." I pointed to Gael's spikes along his forearm. "Your branch magic of augmentation is in constant flux, meaning you can't quell it. So, you're issued a waiver. But this waiver doesn't allow you to practice casting your magic offensively or defensively, right?"

"Oh, that makes sense," Gael Rios-Vega added, pointing to his familiar. "My moms always tell me to be extra careful and follow the waiver to the letter whenever me and King Clucks, Peckfender of the Unhatched Dozen, aren't at home."

A few students chuckled at the rooster's name or Gael's goofy grin. That name. Christ.

"Precisely," I said, burying my judgment. "Once you have your fledgling permits, it'll put each of you one step closer to obtaining an acolyte license before graduating Gemini Academy. As well as interning with an enchanter at an official guild. After all, I imagine most of you came here with the goal of pursuing careers in magic, right?"

Lots of "yeses" followed by added side comments about guilds some already intended on interning at or amazing enchanters with similar branch magics to theirs. With most of the class excited and talking over each other, it created erratic, jumbled, half-composed thoughts which struck through my wall of silence.

"Everyone will know my name..." *"Helping people..."*
"Pointless." *"A career like Evergreen."*
"Demostrar que mi magia es genial." *"Money..."*
"Duh. Why the hell else would we be here?"
"Respect..." *"It's gonna be so cool."*
"The goal, yes. But can I really succeed here?"

I clamped my jaw to stifle a wince. It was a mistake to mention guilds and enchanters to a bunch of first-years. They were all young and eager. Most grew up admiring enchanters and all they'd achieved. But my mind was too unsettled, fractured from the vision, Milo, the dream with… I needed to keep my magic under control and compose myself like a normal fucking teacher.

It was difficult enough not becoming attached to students even when their thoughts didn't ring through my head. Their journeys, desires, hopes, and dreams. It was the kind of thing that stuck with a teacher after seeing them day after day. Thanks to my magic, all those emotions became glued to my mind much faster.

"Yes," I snapped, a bit more firmly than intended. It quieted the class, and without their chatting voices, I quelled their surface thoughts once again. After a calming breath, I continued, "I've reserved the auxiliary gym to evaluate each of your magics in action."

"Hell, yeah." Kenzo's eyes burned with excitement, his electrical hex already in effect.

"But what about the assembly?" Caleb asked. "They said the orientation was required, and if we missed—"

"Screw the so-called required orientation," Kenzo interrupted. "This is a chance to practice magic. Some of us actually came here for that."

Caleb clammed up.

"Yeah." Gael raised a balled fist as his familiar crowed. "Down with the patriarchy, too."

I raised a brow.

"*What?*" chimed many minds.

"Shut up," Kenzo growled.

"What, dude?" Gael grinned. "I was rooting for you. Down with the patriarchy and forced orientations. Live and let live and also f—"

"Don't say it," I interrupted. "Not one more word."

Gael sulked, making an exaggerated frown. These kids were exhausting. Too much energy way too early in the morning. I missed my third-year students because they already knew how to behave and engage, and also, they weren't as hyper. Now, I had to train first-years all over again on my preferred classroom etiquette. There was a reason they said a classroom of children was like herding cats. Impossible and annoying.

"The assembly's long-winded, and I'll email you all the need-to-know information, but I'd prefer seeing your magic in action so we can begin working toward filing your fledgling permits."

Caleb sheepishly nodded. "Mr. Frost, can I ask one more question?"

You just did, but sure. Don't be that guy, Dorian.

"Of course."

"How exactly do you expect us to show off our magics?" Caleb's cheeks trembled with a tight, forced smile.

He wanted to ask what types of magic. I didn't need to peer inside his mind to recognize that kind of anxiety. A branchless kid with no unique magic surrounded by witches all aspiring to be the best of the best with a branch that put them one step closer than him by default.

"I'm glad you asked." I strolled toward the door, ready to wrap up the in-class lesson and move us toward magic. "Does anyone care to tell me the most important job any licensed enchanter is tasked with?"

"Protecting people." "Fame."

"Catching dangerous warlocks."

"Helping where they can." "Inspiration."

"Tracking and eliminating demonic energy." Kenzo's sharp voice and furrowed brow quieted the others.

"Correct," I said, slightly relieved at how he silenced the onslaught of blurted responses. "Demonic energy is an uncommon occurrence in our world because the government and guilds work hand-in-hand to ensure the most dangerous demons don't enter the physical realm."

Students nodded.

"Okay, not to be that guy, but you didn't really answer his question," Gael said, and I braced myself for his familiar's cluck of support.

"Didn't I? You want to know how you're going to display your magic today? For today's evaluation, I'm going to determine your magical proficiency based on how you handle yourselves against demonic energy in combat."

A collective gasp made it difficult to fight the devious smirk that grew on my face. Something about their initial shock always entertained me, year after year.

Chapter Seven

I escorted my class across campus. The layout left some astounded. Anxiety and curiosity bubbled from their thoughts in equal measure. I hadn't spoken since we began the trek toward the auxiliary gym. They weren't in any danger from the demonic energy, but it always gave me a good laugh when their eyes bugged out, paranoia and wonder filling their minds.

I brought my homeroom to the auxiliary gym, a massive dome that made football arenas sheepishly blush at feeling small in comparison. We entered the gym divided into various terrains, from tiny woods simulating a forest to rocky hills creating a cliffside and everything in between, which accommodated all types of training and magics. Along with workout stations so students could condition themselves physically to better maintain their channeling.

Half the students lingered at the entryway. If they'd channeled their sensory root magic, they'd realize there was no active demonic energy and enter with ease. But they were young, and the thought hadn't occurred. Part of why my hit-the-ground running philosophy was important. The sooner I had them casting magic on their own, the faster they'd grow. I ignored the doubt that perhaps this method led Caleb closer to his fate and assured myself a well-trained witch was for the best. And if not, I'd be there ready.

I couldn't do anything for Caleb right now. I still had too many questions and zero answers. What I had to do, what I prided myself on when I got into education, was work with my students to ensure they had the best results at Gemini Academy.

In order to help them improve, I needed to fully assess their skills. Plus, the more I knew these students, the more I understood them, the better my chances of gaining more insight into Caleb's future would become. Peers had a way of seeing layers the rest of us missed. I clamped my jaw. Even telling myself to treat today as a lesson for all my students, my mind continued veering back to Caleb and his impending death.

"There are no fiends lurking around any corners." I waved them inside. "I wouldn't throw you into the deep end on day one. You'll only be encountering wisps during this exercise."

"***Wisps? What a fucking joke. So much for testing our abilities***."

I grimaced.

"Can anyone tell me how demonic energy enters our world?"

"In the form of wisps." One of the girls eased her way inside the gym, clutching a grimoire close to her chest. Sunlight piercing through the glass ceiling illuminated the golden highlights in the large, coily puff tied above her head in a tight bun.

```
Name: Katherine Harris
Branch: Enchantment (Spell Craft)
```

A useful magic that allowed her to channel her essence onto the parchment of the spell book, but without the support item, she'd have no access to her branch.

"Close," I said. "But not exactly."

Katherine wrinkled her forehead, strumming her light brown fingers along the grimoire. She was almost there. Part of teaching came with balancing how much information I threw at them versus the amount I allowed them to gather and share through discussion. It was also a beneficial way to determine who knew what and see if they could express it in a way their classmates would comprehend, sort of a soft skill they'd need the rest of their lives.

Caleb cocked his head. Mutterings ran along the surface of his mind because he believed Katherine had answered correctly, too. Standing next to Gael Martinez, the pair looked even paler under so much direct sunlight, much like myself. Another reason I hid beneath long sleeves, jeans, and a brown mop of hair to cover most of my face.

"Wait. You didn't ask how demonic energy appears in our world, but how it enters." Everyone in class stared at Caleb, who mumbled a few inaudible words before continuing. "You see, all demonic energy begins in our world in the formation of wisps. Fragmented demons attempting to piece themselves back together." He spoke with his hands, gesturing, and retreated into his thoughts, processing the question, leaving everyone, including myself, curious. "But that's not how it enters. Our world is split into various planes of existence. The physical world, which is ours, followed by the temporal realm, where we channel our magic, various other planes that don't really answer the question… And then, of course, the demonic realm, where they dwell in pursuit of more magic to fuel their reality. In order to get to our world—"

"For Christ's sake, no one needs your ramblings." Kenzo sneered. "Demons rip through the planes into our world. This causes them to shatter apart into wisps until they can reform their fragmented energy, creating fiends. There, answered. Now, we can get to the training." His eyes remained locked on Caleb. "How fucking hard was that to say?"

"First, language. This is an academy," I said, groaning at how my apparent inner-Peterson was showing. *Dammit.* "Second, try raising your hand before contributing."

"Why?" Kenzo smirked at Caleb, the anger inside him fading momentarily. "The branchless blunder didn't raise a hand before babbling nonstop."

Caleb shrunk inside himself. *"They all know now. It had to happen, but..."*

I wanted to speak, correct Kenzo's outburst, defend Caleb's place here, but whether astonished by Kenzo's rage or Caleb's doubt or a first day I hadn't prepared enough for or a vision I couldn't prevent— I froze. All the while, every student questioned internally and aloud how he got into the academy.

Gael Martinez slapped his hands together so loudly it silenced everyone. I was relieved.

"Whoa, bro. You got into the best academy in the city without a branch magic?" Gael beamed with pride, his sharklike teeth shimmering under the sunlight. "You must be like super smart and amazing with your root magics. Like, I'm okay with some, but it was definitely my awesome branch that got me into the academy, for sure. But you impressed the panel without one. I'm not jealous of people, but I've got my eye on you, branchless wonder."

His laughter bellowed throughout the entire auxiliary gym. A carefree kindness that carried toward me like a lifejacket in an ocean of drowning emotions.

Caleb's reddened face turned pale again. *"He's right. I'm not a blunder."*

Katherine nudged him with her shoulder as others settled, her grimoire clenched tight.

"I'm basically branchless without this book," she whispered.

He smiled, looking up to meet her eyes since she stood a full foot above him, heart pounding so hard it lurched into his throat and the beat rang between every word he thought.

"Let's return to the time we have." I cleared my raspy throat, aching for a cigarette. "Can anyone tell me why homeroom covens are assigned with twelve students in mind?"

Kenzo scowled, screaming an answer he had no interest in sharing.

"This ties into the origins of when casting and covens first began forming to challenge the demonic energy clawing its way into our world," Katherine answered, adjusting her glasses. "It's because of the twelve branches of witchcraft."

"Correct."

Her smile filled her face.

"I'd also add how the homeroom covens are no longer set up with these same traditions, given how we have more overlap in witches possessing the same branch magics."

"***And apparently for the branchless witches, too.***"

I brushed past Kenzo, grinding my teeth. I reached Gael Rios-Vega and Layla Smythe, then gestured.

"These two, for instance, each possess the bestial branch, yet have completely different variations of the magic."

Gael looked the girl up and down. She was much smaller than him, smaller than everyone in the class, which was only amplified by the oversized academy jacket she wore. It reached the edge of her skirt, almost hiding it entirely.

"Gael's branch provides him with a familiar that he channels his magic with." I nodded to Layla. "Do you care to demonstrate how your bestial branch works?"

"Certainly." Layla ran her fingers through her low-hanging pigtails and snarled. Light brown fur covered her face, and her body expanded, filling out the clothing. The buttons of her shirt barely contained her muscular, animalistic form.

Some students gawked at the transformation. Kenzo balled his fists, gray sparks of static coating his knuckles. Caleb jotted notes.

"She's a therianthrope, most commonly confused for lycanthropy, but that's just because typically, those who adapt their physical form to a specific animal do so in the form of a wolf. Fascinating. Based on the features, I'd say she's a cougar."

```
Name: Layla Smythe
Branch: Bestial (Therianthropy)
```

He'd identified her magic and all the specifics verbatim in my notes after a single glance. This kid was always studying. It was one thing to recognize the twelve branches. It was entirely more complex for a young witch, even a seasoned one, to learn all the variations of each branch.

"Are you a lioness looking for your king?" Gael wiggled his eyebrows.

Layla growled, shrinking back to her human form.

"Hawt," he said, adding a sizzle with his tongue.

I glared, shooing him with a hand to not-so-politely usher him away from Layla.

"That makes sense, I think," Gael Martinez chimed in. "I learned in school that root magics are the foundation of the tree that represents all witches, and the branches are our unique magics stretching out to the world. But I've always thought about how every augmentation magic—like mine—is sort of different from other augmentations, so we're like special leaves lined along that one branch. Guess it makes sense the other branches would have their own special leaves, too."

"That's a clever metaphor," I said.

"A what?" Gael's face scrunched.

"A comparison, symbolic and figurative stuff. You'll cover that more in your general studies courses."

Gael Rios-Vega strolled over, rooster in his arms, looking up at me with a minxy grin. Please no. I didn't even want to scan his mind because whatever he thought was probably tenfold worse than what he'd say.

"Mr. Frosty, is it true genetics play a role in branch magics? King Clucks found our science teacher's answer highly suss."

Oh, an educational question. Now I felt like a dick.

"Obviously." A flame sparked from a lighter, coiling around a student's arm, causing Gael's familiar to crow furiously. "My entire family has primal magic."

```
Name: Melanie Dawson
Branch: Primal (Fire)
```

"But I'm the only one in like forever who's gotten the fire element." She strutted closer, making the rooster flap and Gael sweat. "Hope it's not too *hawt* for you and your cock."

"Never too hot."

I immediately buried his exploding surface thoughts because they were anything but thoughts of fear for him and his familiar. These two were fifteen frickin years old and overtly sexualizing their words like I wasn't standing right in front of them.

I snapped my fingers to draw their focus.

"To answer your question, Gael, genetics only play a small role in branch magics. It's a much more complicated answer you'll learn during your time at Gemini." I rolled my eyes. Why'd I bother? His mind was lost on Melanie. "Anyway, let's move on to the test of magic. I'm sure many of you are excited to put your branch magics on display."

They all started up again, excitement on their faces, boastful words blurted, and doubt hanging on the surface of others.

"I can't wait to show off my branch. Just wait!"

"*Why's it got to be a test on branch magics?*"

"How will this reflect on branch magics that aren't offensive?"

"Oh, man." "I didn't even think of that."

"*I should flip through my grimoire and strategize.*"

"**Get on with it!**"

"Am I allowed to release my spikes or only expand them?"

"My flames can get intense."

"Doesn't matter. King Clucks and I are gonna dominate."

"Bawk."

"Everyone, try to be careful."

"*Even without a branch, I'll keep up.*"

I let them swirl in their joy while fiddling with the controls at the front platform to set up the releases for the wisps. I wanted that excitement to simmer before I took it all away.

"For today's test, I'm splitting you into three groups of four. This is representative of how it's believed a basic coven should have one witch who can call onto each of the four corners when casting."

"Excuse me," Katherine said. "That philosophy is for root magics, I thought."

"You thought correctly," I replied, and Katherine swelled anxiously, much like the others. "Today's evaluation will have nothing to do with your branch magics. My only concern is seeing where you all stand when it comes to your roots."

Dread fluttered about because many lacked the fundamentals, and they knew it. They believed their branch magics would make this training a cakewalk. Not if I could help it. Caleb fought back relief that swam between their nervous waves cascading in the air. This wasn't for him, though. This approach always worked as a proper baseline for evaluating where first-year students stood so we could properly apply for their fledgling permits.

"It's a simple test on how well each of you channels your root magics, which ones need work, and how long your stamina can hold out."

I pressed a button on the panelboard, which controlled the entire layout of the auxiliary gym. A tiny white ball of energy floated in the distance, quickly hovering toward us, seeking magic, craving it even in such a fragmented form.

"We discussed what wisps are, but can someone tell me how to remove them?"

"You'd need an offensive magic," Layla said, holding up her thin fingers. "Theoretically, if I channeled enough magic into a slash, I'd shatter one. Probably."

"My flames could burn them easier."

"I bet King Clucks could peck them into nonexistence. He's quite ferocious."

"Idiots," Kenzo snapped. "He said remove, not disrupt or destroy. Only one magic truly removes wisps from our plane—the root, banishment. Hence, why you're giving us this *basic* test today."

"Correct," I said, biting back the commentary of a growing dislike for Kenzo's attitude. "While enchanters use amazing branch magics to captivate the public, it's their control of the fundamentals that make them vital to everyday society."

"*Banishing a wisp,*" Katherine thought. "*Basically, the Dalton Prep final all over again. I got this.*"

"There will be fifty wisps released throughout the auxiliary gym, and your groups will have fifteen minutes to eliminate as many as possible before time runs out." That shook Katherine and other students who had similar finals at their private schools. "Each group will have three opportunities. Since wisps will be hiding within the terrains, you'll need to access all four roots to find and remove their presence."

I wanted to study all their capabilities, but especially Caleb's. Hopefully, it'd offer enough insight into what I needed to help him with to avert the impending vision. No matter how I pushed his potential fate out of my mind, it haunted me every second of class, fearful the wrong word or lackluster lesson would lead him to his death.

Chapter Eight

I made minor tweaks to the student groupings since I'd put Caleb and Kenzo in a group given their records showed they'd attended the same middle school and high school freshman year, but that clearly wasn't going to work. Students like Caleb, Katherine, and the Gaels chatted it up, collaborating in preparation. Tara distanced herself from her group while Kenzo glared at anyone who attempted to strategize with him.

This test on their skills would also provide insight into their stamina for channeling magic. I smirked. As an added bonus, it'd leave them worn and exhausted the rest of the day, perhaps even the first week. Maybe they'd be less chatty then.

"Group one. You're up."

I went to the proctoring room where the other students joined me. Both Gaels were instantly fascinated by the box office setup at the edge of the auxiliary gym, each staring at their reflections in the wall of black screens until I turned the cameras on, observing the screen where Caleb strode toward the starting line, confidently ahead of his group.

"Careful, though." My raspy voice boomed from the microphones. I studied the reactions of each group member closely with the video and audio throughout the auxiliary gym, along with the wisps already beginning to funnel from vents. "If too many wisps gather in one place, they'll form a fiend. If that happens, I'll have to cancel your evaluation early and secure the area for the next group."

This rattled each of them. Their pained expressions lacked the certainty I had the day my homeroom instructor used this test when I was a student. Even though she kept her mind guarded, prepared for my telepathy, I still skimmed glimpses of its purpose. It helped that Milo had predicted an unprecedented outcome on our behalf, a memory that almost brought a smile to my face.

An important but cruel test that often reflected poorly on the first group having to shake off a new rule moments before beginning. Necessary for any aspiring enchanter, though.

"Don't worry. Stick to the plan," Caleb said with a shaky smile. "*I figured this might be the case.*"

Interesting. What was he up to?

The timer started, and they raced off in pairs, Caleb and Katherine sticking close together by the fitness station where obvious wisps fluttered about.

```
Name: Caleb Huxley
Branch: N/A
```

Caleb motioned his arms in unison from one side of his body to the other, sending a telekinetic burst to disperse a cluster of tiny, white-orbed wisps that looked like little floating lightbulbs. He still needed to use both arms together to cast telekinesis, but a solid technique.

> Name: Katherine Harris
> Branch: Enchantment (Spell Craft)

Katherine kept her grimoire fastened in a satchel slung over her shoulder, resting on her hip, as she worked to divide the wisps Caleb struck. It wasn't paranoia on her part about leaving her support item unattended. She knew it'd serve her no good here, but she wanted to keep it close, training how her body moved with the weighty, leather-bound book attached. Clever.

This lesson wasn't about branch magics, but I needed to learn what branch each of my students possessed, the intricacies and limitations because much of the semester would focus on amplifying the skills of these twelve students.

Caleb and Katherine relied heavily on their telekinesis to shift the wisps apart, keeping their radiating energy bouncing around chasing their telekinetic magic so none merged together and grew in strength. I wasn't certain of their strategy yet, since the actions maintaining their root magic were the loudest thing along the surface of their thoughts.

Five minutes in and Caleb's face reddened, and slick sweat coated Katherine's forehead. As expected, maintaining constant use of their root magic weighed on their bodies.

"Man, they already look tired," Gael Martinez said.

"Well, telekinesis draws upon a witch's muscles, so they're feeling the effects," I said.

"Because they're weak," Kenzo said.

"I'm not worried." Gael Rios-Vega flexed his thin arms. "Look at these guns."

"Casting like this is all about endurance, not strength." It also involved utilizing the full range of a person's muscular system, but it seemed the pair only knew how to draw upon the muscles in their arms where they released the specific root magic. I noted their basic control.

All the telekinetic energy sent wisps further into the air. Eventually, those wisps clustered closer to the glass ceiling, out of range.

"You go high, I go low, right?" Katherine asked.

Caleb channeled magic into his core, levitating toward the wisps.

Gael's rooster crowed and pecked at the air.

"If he's going to do that, please step outside," I huffed.

"Chill, King Clucks." Gael covered his familiar's eyes. "Caleb's not mocking you, I swear."

Wisps followed the trace of Caleb's magic, but Katherine kicked the air, disbursing them quickly, allowing Caleb the opportunity to pull the far-reaching wisps back toward the floor. Her file mentioned the sports she participated in at Dalton Prep, but I suppose I was wrong about only channeling in her arms. Still, she'd need to learn to draw on those muscles without using them for casting. That was the purpose of telekinesis, after all, to draw on the body to move things with one's mind.

Caleb didn't have as much power in his telekinesis as Katherine, given her toned physique, but his bursts were accurate, sending the wisps back to the floor of the gym. The precision didn't weaken midair, and his levitation didn't falter when channeling the two magics simultaneously. I doubted any academy kid would be able to channel all four, but this wasn't about that. I noted each of their abilities.

Meanwhile, their partners had beelined toward the small forest terrain. They avoided casting or handling any wisps along the way. Strange.

```
Name: Jennifer Jung
Branch: Psychic (Empathic)
```

Her gothic getup put my gothiest phase to shame. Long black hair with scarlet bangs covered her eyes but created a heart-shaped frame around her round cheeks and black lips. Even in the uniform, she'd added personal flair in her black nails with skulls etched on each, shiny silver-chained pendants wrapped around her neck, accompanied by matching bracelets, and she trudged forward in black combat boots that were in no way academy regulated. Whatever—I didn't care about enforcing dress codes.

Her mind fixated on the growing swarm of wisps hidden within the thickets of trees. Good. Jennifer utilized her sensory root and prioritized keeping the round from ending early. Figures, given her scores at Brookfield.

"Whoa, how's she know where they all are?" Gael Martinez tapped the screen. "I didn't even see those wisps."

I cleared my throat, glaring at the smudge he'd left.

"Oops. Sorry." Gael licked his palm, careful not to let his spikes along his wrist hit the screen, and rubbed the smudge until it was larger, somehow worse. For Christ's sake, why? My forehead throbbed. Messy children.

"King Clucks says she's got an unfair edge," Gael Rios-Vega said.

Like Milo and me, Jennifer's psychic branch made her better suited for channeling sensory magic. Root magics were equally dispersed to all witches, but it was true our branches sometimes played a role in accessing them. As psychics, we often cast our channeled magic outward in a similar manner, so Jennifer had an affinity for sensory. But just as telekinesis weighed on the body's muscles, sensory magic carried a heavy burden. It drew on the body's water molecules, expelling them into the air to track demonic energy, dehydrating the user with each cast.

I wondered how she'd handle being the only member channeling her sensory.

```
Name: Carter Howe
Branch: Rejuvenation (Vitality)
```

A complete opposite to Jennifer, as in he represented a full-fledged preppy jock in the most pretentious sense with his initial doubts completely buried. Still, I'd taught enough kids from Dalton Prep to understand those kids were more than their parents and money. It didn't help that he had an arrogant smirk and brushed his fingers through his wavy blond hair the entire time he banished wisps, all his nervousness from the classroom had transformed into confidence.

His eyes locked with the camera. Was he actually posing?

"He looks like a model out there," Gael said, slicking back his spiky blond hair.

Not posing. I shook my head. He wanted me to recognize how he kept his composure after eliminating nineteen wisps. Cocky. Banishment was a difficult root to cast without exhausting a witch. It channeled magic which pushed demonic energy back through the cracks of our plane, but that caused a great deal of mental fatigue, leaving the user groggy, more likely to pass out. A witch with rejuvenation would already have grown accustomed to that sensation, however, since by supporting other witches, it would weigh on his mind and body as the price of restoring another's.

This was their strategy. Caleb and Katherine didn't have a branch affinity for a specific root, so they prioritized showcasing telekinesis and levitation while providing Jennifer and Carter the chance to demonstrate their superior skills in sensory and banishment.

The timer buzzed, and I used the control panel to draw the remaining wisps back into storage. Twenty-eight removed. Not bad.

"An okay first round," I said, greeting the tired group one at the starting line. "Interesting how your strategy highlighted the roots you're all clearly proficient in but lacked showcasing anyone's overall comprehension."

"Sorry about that," Caleb said. "That was my idea."

"A good idea." Carter slapped Caleb's back, then pushed past him, standing front and center of his group. "He figured since you were scoring how many wisps we removed, we'd take out as many this round with the roots we're strongest in, then use the next rounds with our other roots."

"A strategy we agreed not to share with the competition," Jennifer said through gritted teeth. "*Moron.*"

"I see, but there's no prize for the number of wisps eliminated. Scoring the number you all eliminated is probably third on my list. The main purpose of this is to see how you all access each root, as well as your teamwork skills. Two important factors for young witches who'd like to become professional enchanters. So far, I've seen some teamwork, but honestly, I'm not the slightest bit impressed by your root magics. Hopefully, you'll change that during your next two rounds."

Group one sulked. Still, it was quite impressive they cleared just over fifty percent of the wisps.

"I would also like to mention that some of your roots faltered when shifting between them," I said. "Channeling multiple roots can be strenuous on the body. Proper breathing can settle the lag between…"

I paused. Caleb wrote every word I said, excited for each tip I had to minimize the delay between casting. Ignoring the delight, I continued explaining, then called group two up and returned to the proctoring room. Gael's spikes grew slightly as he broke away from Melanie and Layla, strolling toward Kenzo. The four of them should make for an interesting group.

"So, me and the others were thinking we should—"

"Stop talking." Kenzo cracked his neck and eyed the clock.

```
Name: Kenzo Ito
Branch: Hex (Disruption)
```

A useful branch magic to prevent others from casting, but no advantages to accessing root magics.

The timer beeped.

Kenzo sprang into the air. His slender frame lingered momentarily, then he guided his arms behind his back, releasing a burst of telekinetic energy. With the mix of levitation, he soared past his group. Rage smothered by the pride he oozed while wind breezed through his short jet-black hair.

I leaned closer toward the screens, tilting my head to examine his movements. That was a sophisticated combination of two root magics. Not the type of thing an unlicensed witch should comprehend. Ever. Kenzo flew, spinning acrobatically, banishing clusters of wisps in one go.

"*Three. Seven. Twelve. I can do this all day.*"

I noted his midair shifts. He'd shown real skill in casting two roots simultaneously and in an advanced manner. Still, he had to completely halt the use of telekinesis and allow his levitation to waver before casting a banishment. That said, I'd had third-years who struggled to shift magical gears like that.

"We can't just stand here." Melanie's freckled face scrunched.

```
Name: Melanie Dawson
Branch: Primal (Fire)
```

She darted toward two stray wisps. Flustered confusion consumed her as she recalled what it took to channel the banishment root. Kenzo leapt between her and the wisps, removing their presence and moving on before she'd fully processed what'd happened.

This was disastrous. I'd had my fair share of showoffs in the past, but he wasn't doing this to impress me. Nope. I'd gathered enough of his surface thoughts to realize he thought very little of me and not much more of Gemini. It could be a desire to intimidate the others, but his surface thoughts were an enigma of calm confidence acting as a thin layer of ice containing the fury brewing beneath.

"We're supposed to be working together." Layla hovered in the air beside Kenzo, her ash-brown pigtails bouncing.

```
Name: Layla Smythe
Branch: Bestial (Therianthropy)
```

"Then keep up." Kenzo released a telekinetic burst of magic that sent Layla spinning toward the ground.

"Gotcha." Gael extended both arms, releasing a bubble of telekinesis to catch her.

```
Name: Gael Martinez
Branch: Augmentation (Spikes)
```

Quite advanced. He might also be proficient in other areas from his time at Chesterton Prep, or maybe he worked better with his telekinesis as a method to carefully distance others from his spikes. Hard to guess when all their minds were scrambling over Kenzo's blatant disregard for their plan or lack of one.

"*Find them all.*"

His sensory root helped sniff out the more elusive wisps tucked within the terrains.

I grabbed the microphone. "And that's the round."

"What?" Gael's jaw dropped. "But we've still got like eight minutes left."

He ran his hands through his spiky hair and tugged it until the frustration faded, and he forced a smile.

"Yes, but it seems your *group* cleared all the wisps." I could funnel more out, but given Kenzo's motivation—not that I fully grasped it—he'd likely remove those too.

Biting back my agitation, I joined group two back at the starting line which, unfortunately, most of them had barely left.

"As far as teamwork, it's hard to know where you all stand"—I glared at Kenzo—"but clearly some of you have great proficiency in the fundamentals. Maybe you'll let your other group members show what they can do in the next round?"

Kenzo scoffed. "Sure."

Witches with hex magic usually acted as support within guilds, given their neutralizing capability, but with such precision on his root magics, Kenzo had identified and worked around that shortcoming to ensure he stood among offensive-fighting enchanters. Interesting.

"I know you're not scoring us primarily on wisps taken out, but group two totally takes first place on that front." Gael beamed. "Thanks to Kenzo, of course."

"Whatever." He stuffed his hands in his pockets, taking slow breaths, but his chest expanded and deflated with exhaustion.

Awe swam along the surface of Gael's thoughts. Irritation along Layla's at losing the chance to showcase her magic. Melanie's mind pivoted between relief Kenzo had stolen the round and dread she was nowhere near his level or the others. Her high school didn't have nearly the same access to training or studying, and that self-conscious nature she'd buried clawed its way out of the earth of her heart in a matter of seconds.

Despite all the worries some teachers had about public-school kids flooding our rosters, only five of my homeroom coven came from them. This made balancing their groups a bit challenging because I'd hoped they wouldn't feel intimidated since they didn't receive the same training. Clearly, that didn't cross Kenzo's mind since his antics intimidated most of the class.

"Well, this is all fantastic." Gael Rios-Vega took a superhero stance—a literal fucking superhero pose, chest puffed, hands on his hips, and broad shoulders with his familiar planted on one. "But it's time for the real winning team to enter. You guys did good warming up the gym, but we're here to conquer it."

"All right, go ahead, group three." I joined the other students observing from the proctoring room, noting that despite going last, group three spent zero time collaborating, only observing the others.

Caleb stood next to me, eyes locked on the screens, pen placed to his notebook, already scribbling. I buried my concerns for him, remembering this moment right here was about education, getting to know all my homeroom students, and that I had time to change his fate.

"You take a lot of notes?" I asked.

"Yes, sir. There's so much magic out there, it's hard to keep track otherwise. The branches alone are filled with variables. Like, Melanie used that lighter as a support tool for her primal branch, which means she can't create flames, only control them." He flipped through his book. "Which is different from two other enchanters who have the same element." He shared the page, which I didn't read since the mental image exploded on the surface of his mind as he'd memorized nearly every fact he chronicled. "They can create and control flames. Is that an experience thing?"

Not in the least. Magic blossomed in everyone differently, or in some cases, never blossomed at all.

The timer beeped.

"Okay—I've got to see the rooster in action." Gael shook his fists.

Spikes sprung between his knuckles. "I bet this is either going to be the coolest or funniest thing in the world, and I want front-row seats."

"Stop channeling your branch," I whispered.

"Oh, sorry." Gael eased, and the newly formed spikes retreated.

I noted heightened emotion—possibly joy—triggering his channeling. That was something we'd need to work on this semester.

"Move your fat head so other people can watch." Melanie stood by Layla, each with crossed arms. "Or are you too busy fawning over everyone else's magic?"

"Maybe ask nicely?" I gave them both a stern expression in equal measure to their attitudes.

"No, it's my bad." Gael scooted to the side.

"Back where you were, porcupine. You're in my space." Kenzo stood firmly and glared, his gaze shifting from Gael to the girls. He pointed to the other end of the cramped proctoring room. "Those lackluster losers can watch from over there."

They waited for my response, but honestly, I didn't have time for their resentment of Kenzo and misdirected anger toward Gael. I'd already missed the opening for group three.

Tara had disappeared into the woods. Her mind was clear of doubt, entirely empty of thought while channeling, which made pinpointing where on the cameras she'd emerge next difficult.

Gael's familiar led the charge toward the small rock-climbing zone with the other members.

```
Name: Gael Rios-Vega
Branch: Bestial (Familiar)
```

"King Clucks, you got this?"

The rooster flapped his wings, clucking and casting waves of banishment onto two wisps.

"Hell yeah. We're rockstars." Gael pointed out another three wisps. Effective use of his sensory but...

"Whoa, King Clucks, Peckfender of the Unhatched Dozen can cast magic?" Gael asked, true sincerity in the damn rooster's name.

"Totally. Those with familiars can channel magic back and forth between each other, so it allows them to share traits and such," Caleb said, clutching his notebook. "Within limitations, I think."

I gripped the microphone. "Gael, you're not permitted to use branch magic during this evaluation. Your familiar is only out there so you can channel your magic. He's not allowed to cast. Another use of branch magic, and your group will be disqualified from the round."

Gael whined. His familiar leered at a nearby camera, pecking the lens. Fucking rooster.

Tara reemerged on a screen, so I followed.

```
Name: Tara Whitlock
Branch: Ward (Sealing)
Branch: Cosmic (Shadows)
Branch: Arcane (Intangibility)
```

She spun in the air horizontally, as if she'd channeled all the levitating magic within her core and coursed it throughout her entire body. Very advanced and difficult to maintain, even for me. Her fingers wiggled ever so gently, releasing light, delicate bursts of telekinetic energy to propel her forward. Tara's long golden blonde hair draped along her body to her waist, like she was an enchanted mermaid far beneath the ocean.

I wasn't surprised by her effortless control of root magics, whether given her massive collection of magics—it was rare for anyone to be born with more than one branch, let alone three—or her prestigious family. It was the serenity cascading off her that perplexed me. Furrowing my brow, I channeled magic farther out, careful not to delve deep into her mind but stunned at how free she'd become in this moment.

Was this the same girl doubting her place at the academy earlier?

Calmly and carefree, she sensed out wisps and banished enough to prevent them from merging. While she distanced herself from the group, she didn't use her magic to dominate the round like Kenzo had.

"Oh, shit," Melanie said, drawing my attention back to the rest of group three.

A cluster of a dozen wisps gathered. Each glowing brighter as their circular forms smooshed together. This wasn't good. I rechanneled magic into my roots. Tensing my jaw, I eased, wanting to give them an opportunity to fix the situation.

"I told you, I can't levitate," Gael shouted.

"Can't or won't?" Jamius asked.

```
Name: Jamius Watson
Branch: Alteration (Duplication)
```

Jamius wobbled in the air like a novice ice skater, only that'd made things worse for him. Clearly, he didn't understand how to center his body when channeling. His branch would've made him better suited for sensory, but Gael took over that role. Apparently, Jamius tried to step in with levitation. He waved a hand to separate the wisps, flailing momentarily once his levitation faltered. I pried through his anxious surface. He'd used to making copies with each assigned a particular root, so casting two roots together was an impossibility in his mind.

Melanie and Layla snickered, whispering jabs and thinking meaner comments.

"Students who barely made it off the starting line should probably reserve judgment."

Self-doubt festered around them, which created a bit of guilt, but my concern was fixated on Jamius' lack in the fundamentals. He didn't attempt banishment. Couldn't maintain levitation for long. His cheeks puffed as he twirled round and round back to the ground.

Gael tensed.

"You need to split them up." Jamius gripped his knees to steady himself, breathing heavy, slick sweat along his deep brown complexion. "I'm spent, and if they form, our round's over."

I noted his areas of weakness, referencing what little I had from his school testing records. Like others who didn't have a private education, he'd need some modifications with instruction this year.

"They're too far for my telekinesis," Gael said.

"Then float up, wave them apart, and drop back down like I did."

"No."

"Why not?"

"King Clucks gets self-conscious when people fly."

"Bawk."

"We're going to be disqualified."

"Fine." Gael closed his eyes, and his feet dangled, almost lifting off the ground. In an instant, his familiar leapt into the air, feathers flying, wings flapping, and pecked Gael's face until he retreated to the ground. Fucking rooster. "I'm done—I'm sorry. No, I wasn't mocking you."

Enough of this.

This group lacked in coordinating—the type of thing to expect from first-years—but not to the point it'd release a fiend. Hell, even third-year interns struggled to grapple with the importance of teamwork, but that was the foundation on which guilds were founded.

I stepped outside the proctoring room, stretching to crack my back and preparing to fly over and end this. Static popped in the air. At this rate, a fiend would form, and that was a lesson best reserved for later in the year. Preferably next semester when I'd have the time to properly introduce them to true demonic threats not because of a fumble, given my wandering mind. I'd fixated on things I couldn't prevent at this moment—Caleb's vision—and it'd distracted me from ending this round earlier.

I sprang up, weightless, letting all the worry blow past me in the breeze that carried me forward. It'd been too long since I simply flew through the sky. I needed to take more advantage of my root magics.

Tara was still off in the forest terrain, handling just enough wisps to keep them from collecting but avoiding the others. Jamius and Gael couldn't muster the right root magics for this test. But where was…

An array of burning pebbles scattered across the auxiliary gym in a wide shot.

```
Name: Yaritza Vargas
Branch: Cosmic (Star Shower)
```

I widened my eyes, having never seen this magic in action. She channeled magic into actual rocks from the nearby terrain and propelled them at the wisps. With a light breath to release telekinesis, I deflected the incoming pebbles that she'd cast in too wide a shot. Then, noticing my error, I clenched a fist and bent my wrist to alter my ricocheted flaming rocks from crashing into Gael or Jamius.

"What the hell are you doing?" I snapped.

"Wait for it." Yaritza winked, pointing to the cluster of wisps, shredded to tiny, shattered light barely distinguishable had I not already locked onto them with my sensory root. "I know you said no branch magics, but this was a massively major extenuating circumstance. Fiend problem solved before it happened. You're welcome."

"You're disqualified this round. Your entire group." I took

careful breaths to channel my magic and compose myself in this infuriating moment.

"But-but wait! I was helping."

"First, I made myself very clear there's no casting branch magics, even allowing your group to continue after Gael's mishap. Second, if I required assistance with handling a potential fiend, I wouldn't ask a first-year student who nearly struck others because of her impulsive need to help."

I slammed my hands together, banishing the remaining wisps in one fell swoop. Static popped, shattering demonic energy one by one until each shining bulb vanished from this realm. An exhausting effort but clearly necessary.

Once I'd cleared the auxiliary gym, I gathered my entire homeroom coven, reviewing with each group what roots I'd observed, how their collaboration fared, and what areas I'd like them to attempt demonstrating during their next two rounds. I also worked to keep my biting attitude reserved; based on their expressions and thoughts, I failed tremendously.

By the end of their third opportunity to showcase their root magics, I sent my weary homeroom coven off to their classes. They dragged their feet out of the auxiliary gym.

The rest of my first day went smoothly enough. A basic introduction to my course, History of Witchcraft, along with classroom expectations and a syllabus for what we'd cover the first semester. My homeroom coven barely kept their eyes open, while the other students had the general exhaustion that came from sitting through a three-hour orientation. Still, despite being a much larger group than years before, their minds were filled with eager expectations of the opportunity many sought to take full advantage of.

At the end of the day, I packed my belongings, ignoring the lingering guilt of still having absolutely no clue how to handle

Caleb's situation. On the way to the parking lot, I debated contacting Milo. He hadn't texted since our argument. No check-in. No pestering. No anything. It wasn't like we didn't go days, weeks, sometimes even months without talking. Years after what happened with…what happened to Finn.

The longing in my heart was unsettling. I grabbed a cigarette, lighting it before reaching my car. I had more important things to fixate on than Milo. Caleb aside, I had lessons to finalize, paperwork for evaluations, and meetings to schedule. Along with a thousand other things.

Chapter Nine

Back at home, I coaxed Charlie up onto the couch while I read through emails. Computer on my lap and paperwork strewn about to my left, I tried to convince him to hop up with my right hand.

He was moody tonight.

"Come on." I strummed my fingers along the cushions. His dilated saucers followed their dance back and forth.

This was a routine he'd grown accustomed to for seven years, yet every single time summer ended, Charlie treated it with resentment. An utter betrayal on my part to leave him alone all day with only Carlie as company.

His butt wiggled, preparing to leap, play, and—crash. Carlie knocked something over in the kitchen. She bolted through the hallway and disappeared to somewhere hidden in a bedroom. Dammit. Charlie blinked, ears alert, and the trance of my fingers' dance broken. He gave a whiny meow and strutted away, playing the victim.

"Oh, sure, resent me for working." I sipped a sour beer, delicately floating it back over to the coffee table, where I rested my feet.

Schoolwork didn't distract me. Quite the opposite, in fact. The more time I focused on lessons, the more it led down a rabbit hole to student records, scores, and achievements. A usual fixation as I prepared for a new batch of kids. But every time I started researching one student, I found myself curious and concerned about Caleb's standing. What he needed, how to circumvent this void vision, and how to help without making things worse.

Could I make things worse than dying? Knowing me, completely possible and probable. I kept waiting for Milo to reach out. He was always better at breaking the ice with conversations between us, especially if there was tension, something our last discussion brought on.

There were answers about his clairvoyance I needed. So much of his branch magic was hazy from vague interviews over the years where he explained his ability enough to pique curiosity but elude the truth, a truth wrapped within memories I preferred remained buried. Whether he wanted to assist in solving this void vision or not, I worried which avenues to pursue.

Would ignoring its presence and simply readying myself be enough? Should I be focusing all my attention on solving it? Could it be solved? Would training Caleb harder help or hinder his chances of survival? How would informing him play out? Would it become more or less likely with his insight?

I shook away the questions, running my fingers through my shaggy, unkempt hair. Something about telling a fifteen-year-old kid their death was imminent felt like opening a whole new box of problems.

Perhaps sitting him down with his grandparents—his legal guardians on file—and informing them all I knew, which was basically nothing, that'd give them the push to contact Cerberus Guild, Enchanter Evergreen himself, and force assistance. Unless that type of meddling was what put Caleb in danger to begin with, like a self-fulfilling prophecy of interference.

I grabbed my phone, checking it for the umpteenth time because Milo remained fixed in my thoughts. Nothing from Milo yet.

Screw it.

> Me: So...
> How've you been?
> Since last time we chatted.

Chatted. Sounded smoother or nicer or more tactful than how last time we spoke, I basically told him to fuck off, which he completely deserved. Still, Milo rarely let my pricklier side push him into silent avoidance. Given what a dick I was most of the time, it would make sense to drop me, but he was the asshat this time around. Guess that made our tally somewhere around one to a million. Shocker—I had the bigger score.

Read. My thumb hovered over the keys. Floating bubbles. Nothing. Floating bubbles. Nothing. Nothing. Nothing. Well, fuck you too, Milo.

I eyed Carlie from the living room as she returned to the kitchen without her brother Charlie, staring at me in the living room. "Seems all the men in my life are too busy for me."

I furrowed my brow, opening my phone to Instagram and Twitter.

Yup. I was that stalker person. But it wasn't really stalking. I mean, I spent most of my days in a daze from the surface thoughts of everyone in a quarter-mile radius, and it was a point of fact that most folks word-vomited these fleeting thoughts onto their feeds.

The Inevitable Future · Making Life Brighter One Person At A Time @MiloEvergreen
Enchanter @CerberusGuild · Consult @ChicagoPsychics · Meme Connoisseur · Often lost in the clouds, sometimes literally · Beautifully Bi 🌈

Him and that damn stage name—The Inevitable Future. He could plug it all day long, but it wouldn't make them a thing anymore. Enchanters hated those signatures. They were dated, difficult, and dorky. Okay, maybe I was the only one thinking about that last part.

I scrolled through Milo's feed. He had three specific strategies for his online persona.

First, so-called witty or charming posts to interact with his audience. Though, by the looks of things, there wasn't much of that as of late. In fact, his last "out with the people" post was a selfie with Chanelle. The night of my—his—our vision.

Next, he'd streamline events that he'd already preordained—he could bullshit all he wanted about the future being a merry-go-round of dominos. He knew what he was doing. Based on his replies, mentions, likes, or whatever, he wasn't interacting much with anyone.

Finally, and possibly most important, came from posting successful updates to Cerberus' movements. The unclassified and completed jobs, of course. None of that for a while either.

I kept flipping through apps, expanding my search, because I was clearly pathetic, and despite having work, something about this was impossible to put down.

Cerberus Guild was trending. Everywhere.

Everywhere and no comment from Milo anywhere? I read through a few quoted retweets and the clickbait articles below them.

> Alexander Devroy Sharing What The Magic Media Won't @AlexDevroy
> Guess this sounds catchier than drops the F***ING BALL AGAIN. @MiloEvergreen talks a big game, but if I saw the future, it wouldn't have even gotten to this point. Here's why...
> **Cerberus Guild Thwarts Warlocks!**

> Cami Castle Enchanter at Heart @CastingCowgirl
> Y'all are stressing me. People are really trying to say @CerberbusGuild and @MiloEvergreen almost lost their money. 😂 These comments need to chill. Here's a (small?) thread on how and why this doesn't affect you. 1/12
> **Whitlock Bank Under Siege! Are Your Funds Safe?**

> Sarah Sunders @EvergreensGirl
> Yeah, #TheInevitableFuture is really out there every day to save the rich. 😳 To the ppl on here saying @MiloEvergreen and @CerberusGuild are only out for money, maybe you need to remember #NightOfTheFiendMassacre. Maybe read up on the countless hours Milo Evergreen donates. Links in the comments.
> **Whose Future Is Enchanter Evergreen Protecting?**

They all more or less said the same thing. A warlock faction stirred up trouble, but Milo led a coven of enchanters to prevent their heist. No one was hurt. Nothing damaged. Except perhaps egos.

He wasn't avoiding me because of our conversation. He had politics to attend to, show the public he cared—which he did—and deflect comments about stocks the Whitlocks had in Cerberus Guild playing a role in this heroic act. My mind wandered to Tara Whitlock, wondering how she coped with such a high social presence considering her family name, then the warlock attack stirred in my thoughts. So strange for a warlock faction to specifically target the most powerful institution of wealth and clout in Illinois. Warlocks were reckless, but this seemed absurd.

All the PR involved exhausted me almost as much as these tweets, so I went to bed. Or attempted to sleep through the prattle of neighboring minds making true rest a distant dream.

I strolled through Gemini's courtyard, my backpack heavily weighing against my shoulders. Oh, great. Another damn dream in record time. Guess my subconscious aimed to remind me of the stress that came with attending an academy, something I needed to consider for each of my new students. Not just… Not the ones with cruel fates along the horizon.

Finn bumped into me, subtle, soft, and secretive. I resisted a smile then. Now, too. Angsty sixteen-year-old me glared. That stage of my life was filled with too much stress. With a workload from advanced classes, root magics I struggled to control simultaneously, and the general anxiety of succeeding at the academy. Add to that the blossoming romantic thoughts mixed with sexual desires I had, and it put me into a constant state of panicked confusion, so I stuck mostly with ignoring them.

I wouldn't kiss Finn this day. Or Milo. Not this memory. I wouldn't kiss them for many days to come. That was a moment I'd love to relive. Something thrilling. Nerve-racking. The intense ecstasy of listening to them sort out our lives and happily ever after as only they could.

"You're not even listening to me."

"Nope," I said, though in truth, I hadn't stopped listening to

Finn's yammering since we'd left English. "Tuning you out is how I get by."

He had kept me motivated the entire first year at the academy. Confidence in every word he said and the thoughts he didn't always believe I'd eavesdropped on.

"We need to start looking into guilds." Finn spun around, walking backward in front of me. "If we have them picked before the end of the semester, we might be able to get an early start on our internships."

I picked up my pace, hopeful of knocking my foot into his and maybe tripping him a bit. Back then, something about that said "I like you" a whole lot more than actually uttering the words.

"That doesn't happen." I scooted around him. "They've been telling us since day one that our internships will be our third year. Stop rushing. It's like you want to get to the end of the story."

"The ending is the best part." Finn winked, quickly strolling next to me. "Besides, Milo says it's a totally high possibility."

I grumbled because of course Finn brought up Milo's visions. Each vision Milo had came with encouragement from Finn about his clairvoyance, even if his probability had the success rate of roulette. Our time at Gemini brought him further out of his shell and well into his emulating Finn phase. In a few more years, he'd transform into his annoyingly chipper, truest self.

Not this day, though. Milo's thoughts were faint and somber. I always had a way of pinpointing him and Finn anywhere on campus above everyone else's minds. The surface thoughts weren't clear, simply sad, and I couldn't recall why. He spent a lot of his early years at Gemini fighting back his anxious bubble.

"And if a man of the future supports it, then I'm totally focusing on our internships." Finn smiled, sunlight brightening his entire face, and the bleached highlights added to his chestnut hair. It drew me out of deep thoughts and gave some layered confusion on where my mind and body drifted. "All we need right now is proper branding. Prospective guilds notice that flashy branding stuff."

"Not this again." I crossed my arms.

"Yes, this." Finn grabbed my shoulders. His firm grip and delicate touch of magic lifted me off the ground, feet dangling in the air. I quelled Milo's distant sorrow, enveloping Finn's joy.

"Put me down."

"Say please." He smirked.

"You're an idiot."

"Come on, Dorian." Finn shook me. The name was ridiculous, and I hated saying it. Perhaps a bit of the resistance of coughing up the absurd name came from the bizarre delight of him holding me tightly with such ease. "I'm The All-Knowing Past, and you're the…?"

He blinked rapidly, long lashes close enough to kiss.

"Enchanters hate that signature naming shit." I broke loose from his hold and backstepped. Because an open campus with fellow students all around wasn't the place to think about kissing the guy I kind of sort of maybe just a little bit potentially liked.

Ugh. If I'd dreamt of a memory a few months down the line, I'd have skipped past this cringeworthy phase and onto a new exhausting stage of my life. At least then, I'd be done with questioning my sexuality whenever I spent time with Finn or Milo.

"Yes, enchanters, but guilds love it. And they're the ones we're trying to impress, so you are..." Finn closed the gap between us, unrelenting.

"The Ubiquitous Present," I huffed, "which is a terrible fucking name."

"I like it. Ubiquitous is catchy. A little hard to say but filled with mystique which sells."

When we finally reached the quad, I sat on a bench, grabbing a book to read. Confusion over classwork felt optimal to confusion over Finn or Milo. My stomach gurgled, having skipped breakfast.

Finn slipped off his crocs, by far the worst choice in footwear, and so against the academy dress code. "Now, we just need to wait for The Inevitable Future."

"He's late. Again," I said. "For someone who can see the future, he's got shit timing."

Finn ignored me, walking barefoot on the grass. He allowed the history to tickle his toes and soak into his magic. He enjoyed the academy history tucked away in every crevice of the campus grounds, but something about this space brought him true peace. The greater Finn's retrocognition grew, the more he used it to search for hidden joys forgotten by time. Moments of history no one knew or cared to discover. It brought him so much happiness; bubbling ideas of journaling these people's histories always popped into his mind as he relived their experiences again and again.

Skimming his thoughts, I only glimpsed his reactions to the layered pasts. Psychic branches perplexed me at this point in my life. I'd believed it had to do with my telepathy lacking in areas but later learned our frequencies differed. It was a challenge matching those branch elements for even a second. Still, somehow in the present, I'd gleaned an entire vision from Milo. Well, a void of one.

Speak of the clairvoyant. Milo walked through the quad, hands tucked inside the kangaroo pocket of his hoodie, curly bangs peeking out of the hood hiding his solemn face. A raincloud of sorrow trailed alongside him as he approached us.

"Why so blue?" Finn asked.

I continued reading my book, pretending not to care, something I did far too often with both of them. Yet, as Finn prodded Milo with curious concern and friendly support, I scanned Milo's thoughts.

Nothing tangible or structured. Simply a downpour of sadness.

"You remember that vision I had with the third-year girl?"

"The one where you planned to strategically save her from making the biggest blunder of her internship before her career ever started while simultaneously networking with someone who already has an in with enchanters at Cerberus?" Finn asked with a devilish grin as his mind drifted to ways Milo's clairvoyance would keep us all in the know on power players in the industry. "Yeah, sort of rings a bell."

"Well, I screwed it up," Milo said. "I tried to work with her by asking questions and asking her to tutor me, but she was too busy for that. Sleuthing and subtly are not my thing, so I just told her about my vision. The parts of it I'd seen which wasn't much."

I recalled this vision or Milo's mention of it. He'd witnessed her casting her primal branch while patrolling with the enchanter mentoring her. The vision predicted a probable outcome of losing control of her earth cast. No fatalities, but an embarrassing and expensive public display for Cerberus Guild to clean up.

"It all happened exactly how I saw it. All that destruction, damaged property, destroyed buildings, that's because I couldn't keep my mouth shut." Milo's raindrops swirled into a whirlpool along his surface thoughts.

"Not true," Finn said. "You tried to help. You've told people about your predictions before, and it's worked out. You couldn't have known."

"I should've known. There were too many pieces missing," Milo said.

Wait. What?

"Even though it was like this weird void, the whole thing snapped together perfectly right after it was too late. Telling her was literally the worst thing."

This was Milo's first void vision. Or the first time he'd had clarity for them, realized the cost of meddling, and grasped how involving the person in question might ultimately weave the events together into the unwanted prediction. Hell, telling the person might've very well been the true cause of the potential future.

Telling Caleb could kill him. I shivered within my own mind, piecing together this memory as my younger self clutched the book, hiding behind it as Finn worked to cheer Milo up.

"One bad call isn't your story. You've got plenty more to tell, live through, change for the better," he said. "You know why? Because you're the…"

Milo pulled his hood further over his eyes.

"No." Finn tugged the hood off. "Come on. Who are you?"

"The Inevitable Future." Milo huffed; his dishwater blond curls bounced.

"Your sour, dour attitude's rubbing off on him, Dorian."

"If only," I said.

Finn rolled his eyes, then tended to Milo's mood. I remained on the bench, content with observing them. I wanted to smile, rewatching this memory, but instead, my younger self crinkled his nose, trying to comprehend why Finn cared so much about always dragging us away from our rainclouds and into the sunlight. It wouldn't be long before Milo's sadness dried up altogether, and he created his own sunlight.

Fixating on their minds, their deepest thoughts, got me through my first year at Gemini. Their belief. Certainty. Joy. All their huge emotions pulled me from the sea of other minds. A complete blessing and, in the end, a curse.

"I think he always got you a bit better than I did."

"What?" My voice trembled.

"Maybe it's because he always knew where you'd end up,

whereas I only knew where you'd been." Finn stood beside me, not the Finn of this memory, that Finn chatted with Milo, both locked in bad puns, sidetracked thoughts, and half giggles while a Finn I'd buried sat on the bench.

Twenty-two years old. So young… So old for him.

"You don't belong here," I said, completely off-script from the memory.

I moved my hand, controlling it, dropping the book, and ignoring the bickering boys so I could reach out on my own accord toward the man I'd lost. This never happened. This couldn't happen. Shouldn't. My muscles tightened, and my whole body shuddered, releasing the proverbial strings that kept me a self-aware puppet in memories past.

"Then again, I think the past is pretty dang important." Finn grinned. "Don't you?"

"There's so much I want to say to you." Tears streamed down my cheeks. "I wish this was real. I wish—"

Finn kissed my forehead softly, sweetly. I froze.

"It's as real as we want it to be. That's how all things work." He wiped away the tears, his hands hauntingly cold. "I wish things, too. Mostly for more time. But right now, I need you to remember something for me."

I shook, struggling to compose myself. "Okay."

"You can't achieve anything if you don't learn from the past. Milo taught you that. I think you were a bit distracted in your last dream to catch the message."

"Wait, what—"

Darkness followed my words, and the dream shattered into broken glass until I slipped further into a silent slumber.

Chapter Ten

Finn's words lingered during classes. Not Finn's words originally because he said Milo's words from our first conversation together held the answer. Was there something important in my past that'd help solve the void vision of Caleb's future? Or was that memory itself the thing from the past I was supposed to learn? Meddling with void visions was precarious, which I already knew thanks in no special part to Milo, but something about the first time I met Milo held a solution. What could it...

"***How fucking long is he going to just stand there?***" Kenzo's rage made me bite back a jolt.

I stood in front of the classroom, a stack of papers in my hand and the semi-memorized lesson drumming inside my head. I passed a test packet out to each student one by one, most identical in every way, but a few modified for those who needed them.

"Before we get into the specifics of History of Witchcraft, I'm giving all of my classes a diagnostic test."

Most of the students in here came from various homerooms, but I had a few from mine scattered within the roster. I walked the aisles, ignoring the external sighs and internal whining. None of them wanted a test during the first week of classes. And they certainly didn't want one with this many questions, written responses, and critical thinking involved. These tests were important to me, not because of state testing—which still played a larger role in the academies than I preferred—but because it helped tailor pacing for the year. It gave me a snapshot of how much they knew, what extra backgrounding I'd have to cover in lessons, and where they struggled to articulate their thoughts. A major benefit to my magic was that it allowed insight into hesitation, trailing minds, or other factors that caused students to answer incorrectly, struggle, or simply lose steam midway.

"I have three simple rules for how testing works in my room." I stood behind Melanie and Layla's desks, leaning between their whispered conversation. "First, no talking. Not while you're testing or after you finish."

I passed out more papers. "Second, no notes. At least not for a diagnostic test." I tapped the open notebook on Caleb's desk.

"Sorry." He quickly closed it and stuffed it in his overpacked book bag, his mind wandering in a thousand different directions on what the test he hadn't even seen yet might cover.

"Finally, no technology. Ever. Believe it or not, your messages will be happily awaiting you after the test." I stood next to Gael Martinez's desk, holding his packet. "You all have the entire class to work, do your best, take your time, and begin."

Gael reached for the packet, attempting to politely pry it from my hand. I placed the test on his desk, hand firmly pressed atop it, while I kept a careful eye on those already opening their packets.

"As I said, this particular test doesn't come with notes because it's more of a baseline on your strengths and weaknesses in the subject."

Gael gulped. His knees bounced; a spike clinked against the metal of the desk.

"However, I've already talked with Ms. Kinsey," I whispered. "Her room is available if you'd like the test read aloud."

Gael's IEP mentioned notes for tests, any assignment exceeding fifteen questions should either be reduced, or he should be offered extended time and an opportunity for separate testing in a smaller setting.

"I'm fine, Mr. Frost." Gael smiled, opening the packet. *"Don't need everyone knowing how stupid I am on the first test."*

This kid was far from stupid. Based on the documentation from his freshman year evaluation, he made massive strides on state tests, succeeded in every class, and met all the goals placed in his IEP, along with a few additions noted by his previous Case Manager.

"You're free to turn down your services, but remember these are in place so you can excel. They don't mean anything else."

"Uh-huh." Gael's foot tapped harder, so I stepped away and allowed him to work.

I went to my desk, channeling magic to tiptoe around the rippling surface thoughts without drowning in the sea of any single student's mind—especially Caleb's.

"I know this, come on."

"**This whole class is a joke.**"

"Skip. Skip. Skip."

"The way it's worded could be a trick. It might be C. No. B."

"Who even cares what the UN passed in 1978?"

"I'll come back to this one later."

"He expects us to answer all these written responses?"

"Fuck this test."

"Seven to ten sentences each? What's short about that?"

"¿Cómo se decía esta palabra en inglés?"

"This is so easy. Wait. Too easy."

Cue the paranoia, self-doubt, and longing for breezy summer days. I took notes as they worked, outlining a rough account of where everyone placed. It was impossible to perfectly teach to a room where most students processed everything differently. But each year, I made a bet with myself that this would be the one I'd master the art of keeping them fully engaged while ensuring the lower-tier learners didn't flounder and the higher-tier learners didn't coast.

Too bad I was really shitty at this stuff. Okay in teaching practical magic usage, but academically, I sucked.

Layla whispered to another student. I walked to the back of the classroom, furrowed my brow, and pressed my finger to my lips.

"But we're finished?"

"Funny how I didn't ask."

Layla sneered. Her blue eyes shifted to Caleb's muttering up front—quiet and mostly unheard, but it clearly helped his auditory learning. It wasn't any different than the student who stood every ten minutes, stretching to keep his mind from tapping out. Or the student chewing on their pencil to fixate as their mind focused on the questions. I took a mental note to write an actual note to remember to bring in my fidgets, which might help the students who needed something to occupy their hands when working.

Layla grabbed a book to read since I wouldn't elaborate. Establishing classroom norms, setting high academic standards, and remaining flexible to different learning behaviors was a true joy. Like playing the world's worst game of Jenga, where one misplaced piece would cause the entire class to descend into a fiery explosion. This would be a hell of a year for several reasons—that much was obvious.

After three classes of anxious students mentally expressing how unprepared they were or how I was the world's biggest dick for assigning a test the first week, I went to the staff lounge to grab my lunch. I put my frozen meal in the microwave and counted along with the timer, desperate to hide back in my classroom.

"Are you really testing your kids this week?" Chanelle waltzed into the lounge.

"Yep." Three minutes to go.

"You're kind of a monster. Or so the kids say with some very colorful word choices."

"What can I say? I delight in their misery. It's what keeps me coming back each year."

"Oh, no. I totally dig it. You being the asshole teacher really lowers the nice bar for me." Chanelle winked. "Keep it up, Mr. Frost."

Two minutes left.

"Have you tested your homeroom coven's root magics yet?" I asked since I'd started working on a channeling exercise for History but wanted to reference other first-year teachers' stats for their students.

Depending on the data—ugh, how I loathed data—I might need to alter the lesson.

"No, because Evans so graciously booked the auxiliary gym for the third-years."

"Okay." One minute remaining. "First, tell her to go fuck herself. Third-year students can train anywhere on or off campus. If she still taught, she'd know that. Second, remind her we need this data completed by the end of the month, per academy requirements."

The microwave beeped. I grabbed my food and skirted around Chanelle.

"Third." I nodded to the opening door. "Enjoy your lunch, Mrs. Whitehurst, kindest educator of them all."

Thompson and Peterson busted into the staff lounge, their cloud of equal annoyance weighing heavily on the energy here.

"*Oh, fuck me.*" Chanelle smiled as Thompson approached.

I zipped past Peterson before he could share his playfully irritating pun of a hello.

"I can't handle one more thing this week." Thompson's mind buzzed with a thousand atrocities she'd endured by the ever-demanding list of expectations.

"I know, dear. Such a stressful time of year," Chanelle said as the door closed behind me. "*Dammit, Dorian.*"

I went back to my classroom. The soggy breaded tilapia and gritty wild grain rice didn't live up to the hype of the picture on the box. Nothing ever lived up to the hype.

The week blurred together in a mash of diagnostic tests, getting-to-know-you activities, staff meetings, lesson planning, and branch magic research. All the while, I kept close attention on Caleb's surface thoughts, along with a few others from my homeroom coven. Nothing in his immediate mind about danger or fearing anything—aside from Kenzo in general. I probably needed to figure out what the hell that was about.

I remained cautious when tiptoeing around students' thoughts, careful not to delve deep into their minds. Otherwise, I'd find myself lost in a memory of their past.

I sprang forward in my seat, nearly dropping my laptop. Everyone's eyes in the staff meeting fell on me, their thoughts piqued with intrigue or confusion. I sank deeper into my seat. Their whispered surface thoughts didn't matter. Everything finally clicked.

"Oooo," Chanelle whispered. "Something happen with Enchanter Loverboy?"

"What?" My gaze wandered, unable to find a place to rest during the department meeting.

The absurd question held merit, though. As my mind fluttered all over the place, my hands had found their way onto Twitter, doom scrolling through Milo's feed. He'd reemerged better than ever, shaking off the trolls, thanking his fans, and promising to always do better than the day before.

"No, it's nothing." I absorbed the surroundings of the teacher's lounge, blinking rapidly. A bland office space that kept us seated too close together under buzzing fluorescent lights.

This shock, this epiphany, wasn't about Milo, not entirely. This was Finn's message about Milo's words of wisdom in my recent dream, where the three of us first interacted together. *"You can't achieve anything if you don't learn from the past."*

Finn wanted me to grasp that, not because it had anything to do with my past but Caleb's.

It was difficult to say how many straws I grasped at because of the void vision. My dreams had jumbled into bizarre, unfamiliar territory since briefly merging magics with Milo. Was it because our magics touched? Was my subconscious evolving? Or did I miss Finn so badly I'd conjured him out of guilt?

I shook away the questions. None of that mattered.

My telepathy was as effective as ever. If snooping through a few guarded memories in Caleb's mind helped ensure he had a future, then I had work to do.

Chapter Eleven

My enchanter license didn't forbid the usage of delving deep into another person's mind, but there were some ethical aspects to contemplate. For one, I rarely used that part of my magic, almost entirely waiting until I'd developed stronger classroom connections with students and promising only to do so with permission. I'd interned with a few telepaths in my youth. My favorite, Caroline Goins, a captivatingly kind woman who used her telepathy to unravel psyches and past traumas through therapy, taught me the dangers of lingering without trust.

I didn't have the personality or patience to help others in such a way, but I'd worked with my second and third-year students to untangle memories that stood between their successful use of root or branch magics.

Diving into the depths of one's memories required a powerful tether of my magic to their mind. And if I did this, I'd have to fully commit to rooting through his memories. An invasive act, no matter the justification. A person's mind was their most private, vulnerable place. It was one thing when their surface thoughts and emotions flew in the air, latching onto my magic. It was different using telepathy to infiltrate.

Still, I had to believe, had to hope the altered memory of Finn meant something. That the kiss with Milo served more purpose than poorly timed lust. That everything in my life wasn't simply a case of random and unfortunate events.

I went to Gemini, intent on seeing this through. Before school began, I lingered in the parking lot with a cigarette. The light breeze trickled and flicked ashes back inside my car. Having reached the filter, I used the ember to light a second smoke. Anything to buy a few more minutes before taking a step I couldn't undo.

Once in my classroom, I waved a hand, rearranging desks into groups of four. My homeroom coven arrived, curious about what it meant.

"This isn't for you. Today's a standard lesson on the paperwork involved for licensing since we still have a lot of work to cover before any of you are ready to fill out your fledgling permits."

Taking a calming breath, I prepared my mind for casting wide telepathic magic. To establish an intact link with Caleb, I needed to fully unleash my branch. Something I hated.

Emotions illuminated surface thoughts with an aura of differing colors. Many students' minds fluctuated in technicolor rainbows depending on their current mental state. Two remained constant. Scarlet red bloomed around Kenzo. Charcoal gray dimly radiated from Tara. It made the lesson challenging, keeping my eyes fixed on reality and not the wafting emotions.

The bell rang, and I quickly prepared for History. Students arrived, some cringing at the stack of papers boldly placed on the corner of my desk. Tones of pale violet and dull yellow bounced over other colors, given the anxiety the work in my class caused.

It was one thing to hear it from their minds, to feel it as a twinge of empathy from time to time, but another to have the emotional colors bombard me every second. I cracked my neck. This sensation would pass once I'd established a link.

"Another test?" Gael sighed, running his hands through his spiky hair.

"No. More of a learning exercise." I turned on the Smart Board, allowing the bright burst of light to blur my vision. A list indicating where and who students were grouped with appeared.

"***Is he fucking kidding?***"   *"Not Kenny."*

"We're all working together. Cool." Gael's sharklike teeth beamed as he joined Kenzo, Caleb, and Katherine.

Sorry, Caleb. But it'd help create a link if his mind was too distracted to notice. The group activity might be sufficient, but whatever perils divided him and Kenzo would definitely divert his attention. Plus, emotions radiating from their present led me to believe their past might hold value.

Not that Kenzo had murderous intent written all over his face, but with an unrelenting scowl toward Caleb since classes started, there was something there. Caleb could hold a potential memory where he'd crossed paths with the person bent on killing him. Then again, like so many things in this world, it could be a random act of violence. Too many variables, and with no real plan in place, I put my trust in Finn. Or my fucking subconscious. Who knew?

I handed a packet to each group.

"You all will be working together to complete this activity."

Bubbling forest greens, pale blues, and deep purples of confusion filled a lot of minds. Katherine traced a finger along the elegant etching at the top of the completely blank packet. Sunshine yellow shone around her. The luminous hues made every member in her group all the paler.

"Is this a trick question test thingy?" Gael asked.

"Nope," Katherine said. "*Mr. Frost clearly doesn't know how lucky my group is. We'll breeze through this.*"

Cocky. Yet, I admired her considering her group. Part of what made learning this lesson effective.

"No trick, simply an expectation."

"We have to break the enchantment, right?" Katherine reached for her grimoire. "I thought Mrs. Whitehurst's class was the only one we'd get to practice this stuff in."

She squealed, startling me or perhaps others in the class. My emotions were melding everywhere. Not good.

"Not exactly." I placed a hand atop the leather cover. "For someone with your specific magic, breaking the enchantment here would be pretty simple, but this isn't a test on branch skills."

Katherine sulked, dimming her sunlight.

"Then what are you testing us on?" Kenzo glared at Caleb. Independently, he'd excel in breaking the enchantment placed with or without his hex branch.

Caleb lowered his eyes, avoiding Kenzo's, and examining the sigils lining the borders of the front page.

"It's simple. After watching my own homeroom coven flounder and hearing how others are doing the same, it's clear this batch of first-year students greatly lack in two of the most important academy fundamentals."

"**No.**" Kenzo studied his group, the answer to today's objective clear in his mind. The fury that I'd dared partner him with someone he considered useless boomed throughout the room.

I winced, facing away from the class and steadying my stance with my desk. The double-edged sword of this situation made it difficult to continue. Caleb's mind was left distracted, but Kenzo's consumed the entire room. An ocean of blood thickened the class, making each breath painful.

Rose pink with edges of orange beamed.

"You all right, Mr. Frost?" Gael's genuine concern smothered the fury.

It was always fascinating how some emotions merged with others. These two had no real connection, not one I knew of aside from our first day of root magic evaluations, yet their auras held chemistry.

"I'm fine. Headache." I grabbed a copy of the packet and channeled magic into the tips of my fingers. "Anyway, this enchantment will help you all work on channeling your magic."

Ink filled the pages, revealing questions.

"I get it," Katherine said. "To complete the packet, we have to maintain a steady flow of channeled energy."

"Correct. It's the only condition that releases the enchantment's glamour."

"But why partner us together?" Caleb thought. *"Unless he expected us to pass the packet around since most people probably struggled with maintaining channeled energy for long periods of time."*

"But there's two conditions on the enchantment," Katherine said, running her slender fingers along the etchings.

"True. The condition requires matching frequencies in a group effort of combining channeled magic; otherwise, the answers will fade entirely. You all need to learn early on how to collaborate with others and their magics to be successful at Gemini." Dread clouded the room. "Don't worry. This isn't something anyone's going to master in a day. For now, work together on learning the rhythm of each other's channeling flow and develop a strategy to keep the enchantment at bay."

I returned to my desk, taking an uneasy seat, and gave a mini-lesson on the ebb and flow of channeled magic, how witches possessed differing frequencies dependent on many factors.

"Like what branch magic someone has," Gael said.

"That's one factor."

"Obviously, not the only one." Kenzo scoffed at Caleb, who shrank into himself.

"Yeah, proficiency in root magics is probably also a factor," Katherine said, her kind face replaced by a slightly furrowed brow with bright red trickling along her sunshine aura. "I'd wager personality is another."

Kenzo folded his arms.

"Also correct." I wrapped up the lesson with a few questions and allowed them to work.

This lesson was useful in training channeling, compatibility, and collaboration–something I still needed to pinpoint for everyone in my homeroom coven. It also gave students a more hands-on day, so I could conjure the necessary magic undisturbed.

Their conversations grew louder than their thoughts as each group tried to figure out the trick. There was no trick here, simply teamwork with a little history mixed into the process of packet questions. It took me all night to decide which groups went where in each class, but I'd probably messed up with Caleb's group. It seemed balanced at the time. Katherine worked well with him. Gael was nice to everyone. And Caleb had mostly survived Kenzo so far.

The air in the room grew thick, this time not from chaotic emotions but the conjured smoke of my manifestation. Gray fumes floated, unseen by anyone else. It puffed inward and out near Caleb, lungs forming into a torso and, soon after, a full-fledged body. I cracked my knuckles against the arms of my chair, steadying myself for the summoning of magic. Paying careful attention to it and my class. They were fine.

A psychic copy of myself stood, fully materialized, and split from my consciousness. The manifestation possessed limited will beyond the direction I'd conjured. Still, I quelled my senses linked to the manifestation, given how our vision synced like getting caught between two mirrors infinitely reflecting back at each other.

He stepped toward Caleb, brushing aside the swirling colors of anxiety, curiosity, and joy. In a blink, my manifestation vanished, hollowing away the rainbowed words from the classroom. I gripped the bridge of my nose, digging my nails into the crevices of my eyes to dull the existence of my magic until it faded. With my magic displaced, drifted apart, and tethered to Caleb's memories, there wasn't much else to do aside from classwork.

Delving into minds was absolutely my least favorite thing. Everyone had such weird shit lying around their psyche, and Caleb was no exception.

Countless marble statues filled a library, replacing the open spaces where furniture would sit. I knew this kid was a nerd, but this had creepy fanboy memorial written all over it. I crept between statues, careful to keep my steps silent inside his mind. It wasn't wise to clunk around, making my presence known. And this mountain of memories in the form of books would take forever to absorb, discern what the other Dorian might find useful, and determine if this was a waste of time and magic.

I walked past a few well-stocked aisles. A woody aroma filled the library with earthy hints. Caleb must spend a lot of time in libraries since this scent wafted in the air of his memories stronger than other smells. New theory. Maybe he pissed off a local librarian, and they decided they'd had enough of him using a dog ear fold instead of grabbing a bookmark.

If only it were that easy.

An entire array of Cerberus Guild members was displayed in the center of the library, stacks of books laid at the base of each statue. Milo stood front and center, posing for an audience even in Caleb's mind, with a bright marble smile.

This wasn't the Milo of today, granted he hadn't aged terribly in the last decade since his rise to fame, but this statue represented the pinnacle of his breakout success. The mission that showed the city Milo was an enchanter to watch. I picked up a book, flipping through the pages all filled with data collected on Enchanter Evergreen: The Inevitable Future.

Wrapped within the margins of all the facts, data, statistics, and details Caleb had accumulated about Enchanter Evergreen were his thoughts and feelings about his idol. The raw information was simple black words etched in pen, but the emotions tied to each piece of information shone as bright glittering scribbles containing where he first learned about Milo—Night of the Fiend Massacre.

The library vanished, replaced by the small, cluttered living room where a five-year-old Caleb sat on the carpeted floor too close to a bright television screen. In skimming the pages of Caleb's emotional connection to these notes, I'd wound up enveloped by a powerful memory. One which established his path, motivation, and desire to become a guild enchanter.

"Fiends have overtaken the city," a reporter said, the screen cutting away to helicopter footage.

Night of the Fiend Massacre. It rarely happened, but when too much demonic energy converged in one place, it carried carnage in the wind that reminded the world of the devastation beasts craving magic caused.

I retreated inward, the anxiety of that night still fresh in my mind. Observing Caleb like a silent specter, he held no fear or concern at the images of tarlike beasts unleashed upon the city, wreaking havoc. Awe filled his eyes at the wonder unfolding as Enchanter Evergreen appeared on the screen, hacking through a dozen fiends, banishing them in the process.

There was a massacre—but not what the media predicted when naming this event where swarms of demonic energy ripped our world asunder. Milo appeared front and center on the screen, smile on his face, plan in hand, and saved everyone he came across.

He flew throughout the city so quickly, most footage only glimpsed blurred images of his arrival and departure. Caleb flipped between television stations, hopeful to catch more sightings. This was where Enchanter Evergreen became a true heroic symbol in Chicago, revered throughout the state, and a household name across the nation.

It was the very thing Finn wanted for the three of us, and Milo achieved it two short years after we'd lost Finn.

Milo had coordinated a strategic plan with clairvoyance that resulted in zero casualties. An effort made possible by the countless enchanters collaborating across multiple guilds. But everyone knew it was Milo's magic that made it possible. He sent the right witch to the perfect spot where their branch played a precise role in thwarting devastation, saving lives, and ending chaos before it began by slaughtering every single fiend.

Steading my breath, I ignored the regret from sitting on the sidelines that day, saving no lives. Instead, I'd quelled my magic and ignored the terror buzzing in the minds of thousands surrounding me. I couldn't continue remaining idle.

I dragged myself out of Caleb's first memory of witnessing Enchanter Evergreen, returning to the mental library filled with countless books on many enchanters and stacks containing information on current and former members of the guild. I skirted away from the Cerberus exhibit. There were statues to every enchanter in the city, the state. Hell, I recognized a dozen or so known nationwide.

Exiting the library, I walked a long corridor lined with oil-painted portraits. The images shifted ever so, unveiling moving memories. A larger painting framed in gold and placed upon a door, the first I'd seen since arriving, showed a young boy sitting alone in a sandbox. The strength of the memory called out, cherished, and always displayed in Caleb's mind.

I ran my fingertips along the smooth canvas with zero texture. Caleb likely had no experience with paintings but subconsciously enjoyed their elegance.

My eyes fluttered. Flashes of sunlight burned my vision, and inside a memory, I stood. His thoughts echoed loudest here, connected to my own, so I kept quiet as events unfolded.

Caleb read a book at the edge of the sandbox, content this was the only place he could find peace from his teacher who encouraged him to enjoy the outdoors or his rowdy classmates exploring the playground during recess. They were all big kids now, halfway through second grade, and no longer had interest in the simplicity of the sandbox. Not when the monkey bars and plastic rock wall leading to the entrance of the twisting slide provided true adventure. Caleb didn't want their adventures. He wanted his own found inside the pages of recorded accounts on notable enchanters.

Maybe this memory held significance because it led to the momentous collection of enchanters he'd studied over the years.

"What're you reading?" A small boy blocked Caleb's light, making the words difficult to read.

"Nothing, really."

"If it's nothing, then why aren't you playing?"

Caleb shrugged, carefully scooting along the bristly wood of the sandbox, avoiding splinters, to reclaim his sunlight.

"It looks like it's about magic."

"It is," Caleb said, trying to concentrate on the bigger words. There were so many he had trouble with inside this book.

"I like magic."

Me, too. The thought lingered in Caleb's head, but he couldn't speak it. Every time he shared his love for magic, the conversation always took a quick turn to a question he hated.

"What kind of magic is it about?" The boy sat next to him, brushing his black bangs out of his eyes. "Are there any cool branch magics in there?"

"It's not about branches exactly."

"That's cool, I guess." The boy twiddled his thumbs. "Do you have a branch magic?"

"No." Caleb dug his tiny shoes deep into the sand. The question he despised most of all.

"Oh, it takes longer for some witches."

"No. My grandma said they're not common in our family." Caleb held his book close to his face, using it to hide the boy's smile and the laughter that would soon begin.

Once kids realized Caleb was branchless, they usually teased him, called him mean names, and said he was stupid for reading about enchanters all day. He hoped the boy would just get it over with and let him return to his book. His dreams.

"That's cool. My parents are branchless, too, and they're the strongest witches in the whole world."

Shock and excitement warmed his chest. His throat was dry, but he couldn't resist asking. "Are they enchanters?" He closed his book, revealing the cover: *Compendium of Enchanters Vol. 28*. His green eyes lit with a joy he only ever felt when reading.

"Not yet, but they're gonna become enchanters really soon. They're working on getting real licenses and everything."

"That's amazing." Caleb bit his lip, nervous he'd say or do the wrong thing, but excitement took over, and he extended a hand. "My name's Caleb, by the way."

"Nice to meet you." The boy took his hand, shaking it vigorously, smiling ear to ear. "My name's Kenzo, but most people just call me Kenny."

Kenzo? Kenzo Ito, the kid with an insufferable scowl glued to his face? The one who screamed his thoughts louder than most death metal singers? I shook away the stunned curiosity remaining in the memory.

Caleb scooted closer to Kenzo, sharing his book.

"Is there anything on Enchanter Evergreen? He's my absolute favorite."

"Not in this book; it's way old."

"Oh." Kenzo's slumped shoulders and sullen expression confused Caleb, giving him anxiety. He dug into his pocket, hopeful to fan the embers and spark the flame of their friendship.

"But we can look up his videos on my phone. I've got lots saved because I'm gonna be just like him when I'm an enchanter."

"Me too."

The memory dimmed. I released my pressed fingertips from the painting. I reached for the knob beneath the golden frame and eased open the door. Inside the room, paintings and trinkets cramped the place from floor to ceiling with recollections of Kenzo Ito and Caleb Huxley.

For a boy who walked around with daily dread because of an angry bully in his class, he carried a lot of cherished memories.

Chapter Twelve

A persistent buzz joined the irritating chime of my phone alarm. I buried my head under a pillow to dull the noise that came with mornings. Since establishing the link a few days ago, a fog clung to me, making waking hours grueling. Fumbling at my nightstand, I finally grabbed my phone and hit the snooze. It buzzed again.

"Dammit." My throat was gravelly.

I brought the phone under the pillow, squinting until I softened the brightness. Milo had sent some late-night texts, which I'd missed.

> Milo: It's been a minute
> Sorry I've been MIA. Not dodging you
> Wondering if you're up

He shared a YouTube link to Bloodhound Gang's "The Bad Touch" video.

> Just a boy w/ 🍆 👀 4 🌊 2 👉 💦
> Guess you're 💀 or 🥵

And the early morning messages:

> Milo: Rise and shine!

He'd also sent a half-dozen gifs screaming GOOD MORNING.

> Me: Morning

> Milo: Oh! You're alive.

> Me: Barely.

> Milo: I feel you. Work is intense. Mountains of paperwork have taken over my life. Send help.

A gif of a woman slapped with a tidal wave popped up. I replied with a gif of two drowning hands high-fiving.

> Me: Welcome to the club.

A tiny smile grew on my face. Whether delirious from my overexerted magic, work exhaustion, or the morning wood tightening my boxer briefs, I found myself excited to finally talk with Milo again. This was probably some reverse psychology clairvoyant trick on his part. Throw himself at me nonstop and then vanish, leaving me craving more. Whatever. It worked. Here I was, typing a highly provocative text with his top five suggestive emojis in the mix.

> Milo: You wanna meet?

I deleted my message before hitting send.

> Me: I have work.

> Milo: Duh, me too. Meant sometime soon. We can hang, bang, I'll give you my wang. That's slang for...

And he sent a dick pic.

I sucked my teeth. Maybe it had been a long minute. I lifted the blanket over my head, tugging my waistband up, and returned the favor.

> Milo: *Gasp* So unprofessional from an academy educator.

> Me: Shut up.

I tossed my phone aside and struggled out of bed. Carlie sat on the edge of the mattress, judgment in her eyes either because I engaged in some morning sexting or was five minutes behind her feeding schedule. Please. Carlie didn't give a fuck what I did so long as she got her food. After feeding the cats and getting dressed for work, I sat slumped on the couch to have a cigarette.

Holding the last puff tight, I resisted the exhale because that meant it was time to check the tether again. My manifestation had collected an assortment of memories, picking through what he deemed useful. Nothing sent thus far showed signs of nearby or potential threats. All most of it showed was that Caleb knew too much about enchanters and that Kenzo wasn't always such an angry little fucker.

I stretched, arching my back, preparing to retrieve yet more messages, sort of like answering your psychic voicemail. In theory, the call between myself and my manifestation could remain constant, but I didn't want to walk around in dual screen all day.

Magic funneled within me, igniting an electrical surge that made my skin crawl. My heart pounded, pumping fiery blood through my veins. Magic drummed my insides, rattling my bones from head to toe.

This was the downside to delving deep for extended periods of time. Or maybe it was because I didn't maintain my magic this way anymore. My eyes rolled back.

Chapter Thirteen

Most of the memories my manifestation sifted through the past few days held little to no insight into the horrors awaiting Caleb. Oftentimes, checking the tether came with a message simply informing me there was no intel worth divulging. I didn't need Caleb's private musings; they could fade away along with my manifestation once this was completed. But the memory shared now held something that still shook Caleb's mind, making him queasy if he thought too long about it.

At age nine, Caleb held an expression of terror in one of the portraits housing his memories. The same face of dread I'd seen in the vision predicting his death. Rarely did Caleb worry about his life in such a way, but here—he felt truly helpless. Useless. Scared.

Crimson blood drops speckled fluffy snow. Caleb cried. He clutched his hand, convinced he'd broken his wrist. His best friend, Kenny, stood a few feet away, his legs deep in the snow, blood dripping from his nose, and fury in his eyes. In the three years since they'd met, Caleb didn't believe Kenny had so much anger. The scowl was deep and unfamiliar to Caleb, but I'd seen that rage on Kenzo's face every single day since he entered Gemini Academy.

"You better run," Kenny screamed, his voice cracking from the high pitch or perhaps the bitter chill in the air.

Caleb wanted to zip his jacket back up, but moving his arm seemed impossible. It might very well crack in half if he released his hold. Already the swelling throbbed, and he couldn't stop crying. The wind stung his wet cheeks.

"You ever mess with me again, and I'll kill you!" Smoky gray static coursed along Kenny's entire body.

"Kenny, stop." Caleb trudged through the snow, reaching his friend and hugging him with his uninjured arm. The pain in his other wrist dulled in the moment; all he could think about was keeping Kenny safe the way Kenny had protected him. "What if they come back?"

"They won't. They're weak cowards." Kenny's eyes swelled, tears he fought back with sniffles, making his nose scrunch with a pained expression.

"You shouldn't have done that," Caleb said, dabbing Kenny's nose with his scarf. "They could've hurt you."

"Yeah, right." Kenny shoved the scarf away. Carefully, he grabbed Caleb's arm, checking the bruised wrist. The delicate touch of Kenny's fingertips throbbed against Caleb's burning bones. "Are you okay?"

Caleb winced. "I think so."

"What they were saying, how they hit you… You can't just let people do that to you." Kenny's angry eyes didn't relent.

Caleb couldn't explain he was used to people mocking him, hurting him because he wanted to be an enchanter. Because he was just a branchless loser with no control over his root magics.

A chill ran through Caleb, confusing him. He couldn't figure out if the cold or Kenzo's icy stare caused it.

"But there were four of them, and they were older." Caleb averted his eyes to the moonlit sky, deep in the wooded park where the city lights almost never reached. "Weren't you scared?"

"Not a chance. Enchanters have to be brave against any threat, no matter what. That's what it means to save lives." Kenny rested his head on Caleb's shoulder. Kenny took sharp, wheezy breaths. "You have to be stronger, Caleb. I don't wanna be an enchanter by myself."

"I will be. I promise." Caleb meant it, too. He knew he didn't have the fury bubbling inside him to make him strong like Kenny or an amazing branch magic to disrupt other magics. But he could be brave and catch up to Kenny.

Caleb helped his weary friend through the snow.

Caleb's memories were a sea of fanboy adoration, meticulous research, and reminiscing when Kenzo was Kenny. Nothing my manifestation sent indicated his past carried the answer. No potential threats lurked in the periphery of his memories or screamed shady murderous intent. This was a waste of time. Maybe.

No. Finn had never led me astray before. Even if this wasn't him but my subconscious stitching together closure, I wanted to follow this thread.

I needed to see this through. Not for me. To save Caleb's life.

The month of September involved a lot of training with my homeroom coven. We met twice a day—three times for those unfortunate enough to have me for History, too. Time spent in class, the auxiliary gym, discussions on licensing, the purpose of covens, and collaborative work. The channeling lesson helped some realize the differing frequencies in witches based on branch types. Our continued review of root magics helped my students gain a basic grasp of the fundamentals. But their groupings were off, not as compatible as they could be. That fell on me. Day one gave a snapshot of their magic, personality shining through in its rawest form, yet I hadn't figured them out enough.

The week blurred together in a haze. Whether due to the extensive use of my magic or simply the overkill workload from the beginning of a new school year, in this current daze, I struggled to compose myself long enough to organize the missing pieces.

I brought everyone to the auxiliary gym so everyone could comfortably train throughout the various terrains inside. Honestly, the imported trees for the forest terrain still excited me. Finn used to hide between them during our trainings, avoiding lessons and studying the long lives of each uprooted tree, exploring the unique past for every speck of bark.

My students' groggy expressions mixed with irritation this early in the morning drew me away from the memories. Memories I happily buried.

"I know you're tired of hearing the importance of the fundamentals, and many of you are eager to jump into practicing your branch magic."

Sullen faces stared, hope in some eyes, doubt in others, and pure contempt in one set.

"Please say root training. I need to catch up, and I don't even have a branch to train."

"**Given the layout, it's another boring sensory lesson.**"

"Please don't say branch training."

"Kenzo looks annoyed. ¿Por qué?" *"You ready, King Clucks?"*

"No wisps, please."

*"Why do I even bother bringing
my grimoire?"*

"Oh, he has enchantments as wisp substitutes again."

"More levitating."

*"More wisp substitutes? I used my
star shower **one** time."*

"No more levitating."

*"I wish Mr. Frost would just spit it out.
Everyone's anxiety is exhausting."*

Their thoughts were difficult to manage currently, but at least their chatty outbursts on top of a flurry of surface thoughts lessened a few weeks in.

"I've reserved the auxiliary gym for the entire day. You'll have free reign to train as you see fit. Think of this as your last opportunity to choose between root, branch, endurance, or channeling. Our October schedule will be branch-focused, November endurance, and in December, I'll be determining if you've pieced it all together well enough to apply for a fledgling permit before winter break."

I sent them to the lockers to change into their gym clothes. No point in wearing the stuffy Gemini uniforms if I wanted them casting all day long.

Kenzo came out first, adjusting the strings to his sleek black joggers and brushing wrinkles out of his white tee. Even Gemini's gym clothes were ridiculously overpriced, given the slightly smoother sweat-resistant material and audacious emblem resembling the zodiac sign they paid way too much to trademark.

Admittedly, I often quelled my telepathy around Kenzo, given his furious mind, but with no one around, his thoughts didn't stir. There was no real rage behind them. Instead, I saw an expression of momentary nothingness, soft and vacant, almost resembling the kind boy Caleb knew once upon a time. How'd he become so angry? Go from the boy awed by his friend's dream of joining a guild and grow into this teen filled with so much hatred for branchless witches.

Caleb walked out of the locker room alongside a chatty Gael Martinez. Kenzo's fury blossomed.

"Hey, man." Gael waved a spiky hand. "Caleb and I were just talking about roots to work on. You wanna practice with us?"

Gael strolled toward Kenzo, unfazed by the rage radiating. Kenzo turned, his eyes meeting mine.

"**Why the fuck is he staring at me? Is he reading my thoughts?**"

I ground my teeth. More like blocking them out. So loud.

Gray static popped, shining against the gel in Kenzo's jet-black hair. He cast disruption to shield his thoughts. Impressive precision, but he lacked an understanding of psychic magic. That might prevent an intrusive visit if he maintained it, but his surface thoughts, and emanating emotions, floated well outside his mind at this point, easily observed with the right magic.

"So cool," Gael Rios-Vega shouted alongside a group of boys exiting the locker room. "King Clucks loves days off."

"This isn't a free day." I glared. "I'll be making my way around to observe and assist."

"Of course, Mr. Frosty. We're going to train our magics very diligently." Gael and his familiar nodded in unison.

"I'm glad you feel that way." My mocking sarcasm lulled a few into a false sense of security. That disappeared when I opened my satchel, withdrew a stack of papers, and released a delicate telekinetic breeze. "I got your other teachers to agree to excuse this absence by ensuring my students would have their missing work completed.

Have to say, it's only the first month, and it's a shame some of my homeroom coven's already falling behind."

Fluttering papers lightly dropped into the hands of Melanie, Jamius, Carter, and both Gaels.

"If you want to practice your magic, feel free once you're caught up in your classes. As for the rest of you, go ahead and get started. Once I have the slackers situated, I'll come around."

Gael Martinez sighed at the handful of papers he held. Gael Rios-Vega crumbled the edges of the stack while his familiar pecked in my direction.

"Bawk." The rooster squinted. Actually squinted. Insufferable.

"Mr. Frost." Katherine raised a hand. "Not to be rude, but you haven't exactly clarified what the requirements are for the fledgling permit. What should we be focusing on?"

Of course I hadn't explained because I'd been so caught up in my own life, my past, Caleb's life, his future, that that simple bit of information slipped my mind.

"I've been waiting for someone to finally ask. Thank you for catching that, Katherine." I mustered the thinnest of smiles. Yes, I was an asshole playing off my own failures as my students' shortcomings. "In order to gain a fledgling permit, you'll need to show capability in each of your root magics. If you want the permit to extend to a branch magic, then you'll need to determine the type of classification you'll be applying for. It doesn't have to be permanent, but if you change classifications, you'll need to reapply again, so this should be a decision you have a solid understanding of by the end of the first semester."

"Classification?" The word left as many lips as minds it bubbled above.

"All magic works differently. Some are better suited offensively," I gestured to Yaritza and Layla, "while others provide support," I pointed a hand to Carter but held off before reaching Kenzo. Everything I'd seen from his display proved he had no intention of playing a supporting role. "There are plenty of classifications to choose from. For instance, when I applied for my fledgling permit, I chose surveillance because my magic allows me to skim the surface thoughts of others, making it easier to obtain intel."

"That's right. He can read our thoughts." Gael eyed his rooster. *"Can he understand you, too?"*

"No, Gael. I can't understand your familiar."

"Whoa. I totally just thought that, and like, you knew it."

"Hence glancing at surface thoughts." My smile disappeared.

"Glancing surface thoughts and a whole lot more, I bet." Caleb's brow scrunched. *"Anyone with an enchanter license should have complete proficiency in their branch magic, which means Mr. Frost can probably do things like observing memories, delving into the psyche, casting telepathic communication links, reading emotional energy, maybe even mind control. No. That's a different branch, right? Psychics have some major overlap, though."*

Caleb bit his lip, flipping through his notebook. His mind was a complete maze of intel he'd memorized over the years. "Question. You have an enchanter license, but you're not classified as an enchanter. Why is that?"

"Great question," I said.

"**Which branchless could've googled and saved us the fucking lecture.**" Kenzo clenched his jaw, frowning. "**Let us train already.**"

I winced. Oh, he wanted a fucking lecture? I'd give him one.

"Fledgling permits allow witches to freely train their magic. An acolyte license allows witches the right to cast magic for personal use, so long as the individual doesn't use their magic to infringe on another person's rights. Acolyte licenses don't allow witches to use their magic for profit, but they're free"—emphasis on the free—"to intern at guilds, eventually qualifying for an enchanter license."

Caleb and Katherine jotted notes. Layla rolled her eyes, among a few who had enchanter family members and found the lesson redundant. Others took a mental note to write this down later, but I could already see those fleeting ideas drifting into the ether of lost thoughts. Good thing we'd have real lessons later to further clarify.

"Working for a guild is the only way to obtain the enchanter title. That said, plenty of witches like myself possess enchanter licenses and work for private firms, academic institutions, city jobs, or government positions. I realize professional enchanter careers are the goal, but it's important to know you all have options."

With that, I sent them off and brought those behind in classes to the bleachers so we could finish their missing assignments. Honestly, most of my coven needed to improve their grades, but that'd be for another day. Right now, I wanted the missing assignments completed and all of them practicing their magic. They needed this time.

"Let's get started." I read over an English prompt they'd all failed to complete.

Gael anxiously followed along, but the words continued flipping out of sequence as he read silently.

```
Name: Gael Martinez
Branch: Augmentation (Spikes)
```

Carter, on the other hand, didn't even attempt to follow. He lay on a bleacher row, arms dangling at his sides and papers covering his face.

```
Name: Carter Howe
Branch: Rejuvenation (Vitality)
```

I nudged his knee. "Need a pencil?"

"No. I'm dying."

"Hmm. Maybe if you finish this work, you'll be able to practice your branch and save yourself."

He snatched the pencil and slumped forward.

Tiny flames trailed along Melanie's paper, singeing the edges.

```
Name: Melanie Dawson
Branch: Primal (Fire)
```

"Stop that." I stole her lighter with a telekinetic grip.

"What? I thought this was an assignment where I needed to use magic to reveal the answers."

"What on earth would give you that impression?"

Melanie held the burnt pages, irritation festering in both our minds. "Obviously, I haven't been keeping up, so how would I know?"

"I'm keeping the lighter until you're finished."

Reluctantly, Melanie agreed. I paired her with Gael and provided some starter-sentence examples.

"No, Gael."

"Huh?" Gael tensed, his spikes shrinking.

"Not you." I shook my head, turning back to Gael Rios-Vega and his rooster with a pen in his claw. "This is your work, not his."

"Trust me, King Clucks' handwriting's way better than my chicken scratch." He stifled a giggle.

```
Name: Gael Rios-Vega
Branch: Bestial (Familiar)
```

Crack. Carter snapped the pencil in half.

"Why'd you do that?"

He shrugged. "I'm not made for this kind of work."

"That was my pencil. That I bought."

Carter put one half on top of his curved lip, creating a mustache, and conveniently dropped the sharpened end between the bleachers. My head hurt. An ache traveled down my neck, reminding me the only thing more frustrating than invasive thoughts was herding reluctant children.

Out of the corner of my eye, Jamius quietly worked. Well, sort of.

```
Name: Jamius Watson
Branch: Alteration (Duplication)
```

Two Jamius' worked while the original lay on the bleachers, arms tucked behind his head as he watched videos on a phone he kept hovering above his face with telekinesis.

"Jamius, while I want you to practice your magic today, that'll only happen after you finish your missing work."

"But I'm better at math than him," each clone said in unison with a thumb to their chest and a finger pointed over their shoulder to the original. "No, you idiot. I'm the one who's good with math. No, I am. Stop copying me. No, you stop copying me." And then the clones were rolling down the bleachers scuffling with each other.

"Ha," Carter said. "Stop hitting yourself."

All the kids burst into laughter. Ugh.

"Get rid of the clones and complete your work." I overpowered the light telekinetic hold Jamius had on his phone and snatched it away. "And no technology."

An academy rule I'd gladly enforce right now.

"You guys ruin everything." Jamius sat up, eyeing his copies.

"It wasn't me; it was him." They pointed at each other. "No, you."

It took time, longer than expected, but I'd gotten them sort of on track and potentially capable of working independently while I checked on the others. Who was I kidding? I kept magic channeled around them in case their minds wandered too far off track.

Sweat drenched Layla's face, competitive with every step she took around the track in the fitness section of the auxiliary gym.

```
Name: Layla Smythe
Branch: Bestial (Therianthropy)
```

Clenching my core, I levitated and cast a telekinetic burst to follow along midair. "And what exactly are you focused on today?"

She ignored me, fixated on her self-imposed time. I spun upside down, hovering in front of her. Unstartled, through expression or thought, she raced toward the finish line. Honestly, the rush of blood to my head and magic channeled elsewhere brought relief from my branch; I relished the silent seconds.

"I'm working on my endurance because I can only maintain my shift for five minutes," Layla said, panting as she reached the end of her sprint. "And then I'm pretty much spent, so that means I can't use my root magic."

All magics, roots and branches, held some physical cost, but therianthropes were the epitome of athletic witches, requiring control for their entire muscular system to channel their animalistic form.

"I see." I dropped to the dirt track. "Have you tried using your branch and roots together?"

"Can't." Layla tucked a leg behind her, gripping the tip of her foot and stretching the muscles.

"Using your root magic while in therianthrope form will increase your body's tolerance to maintaining that form as much as improving your physical stamina."

Layla bit her lip, fighting back curious questions that bubbled to the surface.

"Try meditation to shift between the two states. Channel all your magic into the ferocity of your branch form, then send it cascading into a single root. One you're best suited at."

Layla raised her brows, doubtful of the suggestion since she struggled to quickly transition between the ebb and flow. Shifting gears was often like pulling a U-turn on the interstate while going eighty miles. But like driving, all the simultaneous steps became second nature the more a person did it.

"Until you learn to utilize both simultaneously, this will help you adapt to quicker transitions between the two," I said. "Choosing the root you're best at will wire your body and magic to recognize the mental switch in your mind when adding in the other roots later."

I floated away, using telepathy to seek out those in need of guidance. Jennifer sat alone in the forest terrain. My muscles jumped beneath my skin.

"Shut up. I'm not anxious. Shut up. I'm not angry. Shut up. I'm not bored, happy, sad, tired, or anything. Shut the fuck up."

```
Name: Jennifer Jung
Branch: Psychic (Empathic)
```

I landed, embracing the fresh pine, suppressing the frustration in her mind. "And what exactly are you working on today?"

"I'm trying to figure out what empathy is even good for."

"Lots of things."

"Don't give me the speech on how my magic can help people. I don't want to use my magic to help people figure their annoying shit out."

I fought a smirk. A girl carved from my own bitter heart. I leaned against the tree, sliding next to her.

"Attending an academy, gaining a license so you can work at a guild. That's a great way to find work that'll help you avoid people." My sarcastic tone didn't land well, given her immediate thoughts expressing utter disdain before she buried them.

"My uncle works for the Pegasus Guild and never talks to people. All he does is banish wisps all day." Jennifer plucked bits of grass out of the ground. "That'd be a pretty nice way of using my magic. Flying high above the city, removing demonic energy."

"And not requiring your branch or its proximity when nearby others. You have difficulty quelling your magic," I said, solemn. It was a conversation no one had with me until my third year at Gemini. "Psychic magic is difficult when the witch has strong innate channeling capabilities."

This was my biggest problem. Most psychics didn't channel a constant flow, but those who did always had to double-check, ensuring the stove to our magic was turned off.

"Focus less on quelling your magic. That step will be easier later in life. Right now, you're trying to build a mental dam without any wood."

"*That's what she said.*"

I rolled my eyes. "Keep it up. I'll tell Gael you're after his innuendo crown."

She blushed, running fingers through her long black hair to cover her face.

"Instead of silencing your magic, focus on redistributing it," I said, needing this lesson a bit, too. It was easy to overlook the basics day-to-day. "This will help you actually hone your root magics more, and it'll assist in silencing some of the other emotions glued to your mind."

"How long before I feel more like myself?"

I stood, brushing dirt off my jeans. "We're psychics. We never feel like ourselves."

I moved deeper into the woods, stumbling onto Katherine and Yaritza working together.

"I figured you'd be off at the rock terrain hurling flaming boulders." Endangering other students and herself like she had on day one.

"With Kenzo there, pissing over it to mark his territory? No thanks." Yaritza clumped dirt together into a tiny ball between her palms, breathing onto it until it twinkled with delicate white flames. "Besides, I can channel my magic into any mineral so long as I can identify and understand the basic makeup of the material."

```
Name: Yaritza Vargas
Branch: Cosmic (Star Shower)
```

Interesting. Definitely something to stipulate in her permit.

Yaritza dropped the fiery rock onto a piece of parchment paper. Katherine placed two fingers from each hand on the corner of the page, motioning for Yaritza to follow suit. With their breathing in sync, Katherine muttered something in Latin.

```
Name: Katherine Harris
Branch: Enchantment (Spell Craft)
```

The flaming rock melted onto the page, absorbed into the new form of ink.

"And what exactly is that you're doing there?"

Katherine's eyes lit up, eager to share everything she knew about spell crafting.

"So, I can create my own spells because of my branch, but the types vary. Like, basic spells—I want to float a pencil—I can channel five of those into the parchment of my grimoire a day. Easy. Now, more advanced spells, like, I want to float a flaming pencil to hurl at my enemies—not that I have enemies—I can maybe channel enough magic to make one a week. They're hard, and sometimes the ink implodes if done incorrectly. Then there's significant spells, but my mom won't let me work on those."

I listened, nodding and reacting with interest—as much as a dour face like mine could muster—over stuff I already understood. There was nothing to teach Katherine right now. She knew her magic deeply, even understanding the importance of matching another witch's casting frequency to contain the spell in her grimoire, but what she needed in this moment was an interested ear.

"This, however, is classified as a hybrid spell."

"Really?" I asked.

"Okay, Yaritza has her own branch magic. I could probably create a spell to match it, but it'd be advanced or higher. That said, using her magic, both of us channeling it together, I'm sort of saving a mini version of her casting. Cool, right?"

"The coolest," I said.

The pair went on another five minutes about their magics before shifting topics to God only knows what because I'd capped out on my teen speak. I skirted further away from the forest, reaching its edge where Caleb hovered between the tree lines, preparing banishment on the enchantments. Gemini Academy acquired the best enchantments the industry had to offer. Spells crafted by witches with the same branch as Katherine. These specific enchantments were designed as substitutes for wisps. Without a constant eye on the students and the facility, I couldn't allow them unsupervised training with actual demonic energy.

```
Name: Caleb Huxley
Branch: N/A
```

Using his levitation and banishment roots together caused him to slightly drop. Tara floated next to him, steadying his posture.

"I'm still having trouble maintaining the two," Caleb said.

"It's not easy."

"Thanks for helping with the basics."

"No problem." Tara brushed a stray blonde lock, tucking it behind her ear. "Honestly, I need to spend more time on my root magics anyway."

"Are you kidding? You're already so good at using them together. I figured you'd want to work on one of your branches." Caleb scrunched his face. "Or have you already mastered those too?"

"Not in the least." Tara descended to the ground.

```
Name: Tara Whitlock
Branch: Ward (Sealing)
Branch: Cosmic (Shadows)
Branch: Arcane (Intangibility)
```

Her mind was a desolate cavern of despair. In my current state, if I dove in, her sorrow would swallow me whole. I owed her better. I owed them all more. Instead, I used the excuse of helping Caleb by clinging to my past in hopes it'd shine a light on his future. Just further proof of my shortcomings.

"I'm sure you'll master them soon enough." Caleb followed her, his mind buzzing with everything he knew about the Whitlock family but resisted sharing because he didn't want to come off as a stalker.

Based on the rippling bubble of thoughts rising above Tara's ocean, she was used to everyone knowing a lot about her and her family while not really knowing a thing that wasn't part of carefully crafted public images.

"It's not like my root magic," she said. "I can't pick and choose which branch to train or maintain."

"Huh?"

"They sort of collide when I cast them. It's complicated."

"A channeling overlap," I said, revealing my eavesdropping in a completely uncreepy way. Suppose it'd be weirder to continue listening without chiming in.

"Channeling overlap? I've read about that. Something to do with a witch's branch veins being too close to their roots. It's a medical thing, maybe. When they access one, both trigger or something..." Caleb walked toward his backpack, rifling around for his notebook.

"So, your branches all cast at the same time?" I asked. "Is that why you're not showing them off today?"

"I can use them; it's just a lot to maintain. They differ, but I'll be ready once branch training starts." Tara smiled, forced and fake, then floated toward Caleb for more root training. *"I have to be ready. Like Dad said, if I can't make it at some basic academy, there's only one alternative. Not that there's much for me here."*

Basic academy? Hmph. Figures the Whitlock family wouldn't think much of our academies, especially since the state's new mandate in casting proficiency. Not enough elitism involved anymore.

I'd need to do research on multi-branched witches. Not sure any with more than two existed, but if Tara possessed a channeling overlap with her three branches, maybe I could—

"Train somewhere else," Kenzo snapped at Caleb and Tara, who flew close to the rock terrain.

"He's so irritating."

"Let's head back to the woods," Caleb said. "I want to see how Katherine's project is going, anyway."

I locked eyes with Kenzo, who carefully added another rock to the collection he held in the air above the terrain. A delicate and weighty process keeping a telekinetic hold on two dozen small boulders.

He grimaced as I moved toward him. "**_Fuck off._**"

"What're you working on?"

"Like you weren't listening." Kenzo coated in sweat, muscles tense, mind a flurry of profanities.

```
Name: Kenzo Ito
Branch: Hex (Disruption)
```

"Just checking in," I said, trying to give him the benefit of the doubt. Trying not to assume the worst out of this kid even though he kept setting off red flags.

"I don't need a babysitter to train. Why don't you worry about the branchless blunder?"

Sort of been my biggest focus and problem as of late. I was trying to fix that and be a better instructor. Clearly, I failed on all counts. No. I'd approached Kenzo entirely wrong. He was blunt and rude and straightforward.

"Why do you hate branchless witches so much?" I asked directly because that line would provoke a response from Kenzo.

"**_Skim that from my mind or the branchless blunder's?_**"

"Oh, no. Despite your subtlety, I figured it out all on my own." *Asshole.*

"**_Asshole._**" He sucked his teeth. "I don't hate them. Just wish they'd remember the world isn't going to change for them. The world doesn't need branchless heroes. It doesn't need heroes who rely on flashy branches either."

"Okay. So, what does the world need?"

"Me." Kenzo released the floating rocks, propelling into the air and shattering them in quick succession with powerful punches. Coiling telekinesis around his arms was a proficient skill that most witches with an acolyte license couldn't do. His combined use of his root magics, the advanced expertise, continued to prove impressive.

Too bad his personality was, well, shittier than even mine. Maybe Caleb's past would illuminate a bit of what turned Kenzo so hateful.

Chapter Fourteen

I lounged on the couch, sorting through half-graded papers, poorly scribbled notes, and ideas to assist my homeroom coven that needed tweaking. What I should be doing was pushing all of this aside and preparing for a night off. A night away from the doom of an unforeseen future, along with the daily stress of work. I should be preparing for Milo's arrival since tonight—after canceling on each other four times this month—we'd planned to meet.

A part of me wanted the relief that came with Milo's carefree attitude. Another part of me prepared a half-dozen conversations on how I'd dreamt of Finn, learned clues that didn't really lead anywhere, and how based on all this NOTHING, the grand Enchanter Evergreen should help in solving the void vision he'd written off. The one we still didn't really discuss. The one I'd done a shit job at solving.

My phone buzzed.

> Milo: Gotta postpone. Work stuff.

Seriously? He was blowing me off again. Did he predict my half-concocted conversation to convince him for assistance would go well? Or maybe he predicted a thousand variations on where I'd make a fool out of myself and didn't want to ruin a get-together by politely letting me down.

> Me: That's fine. Another night.

> Milo: Oh, I'm coming. Just not coming as early. There's a joke somewhere in that. 🐙

Insufferable. Honestly, I needed the time to work, think, organize, and do a million other things on my to-do list. Screwing shouldn't be one of them. It certainly shouldn't rise to the top of my list. So, being the productive fuckup I was, I opened a new tab on my laptop and scrolled Milo's Instagram, riling myself up over his most recent pictures. Now, pathetically, checking notifications on his recent trending news. Not in a stalkerish way. After all, Enchanter Evergreen made himself a public symbol, and it wasn't my fault a quick online search offered a more detailed reason behind him running late than his texting innuendos.

Of course.

Milo ran late due to another warlock strike. One the media was in the midst of covering because the propaganda machine loved fixating on the dangers of unlicensed witches casting. I turned on the television to the local news to catch the live feed. Milo, who was absolutely too busy to meet on time, appeared on the screen alongside Enchanter Campbell. It was mildly annoying public appearances and unnecessary interviews counted toward "work stuff" in Milo's world.

"Please step back and allow the local authorities to secure this area," Milo said, arms outstretched but nonaggressive. His friendly smile was inviting. So much so the camera zoomed in, cropping Enchanter Pompous-Barely-Described-It Campbell. "We'll be more than happy to answer any of your questions, but it's important not to interfere with the necessary work of the investigators."

"Is it true the warlock faction is composed entirely of branchless casters?" a reporter asked.

"It's too early in the investigation to know," Milo said.

"Some suggest this faction grew as a way to speak out on the injustice and discrepancies between branchless witches when trying to obtain licenses to cast their magic. Do you think that's why all the targeted victims, as of late, have been guild members or individuals known to frequently contract guild services?"

"Whatever their reasoning," Enchanter Campbell said. "Their targets, as you stated, were killed for no other reason than following—"

"Following guidelines to a system some consider outdated, costly, and preferential," Milo interjected. "Licenses are expensive to maintain. Not every witch, with or without a branch, has the funds to pay these fees for the privilege of using magic. Legislation's changing, which is comforting, but it's understandable some would feel this is a move too little too late."

"So, you think this is a radical message to call out companies such as Whitlock Industries for monopolizing guilds, reinforcing stigmas, and hiring flashy branch users?" a reporter from another station asked, blocking the camera shot. "After all, Whitlock Bank was the first major target this warlock faction struck. Now, all their victims seem closely aligned with their organization."

I scoffed. It was hard not to be aligned with Whitlock Industries. Like they said—it was a fucking monopoly. Whitlock Industries had its hand in every guild's cookie jar, and the few not affiliated with the company rarely rose to the surface. No independent guild ever succeeded in the state. The few enchanters I'd considered for internships over the years were shot down by administration because supporting an independent guild would send a bad message.

"This isn't a discussion on whether companies like Whitlock Industries dictate legislation with their deep corporate pockets. That's something we all know and that I hope can be changed." Milo stared directly into the camera, pausing and allowing that comment to sink in. "This is about lives being taken. This is about unchecked, unregistered magic casting chaos, increasing demonic energy throughout the city, and harming people."

The television quieted. I turned up the volume, convinced I'd hit mute unintentionally.

"There's a huge difference between casting with civil disobedience to force change to outdated policies on licenses versus using magic to destroy lives."

The interview wrapped up, and I turned off the television, hoping Milo knew what he was doing. Stirring the pot of an active case his guild worked alongside the police with screamed industry angst. Milo never shied from controversy, but this was unsettling.

Another thing I hadn't considered about the recent warlock factions—their branchless status. In the same city as Caleb. The one he might very well be meant to die in. Branchless witches made up less than twenty percent of the world. Nothing about the kid struck me as a radical, but who knew what his most recent memories on the current issue held.

I gripped the bridge of my nose, ignoring the tug of my tether. Like an irritating notification flashing on a phone. This soft buzz reminded me of memories collected on Caleb. I lit a cigarette, taking a deep inhale. Full lungs provided momentary clarity. Since Milo was running late, maybe it was time to check for whatever useless intel my manifestation gathered.

I delved into the newest memory my manifestation had sent, involving Caleb at a Guild Convention. Why my manifestation found this particular memory insightful, I didn't understand. The convention whirred with noise from the crowd of people checking out each stand to the enchantments on display for purchase, all the way to the panels with guild members. None of that mattered to Caleb right now. He'd barely afforded a ticket inside, and he didn't want to waste any time gawking at things he couldn't buy.

"I can't believe he signed everything we brought, King Clucks." A stout, round Gael walked past Caleb carrying more memorabilia than his arms could contain. Talk about a major growth spurt between freshman year and entering the academy. "Enchanter Evergreen is the coolest."

He faded as quickly from the memory as he'd arrived. Despite his loudmouth and bubbly laughter, that was all Caleb recalled in this moment. No realization clicked that the kid from the convention was now in his class, which made sense, given how many people we all encounter every day.

All of Caleb's attention was fixated on the winding line leading to Milo. He didn't have anything for the enchanter to sign, but he had a desperate question to ask. One he hoped a brilliant clairvoyant would shine insight on.

"Why, hello there." Milo smiled, inviting Caleb to the table.

Caleb clenched his clammy hands around his notebook. "I wanted to ask…"

"Sign your notebook?" Milo reached for it; Caleb, stunned and shocked to see his favorite enchanter, didn't resist. Milo flipped through the cramped pages, his eyes wide. "Wow. Quite the research you've got going on. I could use an acolyte intern like you in my office."

Caleb's entire body shook with excitement and terror. "You think so?"

"Heck yeah. The attention to detail is incredible." Milo closed the book and pulled a wrapped poster off a stack. "Honestly, wouldn't want to ruin this amazing artifact in the making with my sloppy signature."

Caleb stared at the prices listed next to all the Cerberus souvenirs. He gulped, anxiously reaching for his wallet, which he already knew only had a bus pass and enough for this week's groceries.

"Don't worry about it."

Caleb clutched the signed poster, delighted. But he hadn't come for a keepsake.

"I was wondering if you thought I could be an enchanter like you even if I'm branchless."

"Of course. Truthfully, I don't use my branch day to day. It's all about the fundamentals. I just wish more guilds realized that."

"I actually, um, well, I know it's not part of what enchanters usually offer at these events, but I wondered if maybe you, you know, saw it."

"In your future?"

Caleb nodded, nervously eyeing Milo's fingers strumming along his notebook.

"I bet you have a lot of notes on my branch, huh?"

"Uh-huh." Caleb's mouth was dry, his tongue stuck to the roof of his mouth.

"Then you probably know my magic doesn't work like an exact science." Milo flashed his tiny eight-ball tattoo. "Wish I could give you a clearer answer, but I can't. I can tell you what I do see. A determined, hardworking young witch. One who understands this industry and has the fortitude to make it." Milo opened the notebook one last time before handing it back. "I'm certain I'll see the name Caleb Huxley more in the future."

Joy swept over Caleb, the memory flooded with exhilaration, meeting his idol, notes on panelists, but none of it lessened my seething fury. I severed the link. My chest swelled. Hands shook.

Milo had met him. Knew his name. I thought of the void vision excuse... No understanding of it? Who Caleb was? How to prevent this future?

Fucking liar.

Chapter Fifteen

My telepathy raged, letting countless thoughts into my head. Unable to quell it, I released telekinesis, throwing lamps, hurling knick-knacks, and tearing paintings off the walls. Carlie hissed. Charlie skittered away. I ignored them, tossing anything to satisfy the wrath pumping through my veins.

Was this some form of manipulation on his part? Using his goddamn clairvoyance to push events into place. Did he believe paying Caleb no mind or care would motivate me? Did he know how it'd affect my magic? My dreams? Memories of Finn?

Delight collided against my fury. A provocative tidal wave of emotion sent a tense surge of anticipation, which further infuriated me.

"Knock, knock, grumpy pants. Let your Big Bad Wolf inside so I can strip them off. Don't make me huff and puff and blow."

My chest swelled from Milo's arrival. Biting my lip, I buried his seductive whispers and pining affection before answering the door.

The porchlight illuminated his spiky blond locks, casting a luminous halo above his head and shadows around his scruffy stubble. It looked good. Always did. But he hated a rugged face, preferring clean-shaven for his public image. This was for me. It wouldn't work.

"It's rough." He ran his fingertips along his bristly chin. "Work has been so busy I can't find the time for anything anymore."

"But you can find time to fucking lie to my face?"

"Whoa, what'd I walk in on?" Milo stepped closer, wide-eyed and curious about the destruction in my living room.

I barred the entryway with a firm grip on the doorframe. His cologne wafted in the mere inches that separated our lips.

"I feel like we're having an argument I'm unaware of." Caution bubbled through his mind, along with rehearsed snippets of conversations we'd never had.

"Is that what's going on in your head right now? Replaying potential futures with us so you can lull me into some manipulative distraction?"

"I don't manipulate. I observe, occasionally guide things, and sometimes—very rarely—avoid an argument. It's a tricky balance. You know this."

"Was it observing or guiding when you lied about Caleb?"

"Who?" Genuine confusion was painted across his scrunched face.

"Caleb Huxley. The boy meant to die. The void vision you couldn't grasp. The one you're still ignoring."

"I've got a lot of potential futures on the back burner. You might not realize it, but there's a lot going on right here in the present with warlock factions, Whitlock Industries, and—"

"I don't care about your warlock bullshit." I dug my nails into the wooden frame. "I want to know if this is some game. Met the kid, saw his fate, slipped the intel to me through a kiss and a void vision lie as a way to what? Draw me back into guild life? Remind me how my magic used to save lives? Hurt me? What?"

"I have no clue what you're talking about." Milo shoved his way past me, anxiety about what my neighbors might think bubbled, always considering his fucking image. "It's impossible to keep track of all my interactions, potential interactions, what did happen, will happen, could or should happen. Few things linger in my mind."

I slammed the door, glaring.

"Don't believe me?" Milo stepped closer. "Dive in. My mind's an open book."

I hadn't delved deep into Milo's mind in years. For many reasons. The nearly eight years of silence between us after Finn's death. Honestly, until Milo showed up on my doorstep, birthday cake in hand, bottle of whiskey in the other, demanding I celebrate hitting thirty like a rockstar, I'd believed our paths were never meant to cross again. I'd vanished into obscurity while Milo rose to fame. Surely, he'd forgotten me. That night, he made it clear he hadn't.

During our drift apart, Milo used the time to heal by throwing himself into work, while I used that time to avoid coping. Like anything I couldn't resolve, I ignored the feeling, burying grief by meddling in others' minds.

The other reason I kept out of his mind was how often Finn rose to the surface of his thoughts, lingering like a phantom haunting me with the joy of the past and a future that'd never be.

Rage consumed me. I slapped my hands against Milo's head, tugging his gelled hair. His eyes rolled back as I funneled the memory of the convention into his mind. With a deep breath, I fixated on his immediate reactions, his buried thoughts, the images flashing instantaneously. I searched the depths of darkness in the inner core of his mind and sighed. He knew nothing. It was merely a chance encounter, quickly forgotten, like many others with countless fans, clients, colleagues—a wonder he kept any of it sorted.

Along the edges of his thoughts stood an infinitely tall wall of screens. Each blank.

"*You can't see them, can you?*" Milo's words faintly called out.

"What's this?" I asked aloud, but my words echoed in this hollow place.

My composure waned with a part of me at the doorway of my house, another piece inside Milo's world, and a fragment snapped off, rummaging through Caleb's past.

"*My magic, the inevitable future. You're not the only psychic who can organize their headspace.*"

While our magics had merged during the void visions involving Caleb's future, perfectly synchronized magic so rarely happened, and my telepathy, in all its might, couldn't glimpse Milo's visions here in the privacy of his mind. "It used to be brighter in here."

"Still bright if you could see the screens. I keep everything else dimmer."

"This is your wall of would-be futures?" It'd grown massive since the last time I'd delved deep into his mind. He'd clearly upgraded.

"God, no." Milo traipsed forward out of the darkness his own mind cast; his steps brightened by a spotlight. "These are the ones I'm currently focused on."

"How do you keep it all from overwhelming you?"

"That's the funny thing, I don't."

I stifled a chuckle at the friendly reminder to all the mild psychics envious of those with greater reach. Our lives sucked, no matter the magic.

"Lots of notes, though. Most mental, which you're free to search."

"No. I believe you don't remember him. It's a coincidence and not some malicious clairvoyant trick. Not sure what you'd gain by it."

"I wouldn't gain anything hurting you, deceiving you. The only thing I use my clairvoyance for is to make a better future for everyone I can." Milo walked closer; his steps rippled against a floor of tears he kept at bay behind a constant smile and belief in those potential futures. "I'm not trying to ruin someone's life in the process, but I don't have enough intel on him, on Caleb."

"I know." I pressed my forehead against his. Soft and warm. Our bodies outside this place moved in sync with our thoughts.

"Quite handsy tonight, aren't you, Dorian?" Finn's voice and light laughter sent a shiver through me.

In the distance, seventeen-year-old Finn scrambled with jingling house keys while a very eager younger version of myself caressed his back, kissing his neck. "Someone needs to hurry up."

"I'm trying to find the flipping flapping flopper key."

"Not you." My tongue trailed the back of his ear, teeth nibbling.

An anxious Milo stepped into the free-floating memory. Nervousness permeated this dwelling, eager for what would unfold but equally terrified he had no idea what he was doing. I'd scanned both their thoughts the entire evening while Finn suggestively directed the conversation to this moment, leading us back to his room.

"Is this our first—"

"Time? Yeah. I keep it close at heart. Or mind. Or soul—even if you don't buy that stuff."

Souls. Existence after death. Stuff Finn and Milo and far too many consciously alive people bought into. I'd heard millions of thoughts. None from the dead. Still, no matter how untrue it was, the enthusiasm they carried for it—not the hatred some utilized it for, but the joy held—brought me comfort. Even if it was a lie.

"Sorry. Didn't exactly have time to reorganize my Finn moments. That might've been bubbling along the surface as I drove over."

They vanished into the shadows of Milo's mind while we remained in this quiet space.

"It's fine."

"It's not. I know thinking about him hurts."

"I've actually been thinking about Finn a lot lately." I leaned close, rapid breaths the only thing separating our lips. "Dreaming, really. Weird ones."

"That so?"

"Yeah, I think all that avoidance is finally catching up to me. Or interfering with Caleb's life. My own selfish way to, I don't even know, change or control something."

"You're not selfish."

"But I am. I pushed you away because of the way you held onto Finn, kept holding onto him. Selfishly, all I wanted was to grieve on my own and ignore your pain." I traced my fingers along his biceps. "Letting you back into my life was selfish, too. My way to claim a piece of what we'd had. And I kept you distant in the process, another selfish move on my part, all so I could enjoy the physical without any of the emotions."

"That's because you care. So much it might shatter you."

My vision blurred, eyes watery and cheeks damp. I stepped back, quelling my telepathy. The disheveled—okay, completely wrecked—living room returned.

"I should go." Milo reached for the doorknob, but my fingers caught his, interlocking.

"You see me. Every version. The best. The broken. And selfishly, I want to see that perfect Dorian the way you do."

"There's no perfect you. That's why I love you. Always have, always will." Milo's hand shivered in my grip. He stared at me, not through me, past me, or struggling to keep his gaze. Surface thoughts of sheer honesty bubbled in waves of pure and true emotion, matching his words tenfold.

I trembled. The most delightfully dreadful words to hear. Milo knew it and used the opportunity to make his escape.

"Stay." My voice was weak and gravelly. "Please. I lo… I feel better when you're around."

Milo in my life was a cathartic pain, like mending broken bones.

He kissed me. His lips were plump and soft but hands assertive and already grabbing my waist. I ran my tongue along his, the lightest stubble tickling my chin. Milo spun our stance, pinning me against the door.

"Ouch," I half-chuckled, doorknob hitting my ass.

"My bad." Milo caressed my hips, unfastening my belt. "Not how I planned on poking you tonight."

"No joke flirting. You're not funny."

"Then let's move from humor to hard-ons." He slid a hand inside my pants with a firm, gentle grip.

I kissed his neck, breathing heavily. Tracing my tongue further up, I tugged his earlobe with my teeth. A light bite. Enough to feel the arousal grow in his pants and blossom in his mind. Every sensation of his body guided mine. I didn't need telepathy to know his thrills, the touches that brought the most pleasure, but sometimes I used it to sense his most carnal desire.

My back pinned to the door, hands pressed to his broad shoulders, I lifted my legs and wrapped them around his waist. Milo ran his hands under my thighs, steadying me in his grip. "Bedroom."

He obeyed, carrying me, lips never leaving mine. Milo tossed me onto the mattress, yanking my pants off while I ripped the buttons off his shirt. He shoved me back onto the bed, lifting my shirt and running a practiced tongue along my stomach. His warm mouth enveloped me. I moaned, thrusting my hips.

"Hold on." I pulled Milo's hair, lifting his head. He inched closer, kissing me with sloppy wet lips. "Not what I'm craving."

With a light telekinetic burst, I pinned him to the mattress. I slid further down the bed, unfastening his pants and wrapping my lips around his tip. The subtle shudder in his hips brought a vicarious pleasure as my throat tightened.

His every breath resisted an animalistic groan. My blood pumped faster, and my face warmed. Whether it came from an assertive fuck or being fucked, my versatility was completely reliant on my partner's mood; switching depending on their current pleasures made my skin buzz, a building sensation of arousal that continued growing each moment. Dominant desires fueled his emotions, feeding my longing to answer his call and submit to his needs.

My telekinesis waned, and Milo took full advantage with his released hands, stroking my hair before a firm grip. Each second was a satisfying struggle. Then he released me. Panting, I crawled forward, straddling his hips. He rolled me off onto my side and reached a hand into the nightstand drawer for lube and condoms. His lips pressed to my nape with delicate, tender kisses while one hand gripped my waist, steadying my position, and the other hand guided him as he slowly eased inside me.

I bit my lip, adjusting to his thrusts. I moaned, throbbing harder the faster he moved, craving him.

It was an ecstasy I hadn't felt since the summer. Slick sweat. Loud grunts. Position after position. Milo's delight knew no end. I shook. Begging. Desiring. Exploding.

Afterward, I wrapped my arms around his stomach, holding him tightly, my chest pressed to his back until our breathing moved in sync. I had a dreamless night filled with Milo's stirring subconscious above everything else. An almost peaceful sleep, which rarely happened.

Chapter Sixteen

Grease sizzled. Each crackle sent an aroma of bacon wafting into the bedroom. Charlie sat on my head, licking my messy hair. I stretched until my back cracked. Several small pops of released pressure. Carlie tilted her head with wide eyes at the strange sounds. Not my back, but the human—it was written all over her bewildered face—who did something in this house that just didn't happen. In this case, cooking.

I walked down the hall past the ruined living room that I'd clean—eventually. Milo stood at the stove wearing just his boxers, the buzzed happy trail leading up his abdomen and down his crotch a teasing image this early in this morning. It was an oddly comfortable feeling having him here first thing in the morning. Usually, it was regrettable, filled with memories I'd never escape and possible futures I'd never have. Now, in this instant, I was okay with him here.

"Why're you cooking?" I stepped into the kitchen and poured coffee. Steam rose, and the fresh pot smelled delicious. "What'd you do with the half pot I had?"

"Because food is good, and the coffee was old."

"Such a waste." Because I couldn't simply thank him like a normal fucking person. No. Regret and dread already squirmed inside me, threatening to pull away and hide alone in my house.

Milo opened a cabinet, grabbed plates then moved to stand behind me. His crotch firmly pressed against my butt, only a thin layer of cotton separating us.

"What're you thinking?" A coy and playful question.

"Nothing."

"Something. And despite my best morning wood efforts, it's not sexual." He ran his fingers through my hair. "Your expression's too dour for sex."

"It is not." My jaw clenched tighter. Maybe a little.

"Well, whatcha thinking about?"

"My life. Yours. Finn's. A lot of others. Caleb's. Every shitty choice I've made. But something about this. Our magic doesn't connect, not directly, yet it did. Gave a glimpse of his fate. His death. I can't put it out of my mind. I just wish—"

Milo kissed me. "You can't fix everything, but you're welcome to try."

"That's me. Obsessing over a million things to will change upon." I kissed him back, desperate to hold this happiness even if it only lasted the morning.

Darkness swept between us. All-consuming terror replaced the briefest happiness I had. Heavy footsteps pattered along the shadows. Curly snow-white hair twinkled in the corner of my vision. Frozen, I watched the void vision of Caleb's death play out again. Sweat coated his face, his vibrant green eyes sparkled, and crimson blood against tattered clothes was illuminated in the black emptiness. He collapsed. A silver-hilted blade was embedded in his back, sparkling bright. Another reminder that none of my interference had changed a damn thing.

A hand slipped into view, reaching for the blade, and my heart heaved. No, no, no. Clear as day in this blanketed abyss, Kenzo crouched over a dying Caleb. He withdrew the bloody murder weapon. A strange emblem resembling a fiend lined the hilt in his hand. Tears in eyes. Fury beneath them. The kind of emotional anguish that screamed at my telepathy.

What had happened? What had he done? Had he done it? Would he? My heart raced, trying to conceive all the possibilities that'd lead them to this place.

Reality snapped back. I braced myself against the countertop. Milo held my shoulders, steadying me.

"You know what this means?" My mind whirled, replaying the horrible images.

"Aside from the bizarreness of an expanded void vision. That doesn't happen, just an FYI. They're useless, one-and-done snapshots. The whole reason I call 'em void visions is because I can't do anything except toss 'em to the void."

"No. Not that." His magic merged with mine again, triggering a clearer glimpse into Caleb's fate. "We have a suspect now."

"Suspect? More like a witness. Did you see how devastated he was?"

"Maybe he regretted what he'd done." People made impulsive mistakes all the time that their thoughts didn't register until afterward. "And his rage was massive in that instant. I could definitely see someone with his anger issues acting on whatever it is that'll fuel this attack."

Milo remained quiet. Even his thoughts simmered in silence. Was he giving me the chance to reflect on this? Reserving judgment until he left?

"We have to do something about this," I said.

"Like what?"

"I don't know. Monitor him? Contact the authorities, or I could talk with the academy about his murderous intentions."

"Allegedly, potentially." Milo grabbed me by the shoulders, locking me in place. "You're too close to see this vision clearly."

I wasn't too close. I was invested. "I'm fine."

"Are you? Because right now, you're ready to charge that kid on an out-of-context glimpse."

Milo's mind bubbled with a lecture on how it was unconstitutional to charge someone with something they might do, like I needed the reminder on the psychic amendments. It was the same as me accusing someone of something over a thought.

That said, this added up. Finn's warning. Caleb's sordid past with Kenzo.

"If you knew Kenzo, you'd see what a ticking time bomb he is."

"What fifteen-year-old isn't?" Milo sighed. "Look, we don't know enough about the situation, his involvement, so before you run off confronting him, take a breath."

He was right. There were too many variables. Too much intel not revealed. Too much I needed to investigate. Moving in on this could be what set the events into motion. Then again, doing nothing wasn't an option.

"For all we know, pressing this kid could be what triggers this whole thing." Milo chuckled, a dreary laugh meant to drown the agony of his foresight. "I'll have to tell you sometime what a punch to the gut it was learning about self-fulfilling prophecies. Meddling can make things worse. Please, tread carefully."

"Fine. Of course." I shrugged, ignoring the doubt ringing from his internal reaction. "I won't confront him."

I would discreetly delve into that twisted, murderous mind. Correction, potentially murderous.

Milo squinted, full-on judgment in the tiny wrinkles around his eyes. "***Stop plotting.***"

"I'm not." I cringed. He knew better than to scream his thoughts.

"Lying ass." Milo collected his things. "You're lucky you're so cute. Otherwise, that obsessive stalker thing you do would get so tiresome."

I didn't stalk. I merely used my magic within the purviews of my license.

"Are you just going to leave me with another vision we're not going to discuss?" I grabbed a skillet with scrambled eggs. "And all these dishes?"

"I cook, you clean. Plus, I didn't even eat, so this is a you thing."

"Where are you going?"

"Work. Totally forgot about an early meeting."

"Now who's the liar?"

"Don't think about it. Think about work. Important work stuff. Or sex. Sex is good. Our sex was great. Dorian's dick. Alliteration. Dorian's dick dances? Ugh. English. I don't read enough. I can read about the emblem. No. The Sinclair case. Yes, work-related."

"You have a hunch you're not sharing."

"Hunch? Never. Brunch. With clients. Which I totally forgot about. Hence not filling up here." Milo petted Charlie and reached for the doorknob. *"No hunch on how the toothy fiend emblem resembled—lunch. Rhymes with hunch. I'll need a big lunch today after skipping breakfast. Cutest kitty."*

"Charlie, he's undeserving of giving you affection. Leave." I glared.

Charlie meowed, hopping off the end table and trotting to the back of the house.

"Seriously? Denying your kitty my pets?" Milo opened the door, shaking his head. *"The audacity because he thought I thought of something I won't think of. Not worth thinking of. No need to bring up how the emblem resembles..."* He lingered in the doorway, eyeing me suspiciously until a minxy glint filled his eyes. *"Dorian's butt. I do love that pasty bubble butt."*

I groaned. Milo left, grinning. It didn't matter. I snatched part of the thought and held it close. People really were the worst at avoiding thinking about the one thing they shouldn't. They spent so much time convincing themselves to put it out of their mind it often erupted along the surface.

He wanted to follow a hunch on the emblem. Fine by me. I had my own—Kenzo. I'd delve into his mind, unravel his past, and learn if his angry, venomous attitude held any budding fatalities toward Caleb.

Chapter Seventeen

Gael Martinez strolled to the classroom, sharklike teeth beaming as everyone's eyes fell onto his spiky neon orange hair, signifying the beginning of October.

"What do you think?" Gael stood tall, turning his head so I'd get a full view of the black zigzags. He gripped his backpack straps with his orange and black nails.

"Quite festive."

"I know, right? It's the bestest holiday."

"A little early, though, wouldn't you say?"

"No way. I go all out. Make sure I get my full forty-one days of celebrating."

"You mean thirty-one."

"Oh no, we totally get to enjoy the first ten days of November Christmas free. Mariah Carey be damned. I don't care if her melody magic literally saved Christmas way back when or not. She's not taking my post-holiday celebrations this year."

Once the bell rang, I joined my students in the classroom.

"You've all been asking for an opportunity to show off your branch magics, so today's the day." I ground my teeth in preparation for the onslaught of joy and dread bubbling in the classroom, from the students eager to use their magic, to the ones nervous about where they leveled, to the one who hated her branches, and the one who didn't possess a branch at all. "Let's go."

I took them to the auxiliary gym and led them into the proctoring room.

"Since it's clear you're not ready to fully collaborate as a standard coven, I've chosen to pair you off for today's exercise. This is based less on performances in homeroom and more so from recent history projects."

That jab stung particularly hard at Kenzo, who prided himself on success and independence. His failure to complete the group packet from history class festered in his mind regularly, along with blame for his partners—less so on Gael or Katherine, mostly toward Caleb. It always fell back to Caleb. Truthfully, all my students struggled with the packet since it required synchronized channeling, serving as a project designed to help them comprehend how differing magical frequencies worked. It worked as a true test for compatibility, but even the failures of unifying magical frequencies showed prospective guild witches the challenges in store when working in the field.

I put their pairings on display.

This would give me a better sense of how to work with them as covens of four. My hope was that the pairings based on personality, along with what I knew about their root capabilities and branch types, would make each pairing excel.

"Cool." Gael Martinez punched his palm, smiling at Gael and the rooster. "We got a three-man team."

"I wouldn't even call that a two-man team, given your partner," Layla said.

"Enough," I said before explaining the rules and objectives to my homeroom and sending the first group off to compete while we observed from the monitors.

```
┌ ─ ─ ─ ─ ─ ─ ─ ─ ─ ┐
│  Gael Martinez & Gael Rios-Vega  │
            VS.
│  Layla Smythe & Melanie Dawson   │
└ ─ ─ ─ ─ ─ ─ ─ ─ ─ ┘
```

"This is gonna be so easy." Layla shifted at the starting point, transforming from the smallest girl in class to towering over everyone in her bestial cat form.

"Too easy." Melanie flicked her zippo like she belonged in some angry musical.

"¿Ellas dan miedo, verdad?" Gael gulped.

"No estoy asustado. They underestimate King Clucks, Peckfender of the Unhatched Dozen." Gael Rios-Vega nodded to his familiar. "I didn't tell you this, but I once witnessed Layla and Melanie cackling over fried chicken while mocking vegan lifestyles and supporting the inhumane practices of slaughterhouses. They said it made the chicken taste better!"

"That's awful and not true," Layla said.

"I don't even know what that means." Melanie backed behind Layla.

The rooster crowed, puffing his chest and flapping his wings. My head hurt, and this was only the first round.

The girls' cringed.

For fuck's sake. The rooster—dragging a claw along the dirt—drew an actual line in the sand. I needed a cigarette.

"You all have five minutes to secure your flags and prepare for the match," I said into the mic, desperate to finish this.

As expected, Gael guarded their flag, shooting off his spikes and mounting them into rocks which created caltrops large and small. Melanie protected theirs, high in the trees, providing her a vantage point and shrubbery as protection. Shit. I double-checked the enchantments lined along the auxiliary gym. They'd quell any magic that got too chaotic. I arched my back, stretching to channel magic in case I had to pull some unwitting witches literally out of the frying pan. They had free rein to cast as they saw fit, but I really didn't need any animal or human fatalities today.

The horn sounded. With Layla's cougar senses, she easily avoided Gael and his familiar, tracking the other Gael and the flag. This would end quickly. The boys had powerful magics, but their goofy personalities acted as a deterrent to collaboration.

Gael's familiar plodded ahead so quickly that he left a trail of dust in his wake. I raised a brow. Was the rooster using telekinetic energy to maximize his speed? Fascinating and disturbing.

I'd taught plenty of kids with a familiar companion. Typically, the human channeled most of the magic to utilize their roots, whereas the familiar served as second fiddle. Gael and King Clucks—God, I hated that name—had the opposite approach.

They bulldozed past Layla—who wasted no time sniffing out the other Gael—and reached Melanie.

"Holy shit," Jamius said.

"Language." I turned.

"Daaaaaamn," Carter said.

"Seriously? I'm right here."

"Are you fucking kidding me?" Jennifer shook her head.

"Am I speaking to myself?" I cocked my head just in time for Melanie's bewildered terror to spike, hitting my magic.

I turned back, having missed the entirety of this anticlimactic showdown. Guess I'd spend my planning period reviewing footage.

King fucking Clucks held the burnt flag in his beak, clawed feet perched on Melanie's head, clutching her curly red hair. Gael Rios-Vega mixed a moonwalk with what-the-hell-ever trendy dance routine ran through his mind. Not sure he matched any of the steps properly, but it didn't stop his joy. And now he literally ran in circles slapping his butt. "We won, we won, we won."

"Please clear the terrains so the next pairings can go." I cleared my throat into the microphone until Gael stopped shimmying.

```
Caleb Huxley & Katherine Harris
              VS.
     Tara Whitlock & Kenzo Ito
```

Rattling Caleb worked well as a distraction to psychically delve deep into his mind, but an approach like that wouldn't work with Kenzo. I needed him fixated on a goal, prioritizing his focus and magic elsewhere if I wanted to investigate the remnants of his memories.

Caleb clammed up.

Kenzo stuffed his hands in his pocket, bumping Caleb's shoulder as he left the proctoring room. Tara's cheeks twitched in a weak effort to smile at Caleb before she reluctantly followed her partner.

"Kenny and Tara? I'm screwed. They're both out of my league with root magic, and their branches are amazing and..."

"Relax." Katherine smiled, patting Caleb's shoulder and silencing his trepidation. "We've got this."

Caleb worked well with Katherine, so I hoped the pair would handle the loss well. He wasn't wrong about their pairing. Kenzo and Tara seemed like an unfair advantage, but I wondered if Kenzo would acknowledge that. Or if he'd continue with his superiority act toward Caleb and everyone in this program.

Katherine and Caleb planned in the forest.

"Kenny's going to target you first to take your branch out of play."

"Let him try." Katherine flipped through the pages of her grimoire. "I've collected a few borrowed branches I'd love to test out."

Caleb placed his hand over Katherine's, stopping her short of tearing a page from her grimoire. Their fingers touched, lingered. Excitement skirted across Caleb's mind mixed with dread and anxiety and wonder, and it became impossible to hear a single word over his heart pounding between his muddled thoughts.

"Sorry." His hand retreated. "I've got a different plan."

"Lay it on me." Katherine's face scrunched. "*Did I really have to say it like that?*"

The pair loomed in awkward silence, drowning in overwhelming thoughts. Ugh. This was painful.

"Have you crafted any spells with root magic?"

"Yeah, but our root channeling is on point. I don't see the use."

"I do. Hear me out."

I released my manifestation from Caleb's mind. My vision splintered, half observing the fight from within the proctoring room, another half hovering in the air. The apparition awaited my directive on the next person we'd investigate. It was an odd sensation—grating, in fact, having my vision and telepathic senses splintered yet so close together. I shook off the chaos, steadying trembling hands.

At the other end of the auxiliary gym, Kenzo and Tara stood at the outskirts. Not a bad way to distance their flag from their opponents, but it also left them with more ground to cover to reach the opposition's flag. Who was I kidding? With their proficiency, they'd easily close the distance.

Kenzo's compatibility with others still eluded me, but Tara was skilled and reserved. She wouldn't challenge his strategy. I wanted to not-so-subtly gain insight into Kenzo's hate for Caleb, determine if that rage possessed murderous intent. Combat was a powerful way to draw out the truest and rawest emotions. Hopefully, Milo was right, and I was jumping to conclusions, deluding myself. Yet, the fury in that void vision, their bizarre intertangled history, and a warning to find answers in the past from Finn.

My stomach sank. I was out of my depth.

"Do you want to strategize?" Tara asked.

"No need. Not like you're planning on using this exercise to show off your branches."

"He noticed. Of course he did. I made it so obvious. Bet everyone already knows what a pathetic joke I am."

I shuddered, quelling her whirlpool of sorrow. With my manifestation floating about, I needed to be careful not to fall into her emotional turmoil.

Kenzo slammed their flagpole into the dirt beside Tara. "You've only got one job while I deal with those morons."

The horn sounded.

As predicted, Kenzo bolted forward, barreling through terrains with a balance of levitation and telekinesis, meaning he'd left Tara behind with glorified guard duty. A defensive position was important, but that wasn't running through his mind. No. All Kenzo wanted was to eliminate his opponents single-handedly as swiftly as possible.

Kenzo reached the edge of the trees, high above Katherine running on foot. I raised a brow. Katherine might not move as quickly, but she could've easily flown using two root magics.

Gray static popped along Kenzo's knuckles. He spun in the air, releasing precise strikes of his hex branch, which sparked along Katherine's grimoire.

"No branch casting for you." The disruption took effect.

"Don't need it." Katherine released telekinetic energy, crackling against tree bark.

It'd be nice to see the duration and limitations he possessed on muting magic, but his mind screamed.

"*End her branch. Strike her telekinesis next. Take out her levitation. Then shatter Branchless. Retrieve their flag. End this match with a perfect win.*"

Katherine leapt back, distancing herself from Kenzo. He sped up, releasing stronger bursts of telekinesis. This would end soon.

I cracked my neck, sending my manifestation in pursuit of Kenzo.

"*She can't seriously think she can outrun me.*" Kenzo halted his chase and tilted his head. "*No. Diversion.*"

My heart jumped.

Caleb propelled toward Kenzo, fists first. Kenzo disrupted Caleb's core. I clenched my jaw, ignoring the concern inside the proctoring room.

"*Weak.*"

Caleb was seconds from plummeting headfirst to the ground. I channeled magic, slipping to the exit.

"Whoa. I figured Kenzo's hex branch worked on roots, too," Gael said.

Caleb continued flying at a steady angle directly for Kenzo. I tensed, retreating to the floor as Caleb punched Kenzo in the chin. My manifestation lingered close to the boys awaiting a stealthy opportunity or perhaps for my own nerves to settle since I'd distracted myself. Caleb smacked Kenzo again.

"Talk shit, get hit." Layla snickered.

"*Did I miss his core?*" Kenzo hit Caleb in the stomach, releasing a chaotic spark of gray lightning. "*Impossible.*"

Caleb hovered, intertangled with Kenzo. The boys grasped at each other, Kenzo punched Caleb multiple times, but Caleb didn't relent. He kept a tight grip on Kenzo despite the swift blows. Finally,

Kenzo reeled back and headbutted Caleb, sending him crashing into the grass. I winced at the stinging sensation shooting through Caleb's mind. Kenzo flew higher.

"*It worked.*" Caleb smiled. "Now!"

I buried everyone's mind, studying Katherine's swift flight through the woods, ripped pages from her grimoire in hand, beelining through the forest.

"*Kenzo will take out your branch, so I say we let him. Your spells work with or without the book. It's the pages that hold the magic. You're going to give me a page with levitation...*" Caleb's plan trailed along the surface while Kenzo focused on Caleb's roots, missing the page clutched in his fist. "*I'll stick it to him, sending him propelling upward.*" It worked too. "*That'll leave you against Tara, which is where things get complicated, but I have a plan for her too.*"

I smirked. And it might've also worked, but Caleb and I both underestimated Kenzo's motivation during this test. He continued ascending to the ceiling, patting himself down for the stuffed paper.

I grabbed the mic. "Congratulations. This round goes to Kenzo and Tara."

"Wait, what?" both Gaels shouted.

The shock in their voices matched the perplexed expressions on Caleb and Katherine. Calmly posed on a corner monitor stood Tara, flag in hand. Caleb's plan, my prediction, accounted for her left to guard their flag—leaving an impossibly ferocious foe fighting solo to retrieve his opponent's flag. But we each miscalculated in our thinking. Kenzo acted as a powerhouse distraction so Tara could slip by and secure the win.

"Well, we tried." Katherine assisted Caleb to his feet.

"You tried." Kenzo descended, crinkled grimoire page in his hand. He glared at Caleb. "Nice trick. One that proves you can't do shit on your own, Branchless Blunder."

"Hey," Katherine snapped. "We were this close to winning and already beat you."

"You diverted me temporarily." He cracked his knuckles against his palm, gray electricity sparking. "I'm far from beaten. Had The Whitlock Washout been as incompetent as I'd predicted, you'd have seen that. Besides, it all came down to your magic, anyway. Nothing Branchless did made this a win other than showing he wasn't completely useless."

Kenzo stormed away.

"*I won't underestimate him next time. And if he keeps at it, there won't be a next time.*"

Kenzo's embarrassment was almost invisible, tucked beneath his booming fury, but with my manifestation this close to his mind, I caught a glimpse of the anxiety he buried. He won the round, showed the power of his branch, but failure dwelled in his thoughts. He clung to the simple trick that nearly ended his plan. The branchless boy he shot daggers at, pure hatred in his eyes.

Maybe pitting them against each other was a mistake, the exact type of interference Milo warned against. Caleb embarrassed Kenzo, infuriated him, but to the point only murder would resolve it? No. Too absurd. Or was it? I was fucking all of this up.

I sulked, burying the doubt—Kenzo's and mine. My manifestation leapt within his distracted mind, his protective disruption none the wiser.

Chapter Eighteen

While my other half worked with students on their branch training, I walked through black halls. Everything in here reflected no color except for white words written upon the foreheads of a collection of pitch-black mannequins. It took a second for my eyes to adjust to the subtle shift of blackness cast from the room and that which the mannequins held.

Katherine Harris   Layla Smythe   Gael Rios-Vega
Melanie Dawson   Carter Howe   Yaritza Vargas
Jennifer Jung   Jamius Watson   Tara Whitlock

I tapped the arm of one of the mannequins representing a member of his homeroom coven. It illuminated an array of meticulous observations covering a faceless form from head to toe. A disturbingly fascinating psychosis. He processed everyone in his life absent of color, reflecting nothing, but recorded his knowledge in white, potential for anything on the spectrum. Yet, his reality was pure black and white. Fifteen years old, and everything in his world came as absolutes.

I'd delved into furious minds before. They often came with more chaotic, disjointed views, and sometimes, eerie hatred bubbled along the edges of anger, but Kenzo maintained a calm perspective on everything. A cold, distant one, but no red lens of angry observations.

In the distance, a faint gray light shone. I pushed between the swarm of mannequins cast across the sea of his mind and reached the drab glow.

A door. One that radiated with emotion, rage, confusion, joy, and sorrow. Brimming behind this door was a melody of feelings he hadn't placed absolutes upon. Inside, the mannequins came in a variety of colors.

Two somber blue mannequins clutched each other in an embrace.

Another mannequin had a crimson-red body and emerald-green eyes. Was this Kenzo's fury for Caleb or bloodlust?

I reached for the mannequin's arm, hesitating at what hidden truths lay dormant within Kenzo's memories.

A shark-toothed smile on a gray mannequin with pink emanating from his chest caught my eye. Gael Martinez. The only classmate thus far in this hollow place aside from Caleb.

I didn't trust or like Kenzo. I came here with the intent of painting him as the villain. Milo was right. I lacked objectivity. But maybe there was something good in this angry kid. Maybe he didn't hate all things. Memories swirled within Gael's mannequin, and I plummeted deeper into the canyon of Kenzo's mind.

Gael sat with Layla and Katherine at a cafeteria table. Fury boomed from a distant Kenzo, observing from the corner.

"Caleb thinks we should just write down the answers on a separate sheet of paper, then transfer them to the packet at the end." Gael was talking about my history packet they had to channel their magic together to complete.

"Not a bad idea since all the answers disappear every time our channeling is off," Katherine said.

"Because of the branchless boy?" Layla asked.

"No." Katherine furrowed her brow. "Because Kenzo keeps taking over. He overexerts his magic, which pushes the rest of us out and reactivates the enchantment."

"Personally, I think that bag of dicks, Mr. Frost, assigned this on purpose," Layla said. I'd say screw her, but I never made much effort in coddling kids. "He just wants to watch us all slowly fail."

Okay, fuck her. That wasn't true.

I eased the emotional wave in this memory, distancing my feelings because they latched to the anger wafting in Kenzo and amplified my own reactions.

"I don't know," Gael said with a mouthful of fries. "My channeling has gotten way better since this started. Like, trying to keep up with Kenzo and everyone else. Plus, seeing the questions every single class, it's like I'm learning this shit."

Having them work on the enchanted packet at the end of each class did benefit them. It allowed students to practice channeling, collaborate, and review material indirectly. Learning without learning or some shit.

Kenzo glared at the loud table. Gael's eyes lit up when he noticed Kenzo watching.

"Hey, man." He waved. "Come join us."

"Dear God, no." Katherine turned her head to mumble but spoke clear as day.

Kenzo scoffed as if he wanted to spend any more time with that know-it-all entitled brat than he had to. Not that I agreed with the sentiment of considering Katherine a brat, but I grasped the jealousy he possessed for her and her family's business.

Gael smiled at the girls, then grabbed his tray to join Kenzo.

"Go away."

"You're funny. A little hostile." Gael laughed, reaching into his Cerberus-themed backpack, and pulled out notes. "I wanted to return these. They were super helpful."

"Whatever." Kenzo snatched his notes.

He couldn't fathom why he'd loaned them to Gael. Something about watching him stay late at the academy, racking his brain to study in the library during Mrs. Whitehurst's tutoring sessions, so he wouldn't fall further behind. It pinched at his chest. Kenzo loved the isolation of the library, the calm of learning, but Gael kept pestering him to be study buddies every day. Porcupine was annoying, infuriating, and too happy all the fucking time. That was why he gave him the notes. The only reason. He ground his teeth, burying confusion, and convinced himself of this truth. A sentiment I oddly understood.

"You know, you should come to Gael's party this weekend." Gael's sharklike teeth shone against the sunlight cast inside the cafeteria. "His moms are gonna be out of town, so it should be pretty fun."

"Pass." Kenzo's hands were clammy. He popped dry gray static along his palms, desperate to shake away his body's bizarre reaction. *Holy hell, what's this feeling? What's my fucking problem?* His questions echoed in this memory.

"Well, if you change your mind." Gael scribbled his number on the notes. "Text me. You can sulk in the corner with Jennifer."

Kenzo's cheeks burned, which made Gael's smile bigger and

Kenzo's head more frustrated. He averted his gaze, trying to place the name, running through a mental roster of classmates until he landed on the gothic empath.

"I got her to agree to come, too. But only ironically, whatever that means." Gael stuffed more fries in his mouth. "I'll whittle you down before the weekend hits."

He winked, and Kenzo stood, tray in hand. "I have to go."

His chest pounded as he stormed out of the cafeteria.

"You forgot your notes, dude," Gael shouted.

I trained my homeroom on their branches, taught lessons to my students, attended staff meetings, and worked during off hours while my other half scoured Kenzo's memories. My manifestation bombarded me with interactions he'd had with Gael since the beginning of the semester, all in an effort to avoid delving into the core of my pursuit—his hatred for Caleb. Though Kenzo's fear of allowing someone to get close to him was a familiar paranoia. Fucking manifestations, always working through subconscious baggage opposed to their damn job.

The tension of maintaining a split psyche was like sleepwalking through life. More so than normal sleepless nights.

Each moment with Caleb this semester was filled with resentment, jealousy, and a strange twinge of concern. Kenzo didn't care about fitting in, but it bothered him every time someone complimented Caleb. Every time the branchless blunder deluded himself into thinking he belonged at Gemini. I needed to delve deeper into the past, but everything about their childhood was shattered glass inside this gray room. Piecing them together took extraordinary effort. The fragments repelled each other like magnet poles placed incorrectly. Memories flickering away with a similar desire I had to block my own past.

I set the broken glass at the feet of Caleb's mannequin, wishing their complex history was easier to read, like his confusion about Gael. An enigmatic room warped with contradictions he worked to sort until they were absolutes like everything else. This barren place held few people or things. Some, lost enchanter idols he strove to emulate yet despised for their place in the system. Others, ideals he hoped to live up to while discrediting the concepts altogether. Finally, desires he held for a guild dream he believed foolhardy, pointless, and an all-consuming fire.

The somber mannequins embraced in the corner cast a chill. Unable to glean much from Caleb's interactions, I waded through the trepidation wafting off them and allowed it to envelop me.

A literal lake of sorrow crafted to contain the memories of his parents filled these quarters of his guarded mind. Dark and crushing like the depths of the seafloor, where he'd buried the treasures of his past. Why hide joyful gems from himself? Why cling to the anger floating so close to the surface? I kicked through the water, desperate to escape this pain yet craving an understanding of it.

The depths felt endless, but finally, a memory approached.

I wheezed, soaking wet on a carpeted floor where ten-year-old Kenzo sat, ignoring my disruptive presence in the memory where so much sorrow collided with fury, his memories fixated on the loss of his parents. A fresh wound in this hollow place. Their dreams smothered. His life changed. All the passion he held for the industry he understood so little of shattered in this moment.

Kenzo couldn't grasp why Enchanter Evergreen wasn't there.

The most iconic witch in Chicago, but despite everything in Milo's capability, he didn't venture much to the outlier cities in Illinois where Kenzo's parents worked. Kenzo couldn't fathom why his parents had to leave forever. Why they had to leave at all. My heart wrenched at this memory. It was a complex sensation knowing everything in his mind, yet nothing at all.

"Do you wanna watch something different, maybe?" Caleb asked, the desperation and concern in his tone too much for Kenzo.

Kenzo's aggravation radiated, burning brighter and filling this memory.

This was the month everything had fallen apart. I didn't want to care. The tragedy looming in his memory didn't excuse his behavior, then or now. Yet, every nerve ending seared, agonized by his pain. No. Kenzo's rage swelled. An unfriendly reminder that this moment triggered his hatred for Caleb. I stayed to understand how and why it blossomed.

Caleb had come around to talk, to listen, to sit in silence. Kenzo couldn't grasp it. Someone willing to be whatever he needed when he needed it most, yet nothing Caleb offered calmed the festering anger.

Still, Caleb's weak smile hurt most. Kenzo ignored it, unwilling to allow it to break the anger that held back a sea of sorrow. He had to know. Understand. Comprehend death. Everything was perfect, better than perfect, better than even his greatest memories could fathom—he truly believed it—but suddenly, it vanished. No warning. No cause. No reason. Kenzo hated not understanding this. He hated the happiness of the world around him. He hated the sympathy for his pain.

This was a reeling sensation. I didn't comprehend his exact emotional strife, even this close, but I'd grappled with doubting the value of joy and sincerity after deep loss. Emotions that hit like a mountain of betrayal. A million unsaid words.

I buried my thoughts, fixating on Kenzo's past.

Nothing on television made sense. Nothing he read made sense. Nothing his aunt compassionately expressed made sense. All Kenzo knew was he hated this feeling. He hadn't understood hate. Not really. But the bellowing tidal waves it caused soothed him; feeding this beast allowed him to ignore the hunger that came with missing his parents.

The news came on. Caleb reached for the controller, swiftly attempting to push a button.

"Stop it," Kenzo snapped. He didn't know his voice could carry such a deep tone, but when Caleb quivered, it calmed him. He didn't want to lose that feeling.

I wanted to shake him. Change this memory, but I clung like a ghost, haunting a reality with only observation aiding me.

"What happened to Phoenix Guild was a tragedy." Tobias Whitlock appeared on the screen. The most illustrious man in all of Chicago and one of the top business moguls in the United States. Whitlock Industries kept Illinois' guilds at the peak of the industry.

It was bizarre seeing Tobias Whitlock—Tara Whitlock's father—so deeply tethered in Kenzo's most vulnerable memories, a truly defining moment involving Caleb.

Tobias' sullen eyes were unforgiving. His stern voice, unyielding. His comment on the news, phony. Something Kenzo and I both registered immediately. More than anything else, that ate at Kenzo.

Whenever something good or ill happened, Tobias commented. I'd often rolled my eyes at his absurdity over the years. The man wielded more power than anyone in Illinois. But why run a state when you could own it or all the guilds which kept it safe.

"The travesty that befell Phoenix Guild was an unnecessary one," Tobias said. It ignited rage. Flames burned the edges of the room, quelled only by a desire to hold this moment close as opposed to searing it from Kenzo's mind entirely. "The strict measures in place for licensing aren't designed to exploit individuals; it ensures certain reckless casting doesn't draw demonic energy. Those casting need to be fully capable of handling any problem. Phoenix Guild desired to cut corners, declare their independence, and doomed those poor branchless acolytes they promoted far too soon."

Kenzo seethed. Each time his chest swelled, Caleb shrank.

"The academy model isn't meant to hold witches back. It's meant to prepare them. Ensure they're qualified to handle any situation. Phoenix Guild—like others declaring independence—isn't admirable. It's reckless. It's damning. They skirt rules in place for a reason, condemning those they help license with unqualified skill sets."

Kenzo's rage exploded, clicking in place with each staged word that left Tobias's mouth.

"My branchless son also dreamed of guild work. A life people often forget is less about fame and more about serving the public. It's with a heavy heart I use my resources to reach out to the families affected by the tragedy that struck Waukegan and devastated so many."

Kenzo tuned out the humble tidings Tobias offered to compensate through grandiose charity. All his rage funneled toward Caleb, an inferno exploding.

"I keep trying to understand it," Kenzo said, his voice quivering. "They were only at that guild because of you. You and your stupid fucking research."

Caleb shrunk, teeth chattering. "Kenny…"

"Shut up." Kenzo jumped from his seat. "You're always studying something, trying to find reasons and places you and your magic belong in this world. Inspiring others. Inspiring them."

Caleb remained seated, close to Kenzo. Too close for Kenzo's liking. Irritation festered like a sick wound creating an infection of rage and hatred inside Kenzo.

"Your parents wanted to find a guild to intern at. They couldn't know that Phoenix—"

"Was dangerous? Underfunded? Useless? No. All they knew how to do was chase stupid fucking dreams." Kenzo hurled the controller at the television, hitting Tobias Whitlock in his smug face. "He's right, you know? You're useless. Weak. Pathetic. A branchless witch like you will never make it out there."

There it was. In order to silence his hatred for Tobias sharing fragments of truth on an industry Kenzo wanted to join, to avoid the sorrow that chased him with memories of his parents, to quell the guilt for being too weak and young to help, he directed all his anger toward Caleb. It was a strange, soothing sensation. Focused. Precise. Protective.

In this moment, Kenzo decided to shield Caleb and others too weak to protect themselves from their own reckless desires. Watching Caleb recoil, he knew what it meant. He'd be their monster if that was what they needed, anything to keep them away from the true horrors of this world.

I backstepped from the enveloping certainty in this memory, fading from Kenzo's mind and merging with my other half.

Kenzo didn't want Caleb dead. The kid didn't know what he wanted other than to avoid his pain. I'd deluded myself into thinking I could solve a void vision Milo saw as pointless from the beginning. I buried my manifestation, searing the echo back to the depths of my subconscious.

Chapter Nineteen

After drinking away the guilt of searching through these boys' most guarded histories, I researched Milo's potential lead. The one he carefully avoided thinking directly too hard on. It'd taken time and lots of wasted effort—much like everything in my life. But I'd found the fiend emblem.

I winced, sipping a screwdriver, hold the OJ.

The emblem belonged to a faction of warlocks. I scanned articles. My phone buzzed.

> Milo: Stop drinking. I need you sober.

I finished my drink and typed a response.

> Me: I'm not 🦴 -ing you.

Send. Ri*dick*ulous bone emoji included. Screw Milo, without actual screwing.

> Milo: Too much whiskey dick? Or vodka cock? 😉
> Not trying to bang you anyway. Just solve your void vision vobsession

I gritted my teeth, practically feeling his annoyance at the fact there were no words for obsession beginning with V.

"Fuck you," I muttered.

"Thought we established there'd be none of that tonight," Milo shouted outside my house.

Wait. Did he hear me or use clairvoyance to predict what I'd say? Damn clairvoyants.

I scrambled to the door. "Why are you here?"

"Missed your surly face," Milo said, forcing his way inside almost as quickly as the chilly night breeze. "Kidding. Well, not really, but put a pin in that. I've got a lead."

"The branchless warlock faction? Yeah. I did some research."

"Caught the thought? Sneaky, sneaky. There's a joke there, meme, something." Milo slid his rough fingers against my stubbly chin. It was a comforting, gentle touch that I wanted to last longer. "But before we catch that humor, I need your help catching a baddie."

I gripped his playful hand, squeezing his wrist because his banter had a way of enticing and irritating me in equal measure.

"So forceful." Milo bit the air playfully. "Hot."

"Spit it out already."

"Now you're just taunting me with jokes. Fine," Milo said. His demeanor shifted, cold and calm, as he adjusted his jacket and tightened his tie. "I might've found a way to put my void vision to rest and resolve the danger. Potentially. Certainties are never guaranteed, but this may be associated with some terrible impending events. All I need is a powerful telepath."

"There are telepaths—"

"Everyone working with the police keeps falling short. They claim it's because of a psychic block, but I need someone who can unravel the truth before this warlock's lawyer finds a loophole."

I huffed. "You want me to skirt the law, within some licensed advantage, of course."

"I want you to discover if this warlock knows something. Something connected to the guild witches dying because of his faction. Something that might buy this city a few days of peace. Something connected to Caleb and that void vision."

"And you don't have any insight on this guy's involvement or potential future involvement?"

"None."

Embarrassment rose to the surface of his mind and reddened his face. This could be the answer I needed. This could be the reason Milo's vision wasn't coming in clearly. Someone shielding their mind from psychic magic.

"Screw it." I slapped the flush out of my cheeks until my buzz faded. I'd shatter that block. "Let's go."

On the drive to the station, Milo explained the basics behind this warlock faction of branchless witches. A lot of already public information, but he shared a file containing some omitted intel.

I squinted, using each passing streetlight to help read.

"Borrow my readers."

"Since when do you wear glasses?"

"I don't. My guild rep says they're bad for my image."

I took the glasses, grumbling at the aggravation behind public appeal for all things enchanter related. "Seeing's bad for your image?"

"Apparently, my brand doesn't scream smart and sexy. Smexy?"

"Shocking. You realize glasses don't make you smarter, right?"

"If that's true, then tell me why Clark Kent can hold a full-time job exposing corporations while Superman falls for the same damn kryptonite trick every time."

Milo took a swift turn, cutting between traffic, and I used his distraction to focus.

Alexander Gillett, alleged lieutenant of faction inciting violence and conspiring against guilds.

More than two dozen warlocks detained.

Two enchanters killed.   Eight clients dead.

Four cases pending with suspected foul play..

Branchless possessing incredibly heightened root magics, some using branch magics.

Enchantment magic suspected.

"Please tell me this case doesn't come down to some bullshit warlock's right to bear arms by using unregistered enchantments?"

"That's the thing. We suspect them but haven't found any on their person. And their magic hasn't lessened since being detained. If they're using enchantments—spell crafts, some magical alteration—it's unlike any I've ever seen before." Milo pulled up to the police station. "Hell, maybe they're all just late bloomers."

"Yeah, makes sense." I scoffed.

Over two dozen warlocks developing new magics, despite most witches inheriting their branch around puberty.

Milo led the way inside, bypassing security and leading me to a holding cell.

"You can't bring whoever you want in, Enchanter Evergreen." A hefty older officer gripped his weighty belt as if it somehow strengthened his stature. "There are protocols."

"Yeah, yeah," Milo said, waving a dismissive hand and strolling past him. "Cerberus has already filed the appropriate paperwork. Dorian Frost is acting as our official consultant. Unless, of course, your skillful telepaths have unlocked Alex's mind."

He leaned against the door, blinking to fill the officer's silence, cocking his head to show how sarcastically he awaited to hear the nonexistent good news.

"Consult or not, he's not going anywhere without an officer. I don't need some civilian getting evidence thrown out because he didn't follow the rules."

I pushed ahead, ignoring the headache this precinct captain caused.

We walked into the holding cell where Alexander Gillett sat cuffed to a table, smugly grinning. It was difficult interpreting his thoughts, but he radiated a confidence that suggested he was completely free. Damn. I tensed. He possessed some serious psychic pushback. Or I'd spent too much time delving deep into Caleb and Kenzo's memories, and my magic hadn't fully recovered.

"His resistance is unlike any I've encountered," Specialist Amin thought, linking her mind to mine the second I stepped into the room. A young woman with olive skin and long brown hair. Despite my own invasive telepathy, it was always off-putting having someone rummage through my thoughts.

Specialist—a title reserved for witches in particular fields with clearance to cast their branch magic. More freedom than a permit or acolyte license, less than enchanter licenses or those working for guilds.

"What happened to your guild internship, Farah?" I scanned her surface thoughts as quickly as she gleaned mine.

Farah Amin graduated from Gemini a few years back. She was in Chanelle's homeroom, but I'd spent time helping her fine-tune her telepathy for her licensing test.

Turned out the spotlight irritated her almost as much as me. Farah believed despite all the red tape, this career truly allowed her to do real good. Scanning the minds of the accused, sorting out the wronged and the wicked, but a darkness trailed along the surface of her mind like a snapping viper. I shuddered. The price a telepath paid when rummaging through too many hateful personalities. We adopted pieces of them, retained them in our psyches, and found it difficult to smother.

I walked around the table, placing a hand on Alex's shoulder. "Shall we begin?"

"Please." He looked up, smiling like the Cheshire Cat, only it wasn't his body vanishing, but his thoughts. "Do be gentle. You look like a bull in a China shop, and my mind's oh so delicate."

"Has he been like this the entire time?" I asked.

Milo didn't respond. He stood with crossed arms, fixating on his clairvoyance, willing it to trigger so he could uncover the mysteries of Alexander Gillett.

"*Yes. We need to be cautious. There's something deflecting my telepathy,*" Farah thought.

"*I've got a better idea.*"

I lunged into his psyche headfirst because this type of hex required a bulldozer to break.

Chapter Twenty

Every nerve ending burned. My muscles ached. My bones cracked. In the depths of this warlock's mind, he fought against my telepathy. I dug my nails into the pristine tile of my elegant core. Somehow, I'd been rebuffed from his mind into my own. That'd never happened before. How'd this guy without an ounce of psychic magic manage it?

I stepped through the picturesque ballroom with marble flooring and chandeliers to brighten even the darkest corners of my mind, a pure fabrication crafted to create a tiny comfort. Some deluded lie I'd bought into about being the version of yourself you wanted to see in the future. Fake it till you make it was garbage.

Something stabbed at my back. I recoiled.

"It's not real. It's resistance."

I gasped. "Am I dreaming?"

Finn stood in front of me, a captivating smile almost erasing the pain.

"Nope. It's strange, though, right? It's like we're in your mind, but we're not. Memory, no. Deep delve, no. Weird shiitake magic at work, possibly." Finn smiled, helping me to my feet. His kind touch was such solace against the agony slicing my magic apart. "Based on what I know about the hex branch, this is quite a powerful counter. But how's this branchless warlock countering your magic?"

"He's not." I gritted my teeth. "Someone's helping him."

"Hexes require direction, precision, aim." Finn's knowledge of branches was always superior to mine. If he were here, truly, he wouldn't muse over this. "Something his partner lacks access to while he's in custody."

"How'd you—"

"Worry about answers later. We've got a case to solve."

I dragged myself forward, searching my mind for answers. Every blink, the second between vision and closed eyes, revealed a subtle shift of my brightly lit ballroom and a dank dwelling.

"You see it, right?" Finn asked, running his fingers along the elegant walls.

"These aren't mine."

"Not exactly."

Beneath the wallpaper was damp concrete because I'd failed to fully infiltrate this warlock's mind. I clawed at the frivolous comforts of my core I'd conjured. This wasn't my mind but an illusion of my making to compensate for nearly being repelled from another's mind. Bounced back but not really.

"There it is." Finn rested his palm along a sigil. "Hard to find illegal enchantments when someone's branding magic is inside someone else's head."

The enchantment branch possessed a lot of variations. Katherine's spell craft was common among the branch users but not as effective as a brand, which acted as a literal tattoo of magic.

"How's it in his head, though?" Brands were supposed to be visible on the skin.

"Seems like this branchless warlock has a lot of branch-casting friends. Someone to provide a hex to counter psychic magics, someone to brand the power in place, and some crafty psychic placing these sigils somewhere undetectable."

I struggled to breathe. Hearing Finn's voice hurt almost as much as the fiery sting consuming me. Needles stabbed my body.

"I wish you were really here," I said. He wasn't, though. This was some subconscious ploy to process the effects of complex magics pushing against my telepathy.

"We can unpack reality versus fiction another time." Finn reached for the sigil, but I grabbed his wrist, pulling him closer for an embrace.

"Wait." All the pain was quelled by the simple touch I longed for again. I'd endure this torment tenfold if it gave me another minute with him.

"Dwell on the past later. Fix the future now." Finn cupped my face, leaning forward. A soft kiss that didn't come as an invitation but a goodbye. "After all, that's what the ultimate trio is all about."

He scratched the sigil, shattering the brand containing the counter hex, vanishing in my embrace.

Black sludge pooled along the floor, rising to my knees, lights flickered and decayed, and the damp, gravelly walls resembled a chilling catacomb.

"*How did you do that?*" Farah called out, entering Alex's mind.

"Come on. We're not done here." I waded through the thick sewage of his mind.

"Remind me this isn't real, that I'm not sloshing through shit water."

Alex's perception of his core was revolting. Real or not, the stench of rot clung to everything. The putrid smell brought him comfort. I gagged, pressing forward.

A twinkle of silver floated along the sewage.

Rage and panic swirled ahead. Alexander Gillett stood within his wretched mind, coated in sweat and panting. Someone had taught him how to follow a telepath's tether, and I planned on finding out who.

"You can't be here."

"Don't worry, I'm being gentle." I mused the catacombs even in the darkness, the blood splatter smearing the walls held Alexander's sadistic pleasures. "Have to say, this place doesn't look as delicate as you described."

"This is my mind. Leave."

"Despite all your borrowed magics, I barged right inside."

"Get out," he shouted.

"Whether in a few minutes or a few hours, we're going to uncover every memory you hold. Expose whatever secrets you're desperate to hide."

"*Those covered by the warrant.*" Farah eyed me, sharing the limitations of searching memories past particular dates, fragmented fantasies, and other things not directly tied to his alleged crimes.

"Resist if you want, but I'm not leaving until I know everything about your warlock faction and those supporting you, and I'm starting with memories attached to this."

I picked up the sparkling silver, holding the same dagger meant to kill Caleb.

"No, no, no." Alex's fury boomed, exploding into hatred, disgust, envy, and an inconceivably erratic desire to slaughter us where we stood.

Farah backstepped.

"*Relax. He can stomp around all he wants. But without that sigil, here inside his mind, I run this place.*"

Alex ran forward, sloshing through the sludge. A whirlpool shifted his conjured sewage and unveiled the floor he pounded against.

I trembled.

His fists punched at a partially exposed sigil.

"Stop." I released a telekinetic burst, throwing him back against a wall.

My roots didn't exist in this place, but reality was what a telepath made of it. With enough magic and willpower, if I believed it, it existed. Not as magical as when I always had to stand on the other side of the curtain when casting within someone's mind.

"You're too late." Alexander grinned, still pinned to the wall with blood pooling under his eyes like tears welling up. "You'll learn nothing. You'll die here with me."

Farah approached the exposed sigil, a single crack along the brand. Shit. Any alteration to a sigil broke its hold. He wouldn't do that if he wanted to use magic.

"He's unleashing something." But what?

The sludge boiled and burned. Farah and I floated upward. I didn't want to leave, not without finding something connected to the faction. I clutched the dagger, desperate to unravel memories.

Emerging from the muck stood a fiend. A furious steam radiated from the monster. Its red eyes were the only feature not coated in a tarlike form. The snout of a hound with yellow fangs. A humanoid body with elongated arms that reached its crooked knees.

Impossible. He'd bound demonic energy within himself. That was how they'd gained so much magic. But how?

The fiend leapt forward.

I unboxed chunks of the memory tied to the blade. Images of a woman in a white coat. Doctor? A man with a perfect smile. Cold blue eyes. Their faces were blurry. I needed more time. A few more seconds.

"Dorian!" Milo's voice rang in my ear.

He jolted me into reality. My back slammed against the wall next to Farah. Alexander's body convulsed; black blood oozed from every orifice. His mind was completely dampened by an incomprehensible fiend.

"Milo, he's—"

"I know."

Alex's body swelled, skin turning bright red like he was on the verge of exploding. His mouth opened, jaw cracking apart and dislocating wide. I buried my anxiety and channeled telekinetic energy. A slimy snout tunneled its way through the dead warlock's gaping mouth. Once the fiend's head became exposed, Milo punched a hole through it with immense telekinetic force. Tar splattered the walls. Acidic droplets singed my face.

Alex's body slumped over like a deflated, bouncy house. I dry-heaved at the squishy mess and wretched smell. The tarlike remains glowed. A flurry of tiny white wisps scurried about the room, merging. In the time it took me to redirect my telekinetic root to my banishment, Milo had released a powerful banishment that eradicated every single wisp instantaneously.

"Fuck," I muttered.

How could I have been so careless?

Chapter Twenty-One

I smoked a cigarette outside the station while Enchanter Evergreen dealt with the debacle my arrogance caused. I'd survived but utterly failed. Milo was no closer to untangling this warlock faction, and my efforts were wasted. Caleb was still in danger. Everyone in the city these warlocks despised was in danger, and that was because I got cocky after one tiny success.

The precinct captain unloaded every profane thought he'd ever held back. I wanted to run inside, take the brunt of this envious man's fury, but beneath the booming rage that consumed this entire building, Milo's calm showed how little this venom fazed him.

Something happy beamed within him, the kind where his head buzzed, but I couldn't read it. I was exhausted. Or weak. Or useless.

Milo stepped outside, taking a deep, satisfied inhale of the crisp night air.

"I'm sorry I screwed up." I tossed my cigarette. "His magic

messed with my head. There was a brand holding a hex branch that countered psychic magic. It made me delirious. I saw… I hallucinated Finn. A kind of way to handle the hex, which made me high on overconfidence, and I got careless, and your lead is—"

Milo kissed my forehead. A wet, heavy smack like we were seventeen again, and he was bubbling with feelings.

"It all clicked. Everything."

"What?"

"Every vision I've been trying to piece together since this faction showed up in Chicago. Whatever you did, Finn did, it opened Alex's mind to my clairvoyance. The instant before he died, I saw every potential future he'd never see since the fiend ultimately got him."

"I don't understand."

"I know everyone he's worked with, could work with, where they're at, what they're plotting, and how to end it."

"Just like that?" I gripped his jacket, keeping his restless body in place.

"Go home, Dorian. Go to work. Live your life. Enjoy that Enchanter Evergreen will fix this soon."

"How?"

"Sorry, that's above your clearance."

"Milo."

He broke my hold, gripped my shoulders, and kissed me on the lips. Again, sloppy and wet because he knew I hated it.

"Take my keys. I've got so much work to do." He backstepped, brimming with bliss and guarding his thoughts. "And don't think I'm not going to make you elaborate on that Finn daze. As he'd say, I want every flipping detail."

Milo channeled his levitation and telekinesis seamlessly, flying into the sky and blurring out of existence between the conflicting darkness of night and bright city lights.

I did as Milo suggested. Home and work and repeat. I'd never found the mundane routine so excruciating. I kept out of the students' minds, aside from skimming the surface, because Enchanter Evergreen was on the case. Or so he said. Two weeks in, and nothing'd happened. No reports on exposing warlocks. No decrease in their strikes. No response from my texts asking about the void vision or the others he'd suddenly pieced together.

As someone who was constantly bombarded with everyone's insider information, it was frustrating being left in the dark. Fucking Milo. Insufferable.

"Stop making that face." Chanelle nudged my ribs.

I stood in the hallway, lost in the haze of my life. Or lack of one. Or lack of… *Caleb's hair.*

My face flushed.

"It doesn't look that bad. God, Dorian. You're gonna give the kid a complex."

Caleb sheepishly walked down the hall, his shoulders hunched high, doing no good to hide the hair he hated. Spiky white. No curls or brown roots, but close enough to the look he had in the void vision where he died. Would die. Could die. My chest caved.

"It's not as bad as you think." Gael Martinez walked beside him in a blue fishy onesie.

"I think it's wonderful. I'm so glad the academy allowed students to dress up this year." Chanelle raised a thin brow. "What do you think, Mr. Frost?"

"It's nice. What're you supposed to be?"

"Who," Gael corrected. "Full disclosure. I might've left the dye in a little too long or mixed chemicals wrong or not taken his color fully into account, or been slightly distracted by a baking project."

"**Slightly?**" Caleb sulked in his tiny mix of anger and dread.

"But he basically looks just like Enchanter Evergreen, right?"

"Not even a little," I said.

"Yeah, huh. He's got the spiky hair. The Cerberus emblem. FYI—the replicas are super hard to find online—you're welcome, Caleb. Plus, he's wearing the fancy suit."

"He's in his academy clothes," I said.

"He's Enchanter Evergreen as an intern." Gael rolled his eyes. "Duh."

"Yeah, duh, Mr. Frost." Chanelle cackled internally.

"Nice costume." Kenzo brushed past Caleb.

"Thank you," Gael said, truly sincere and oblivious to Kenzo's mocking tone. "What do you think of mine? It took forever taping my spikes so they wouldn't poke holes."

He raised his finned arms, sharklike teeth beaming. Kenzo remained silent, his face reddened.

"I think the shark costume is adorable," Chanelle said, truly incapable of bearing silence for more than a minute.

"I'm not a shark."

"He's obviously Enchanter Miller," Kenzo huffed.

Ah, yeah. I saw it now. The marina enchanter who kept demonic energy from clustering in the ocean by traveling deep into the watery depths. Gael's costume represented Enchanter Miller in her dolphin therianthrope form.

"Exactly." Gael shook his finned hands with excitement. "She's totally cool. She just got a Netflix special where they follow her underwater."

"I didn't realize that," Chanelle said.

"Maybe spend less time babbling nonsense and more time getting your old-ass eyes checked." Kenzo stormed into the classroom.

"Old? If he says one more smartass comment…"

I whispered in her ear, giddy at her near implosion. "I forgot how annoyingly obsessed you are with being loved by the kids."

"I'm not obsessed. I'm fabulous. The kids relate to my humor, fun lessons, and classroom engagement. He's just an exasperating little shit, and I have no idea what his problem is."

I did. Partially. Not enough to help him.

It was impossible to remain focused at work. Afterward, I drove to Cerberus Guild. Caleb's hair didn't mean he was going to die. For all I knew, Alex was the one meant to harm him. But Milo would've said that. He hadn't said anything. Explained anything. Resolved anything. I wanted answers.

"I've got an appointment." I brushed past the intern greeting everyone and pushed the elevator button.

"You can't just let yourself in. Your name?"

"The fact that you have to ask that makes me question your position here." I stepped into the elevator. "I'll be sure to mention that during my meeting with Enchanter Evergreen."

She recoiled, her frightened mind scrambling long enough for me to make my way up. I was an asshole most of the time, but not the type who pissed everywhere to get what I wanted. It was amazing, though, how much those aggressive, rude pricks got whatever they wanted.

"No, no. Not a walk-in. Just a priority case." Milo hung up the phone as I stormed into his office. He had deep bags under his eyes, intensified by a bright grin that made my heart thump faster and my throat grow dry. "Well, well, I'd say leaving you on read so long left ya desperate and craving a piece of me, but that grumpy face paints a different picture."

"You said you've solved this." I ignored my feelings and fixated on the void vision.

"I did."

"Then why hasn't anything happened? No news?"

"No news is good news."

"Milo." I ground my teeth.

"It's classified. And no, I can't breach a little Cerberus policy for you because this is bigger than my guild."

"How big?"

"The number of times I've been asked that would astound you." Milo winked.

A knock at the door broke his irksome, minxy gaze. The intern entered, frantic and probably here to usher me out. Not fucking happening.

"I know you said not to disturb you, Enchanter Evergreen, but it's an emergency."

"What is it?"

"The guilds are making their move."

"Guilds?" I asked.

"No, they're not." Milo took a deep breath, exhaling frustration that wafted through his office. "We're not moving for another week."

"Another week?" I asked and again was ignored.

"An operative from Kraken Guild was exposed, so their enchanters made a judgment call and—"

"Of course they did." The portraits on the walls rattled from Milo's stirring magic. "Reach out to our enchanters, inform the other guilds, and tell everyone to expect my updated plan."

She trembled.

"Now!"

She scurried away.

"How can I help?"

"I don't need your help, Dorian. I need another week for the necessary psychics to arrive. I need people to stop screwing with my perfect plans."

"You need a psychic." I pressed a hand to his chest; images of incomplete carnage flooded his mind. These weren't visions but paranoia. I recognized the illusions of 'what if' immediately. "Who's better than me?"

"You? The washed-up enchanter moonlighting as a consultant?" Milo squeezed my wrists, pushing me away. "You worked with me once and managed to allow a fully restrained warlock to kill himself with that demonic brand while in our custody. The questions my guild has had. The number of headaches it's caused. Rapport with the police lost." Milo stepped away, mind spinning through a million different scenarios. Hearing his mind work through new potential futures was difficult. The speed of his thoughts weighed on my telepathy. I processed his reactions, his ideas, but only saw pieces to the puzzle he worked on. Some vanished mid-thought, wrapped back inside his magic. "I get it. You're worried about that kid. You've got one potential life in your hands. I've got thousands. And I don't have time to coddle you."

I retreated inward, small and hurt. His anger was fueled by the alteration of his plan, unaccounted losses, damage he re-strategized to mitigate. His composure crumbled. The anger was misdirected but not entirely wrong. I was useless. I spiraled into growing self-doubt and slumped onto the office couch. Milo texted and made calls.

A few minutes passed, and he stepped over, leaning close, and pressed his forehead against mine. Ever the puppy, apologetic, he'd bared his teeth. In this brief touch, I gleaned fleeting thoughts from Milo's plan.

"I'm sorry, Dorian. You've got more than one future in your hands. Go home, shape some futures while I do what I do to save some."

That wasn't happening. Milo was paranoid about fatalities, about collateral spilling out, about warlocks escaping. That dread consumed him in a way I hadn't seen since the day Finn was snatched away and murdered.

I refused to accept the sidelines.

I flew above the bright lights and busy streets of Chicago, piecing together the images and plans from Milo's mind. The pleasure of coasting high in the sky was something I hadn't found time for in years, but chasing Milo didn't offer much opportunity to enjoy it. Frigid wind slapped my face, burning my cheeks and nose. If I hadn't maintained a connection to his mind, I'd have lost his trail six times over. His roots were more effective. His knowledge of the city led him with ease. His determination was greater than mine.

But he made the careless mistake of touching my forehead, leaving his mind vulnerable to my magic, an exploitative move I could regret later. I could regret it all later. First, I needed assurance this went right. I opened his guarded mind with ease. Picking a lock to an open door would've been easier.

Careful and observant, I landed at one of the hideouts. Thirty in total scattered across the city. Milo planned to obliterate the faction in one fell swoop, simultaneously striking each operation before the warlocks could counter, fall back, or fathom a way out.

Frantic and angry minds clashed with calm and resolute thoughts. The enchanters had made their move on the warehouse. The air hummed with magic.

Instinct versus strategy created a storm of chaotic emotions in their rawest form. Milo's mind soared, buzzing above the conflict, withdrawing to contact others, supporting allies, fighting, and thinking of every possible alternative for himself and everyone else at this location and others. How he maintained composure in combat floored me. I pressed my palms against my throbbing head, quelling my telepathy from so many surging, erratic thoughts.

What was I doing here? I trembled. Milo was right. They didn't need me.

White lights twinkled as wisps trickled outside the warehouse. Fiends within roared. Their stench carried a humidity that sliced through the cold. Were they drawn by the massive collision of magic?

I skirted around the back of the building, banishing wisps along the way. Even if I couldn't offer much, I'd help in some small way.

Wisps bounced along a watery doorway as it rippled from their touch but were unable to cross the crystal blue threshold. A warp portal conjured by the cosmic branch. It allowed witches to travel between different planes of existence and reappear somewhere else almost instantly. Teleportation that allowed the casting witch to move groups.

Hesitantly, I crept forward. My skin twinged at the pulse of the passageway and nerves crawling along my flesh. Had Milo taken this magic into account? Would an enchanter swoop in to stop whatever threats emerged? Had the sudden change in his plan not accounted for this variable? Did he expect me to handle it? Was that why he allowed the intel to slip between us?

I balled my fists, channeling telekinetic energy. It was impossible to comprehend how much Milo's clairvoyance pushed events into play and what happened by chance. If he had placed me in this situation, I needed to prove I could handle it. If he hadn't, I couldn't waver and allow this variable to ruin everything.

"Pardon me." A delicate hand slid along my nape, carrying with it the weight of an anvil crushing my skull with psychic energy.

I gasped. My knees buckled.

A finely dressed woman sauntered toward the portal while I

struggled to breathe. Our eyes met. Her face was from Milo's mind. The most vital piece I'd gathered from our momentary touch.

Dr. Kendall. The warlock behind this all. The warlock who held the highest priority in Milo's mind. The one he wanted more than any other to detain. She was the one who I'd glimpsed in Alexander's mind alongside a man with hollow blue eyes. If this had to do with the void vision and Caleb's death, I couldn't allow her to escape.

"Stop," I groaned.

She paused at the portal; the blue reflected against her face. My vision blurred. Small cracks within my head traveled down my spine, twisting my body inward.

"You're strong." Click. Like little magnets snapping together, our magic's linked. *"A telepath. No wonder you're still standing. Well, conscious at the very least."*

Seconds ticked by as we sifted through each other's thoughts. I hurled mundane memories, hoping to bombard her as I swept secrets from her.

They came as fragments.

She'd orchestrated the incursion on the city.

Images of experiments, both cruel and kind, flashed. All branchless witches, some content with her offer of power, others begging for it to end. A plan to collect every branchless witch in the state.

Not all sigils held fiends in place. Bodies ripped to shreds. Blood. Tears. Agony. And simple notes jotted down the learning process.

"It's not working." Her voice carried distress, panic, doubt.

The barrage of flashing memories made it impossible to discern this one entirely, only the significance it held for her.

"It'll work. It doesn't matter how many die. A hundred. A thousand. You'll find a way to apply these new enchantments," a deep scratchy man's voice said. *"I believe in you. You're the catalyst*

that'll overturn this entire corrupt system."

Pride swelled within her, an arrogance high above any I'd felt.

Scattered documents with scientific words that looked like mismatched scrabble pieces fluttered.

The brandings holding fiends provided power to the powerless. Magic to the ungifted. Unlocked…the words, the images, the emotions, all slipped away.

I wheezed.

Her telepathy was intricate. She utilized it to delve deep into a mind, strike it asunder with psychic attacks, but she didn't gloss the over minds of the many. We used our branch differently.

"*You tried to assault me.*" I dragged her toward me with telekinesis. "*But you don't realize how much damage my psyche takes every minute.*"

She would now, since the link still held. I squeezed her wrists, unleashing my magic. Every person, every thought, every feeling in a quarter mile burrowed between us. Fleeting and permanent alike rattled to the core. A monsoon of minds.

"Stop," she shrieked.

"*Your telepathy possesses powerful precision.*" I chuckled, lost in my delirium, and clawed at her wrists the harder she yanked away. "*Must be nice to have an off switch. I'll tell you, though, it makes that hammer you hit me with an average fucking Tuesday.*"

The link shattered. Her mind simmered, and she collapsed. Her body twitched, her mind flickering in and out.

Dr. Kendall was the one meant to kill Caleb. I could see that now. It was the only thing that made sense. She collected branchless witches for some test of containing and controlling demonic energy. Willing or not, she needed them. Maybe that was why he was running in the vision. Maybe her supporters chased him. Maybe he tried to escape. Maybe… It didn't matter.

I'd stopped her.

Everything became hazy, a fog thickened by the countless wails of suffering souls collected from our brief encounter. Pure apathy radiated in waves. So much death, for what? I crawled toward her, my fingers wrapped around her neck, possessing a will of their own. Maybe I was asking the wrong questions. This was about more than Caleb. More than some warlock faction. She was vile. Horrid. I squeezed.

Dr. Kendall flailed, slapping me and tugging at my sleeves. Numbness took hold. Her gasps were faint. The stench of fiends dulled. Her red face was cloudy. The taste of venom grew like a thick lump in my throat. Perhaps I'd touched her darkness too long. Maybe delirium played a role. Or this was a necessary evil that'd make the world a little brighter.

My surroundings faded, dragging me into a silent slumber, but I couldn't rest until I'd stopped her, ended her, here and now.

Chapter Twenty-Two

"You can't just kill someone," Milo said, sprawled out on Finn's bed with scattered papers. He was younger, nineteen, and at a point in his life where he jotted all the potential futures he saw on paper. I'd shared a way to develop the space in his mind to sort that intel, but he liked the cathartic process of writing out woes. A part of me wanted to antagonize the futility of his process.

Instead, I sat on the windowsill, taking icy breaths and blowing smoke out into the blaring city. The death of winter didn't slow anyone down. Traffic and the bustle of pedestrians did little to quiet the conversation inside. Dread consumed me. Not the me in this memory, the present me currently fumbling in this dream state. What had happened in the alley? Had I fallen unconscious? Had I killed Dr. Kendall? Why else would I be locked in this memory, reexamining the hypotheticals on the value of life?

"I don't think he meant someone in some arbitrary philosophical trolley problem way," Finn said, ever protective of my crude commentary.

Truthfully, I meant it in that exact sense. I'd become jaded since graduation.

Their debating minds helped quell the ramblings of nearby strangers in the dream, but not my current guilt.

"I'm just saying since joining Cerberus, I've touched some wicked minds and seen some people continuously desire the wrong choice." I blew smoke into the apartment, annoying Finn. "A choice that harms. One that damages. Breaks. And if I had to decide between their so-called potential future and someone else. Something else more certain…"

"That's just it. Nothing's certain," Milo said. "Take it from the expert."

"There's only one thing I'm taking from you tonight, buddy boy," Finn said, attempting to use humor to diffuse the conversation. Our new relationship daunted him—all of us, in fact—but he'd gone from speaking his mind to interpreting what we'd meant. A peacemaker at heart.

"You want to talk about experts?" I asked, recoiling at this memory of my enraged youth, determined to change everything. "Take it from someone who's had the pleasure of delving into some of the most vile minds this year; some people don't deserve possibility. They don't deserve being pushed toward their best selves when other potential futures are at stake."

"I can totally see that," Finn said, balancing Milo's outspoken nature and my annoyingly bitter phase for someone who hadn't even entered his twenties yet. It also happened to be where my true disgust for the world blossomed. Still, Finn quelled our spout. Poorly, but I chuckled all the same, reliving this phase of Finn.

He chased his dreams more than anything, but part of him was always splintered, seeking to keep us bonded. A piece of him was always lost in every broken relationship he'd ever chronicled through the long past of humanity. Not all, but enough to believe he could perfect something so pointless. That was how I saw it then. If I'd tried harder for him during those years, maybe we wouldn't have been split. Maybe he'd have survived.

Finn had always possessed the ability to read past events. He'd absorb a place's entire story standing there, every second. Follow an item's complete journey and every life it interacted with. Unravel a person's entirety with a simple touch. His retrocognition had grown since becoming an acolyte at Cerberus and took him on a journey to stop society from repeating the same history again and again. As if one person could change the world.

Finn's retrocognition made him a literal phantom looming in the past, similar to how my telepathy transformed me into an apparition haunting the present or how Milo's clairvoyance made him a specter with omens of the future. Each of us was dead in some way, fighting for whoever lived, but I was the only one who wore a ghostly expression.

Finn strutted toward the window, rubbing the chill away from my hunched shoulders. "Hope that nicotine fix is worth us freezing our butts off."

"Absolutely." I exhaled, mixing smoke with falling snowflakes. "Besides, I told you not to get this tiny apartment. I specifically said somewhere with a balcony if you intended on dragging me to your place all the God-awful time."

The words fell off my hollow tongue, unable to interact or dwell on what I'd done. What had I done?

"Well, we can't exactly go to your place, Mr. I got a shoebox apartment with a twin bed to spite my boyfriends."

"I'm saving up. I want a nice house," I said, tossing my cigarette.

"It'll lose its value in three years, tops." Milo slapped his pen against a piece of paper, then shoved the pages off the bed. "Call it a possibility."

"Plus, I don't like sleeping with people. Sex, yes. Sleep, pass."

"I'm gonna cuddle the fuck outta you tonight." Milo thrusted his hips. "So hard. You're gonna be the littlest spoon that ever spooned."

"Can we avoid rage-pounding each other unless explicitly requested?" Finn asked. "Because I'd like the joy of exploring bodies, not having a conversation that ends up heated."

Finn quieted.

Milo and I eyed each other, eyes softening, recalling every time we'd avoided confrontation for Finn's sake. For each other, too. We weren't compatible. There was a gentle softness to Finn which glued us together, but without it, we became toxic. Even with him, our venom spit occasionally. Still, we cared for each other. Our words simply lost themselves when colliding.

Gently kissing Finn's neck, I ignored the poor decisions of my life. It might be falling apart out there, but at least I could relive something enjoyable. Enjoyable to a point. It might've been a broken moment in our lives, but the sex was good, and the emotions were true, which accounted for most of my thoughts at that point in my life.

"You never finished chiming in during this discussion." Finn dragged me away from the window, shattering the truth of this memory, while Milo undressed, surly eyed, and unaware we'd gone off script, veering away from the memory. "What is the value of life to you versus another?"

"I have no opinion." I trembled, cold from the window, scared of what I'd done, and nervous about what Finn would say. How would Milo react to finding me in the alley?

"Your entire life seems to have become a trolley problem, but you need to let the weight of the world go for a breath." Finn brushed my hair. "I wish I'd done that. Somewhere along the way, my dreams of fame and helping turned into this obsession with fixing everything. Regrettably, I think I've passed that on to Milo. I've possibly passed on something worse to you."

Regret? Guilt? Isolation? I deserved all those things.

"I don't know what to do." I never did.

"I wish you'd spend more time enjoying life instead of regretting what you didn't. I wish you didn't dwell so much on what we all had and remembered what you still could have with…"

His words fell away, whiteness filled the void between us, and I sank into a dreamless state.

I awoke in a sterile room with a false sense of homey vibes, like an overpriced hotel lacking personality. A Cerberus recovery room. Stirring thoughts thrummed along my skull, rapping on the chamber door of my mind, ready to kick it down. I groaned, quelling magic, desperate for these unpredictable, incomplete ramblings to cease.

"You're awake?" Milo strolled inside with a genial smile, his mind an open book inviting me to roam. Ignoring everyone and everything else, I gently traced my fingertips along the lines of his palm. Seconds turned to moments that clung as time slowed from our simple touch. I absorbed as much of the events as his memories provided.

Milo had stepped outside the warehouse, surveying for warlocks attempting to flee, and found my unconscious body slumped over Dr. Kendall. His hands were clammy, his breaths shaky. Terror consumed him as he approached us. I almost broke the connection right there. Had I killed her?

Flashes of the days I'd lost played.

Milo's multi-guild tactical strike made national headlines. Cerberus made headlines. All the guilds involved did. Enchanter Evergreen, ever the hero, front and center among it all, explaining to reporters a plan aligned with local authorities to apprehend and arrest over one-hundred warlocks.

Illegal enchantments seized. Locations sealed off due to surges in demonic energy. Fiends suspected. Whitlock Industries celebrated the success while inviting feds to handle the ringleader orchestrating it all.

Former government researcher Dr. Stephanie Kendall was taken into custody. Her entire life story lain bare in articles by every news site.

She was alive.

I sighed with relief, unraveling more of the three days that'd passed.

"Fuck. My classes. Who knows I'm—"

"Keep reading—scanning, thinking, something—or should I just provide spoilers?"

I glared.

Milo scrolled through a thread of texts with Chanelle. Since when did they talk so much?

> Chanelle: He has zero lesson plans.
> Seriously. None.
> Maybe on his computer?

> Milo: Password locked.
> I can't get in. Sad face.

> Chanelle: Can't you just predict the password?

> Milo: No. Sadder face.

> Chanelle: Uuuuggghhh. I'll figure something out.
> His classes are covered.
> You're welcome.

> Milo: You're a lifesaver. 😊

> Chanelle: You're charming AF, but I want the real story when he's back.

"You can't tell her the real story, by the way," Milo said.

"Imagine I can't tell anyone about my attempted murder."

"I'd say that was an aggressive takedown, not attempted anything. Besides, the guilds and government just want to keep the involvement of an official consultant discreet. It's more of a bureaucratic headache otherwise, which I've already got ten thousand of those."

"I'm not an official consultant."

"Paperwork says you are. I dotted the i in your signature with a heart and everything."

"What happens next?"

"Nothing. It's done. A few stragglers, but the faction's over. Feds have their big fish and will use her to catch those elusive whales or some shit." Milo stroked my hair, brushing bangs off my face. "Mostly because of you and your successfully reckless actions."

"Did you plan it that way?"

"Did I plan for you to end up in that situation?"

Silence lingered between us. His mind remained inviting and willing, but I crept along the edges, frightened by what the truth held.

"My plan was to trace her portal and find a few others. A lot of that night was improvised."

"And I screwed that up."

"No, you didn't. Like I said, a few stragglers. Detaining Dr. Kendall was the lowest probable success, and you made that happen. If anyone screwed up, it was me." Milo kissed my forehead. "Get some rest. They said you took a lot of psychic damage. When you're better, you can go back to your life. Routine. Boring classroom antics. Annoying kids. Irritating teachers. And avoiding me until you just can't take it any longer and find yourself in my bed again."

"You're insufferable." I lay back on the bed, resisting the faint smile I had for Milo's calm charm as he covered me with the blanket.

Milo was right. The events were abuzz as the city rejoiced, but in the days since returning to the academy, it quickly died down. It was fascinating how the media fixated on something for months and invested the entire nation, then swept it away for a new trending story. I took a breath, welcoming the simplicity of teaching classes, networking, and helping my homeroom harness their magic. Relishing the return to reality and using my telepathy with the best intentions instead of navigating unknown futures.

Gael Martinez stalked close to an anxious Caleb in the hallway. Caleb's curly white hair had grown out, brown roots showing like muddy snow. I smiled. It meant nothing. His hair hadn't changed, but his fate had.

"It won't fall out, dude. Gimme another chance. I know what I'm doing." Gael ran his fingers through a medley of yellow, red, orange, and brown spiky hair perfectly blended like he himself signified the arrival of autumn.

"No," Caleb said, skirting into the classroom. "I'm just letting it grow out, then chop it off."

"Es demasiado hermoso para cortarlo," Gael said.

Tara made her way down the hall. My grip tightened on the book I'd bought. I pulled her aside before the start of homeroom, resigned to stop prioritizing Caleb. I would help him like any student, ensuring he didn't slip between the cracks simply because he lacked a branch. But I had other students who needed guidance.

"I wanted to discuss your channeling overlap."

I handed her the book.

> Clash of Fire & Ice: A Journey to Steam Magic

"Nya Desmond released an accounting of her struggles with a channeling overlap. Her workaround was to mix the heat of the flames in constant succession with her ice. Thus, creating steam magic. It discusses different strategies she worked with to bridge the two magics. Maybe there's a way to use your three together."

Tara blinked. Complete silence between us and in her mind. It was like she felt me tiptoeing and quieted all stirring emotion.

"It's not a technique you'll learn overnight," I said, unable to bear another second of uncomfortable silence. "But perhaps it's something we can work on this semester."

"Thank you, Mr. Frost." Tara walked into the room. "*It's useless, like every effort.*"

For the life of me, I couldn't think of a way to merge her three magics from the shadows that controlled darkness to intangibility that altered physical properties and, finally, the sealing which could bound or encase anything. For the sake of lessening the sorrow consuming Tara, I'd make the effort.

Rage barreled through the halls, squashing all other emotions.

Kenzo. He stood on the precipice of change. He could fall off the cliff into a valley of hatred or soar high, using that anger as fuel to process other emotions. All he needed was guidance. I wasn't deluded enough to think I understood him or could help him, but I needed to find someone or something to steer him from this self-destructive isolation before it became permanent stone.

I joined my homeroom.

"Mr. Frosty, this had better not be another bookwork day. You swore by November we'd be focusing on our branches."

"And we are. Researching existing enchanters with your specific branches will assist in cultivating your own and streamline your training." By research, it often meant reviewing sources I'd already scoured for them and finding the helpful hints along the way.

"Cluck."

"That's right, there's no enchanter with a cock as cool as mine."

I cleared my throat, actually enjoying Gael's crass humor and the giggles it brought to the classroom. This was their feelings creeping in. So annoying.

To silence the joy from invading my magic, I dropped the bomb none of them wanted to hear. "Essay." Oh, the misery that filled the room at the idea they'd have to take this research and turn it into a paper.

"Stop whining," I said. "Understanding how your magic can assist others, what makes it marketable, other successful enchanters wielding your magic, or why you have something new to offer that they've never seen, is all important if you truly want to be a part of this industry."

"But why do we need an essay?"

"Gemini prepares you for all the stages of licensing, including offering fledging permits, but it's a separate panel that decides if you obtain those permits. These essays are your resume, cover letter, and introduction to the panelists."

"*What happens if we fail?*" Caleb thought.

"You reapply after ninety days," I said, turning to him.

Caleb clammed up, and I froze. I was usually better at answering a thought bubble without exposing them or myself for eavesdropping.

The panelist reviewing first-semester student essays and their displays of magic was relatively easy, but the academy liked to make the process appear more stressful. Our way of preparing students for the actual stress that came with licensing, which was handled by the government and completely out of our hands.

I spent the rest of class answering questions correctly and not outing someone's private doubts. The December deadlines. The breakdown for the fledgling permits. How much they actually permitted. Turnaround time for getting their results. And, of course, everyone's favorite—when we'd be practicing magic again.

I smoked a cigarette on the way to my car, finally enjoying a bit of the typical work-related stress instead of the added void vision.

My phone buzzed. Milo was calling. He never called. Not that his silky voice and wit couldn't convey the same tone as suggestive and inappropriate emojis, but he avoided calling anyone. Too much business involved. Plus, I hated phone calls.

My thumb trembled over the green 'accept' because this could only mean one thing—something bad happened. The vision wasn't over. Or my involvement compromised the case. Happiness was stupid. I fucked fate up by interfering.

"Hello." I uttered the word, resisting chattering teeth.

"So stiff and formal. Not at all the stiff I like." His snicker released the tension in my shoulders. "And that stiff would be a drink, which you should join me for, at a dinner party, with a selectively well-connected guestlist, that'd benefit you and any stiff parts of you."

"I don't have time for parties. I'm swimming in work. Believe it or not, that unproductive vacation I took added a mountain to my to-do list."

"You should probably consult someone in the English department, maybe Chanelle, because you're mixing metaphors." Now, the snickers at his terrible humor became grating. "Dorian, this isn't a party-party. It's a benefit for all those affected by this warlock chaos and a celebration for all the nonsense we enchanters averted. Also, total networking opportunity. Think of the children and be my plus one."

Finn's words about taking pleasure in the small joys of life echoed.

"What time does it start?"

Chapter Twenty-Three

Here I was, forcing myself into a stuffy suit for a black-tie dinner I had no desire to attend, like this was somehow the first step to enjoying life. Still, as I drove to the Whitlock Estate, fizzling the thoughts of nervous staff and arrogant guests, I reminded myself—this was, in fact, a networking opportunity. It was never too early to start searching for potential guilds and skilled enchanters to work with my homeroom coven. That was why I came.

The pristine stone driveway with a valet at the ready didn't prepare me for the absurdly opulent manor. After dropping my name with the attendant who blushed, realizing I was *the* Enchanter Evergreen's plus-one, I entered an inviting foyer with expensive artifacts on display like household knickknacks. Any one of these could cover my salary for an entire year with an ample bonus added. It was astounding that the Whitlocks chose to send Tara. Certainly, their connections offered more than even the prestigious Gemini, especially after opening its doors to the state mandate.

Guests quickly made their way inside, from high-ranking enchanters to guild masters to entrepreneurs developing products offering the best of tech and magic combined, all the way to the business elites who proved the greatest magic at the end of the day was money. Quite the eclectic guest list.

Selective, yes. Small, nope. Shockingly, Milo got that one wrong. Still, some of the guests also happened to be mentoring my former third-year students, whom I hadn't checked in on once this semester. I got a new schedule and cut ties, thoroughly abandoning them during their internships. Another reason to come tonight. The only reason. The kids. Networking. Trivial conversation with enchanters and guild masters while stroking their egos.

This was in no way related to Milo or stroking anything else. I cringed. From the other end of a crowded room, his lust called out. Between guests dressed in anything finer than I had—not that I cared to try—and caterers serving drinks and appetizers far too elegant for my cheap palette stood Milo. Despite the elegant floral arrangements casting a lovely fragrance throughout, the hors d'oeuvres reeked of fish and stinky cheeses.

His eyes were locked on a woman in the midst of a conversation. Had he averted his gaze once he spotted me? Had he simply thought of me before I'd arrived? My cheeks flushed. I bit my trembling lip to silence curious anticipation.

Chandelier lights reflected off the sapphire silk of his vest, illuminating his midnight black suit—tighter than appropriate and not at all functional for work. But he wasn't working. Well, he was, but he wasn't casting. Okay, he casted charm, not magic. I wasn't the only one here tempted to peel him out of those confining layers, either.

I quelled my telepathy, downing a flute of champagne before grabbing a second one. That was all this desire was. My emotions mixed with adoring fans. Surely, there were some bitter or envious enchanters' minds I could latch onto because this place was far too crowded and my pants far too revealing to be sporting a boner.

"You're telling me you wouldn't hit that?" Gael's voice boomed above others.

Regrettably, I turned to see him in a suit with a sunshine yellow bowtie next to a vacant-eyed Tara in a strapless golden gown staring at Milo. Somehow, Gael had convinced, manipulated, or forced Tara to invite him as a plus-one to this event.

"Oh, come on. I don't even swing that way, and I can objectively see his hotness. Pretty sure even my moms have a secret crush on him. I mean, they're hella old—too old for him—but he's Enchanter fucking Evergreen. How can you not recognize the awesomeness of that?"

"You're asking the wrong girl." Tara slipped two glasses from a passing tray, and Gael's deep brown eyes lit up when she handed him one. His eagerness to drink among adults without question clouded his festering thoughts on the topic. Tara sipped her drink, knowing she'd successfully pulled off a diversion.

Wrong.

"Okay, but look at that swagger." Gael pointed to Milo, who was making his way across the marble floor. "You're telling me all those *ass*ets don't register in any way?"

"Look, I can respect the aesthetics of a supposedly hot guy." Tara shrugged. "Sure, he's got the chiseled jaw, big muscles, small waist, and bubbly butt or whatever. But that doesn't mean it does anything for me. Though I'm starting to think it does for you."

"*Supposedly?*" Gael thought because that was his takeaway.

"Ba-ba-bawk." King Clucks, the world's most irritating rooster, also happened to be the world's most sharply dressed in a fancy bird vest. Who made those? I downed my drink.

Gael glared at his familiar. "*Yeah, I know she's ace. This isn't about that. This is about teaching a friend who's hot and who's not. Honestly, could you imagine how cool it'd be if we got to intern with Enchanter Evergreen? He's so amazing.*"

His mind trailed off to pining, followed by a dozen other random thoughts.

The rooster screamed, drawing everyone's attention, to which Tara giggled. Actually, fucking giggled. My heart raced, searching for hidden fear beneath anxious laughter, but there was none. Simply sincere and giddy excitement as so many eyes fell on her for something unrelated to the Whitlock family.

Of all the students at Gemini to gravitate toward, to invite to this exclusive event, Tara brought Gael. Trailing along their surface, it seemed they'd bonded. I scrunched my face. Something about his crass humor entertained and distracted her from the well of sorrow constantly consuming her. Gael's juvenile delights kept him from realizing the power behind Tara's connections, making him ideal for genuine friendship.

I slipped away into the thick of the crowd unnoticed, breaking free from the lively herd of enchanters and sponsors to enter a quieter place. But there were no simple rooms in the Whitlock Estate. I smiled, truly awed in a room with elegant paintings on display. Few guests strayed into this space, and I took full opportunity to admire the sheer beauty of the detail, effort, and time for each piece. From old relics any museum would snap at an opportunity to showcase to newer works by amazing young artists who I followed when seeking to ignite my own artistic joys.

A calm overtook me, silencing the internal chatter of the party. Were these the simple pleasures Finn meant? Finn. Like it was actually him talking. Either way, it worked. I could spend the entire night in this room.

"Admiring the art?" Tonight's host, Tobias Whitlock, stood beside me, pride pulsating over the exquisite display he'd locked away from unworthy eyes.

"I guess. Hard to make any sense of this stuff."

He chuckled gruffly, stifled and stunted with a pained expression. "Who are you again?"

"Just a plus one, not a memorable one at that," I said, ready to take my leave because the hubris permeating from Tobias Whitlock intertwined intoxicating arrogance within my emotions.

"*I wouldn't say that, Mr. Frost.*"

I paused. Motherfucker already knew me, which I'd have caught if I'd kept my guard up.

"The name Dorian Frost has crossed my desk many times over the years. A lot of our current enchanters began as interns brought in by great academies such as Gemini. More than a few based on recommendations from you. I'd say your keen eye for turning out successful enchanters like that is quite memorable."

"Here I figured someone of your stature, with a few dozen guilds to oversee—countless other businesses, real estate, an estate—wouldn't notice little things like teacher recommendations." I feigned a tight smile.

"There's nothing I overlook." His hollow blue eyes held a menacing stare. Why'd his observant nature sound more like a threat than boasting? "I picked Gemini specifically for your skill set. You've taken plenty of bland coals and crafted diamonds. My hope was Tara might be one of those lumps you reshaped. I have to wonder if her continued failures come from her own incompetence or more so with your rekindled passion for guild life."

"Excuse me?"

My attempt to clarify his cold tone with honest thoughts was met with silence. A literal golden wall inside his head blocked his mind from prodding. Figured. The Whitlocks didn't rise to the top on their business sense alone. Most possessed a magic from the arcane branch, which in itself was one of the most versatile branches, given it usually came as a magical fusion of two types of branches. Tobias, for instance, possessed abjuration, which allowed the caster to create shields repelling magic—even my psychic snooping—like the hex branch, but it also held healing properties like the rejuvenation branch.

He allowed pieces of his mind to trickle through freely, interacting with my magic, but kept the rest guarded. To what end?

"Your recent role as a consultant for Enchanter Evergreen. That, too, has caught my attention." Tobias grabbed two glasses of wine and handed me one. "So, which is it? Is Tara truly a lost cause, or have you lost your passion for education? I hear that happens quite often for people in stressful yet mundane careers."

Questioning my dedication, I could live with. Lightheartedly stabbing at my career choice as mundane, not the first time I'd ignored a similar insult. But what furiously stirred within my stomach and exploded into rage swelling in my chest was his shallow, hateful disregard for his own daughter. Hell, I preferred parents who insulted my competency when it came to their children's success over this.

I swallowed the wine quickly, hoping to drown the desire to spit venom at this man, but alcohol only exacerbated the urge.

"Ah, I found you." Milo strolled into the art display, swaying his hips with each step.

"Enchanter Evergreen, good of you to join us. Mr. Frost was just explaining his recent desire to serve as a consultant for Cerberus."

Milo's minxy grin faltered, and he eyed my furrowed brow.

"I'm not rekindling anything for guild life. Clearly, you're not as observant as you claim. Probably why your da—"

"Truthfully, I've been using him as a consultant to my own ends, so we can spend time together," Milo interjected, smirking. "What can I say? That dick really does it for me."

Tobias and I both choked on our drinks. My cheeks burned, likely matching Tobias's reddened face.

"Wonderful conversation, Mr. Whitlock, but I have loads of people—yes, that was an intended pun—to introduce Dorian to." Milo locked arms with me, dragging me away.

"What's your problem?"

"Saving you from an impulsive, sharp, yet regrettable exchange."

"By mentioning my dick?"

"Please. Vulgar conversation always rattles elitists who find themselves oh so above it. Well, him, at the very least. The only thing that man hates more than lude queer commentary—or me being his top-*mostly*-ranked enchanter in the state—is being insulted by someone attempting to put him in his place. Trust me, he's more spiteful than mountains are tall."

I'd say his child also ranked high on the list of things he hated. Was this where Tara's depression stemmed from? Or was it merely another facet of her I didn't understand?

"Whatever. I don't need you to save me from speaking my mind. If I want to tell someone to fuck off, then let me make my own bed and—"

"You never make your bed."

I broke free of Milo's grip.

"I'm going for a smoke."

"Fine. Kiss ya later." Milo strutted toward an elderly woman with so much gaudy jewelry I was convinced it added to the hunch in her back. "Evelyn, my darling, I've been searching for you all evening. I wanted to thank you personally for your skillful enchanters at Kraken Guild. How'd you acquire such fantastic taste?"

"Ugh." I gagged on his phoniness.

He hated Kraken Guild. Hell, their guild nearly screwed up his entire plan before it began. But he always had to play the game of politics and niceties. And yes, I did it too. At least when I did it, it was for kids and their futures. Not a fucking career move on my part.

Evelyn bellowed with laughter; her yearning screamed all the way to me at the balcony doors. Delight danced along the surface, which almost masked her insecurity and loneliness as Milo gripped her gloved fingers.

I braced myself for the bitter breeze and lit a cigarette. Snowflakes twinkled in the lights that shone on the ostentatious statues symbolling the mythical creatures for which many guilds earned their name. Manicured hedges and lovely flowers hid the metallic lamps that kept the beasts illuminated at all hours. Proudly on display stood some of Tobias Whitlock's guild mascots. A Cerberus, Pegasus, Kraken, but it didn't seem he acquired displays for just his own guilds. Further down the acres of land, which secluded this home from the cramped city, stood a Phoenix statue.

Perhaps a tribute to the fallen independent guild. Doubtful. The crack lining the bird's face while all other statues were carved and maintained without a sliver of a fracture felt intentional. I grumbled with an exhale of smoke. A crude reminder from a man who aspired to own the world.

Tara's heels clicked along the cobblestone below as she dragged a hooded person—not anywhere close enough to blending in this crowd—by the arm and into the shadows next to a monstrous stone tentacle. "You can't be here."

"I'm not afraid," said a man with a scratchy baritone.

"You should be," Tara snapped. I didn't realize she had fury in her voice. Perhaps some of her father's fury was buried beneath all that sorrow.

I studied the hooded man. He chewed on his lip. His fingers tugged at the strings along the rips of his jeans covered in grime.

"Do you realize how many enchanters are here?"

"I could cut through them if it pleased me."

I froze, resisting the shudder traveling along my spine. Hatred boomed from him, but his surface thoughts were jumbled, choppy, and erratic.

"Then why don't you?" Tara asked. *Regret. Please say regret.*

"As much fun as it'd be seeing the Old Man's reaction by announcing myself in front of the swarm of leeches who'd delight in his fall, that's not why I came."

Tara trembled, either from the frigid gust or the terror that clung inside her throat, making it impossible for her to speak.

"I want to know where he's hiding the doctor."

Doctor?

"Everything about her detainment is off the books. Very hush-hush. Even when I questioned the feds—incredibly politely, might I add—supposedly holding her in custody, it bore no fruit. Only blood. But you, tragic little Tara, can find out. Can't you?" He inched toward her, snatching her bare shoulders and squeezing tightly.

I leapt off the balcony, using telekinesis and levitation to target my descent between them.

"What seems to be the problem here?" I balled my fists, ready to snatch Tara back with a telekinetic grip and break a piece of the statue off to crush him if necessary.

He released her.

"It's nothing," she said.

"It doesn't look like nothing."

"You heard her. Everything's fine. Why don't you go back inside?" He lifted his head, hollow blue eyes meeting mine before his head dropped. Seething hatred flooded the courtyard, darkening my vision. Deranged minds were the most difficult to hone in on. They carried such gruesome weight.

"*You're the filthy telepath that attacked my Kendall,*" he thought, directing his psychopathy at my magic.

I recoiled, gritting my teeth.

He cocked his head, eyes hidden but smile bright in the shadows. An attempt to sever his mind from mine and distill his thoughts yet again, something I should've relished, but I latched onto the madness, unwilling to relent until I knew what else he had to share.

"*Not him. Not here. It'll ruin what's in store.*" He hovered inches above the ground. "*I need to leave before that wretched telepath alerts someone.*"

He barreled back through the air; a glint of silver slipped from his sleeve. I backstepped, wide-eyed at the dagger's hilt in his palm.

He wasn't going anywhere. Subduing the shiver in my body, I gave chase, drifting between statues and hedges, tracking his chaotic laughter in the dark.

"Mr. Frost, wait."

Crystalized blue flashed as I turned the corner. The erratic mind of the hooded man vanished instantaneously. I ran my fingertips along sparkling droplets as they faded to nothingness, exactly the same as what Dr. Kendall attempted to escape through.

Tara arrived, calm and composed, straightening the ruffles in her dress.

"Who was that?" I asked.

"No idea. Said he was a former enchanter mad at my dad about some licensing restriction. Happens all the time. Honestly, Mr. Frost, it's not a big deal." The lie rolled out instinctively, but her mind exposed the truth with a whirlpool of regret. "*This is all dad's fault. Mine too. Everyone paying for our mistakes.*"

I'd gathered enough to know he was connected to the warlock faction, to the doctor, to the Whitlocks. I shivered. He was potentially the reason behind the void vision I'd foolishly believed was over.

Chapter Twenty-Four

I escorted a reluctantly quiet Tara inside. Her insistence did little to sway my one-track mind, especially since she worked so hard to keep her thoughts fixated on the party as if five minutes ago never happened. Still, I let her slip away and tend to guests with whatever fake daughter-of-the-hosts task she'd conjured. I had to find Milo. A bell chimed; droves of guests were ushered toward the dining room. With so many people talking, minds buzzing, and my own concern, it was impossible to pinpoint Milo in this thicket of pretentious riches.

"Dude, you're here." Gael Martinez smiled, sharklike teeth beaming, in a flashy red suit with short sleeves and capri cutoffs, providing his spikes breathing room and reminding wary guests to also offer some wiggle room as they shuffled past.

I blinked, momentarily bewildered by being called dude as he strolled toward me, opposite of the moving crowd. It figures Gael landed an invitation to this exclusive event. His grandparents were the former guild masters of Basilisk Guild and quite influential in these circles.

"Yep. King Clucks and I got the best table in the whole damn house." Gael Rios-Vega strutted by me. Suddenly it registered I was, in fact, not being called dude.

The rooster clucked.

"You're right," Gael said to his familiar. "Gael, you should totally join us at our table."

They stood a few feet away, enamored in conversation, completely oblivious to my presence.

"This isn't the cafeteria, man. That's not how these banquets work." Boredom bubbled along the surface, recalling how many of these stuffy events he'd been invited to only to end up secluded in some distant seating.

"We're right by Enchanter Evergreen's table! Like in talking distance. We can just squeeze in another chair, or maybe Tara will switch with ya. She doesn't even wanna be here. You seriously okay passing up being that close?"

"Ugh. Don't say that. My abuela would throw a fit if I caused a scene trying to trade seats." Gael huffed; his perfectly gelled autumn bangs remained in place. "Plus, Kenzo would get super pissed if I ditched him after dragging him here."

Hours of pleading, coaxing, and well-timed reverse psychology lined Gael's mind as he replayed how he'd convinced Kenzo to be his plus one. *Convinced.* His tactics, much like his spiky hair, were reminiscent of how Milo used to drag me to these galas.

"Bawk."

"Exactly. Kenzo's always pissed. So ditch him for awesomeness." Gael followed his familiar's pecking beak and pointed through the crowd to Milo, chatting with a couple of enchanters as they entered the dining room. They had a better knack for tracking than I realized. Guess obsession played a role in that. "It's Enchanter Evergreen. But if you wanna hang in the back somewhere with all the forgettable witches, who are we to judge?"

Gael and his rooster created a strange unison of his laughter mixed with his familiar's timely clucks, which could only be properly described as a cluckle.

"Déjame en paz," Gael said, waving a spiky hand dismissively.

I beelined for Milo.

"Whoa. Was that Mr. Frosty?"

Wading through the crowd, I slipped a hand under Milo's arm and squeezed tightly, not-so-politely, pulling his attention from idle chit-chat.

"So handsy. And I thought you hated PDA." Milo flexed his bicep in my grip and bit the air playfully.

I shrugged away his flirtation. "We have a problem."

"I know. Paige Portman's at our table. She's so dreadful. I swear if her family hadn't founded half the guilds in the city, I doubt anyone would remember to add her to the guest lists."

The dining hall was closer in size to an arena than a room, filled with elegant tables, each with its own individualized centerpieces staggered in a crescent shape that faced a nearby stage.

"This is serious," I whispered. "One of your warlock stragglers was here."

Milo paused, an expressionless face as he scanned the banquet, and his thoughts fizzled to nothingness. His eyes fluttered, momentarily lost in his clairvoyance. "I see. He's clearly gone now. What happened?"

"Something about Dr. Kendall. About the Whitlock's. About—"

"We'll discuss this later, privately." Milo escorted me to our table, where I released my hand when mental whispers of curiosity at the table questioned if I was a date, a joke, or a grungy charity case. So much for all that wasted debate on which suit looked best. Clearly, nothing I could've worn would impress this crowd.

I kept a dour expression as I took a seat next to Milo, not bothering with niceties for this group because I didn't have the time or concern about what they thought of me. What they continued thinking—loudly.

Tobias Whitlock walked up to a podium on a stage. "I'd like to thank all of you for attending this evening. Truly, such an honor to have so many witches dedicating their magic to protecting the city."

Pride swelled amongst the audience as Tobias named off guild masters for their commitment. As egos inflated, everyone applauded name after name, and this felt less like a benefit and more like some expensive self-congratulatory jerkoff fest.

Milo eyed my fumbling hands, which made minimal effort at faking the applause. In my defense, everyone in our vicinity was too fixated on their own accolades to notice.

"What? Just feels a bit premature, wouldn't you say?"

Milo's smile filled his face, nodding past me and to some foolish guild master over my shoulder.

I leaned in to keep my voice low. "When you said there were a few stragglers, you made it sound like something simpler. Like this was over."

"This is simple."

"Milo, you didn't feel this guy's hatred."

"I've seen it. The potential danger it carries."

"And you said nothing," I hissed.

"It is nothing. I'm handling it. There are still too many moving pieces. Telling you would've made you worry, obsess, dwell."

"Is the void vision gone or not?"

"I don't get a checklist of successfully completed side quests every time a future shifts."

Truth rattled along the surface of his mind before he buried it. This warlock was the one meant to kill Caleb. My pulse quickened, pounding against my neck. I swallowed hard, trying to make sense of everything.

"I'd like to give a very special thanks to Harris Enchant Tech," Tobias said. "Their innovation over the years by creating accessible enchantments for witches in the guild industry has been instrumental in assisting all of our enchanters in the field."

Applause rumbled as a spotlight shone on a nearby table housing the picture-perfect Harris family. Quite a humble family until recent years when their eldest son found a way to easily decipher illegal enchantments, patent-pending, and sent their company skyrocketing to the top in the state. Mr. Harris's earth-brown cheeks tightened at the audience's attention, and Mrs. Harris smiled, resisting the urge to fidget with her drooping shawl that exposed her pale, freckled shoulders.

The only one at the table truly at ease having all these eyes on her was Katherine who, thanks to her parents' successes, grew up quite comfortable with the spotlight. Her demurred smile and polite half-wave screamed shy, but confidence roared within her even louder. Hmph. Background of a rising family with a powerful branch magic of her own. Self-assurance with the crowd, yet the humility not to show it. She'd make a quality guild enchanter at this rate.

Her plus one, on the other hand, was surprising for more than one reason. She'd brought Caleb with her. His sweaty face and twitchy smile as he inched his chair out of the spotlight made it clear that, like so many students, he wasn't ready for the unrelenting eyes. My chest ached from the returning concern of the void vision. Did Milo worry my interference would harm Caleb?

Caleb stopped scooting his chair. He pinched his eyes closed for a second and then replaced the sheepish smile with something sort of resembling confidence. *"Katherine's right. This is an opportunity. Meet people. Impress them. I'd never get a real chance to talk with so many influential witches otherwise. I'll have to prove a lot more and convince them that, even without a branch, I'll be valuable at any of their guilds. Yes, some of my top enchanter interning choices are here, but I should probably take notes on the acolytes in attendance, cross-reference that with the public records of those involved in that recent warlock takedown, and check out their backgrounds. If I ran a few figures, I might be able to predict which of these acolytes would be new, eager enchanters willing to take more chances with branchless witches in a few years' time. All I need..."*

Geez, this kid never took a night off from overanalyzing his future. And if he wouldn't stop thinking about his future, then how the hell could I? I released my telepathy, allowing the pompous overflow of the audience to take hold. So much fawning and envy all directed toward the arrogant host.

Tobias prattled on about Chicago returning to one of the nation's safest cities to live by maintaining a low percentage of illegal casting and keeping demonic energy an almost invisible blip on the radar. Sure, if we only ran those stats, ignoring our higher-than-average poverty rate, violent crimes, homeless population, stubborn police force, or a million other factors keeping the windy city from being safe for all. Something that didn't register with this crowd of witches. Occasionally, I wondered how Chicago would've turned out if a magic-based market hadn't hit the world so hard.

I leaned into Milo, ignoring Tobias's blathering. "Are you keeping things from me because you're worried my interference could skew something worse or the potential Whitlock involvement?"

My tone was perhaps a bit more accusatory than intended, but the question stood. It stood silently between us as beads of sweat pooled along Milo's brow. I didn't want to harm Caleb's chances like I clearly did by intervening with Milo's raid on Dr. Kendall and this hooded warlock straggler affiliated with the Whitlocks somehow.

"It's a precarious situation. One best discussed in private."

"We have lots in store for you all this evening, including opportunities to help those affected by the warlock incursion, but before that, I'd like to give a special thank you to the enchanter who helped make this success possible." Light stung my eyes, exposing our table. Hopefully, Tobias neared the end of his goddamn telethon speech. "Enchanter Evergreen organized a flawless success, removing the blemish on our beautiful city."

Scooting my chair away from the spotlight, I glared at Milo's smile, refusing to join in with the others and their fucking seal clapping.

Dinner finally began, and Milo responded to Gael's not-so-subtle *pssst* with a polite wave and small talk before jumping back into conversation with those I lacked the energy or desire to speak with at our table.

"And who is your friend?" The curiosity finally escaped someone's lips before the end of the first course.

Milo placed a hand atop mine, his fingertips gently massaging my knuckles. The affection was nice. The illusion was enjoyable. But navigating this world, his world, from the sidelines was difficult enough. Add in our tangled past, my regrets, and my need to detach from anyone, and guilt crept along the goosebumps his touch caused.

"This is Dorian. Sort of keeps me grounded, reminding me no matter how big my head gets, there's a lot of empty space up there." He chuckled. "It reminds me of this story when we were both still acolytes. Oh my God, never meet your idols because…"

Darkness swept across the table. The dinner conversation was silenced by the patter of fatigued footsteps running on shadows. Caleb collapsed. Kenzo grabbed the bloody dagger. A tiny snippet returning to show nothing I'd done helped. Kenzo's rage unhinged like an inferno, ready to burn this future to ash. But an ocean of guilt came crashing, dousing the anger. Tara stood, trembling, eyes locked on Caleb's body.

"This is all my fault." Remorse and blame fluttered about her like wicked songbirds carrying a tune of regret.

Kenzo rose, dagger firmly in his grasp. "Always the fucking Whitlocks taking everything from me."

Tara fell to her knees, brushing a hand along Caleb's white curls. Confusion in her eyes. Kenzo stormed forward, blade raised.

And then, nothing…

"…I swear. I still blush every time Enchanter Lawless comes to town."

The table roared with laughter at Milo's story he completed in the midst of a vision without missing a beat. I blinked away the darkness still clinging to my sight.

I shook, staring at an oblivious Caleb, unaware of a future I continued failing to prevent. He overthought everyone's words at his table and tensed when Katherine squeezed his clammy hand beneath the tablecloth, a gentle reassurance on her part that perplexed him even more.

It didn't take much to catch a whiff of Kenzo's rage percolating at the far end of the banquet, furious by the guestlist, his seating, Gael's smile which he professed annoyed him despite his rage softening every time he looked at it.

Tara sat at a neighboring table, softly thinking of the hooded warlock. I wanted to investigate, but a tidal wave of haunting emotions from the depths of her core collided along the surface, making it impossible to glean anything else without delving deep into that dangerous abyss of sorrow.

I stayed quiet during the dinner, quelling magic and insecurity. Caleb, Kenzo, and Tara were all connected to this void vision, this future of death, anger, and remorse.

Afterward, everyone was funneled into some auction exhibit hosted in another lavish location to this infinite manor. Milo pulled me aside, walking down an empty corridor.

"It's not a coincidence that a warlock shows up to the Whitlocks, and Tara's piece in the void vision revealed itself." Milo's thoughts were a whirlwind of incomplete theories and suspicions. "I've suspected Tobias possessed some role in this upstart faction. The enchantments the warlocks used prevented me from gaining intel until our strike, and now he's trying to close the book to this mystery before we reach the ending."

"And Tobias's magic allows him to guard his mind and intentions unless he allows for it."

"Precisely. I can't very well investigate Tara without Tobias catching wind, but my clairvoyance works through many degrees of separation. The better I know someone, the more tangible their futures become in my mind. And the futures of those close to them. Delve into her mind like you did with Caleb and Kenzo. It could help me find the missing pieces to this void vision future."

I retreated behind my bangs, covering my eyes. He knew about that. Before or after I rummaged through their pasts?

"Just explain it. What're you planning?"

"It's not that simple. There's a reason I don't tell people their dream will come true on X date, the name of their soulmate is so-and-so, or the way to avoid that death is by following steps A-B-C. Self-awareness creates its own variables. Knowing a dream's finally coming true might stunt the person's drive that served as the catalyst to achieve it. Knowing a true love's name might ruin the chemistry that sparked between those hearts. Knowing how to avoid a dangerous future might cause them to overlook a hundred other tiny precautions that played a role in their survival."

Doors at the end of the hall opened, and caterers carried trays. Milo nodded as they walked by and grabbed my hand.

"*I don't withhold to be cruel, but when every breath a person takes creates a subtle alteration to those futures, I find it impossible to keep anyone other than myself up to date on the strategy.*"

Milo needed assistance, and I needed closure on this vision that brought the three of us back together in the strangest of ways. I would delve into Tara's past, unravel where this guilt and sorrow she carried stemmed from, and how it tied to the hooded warlock.

Chapter Twenty-Five

Back at the academy, it was obvious Tara's mind was the easiest to delve within, but also unlike any I'd explored. I'd wandered the edges of many minds drowning in sadness, too frightened to jump in, knowing I didn't have the skills to pull them up for air. I gasped, choking on the overflowing ocean, which represented her core consciousness. How she functioned day-to-day with memories dragged through such a powerful vortex of opposing currents, I couldn't fathom. Voices muffled by crashing waves led me deeper.

"You still can't control your branches."   *"Such a waste."*
        "She didn't love us; that's why she left."
"You're the future of this family."
            "We have each other.
            I'll always protect you."

"He may not love you, but at least he's not ashamed of you."

"Try harder."   *"I don't need treatment!"*

"I wish you were all dead."

"I wonder if things would've been different had Theo been gifted your magics."

"I love you, Tara."   *"I miss you, Tara."*

"This is all your fault, Tara."

"Their blood is on your hands. Remember that every time you fail to master your magics."

I swam, unable to discern direction, but sought something stable in this abyss. A fully formed memory. Anything. Because even in an illusion of her mind, I couldn't sway or control it. Fatigue consumed me, my body numb and adrift in this cold place.

Somewhere in this sea of sorrow, Tara trembled. I reached out. Inhaling the small air bubble, I let the moment envelop me.

"You're seriously not going to let me attend an academy?" a boy's voice asked.

"There's not an academy in the state that wants a branchless student," Tobias said. "If you think I'm going to pull strings—"

"I'm not fucking branchless!"

Tara was young here, too young for the memory to fully form. It dwelled in this grim space with so many others.

"Careful what magic you inherit, Tara. He might disown you, too."

"Shut your goddamn mouth, Theodore."

The bubble burst. I held my breath again, searching the dark waters for relief. A vacuum of pressure dragged me to the ocean's floor, where it pinned me beneath so much misery. I dug numb fingers into the dirt.

I couldn't rest…

Maybe for just a minute…

My other half could conjure another manifestation…

I collapsed onto a marble floor, choking in deep breaths. Overwhelming joy took hold. Relief for finding a firm and safe memory came from me, but the joy—that was Tara's. Strange how her happiness lay buried below everything else.

"Oh, no." Tara clutched the blanket close, covering her face but peering at the screen, unable to tear her eyes away.

Like so many other children in the city, the nation, the fiends unleashed upon Chicago captivated five-year-old Tara. The camera rattled as a tarlike fiend trampled forward. Tara panicked until Enchanter Evergreen showed up yet again, one swift punch and the fiend flew out of frame. By the time it panned over to the beast, Milo had banished it.

Tara rejoiced. All night, Enchanter Evergreen and other amazing witches were caught on video protecting everyone. An impressive feat to stop so many monsters and ensure no one was injured. Her smile was tight and painful but matched the amazing Enchanter Evergreen on the screen before he leapt into the air and flew off. Desire blossomed in her heart while watching the news. She hoped to develop an amazing magic like Milo someday.

I haunted this memory, bewildered by how little I truly knew about the girl. Here I assumed her attendance at the academy was forced upon her by family obligations, but deep within her core blossomed the origin of that dream. I needed to discover how she connected to the void vision, how she was tied to the warlock faction, the one filled with such deep-seated hatred. More than anything, though, I needed to do better by Tara and all my other students.

As the news cutaway for a commercial, Tara climbed off the couch and raced through the dark hallways, a blanket protecting her from all the monsters lurking in the shadows of her imagination. She had to tell her father all about the amazing Enchanter Evergreen. He needed to know she wanted to be just like him. I floated behind her like a sopping ghost.

"That bitch Kendall was supposed to help Theodore with his branch, not let him destroy my city," Tobias said into a phone.

Tara froze at the ajar office door. I peered inside, which revealed Tobias's head, half torso, and arm were all that'd formed in this vacant white space. Since Tara clearly never crept inside, this memory, though strong, lacked in full creation.

Fear of her father's shouting—even if it wasn't directed toward her this time—kept her stuck in place. She tried to recall what Theo told her to do when she was scared, but she hadn't seen him since he went to the hospital to get better. Based on her father's anger, she worried they might not get to write letters anymore.

Theo. That was her brother. The one in those scattered and fractured memories swirling in her ocean above. I knew he'd died but never realized it had to do with a connection to the Night of the Fiend Massacre. And what the hell did Tobias mean by his branch destroying the city?

"We need to control the narrative before this gets out. I won't allow everything I've worked so hard to build to end up ruined because of a spoiled brat's temper tantrum. This whole operation needs to be scrubbed. Every record. Find the doctor. Detain her and Theodore before he unleashes more fiends."

I shuddered, synced with Tara's anxiety. Unleashing fiends? What the hell kind of magic was that?

"If you can't take them in quietly, then you know how to deal with this problem."

At five, Tara didn't grasp what his selective words meant. I did. Disgusting and not at all shocking Tobias Whitlock would plan a contingency to kill his child off to maintain his position. Sickening how he painted his son's death as a tragedy to fuel his agenda of spreading prejudice toward branchless witches masked as precautions for limiting their licensing. And all the while, his son had a branch magic, simply not one palatable to the Whitlock name.

Nearly two weeks later, and my manifestation hadn't made any contact. As class began, I tried to reach out and grab a message through Tara's close proximity. I ground my teeth, biting back a shiver. Not happening with her well of sorrow.

I distributed the application essay rough drafts back to my homeroom coven with notes for each of them to review.

"Gah. Why are we always writing about magic instead of casting it?" Gael Rios-Vega slammed his hands on the desk, huffing so dramatically it sent a shock through half the minds in the room.

"**Idiot**." Kenzo glared.

"Bawk."

"You're right, King Clucks. He's just afraid of all the awesomeness we bring."

"I assure you, your awesomeness does not intimidate me." I slapped his paper on the desk.

His essay was a bloody mess from all the red ink splattered across the pages. Was red a demoralizing color to cover in a paper? Yes. Did it spark anxiety in each of the students as they read through their comments? Also, yes. Had I found it crudely successful over the years? Hit or miss, but unlike most, I always knew how to steer a lost mind if the comments bogged them down too much.

"How is this 'unessential material' to my essay?" Gael held up the paper, crinkling it with a pointed finger.

"You went on a tangent for two pages about how Chick-Fil-A is systematically pitting animals against each other."

"They are. Cows do not hate chickens or want you to eat more. King Clucks is actually best friends with a cow. She's a little shady and cheats at Blackjack, but that's a whole other story."

"That may be, but your essay is supposed to inform the panel why you should receive a permit and eventually have your magic licensed."

Gael groaned, long, drawn out, and suffocating for the rest of the room.

Frustration festered in the class as students reviewed their comments. They were justified. My notes were hard-hitting and tougher than most of the teachers at Gemini. That said, most of my students flourished during their internships in their third year, and fewer of my students had to retake their licensing exam after graduation. I took a bit too much pride in how my tactics prepared them for the harshness of this industry.

I went to Caleb's desk. His mind buzzed with a thousand different questions about where he went wrong over what I must say was my lightest revision. Kenzo had more notes—and he certainly let me know he disagreed with nearly every comment through his enraged thoughts. I squeezed the bridge of my nose until the pain in my tear ducts distracted from his explosive commentary.

"You're concerned," I said.

"Just making sense of it," Caleb said, his thoughts spinning like the fastest teacup ride in the world.

"Your essay describes the proficiency you've developed with your roots this semester and how you're utilizing more than one at a time. But I'd like to see you explain your other skills."

That was where Caleb's concern bubbled loudest.

"Let me elaborate. There are plenty of enchanters with unimpressive branch magics that provide invaluable service to their guilds through other means—their deductive reasoning, analytic detail, charisma with clients. These are all components that guilds seek from prospective acolytes. Show the panel you already understand these factors. Show them your other talents."

"Because I don't have a branch to show off." That teacup whirl winded off the tracks, casting doubt, regret, premature failure, and more emotions than I could make sense of.

I cracked my neck, focused on the short relief in the snap that eased tension in my spine.

"Because you don't need one. You've improved your root magics since arriving. Your test scores are sharp. Your channeling is impressive. And your understanding of so many different branches makes you an asset for guilds that often have witches working in teams."

Caleb nodded. "*Yeah. Like Enchanter Evergreen's multi-guild strike. I might not be able to predict the future, but I can statistically guess an outcome based on someone's magic.*"

As Caleb's doubt eased, I worked with all the other students, including an unwilling Kenzo before uneasily making my way to Tara's desk. Her essay hadn't provided any insight into how she intended to merge her magics but instead took a standard approach to how the magics worked. All well written, but she wouldn't be able to show the panel that when displaying her magic. I still didn't have a solution to merging the three branches.

"Hey, I almost forgot." Caleb withdrew the book I'd given Tara about channeling overlaps from his backpack. "It was really insightful stuff. I always found Nya's steam magic fascinating but had no idea so much thought went into it."

"Yeah," she said.

I stood close behind them.

"It actually gave me a couple ideas on your branches. I mean, not that you need them, but maybe if you're like open to hearing…"

Caleb and I both hung onto Tara's unmoving face. Each second of her unresponsive reaction created doubt.

"Well?" she asked.

"Oh. Sorry," Caleb said. "Anyway, your sealing magic constricts anything physical to a confined space. A sort of impenetrable wall which counters your intangibility magic by allowing affected things to phase through anything warded or not. This got me thinking how you can't not cast any of the three, so you have to find a way to make them work in tandem. Those two magics, in particular, being opposing forces made it hard. But then I realized your shadow manipulation is actually the perfect conduit to bridge all three."

Tara's perplexed expression likely matched mine. Caleb rambled on about his hamster ball theory. I fixated on his powerful mental image of said hamster ball. The ball, in its entirety, represented her shadows circulating in a concentrated area. The hamster's entrance served as where Tara would pinpoint her intangibility.

"And then, by sealing off the rest of the shadows, you pretty much prevent anything held in that space from escaping. Of course, you'd have to rotate the shadows, or else those contained would find the exit and phase back out."

"That'd force me to change my classification type to a support role," Tara said.

"Yeah, I couldn't think of a way to use all three simultaneously in an offensive manner."

"Not a huge deal," I said. "Just a few changes to your essay and your permit request."

"Exactly," Tara said. "*I prefer that over something offensive, anyway. Even if that's what dad thinks is best for my magics.*"

Honestly, I didn't fully comprehend Caleb's answer, even skimming his mental image confused me. But Tara understood, which was good. It was a friendly reminder kids were often more capable of teaching each other when the adults in their life dropped the ball.

A twinge of guilt hit, related to a sad thought that maybe I'd become one of those adults. Not become. Was. By looking out for Caleb, and failing terribly, my goal of being half-competent at helping students achieve their goals was superseded by a desire to keep him alive.

Another thing I failed at. I winced. The pulsating twinge of unread calls from my manifestation ached. Every muscle in my body receded. Ignoring it, I managed to survive the end of classes until my planning period, where I foolishly dove into memories, desperate for answers.

Somehow, I'd dragged myself through the pits of Tara's mind and found a memory with Theo. Him and her. Alone. No Tobias. So much regret clung to this single event.

Eight years old, with no idea what to do in this situation, Tara stood on the steps leading to the cellar with a cage containing her brother.

Her branches blossomed in quick succession to one another, yet despite being the blessed branches her father craved over Theo's dreadful curse, she couldn't use them yet. Someday she would. She knew it. Believed it. Like Enchanter Evergreen said, *"magic's more about training and determination than anything else."*

The imaginary monsters were powerful as Tara walked down the stairs toward her brother. Each creature clawed at an anxious Tara, who braved the steps to see him after three years. Three years of being told not to utter his name. Three years of hearing he was evil. Three years of choosing family—whatever that was—over him.

Still, three years weren't enough to silence the longing she had. She'd face her horrors and crept down the creaky stairs to hear his almost fading voice.

"Come to see me die?" Theo's bloody and bludgeoned face made Tara's eyes watery, goosebumps shivering up her arms. His limp body lay against a stone wall.

"You're not going to die. Dad said—"

"Daddy says lots of things, tragic little Tara. You don't realize the horrors he has in store for me simply for existing."

He leaned forward, his fingertips reaching for the bars we both understood he couldn't touch. A single attempt would cinder his flesh to ash, but Tara didn't comprehend the dangerous sigils lined on the bars casting powerful enchantments to hold him in place. To say it was unethical was an understatement.

Tobias painted his branchless son's death as a tragic accident. Did he end his own son's life down here in the dark, hidden from the world?

"He said you'd get to leave soon."

"Only after I submit to having my magic bound."

Tara shook, confused why that sounded so appealing. Though she desperately wanted to master her branches, her father continued reminding her of the failures every day.

Legally stripping someone of their branch was weighty, time-consuming, expensive, and often met with much public backlash. Many considered it a cruel, archaic practice.

"You can help me, little sister." Theo pointed to the enchantment opposite the cell imbuing the sigils to confine him.

"No," she said. "Your branch is dangerous. You tried to hurt people."

"I didn't. That happened because I couldn't control my magic. But no one was hurt, remember?"

Tara replayed the videos in her mind, holding that single shred of joy she carried with her as Enchanter Evergreen protected everyone during the Night of the Fiend Massacre.

"My doctor, the one our old man discredited, taught me how to control my branch. She only wants to help people. I want to help people. Maybe we can help you, too. I know you've inherited some very complex branches."

"You know about that?"

"Of course," he said. "Father may have forced me into hiding, but I always kept an eye on you. I'd never abandon my baby sister. Not like our mother or our absent-hearted father."

His pitiful expression weighed heavily on Tara's mind and heart. All she wanted was to hug him, protect him, free him.

"I don't know how to break the enchantment." Tara fidgeted.

"Do you want me to tell you?"

She nodded, approaching the complex enchantment, which, honestly, even I didn't fully comprehend. The construction of many rules applied to a single spell was a work of art. All the same, young Tara listened to her big brother's instructions, happily helping free him because she believed it'd finally fix their family.

As the memory faded, I returned to the reality of my empty classroom.

Gael led the way to the auxiliary gym, humming a holiday song in his ugly Christmas sweater, made worse with each step, given he'd attached tiny, jingling ornaments to the tips of his spikes.

"*Ridiculous.*" Kenzo rolled his eyes, walking alongside a smiling Gael as they trailed ahead.

I firmly agreed with Kenzo's sentiment, but admittedly, Gael's frosted blue hair with snow-white streaks was much subtler than the bright green and red I'd predicted he'd choose for the festive season.

Once we arrived, I kept everyone gathered together before letting them disperse.

"The closer we get to the fledgling permit exams, the fewer available slots there are to reserve this space." I quelled the concern of my homeroom, believing this was the final trip we'd have here before the end of the year. "No. That doesn't mean branch training is over. In fact, quite the opposite."

Most teachers with first-year homerooms scrambled to make sure their students had as much time in the auxiliary gym as possible. No one wanted their kids failing to obtain their fledgling permits in the first semester. Our jobs were to educate, and those outside the classroom ensured we did that by evaluating our stats because nothing said dedicated educator quite as much as cold, hard data.

I definitely fought alongside the rest of the teachers, reserving days on the calendar, sharing the space when possible, but that wasn't the only measure I took to give my students all the time they'd need to train their magic.

"Hello, little lovelies." Chanelle burst into the auxiliary gym and immediately unleashed her students to claim a terrain that suited their magical skill sets.

"We'll be sharing this space with other homerooms for the time being."

Mostly sighs of relief followed, with a few agitated about sharing the space and one mind grumbling about Mrs. Whitehurst waltzing right in and sending her kids off without a drawn-out lecture. Seriously? I huffed. Time to rip off the band-aid that'd send them all into a tizzy.

"I'll be reserving this place explicitly for our class every Saturday leading up to winter break."

"What about those of us with jobs?" Carter asked, hand raised for no reason at all.

"You don't have a job," I said.

"I know that, duh. That's why I said *us*. I'm a man of the people." He adjusted his tie, winking at the others.

Their minds and mouths immediately collided together in a kerfuffle.

"I have to babysit."

"My DnD group meets Saturdays."

"Shopping."

"I could probably flip my schedule and work a double on Sundays."

"But I have a date." "I need my weekends."

"Is this necessary for a permit?"

"**Lazy losers don't deserve licenses if they can't give up a few Saturdays**."

"Some of us have holiday parties." "Every weekend?"

"Better than being home."

"These Saturday trainings are not mandatory, and they'll only run till noon." I cared they got in as much training as possible but not enough to eat into my entire weekend. "While not required, I encourage you all to find time to attend some. It'll improve your odds of receiving your permit before the new year. Once you have those, you'll be able to train wherever and whenever you like."

They buzzed with excitement. Suddenly, the loss of a few Saturdays didn't feel life ending. I released them to change into uniforms and make the most of their class time practicing magic.

"Ah, yes. The noble act of sacrificing your Saturdays does not go unnoticed," Chanelle said. "It's annoying. But eventually, overworking yourself will be the death of you. While dancing on your grave, I'll try not to say I told you so."

Mockery from the woman who ran after-school tutoring three times a week. A couple of Saturdays was a minimal sacrifice.

"Dude, wait up." Gael and King Clucks raced behind Gael.

"Sorry, man." He hovered above the pair. "Kenzo's gonna help me with my levitation today. I know that's not your favorite."

"Bawk." The rooster flapped his wings with fury at the flying Gael Martinez.

"*So much for bros before hoes.*" Gael joined his familiar in a squinted glare.

Students began breaking into groups casting together.

Katherine pulled Jamius aside. "Can I borrow you for a bit?"

"What'cha need?" he asked, eyebrows raised.

"Your magic, one of your clones, if you don't mind."

"Oh, for your little spell book." Jamius burst into two, then three. "We'd totally be down for that."

"Thank you." Katherine and all the Jamius' wandered off to join Katherine's growing grimoire.

I drifted through the forest terrain, watching Caleb spin in the air, kicking telekinetic bursts. Bark cracked. Each kick possessed more channeled magic, yet didn't pull away from the magic in his core, levitating.

"When'd you pick that up?"

Caleb took heavy breaths, steadying them to keep his channeled magic from faltering or his midair pose from dropping.

"Katherine showed me, she's um," *pretty, smart, tall, s...* He cleared his throat and wandering mind. "She's really good with her root magics."

I spent time working with Caleb on his roots, impressed by his observations that continued making his roots improve each day.

Things might've changed sooner if I'd confronted Caleb with his fate. Maybe I could've trained him one-on-one, dedicated everything

I had to improving his skills and preparing for what would soon arrive. It wasn't too late. I could tell him everything. Inform his family. Remove him from the city, hidden away until his future had no choice but to change. Unless the lingering warlock faction also hid outside the city, biding their time. Then they might... No. It was impossible to know what choices were right or wrong, even with failure looming ahead.

My phone's buzz distracted me from doubt.

> Milo: Whatever you're learning with your inquisitive mind it has made the future ☀️

Inquisitive mind? Was that code because he didn't want to drop Tara's name? Sunshine emoji. Did that make the future hotter, brighter, or happier? Maybe it meant nothing would happen until summer. Since entering the first stages of the dead of winter that would hang around for several months, we had time. No. He definitely didn't mean that. Him and his fucking emojis.

> Milo: Stop obsessing. I wanna meet later this week. Talk then.

The depths of Tara's ocean no longer suffocated me. Yes, the currents were powerful, impossible to swim through, but I'd learned they also held no secrets. No places they wouldn't take me. Her mind cycled in a depressing pattern through her entire history, so long as I followed its guiding tug.

I braced for the undercurrent, the immense pressure almost

crushing the psychic energy keeping my form manifested. Yet, in one swift split—it all vanished. I released my breath and soaked in the gloomy environment I'd landed in.

Ten-year-old Tara sat alone, like most days, watching television while she worked on her studies. Bookwork that was far easier than any magical training despite the many expert trainers she worked with. Her root magics were coming along nicely, but that didn't impress her father. She sank into the couch, trying not to dwell on that fact.

A special news alert flashed on the screen.

"Fiends have struck Waukegan, leaving twelve acolytes and three enchanters in critical condition."

Tara's mind splintered, casting a haze that fogged everything in the room, only allowing pieces of the news report to cement in her memory.

"Phoenix Guild hasn't commented on the condition of their guild witches or how so many fiends managed to gather in the city."

Phoenix Guild. The same one Kenzo's parents worked for.

"There hasn't been a convergence of this many fiends at once in Illinois since the Night of the Fiend Massacre five years ago in Chicago. Unfortunately, this event has unfolded with more casualties."

Guilt swelled inside Tara. Theo had abandoned her after gaining his freedom. But he kept his word—no one was hurt by his magic. This couldn't be him. It couldn't.

Sobbing family members on the screen blurred together. My breathing hastened, unsteady, along with Tara's, as I found myself dragged into her sadness. She screamed, tears rolling down her cheeks. I wanted to tell her this wasn't her fault, grab her before she fell into an ocean of regrets. But this was only a memory. She collapsed, slipping through the floor, and was consumed by the ocean of sorrow entirely.

Her branches unleashed erratically. Shadows thrashed throughout the manor, destroying everything in sight except the marble floor her sealing magic enforced. The sleek sheen of white marble was brightened by the golden hue of her sealing magic.

"Control yourself, Tara." Tobias towered above her, a golden barrier of his own shielding from Tara's disjointed shadows whipping about. "You've seen the tragedy you caused."

Tara collapsed to her knees, struggling to breathe, and quelled her magic but not the guilt. The sorrow. "I didn't."

"Theodore's out there because of you. Their blood is on your hands. Remember that every time you fail to master your magics." Tobias knelt next to her, not an ounce of compassion in his fiery eyes. "That trash warlock's been dead to this family for years now. Since he decided to reemerge, I'll remind him why he should've stayed dead."

I drifted away, unable to bear any more of Tara's memories. She needed help, and perhaps the other half of my mind, the true Dorian, could make sense of how to begin that process.

Everything happening. Everything that happened. The attack on Chicago that cemented Milo's fame, the death of Kenzo's parents, Tara's fractured mind, the warlock faction that swelled in our city, Dr. Kendall's cruel experiments, and the void vision meant to be Caleb's death all stemmed back to Tobias and Theodore Whitlock. Their family feud harmed so many.

Chapter Twenty-Six

On Friday night before the first Saturday meeting, I texted Milo a reminder about meeting, where I intended to share what I'd learned about Tara and how the guilt consuming her connected to the warlock faction in question. Waiting for his late arrival, I fed Carlie and Charlie, ignoring my own appetite because of the fuzziness from all the deep delving I'd done inside Tara's memories. So much time in her mind left a foul feeling. Theodore's hatred seeped deeply into all her thoughts, new and old, like an infection eating away at Tara. The prideful discontent from her father, Tobias, didn't help matters. But that hatred of Theodore's radiated, an echoed fragment that must've come from her memories.

Minds in the neighborhood hummed until a restful silence took hold, like the silence of chirping crickets. All that remained was hatred at my front door. I trembled, channeling magic into my telekinesis, and attempting to simmer the disgust outside my home. Keeping my distance, I flung the door open and saw nothing. I stared at the fleeting sunlight. As quickly as a heartbeat, the foul feeling vanished.

It was nothing but twisted delusions from overexerting my magic. The blissful certainty of Milo's approach replaced the strange sensation and I took an easy breath.

"Came straight from work, I see," I said, eyeing the Cerberus emblem on his blazer.

"When am I not working?"

"True. Hungry after a long day?" I asked. "I can make something."

"Since when do you cook?"

"Hmm. Want a drink?"

"I'm fine."

"Okay. Care if I have a smoke?" I asked.

He shrugged, joining me by the couch, which made it difficult to stall, so I divulged everything about Tara and the Whitlock family. I hoped we'd piece it together, find a potential future where the void vision never occurred. More than anything, I wanted him to fix everything broken. In me. In the world. In the past. In the future. I demanded too much from Milo, but he'd accomplished everything Finn dreamt of and more. He was the best of us. Realistic, idealistic, optimistic.

Milo's eyes glossed over, sadness or a vision. Perhaps both. I grabbed his hand, frightened of the answer he'd say or think.

"I think I've got the answer." Milo smiled, eyes still glassy.

"How bad is it?"

"It's not. Not really. It's exactly what you've wanted." Milo squeezed my hand.

"But you can't tell me because that might somehow influence events to unfold differently."

"Precisely." He forced a laugh until the glint of sadness faded.

"Besides, no matter what I tell you, you're going to do whatever it takes to help that kid."

"To help them all. Kenzo and Tara might not be dying, but they're both so broken already. I can't let that future happen to them either."

"Well, on that dreary note, I should probably get home." Milo slapped his thighs, a gesture reminding me of the long Saturday I had in store. "I gotta ask, what sort of masochist works on their day off?"

"More of a sadistic move, forcing others to work on a weekend."

"Too bad about the early morning. I could really use an aggressive Dorian right about now."

Loneliness clung to Milo as I escorted him to the door. His longing to be held called out. His heart was desperate for love, exhausted from being alone. He didn't want what came with frivolous dates or better people than I could ever be. No, this longing came from what was, what we had… The three of us.

I couldn't prevent the future, only play my part. I couldn't be everything Milo needed, but I wanted to. I held the door shut, grabbing his tie. He trembled, refusing to bring himself closer. I leaned in and kissed him, his lips soft and desires shouting. Channeling magic, I carried him through the hallway.

He gripped my hair, pulling my head away, biting air between us. I envied that air. He released me, nuzzling my neck. I nibbled his shoulder every step into the bedroom, half undressed before we crossed the threshold. Stripping off what remained, I shoved him back. I craved his lips, his body, but his satisfaction above all. Hesitation hit. Milo didn't want foreplay. He wanted me this second, and his yearning sent a primal urge through all my tingling muscles.

I propped Milo's legs over my shoulders. Milo ran his fingers along my stomach, reminding me to ease my way inside him. As much as he wanted more, he needed a gentle touch. With our foreheads pressed together, it allowed me to focus on his unsteady panting. I slowed my strokes until his breathing eased.

Flashes of a blue comforter funneled from Milo, a memory surfacing louder with each thrust of my hips. He was bent over, fingers wrapped against the blanket, his teeth gritted nervously. Warm hands rubbed his back; my spine prickled with excitement. He quivered. Their soothing touch guided him into an arch.

"Relax, Milo." That was my gravelly voice of the past echoing in his mind. I froze, only continuing because the current Milo wrapped his legs around my waist which pushed my cock all the way inside him. He moaned, louder than he had in the memory which surfaced. He wanted this. Needed it. And I wanted him to be happy. Craved it. I shook away the memory of us, but it remained locked on the surface.

Milo nodded. My thrusts synced with my younger self, wrapped in a blissful sensation of understanding how my touch aroused him. Where to move my hands along his body. Shoulders to back to hips to abs. What he desired the instant pleasure struck. A commanding slap to his ass coupled with a grip below his jaw. When to speed up, slow down, and shift. Sweet sweat from then and now intoxicated me, casting a delirious ecstasy.

The significance of this memory revealed itself through the smack of rough lips. Then. Not now. Mine. But not ours. Despite craving his lips, ours didn't touch, but the passion of another reminded me of what we had.

I paused, my chest pressed to Milo's as he wrapped his arms around me, holding me almost as tightly as his mind held the last night Finn, him, and I spent together. Normally, I'd pull away, wait for the memory to fade, and continue. I had to; it was the only way to keep a piece of Milo in my life without the haunting memories of Finn. But here and now, I found myself longing to swim in this powerful moment no matter the tragic result of time. I thrust harder, grunting over his shallow breaths, allowing my buried memories to return.

Finn pressed to my back, a hand wrapped around my throat, another on my hip, directing my strokes as the three of us entangled in blissful sex. Finn bit my earlobe.

"I love you," he whispered.

I moaned, tugging a younger Milo's hair to pull him closer. Back then I did anything to silence myself from uttering those words, reciprocating my feelings. I kissed Milo's nape. Again and again. Milo panted. My teeth chattered so I bit him, softly, delicate, but enough to quell my own eruption. Finn pushed me forward atop Milo, who squeezed my wrists, mouth searching for mine. Finn's hand on the small of my back guided my every movement.

Close. So close here and then, I couldn't tell which was happening when. I kissed Milo, eager to relive every second of what we had. What we could've had. What we might still have.

Finn rolled me aside. I lay next to him while he straddled Milo, whose hands found both our most sensitive parts. Joining Milo, I ran a hand along Finn's slick chest, and my mouth finally found Milo's. Then and now. Living this magical joy made it impossible not to allow their wave of passion to engulf me. I could feel my excitement. I could feel everyone's orgasm inching closer. But I wasn't ready. I needed more. For him. For me. For them.

Milo of now throbbed against my stomach. His pleasure then, as his hips popped against Finn. The sheer thrill of our bodies locked in constant motion. Magics flowing. The bed became distant as we channeled together, lost in an endless space.

"I can't. I'm going to…"

"Wait." Milo gripped my face, kissing my chin, unable to find my mouth but drawing me back to the now. His memories quelled. Mine, lost because all I wanted in this exact moment was him and his pleasure. I stared at his beautiful glossy blue eyes, lips trembling. This was the present.

Milo whimpered as I continued. I hugged him tightly, unwilling to let this moment between us end so suddenly. I wanted to hold on to it forever. To us forever. To him forever.

"Fuck," Milo said.

I'd finally released him, resting my head on his shoulder, wheezing.

"This is why I don't bottom."

"You just did," I said, reaching for a cigarette.

"Gimme one."

I lit a cigarette for each of us. Milo hated the first drag. Fire engulfed the inhale, making the hit harder as embers at the tip sparked. I set an ashtray neatly tucked between our thighs, which didn't prevent our calves from overlapping or our toes from curling against each other.

"I thought you hated smoking."

"Who turns down a smoke after a good fuck?" Milo inhaled lightly. "I know it's what I wanted, but damn, I had forgotten that feeling."

I blew smoke against his, slightly eager to mount him again, but settled on my smoke overtaking his. Gray haze collided, smokey silhouettes recreating our passion with a bit of telekinesis to assist the smoke.

Milo ran his fingers through my hair, massaging the tension that built from telepathy. He knew the spots better than anyone especially for the headaches that hadn't quite formed. I could read where he carried his tension, and he could predict where mine would soon explode. It should have been picture-perfect. But the best pictures had a glimpse of the past, where they came from, so they'd know how they ended up there. We'd lost that.

Something which continuously ate away at me.

"You want me to go home?" Milo rubbed my neck.

"Not a chance. Just thinking. Overthinking."

"You can't have my crown." He leaned in close, and I combed my fingers through his spiky blond hair. Sweat drooped their points. I inhaled his cologne mixed with the smell of us. "Maybe we just stay up all night, blow off our weekend plans. You cancel your little Saturday teaching thing; I'll reschedule my guild mission thingy. We can blow something better for the weekend." Those playful eyes stilled, casting an expression of longing, concern, quiet. "*I should just say it. Tell him how I...*"

Feel? Likely, but he buried the thought. I wanted that to be what he thought. I wanted him to tell me how he felt for me. I wanted the courage to tell him how I felt, how I'd always felt, how I always would. Instead, I did what I do best, and kept it to myself.

"I've been so preoccupied this semester, dropping the ball every chance I get. I'd like to make sure the kids get these little opportunities to practice."

His eyes were vacant, lost in a daze. I traced my fingertips down his sharp jaw, tickling his chin. Milo's minxy grin returned. "Please, I've been on a dozen of those panels. They just hand out fledgling permits."

"I know fledgling permits aren't the be-all-end-all for the kids, but it's their first stepping-stone into the industry. I wanna make sure they have a successful introduction." I kissed his neck. "That said, we can still stay up. I'm fine functioning like a zombie tomorrow."

Milo kissed my hand. "No. You need your rest. Gotta be in tiptop shape for the kiddos."

Every part of Milo captivated me. Always had. Always would. I wanted to hold onto that. I drifted off, lying against Milo's chest, his arms wrapped around me. Another dreamless night where his dreams, his hopes for the future, his longing memories of Finn allowed me to finally put a piece of the past to rest.

Chapter Twenty-Seven

I arrived at Gemini Academy early, savoring a cigarette before the kids arrived for our Saturday training. It was doubtful more than a handful would show, given all the grief they gave me over losing their weekend.

I wanted to spend more time with Milo. It was exciting and unnerving. But he had a big day of his own planned, something to prevent the wrong future. He always had a plan. So here I was in the staff parking lot, missing him.

Missing him.

I couldn't make sense of any of it. After avoiding my grief for so long, it felt wrong to unearth it. Worse still to let it go. Looking forward felt a lot like abandoning Finn and failing him again. But as uneasy as it was, having Milo there beside me kept me steady. I couldn't continue making the same mistakes by rejecting happiness because the potential fallout made all the joy unbearable. I'd chase it, embrace it, accept all the ridiculousness of love.

More than anything, I wanted to tell Milo I loved him. Milo was a piece of me. A piece I couldn't let go of.

"Ew, so gross. Are you seriously smoking, Mr. Frosty?" Gael strolled alongside his familiar. About a hundred Tobacco Truth campaigns played on a loop in his head, while his rooster faked a cough. That fucking bird.

More students walked across the parking lot, the entire class trickling in one by one. I dropped my cigarette, smashing the butt into the gravel.

"It seems everyone made it. Good. Means we won't have uneven numbers for today's game."

Curiosity popped up in them all.

"Having reviewed the classification types you're each applying for, I think everyone will enjoy today's training." Okay—they'd be miserable by noon, but it'd do them good, and it was nice putting things aside, leaving it to Milo. "Hope no one's afraid of a few bruises. We're gonna be playing an ole fashioned game of offense versus defense."

Among the twelve students, three rose to the top. Three I'd followed closely this semester.

"With the work I've put into my roots this semester, I can handle either."

"Hell yeah. I've got the best offense here. I'll win this."

"It needs more work, but if I end up on the defensive side, I might be ready."

"Let's go."

Once inside, I went to the proctoring room to engage the enchantment system and make sure every safety protocol was in place. I didn't need any students injured. Despite Kenzo's aggressive nature, he was the best at holding back his magic. A few others casted too wildly—something we'd need to fine tune before their exam. No need for any red flags preventing them from obtaining fledgling permits.

"Is this gonna be like the capture the flag training we did?" Gael asked as I joined them by the fitness section. "Because King Clucks and I crushed that."

Kenzo glared at Caleb and Katherine, unwilling to drop his guard if paired against them a second time. I wouldn't make that mistake again. Those two had a lot of baggage to unravel, not the kind that'd resolve itself overnight, and something I hoped to subtly mend over the next three years. Well, two. Since the new academy motto meant stealing our third-year students and throwing them into the deep end.

I grinned. The next three years. Because they'd have those three years to grow and learn. They'd have more to follow. I believed it fully in my heart.

"Oh no. Mr. Frosty's smiling." Gael sighed in unison with his rooster's cluck. "That can only mean he's got something pure evil planned."

"Nothing nefarious, honestly. Think of today like a marathon of magic. I've set up several games—I use the term loosely—because this won't be fun for anyone." I glared, hiding joy as they squirmed at what they'd signed up for. They'd struggle now, but I could guarantee they'd all perform better when applying for their fledgling permits. "Everyone will get the chance to show off all they've learned this semester and gain a few new skills. Before we begin, I want to explain how each event works, from the obstacle course, wisp hunting, the relay race…"

Confusion and anxiety swirled, but someone's unyielding hatred hacked through the students' thoughts. I shuddered.

"I thought you said this was only for our class."
"What kind of magic is that?"

"*That's a warp portal from the cosmic branch.*"
"**No one at our academy uses that magic.**"
"Is this part of the training?"
"What's with those masks?"   "*Siniestro.*"
"*They look like fiends.*"
"*That feeling of hatred is too intense.*"   "No. He can't be here."

I gulped, quelling their minds and tuning out their voices. My insides completely hollowed as I turned. Standing before a crystallized blue doorway stood four warlocks. Each wore a disfigured, sleek black mask in the form of a fiendish face. The erratic mind standing in the center was a familiar one I'd encountered, one I'd observed in the depths of Tara's ocean.

Theodore Whitlock.

He wore a tattered bloody hoodie and strolled ahead of the other three warlocks toward my class.

"Oh, I get it. This is one of the games. They're supposed to be playing fiends or some shit. Super creepy, Mr. Frosty, but King Clucks and I came to win."

I scanned the enchantments lined along the walls of the auxiliary gym where none had triggered from the unregistered magic which brought these warlocks. So much for academy precautions. Gael waltzed forward.

"Stop moving, Gael," I snapped, hoping it covered the quiver in my voice.

A man with a blue tie traced his fingers against the blue portal. It rippled, vanishing into droplets. The man next to him wiggled his fingers, tightening the leather gloves over his hands, and traced a glowing green sigil in the air.

A searing pop hit my thigh. Lights in the auxiliary gym flickered, dying out. The kids panicked, but we weren't in complete darkness, with the glass ceilings allowing a cloudy overcast to illuminate the area. I pulled my phone from my pocket. Dead instantly. That sigil was a branding placed on the area. The warlock faction had someone who branded fiends within the minds of branchless witches. Given the dead phones, it was easy to guess he'd cast a rule to disrupt nearby technology. Did he also affect the enchantments of the academy? So quickly?

There were four warlocks here. Theodore possessed some ungodly branch involving fiends, one I didn't fully understand but knew held destructive capability and likely helped Dr. Kendall with her experiments. Blue Tie was the warlock who could travel between planes; he was one to carefully watch since he could open and close doorways, traveling instantaneously. Leather Gloves provided the brands. Clearly, he channeled quickly since it took him seconds to isolate us in the dark without triggering the safety alarms.

I eyed the lone woman in a white dress, backlit by the portal, stained by trickling black ooze. Her silent mind made it impossible to gauge anything from her just like the branchless warlock, Alexander, whose mind was silenced by a brand containing someone else's hex magic. If I were a guessing man, which I hated doing, I'd say she possessed counter. If I tried to force myself deep into her thoughts or the others, she might put me out of commission by knocking my magic back at me tenfold.

Fuck. They were all dangerous. Of course they were.

My fingers trembled. My knees shook. Was this dread mine or the students? I took a shaky breath, resisting chattering teeth. I needed to end this fast.

"I need you all to find the exit, get out of the academy, and—"

"But Mr. Frost…" Tara's fear and guilt collided with mine, creating a whirlpool of doubt.

"Now." I couldn't fixate on their minds and keep them safe.

Was this it? The void vision come to fruition? No. Milo had a plan. He saw the ending; I helped him piece it together. Maybe he was on the way. He'd storm through the doors with a dozen enchanters any second. Bust through the glass ceiling, providing sunshine to the dreary gray sky above.

"No, no, no. No one's going anywhere." Theodore shook his finger. "Ernesto, be a dear."

Blue Tie extended his arms like a showman about to take a dramatic bow. Multiple portal doorways formed around me and my students, each permeating a foul stench. It carried rot and death into the auxiliary gym.

"Wait," I said. If they fell through any of those doorways, I might never find where they'd landed.

What did these warlocks want?

"Come now. I'm summoning you. Feed upon these sycophants to a system opposing our existence." Theodore panted heavily beneath his mask, hollow blue eyes twinkling behind the fiendish face he wore. *"My fiends are going to devour all of your students, Dorian Frost."*

I backstepped, channeling magic, uncertain where to prioritize my power.

Humidity wafted from the blue portals. Hot and sparking. These portals weren't meant to take the students anywhere; they were designed to bring something through. Static popped. Gray electricity snapped against blue, crackling with a whip of lightning. Three doors vanished. Two more. The air cooled. Kenzo's eyes fluttered, searching for the next one producing heat. He didn't cast indiscriminately. He studied them, reserving his magic for when he needed to utilize his branch most. He'd figured out they were being used to usher in fiends.

Fiends Theodore Whitlock controlled.

"Kenzo," I said, eyes locked on Theodore. "Create a clear path for the others and leave."

"No. I can help."

"Me too." Caleb boldly stepped forward, the absolute last person I wanted here in this dire situation.

    "Yeah."   "*Maybe.*"   "I'm not ready for this."
"These are actual warlocks."   "*I don't wanna die.*"
    "We should contact enchanters."
"*That guy's using sigils. I could probably decipher them.*"
    "Don't do this, Theo."

"Enough. This isn't a suggestion. Get out of here." I clenched my abdomen, barely levitating off the ground. With a powerful telekinetic burst, I soared ahead, the tips of my shoes dragging along the dirt. No real flight. Not yet. Not until I reached Theodore. He quickly struck out with telekinesis, as predicted.

I propelled above, all levitation, swung behind him, and gripped his shoulders. With a knee to his back, I channeled telekinetic energy into the strike, dropping him to the ground hard. I'd break him first then the others.

I reeled back my fist, enough magic to create a telekinetic burst that'd render him unconscious. His mind went silent. The others became hazy. I leapt back. Silver shimmered as the woman in white sliced where I'd been a second ago.

"Missed." Her voice was light and playful. "Well, if at first you don't succeed."

"No games, Darla," Theodore said.

"Boo. That's no fun," she said, slashing the air between us.

I unclenched my abdomen, releasing the levitation. Hitting the ground, I quickly skirted by Darla. The counter was invisible to the naked eye, but if she'd hit me while using levitation, who knew how my magic would react. I sent a telekinetic strike, knocking her off her feet. She flipped backward, silencing my next two attempts.

Bright blue illuminated my shadow. I spun around, tilting my head as outstretched glowing green fingertips reached out.

"So close," he said.

"Vincent, fall back," Ernesto said as his warp portal grew.

"No, stay." I clutched his wrist, preventing him from entering the portal.

Channeling telekinesis, I headbutted Vincent. No escaping. Again, I channeled another headbutt.

They coordinated well. Ernesto's warp portals sent them striking from all directions. Darla's counter made it impossible to get a clean read off them. I kept up with my combat training so I could best instruct students, but clashing with magic at this level, lives at stake, wasn't something I could do for long. Without being able to rely on my branch, I couldn't hold them forever.

That said, I had Vincent in my grasp. Taking him out of commission wouldn't undo the enchantment brands he'd already set, but it'd prevent a further headache.

Releasing his wrist, I directed telekinesis into my palms and knee. I'd give him a concussion that'd last for days. My foot slipped. Blue rippled beneath.

Floating to escape, I ground my teeth. Vincent waved, vanishing in blue. Darla's giggle drew my attention. Her blades slashed, sending unseen threats. Sweat pooled on my forehead.

With the portal below, I couldn't release my levitation. With a newly formed one above, I couldn't fly up. Any move I made would lead to a new trap.

Flaming spikes splintered apart in front of me. The fire smothered to embers, absorbing the counter Darla hurled.

"Not fair," she whined.

Gael stood poised with outstretched arms, his spikes swelling. Melanie stayed behind him, her lighter trembling in her grip.

"Hex this, bitch." Kenzo soared toward Darla.

"No," I shouted.

Gray static engulfed Kenzo, his rage contained, mind clear. Unable to predict Darla's intentions, I rushed toward them. He was skilled but not at the level meant to hold his own against warlocks; he was fifteen years old. She sliced chaotically. Kenzo bounced back and forth in the air, dodging her invisible strikes, aiming his disruption. Her hand sizzled, and she dropped a blade.

"Ow. Not nice. Not nice at all." Darla sliced the rest of Kenzo's gray static, fizzling his electricity to nothing.

I hovered between them. "I told you to leave."

"Don't be stupid. You need our help."

That might be true, but if they stayed, it'd put Caleb's life in danger. All their lives. No one was harming my students. Nothing was going to make that void vision occur.

Darla slipped through a portal, falling back to join the others. I needed to keep an eye on their next move.

"*Where the hell are my fiends?*" Theodore stormed toward my students, and I braced my magic, preparing to attack. "Why haven't they crossed through?"

The portals surrounding the students widened.

"It's not my gates," Ernesto said, his voice shaky.

"Well, if the ones I prepared don't want to come out and play, I'll make new fiends."

Theodore's mind raged, searching the auxiliary gym. His eyes lingered on the vents containing wisps. Tara approached Theodore, floating between him and the class, blocking my shot. Dammit. "Why are you doing this?"

"Why?" He cackled. "All I've ever wanted was to spit in our old man's face. Show the world the absurdity of this system we feed into. My dalliance with the Night of the Fiend Massacre was too bold. I see that now. Too many factors I didn't comprehend. Like that trash enchanter meddling where he doesn't belong."

A bloody filter coated the image of Milo that Theodore held in his thoughts. Where was Milo? Didn't he predict this happening? I couldn't fight them alone.

"You choose to attack guilds? Hurt people, kill them?" Tara quivered.

"Merely me stabbing Daddy's pride."

"And Waukegan? You massacred so many people. They weren't even connected to Whitlock Industries."

"Huh?" Theodore's mind buzzed over countless horrors he'd involved himself in over the years, across the nation, the globe. I ground my teeth, quelling the death blissfully booming inside him. "Oh, tragic little Tara. How much you don't know. But yes, I recall the massacre—if you'd call it that—of the tiny free bird guild. The one deluding itself with independence from the machine we call established order. They were lying to themselves, so I released them from their delusions of grandeur. Besides, you don't wage wars without a few simulations."

Somber tears splashed against the rage within Kenzo. He cocked his head, absorbing the fiend attacks Theodore orchestrated. Fury melded with his magic. Static coated his entire body.

"You attacked Phoenix Guild?"

"I'm sorry, who are you?" Theodore peered around Tara. His blue eyes were haunting in their hollow curiosity.

"Five years ago. Were you involved in the attack that led to eighteen deaths?" Gray static sparkled along Kenzo's sharp jaw, his entire body tense and trembling.

"I may've sent a few fiends. It's a nifty branch I've got. Wanna know how it works?"

Kenzo flicked his fingers, and Darla's discarded dagger whipped into his hand by telekinesis. He soared ahead, no hesitation. Disruption erupted from him, coiling around Theodore. I raced behind Kenzo, his emotions too erratic to catch up to his mind or the movements of his body.

"Nice hex magic." Theodore blocked Kenzo's blade with his own. "But it can't affect me unless I'm casting."

Kenzo punched Theodore's chest, propelling him back with concentrated telekinesis. He flopped against the ground, toppling over a few times before digging the blade into the dirt. Steadying himself, he rose as Kenzo's gray lightning gave chase.

"Don't need to disrupt your magic, just keep you from casting while I gut you!" Kenzo leapt again, closing their distance, disrupting the portal behind Theodore, and cutting off escape.

"Wait!" I flew faster. The doorway was a diversion.

I grabbed Kenzo by his sleeve, keeping him from falling into another. A petite hand slipped through a tiny blue bubble, stabbing my shoulder. I winced. Hovering next to Kenzo, I surveyed the terrain. No one.

"Let go of me." He resisted my grip.

Blue light. A slice along my calf sent a searing pain up my leg.

Pocket portals opened and closed in every direction. Anxiety swimming in the auxiliary gym made it impossible to focus. Constant blue lights left spots in my vision. I hurled Kenzo away. Tiny cuts hacking at my back, chest, arms, legs, and face.

I descended, but the lights followed, swift slashes chasing. Kenzo's disruption mixed with the portals, removing them as I landed.

He dropped to the ground, running toward me. "***I'm supposed to be better than this. Stronger. Think, idiot.***"

A hand gripped my shoulder, and fingers dug into the wound. Pressure throbbed, coursing down my entire arm and spreading across my chest like an agonizing web of shooting pain through my nerves. I shouted, but a cold blade to my throat kept my movements limited.

Kenzo froze. His angry face softened. "*No.*"

His frightened sadness blurred by my teary eyes.

"*I want you to understand why I'm doing this.*" Theodore jabbed his fingers deeper into my shoulder. I clamped my jaw, stifling a scream. His memories collided against my telepathy, exploiting pain to worm his way inside my head.

Darkness crashed alongside a dimly lit bedroom until all I could see was the mattress. I clenched my fingers, no sensation from the blanket. This wasn't happening. It had happened. I'd fallen into a mind.

"This won't be like last time." Dr. Kendall slinked toward me, her delicate touch the only thing settling the chaos in this room.

No. Not me. Theodore sat in a nearby chair. His hate slithered around, coiling across my chest like a serpent. I gasped.

"Why are you in such a good mood?" he asked.

Dr. Kendall straddled his hips, her telepathy humming a sweet tune, which eased the venom making my breathing shallow in this memory. "We had our first success today. Vincent's brands are truly flawless. You'll have to tell me where you found him."

There was a yearning to share. To trust. To give her every piece of himself. Doubt tore those desires apart. He'd given himself to others before. Trust was a daring thing he no longer possessed.

She kissed him. The flavor of strawberry beamed within him. Her hands unfastened his zipper. Theodore was swept into a primal urge, one met by the doctor who saw his truth, his face, his branch, and didn't shy.

"Stop." He pressed his forehead against hers, desperate for her to take all his hate but believing only one thing would rid him of it.

"Enjoy what we've achieved," she said, her voice rattling in his mind alongside songbird humming.

"No. I need to secure our little reservoir of fiends. This haunted hovel has become too cramped and drawn far too many eyes."

Disgust poured from him, a toxic fume casting a haze around the room. Each instinctive breath was like swallowing shards of glass. As someone who actively avoided menthols, it was a truly discerning sensation. How he hated scrounging in shadows to avoid Tobias Whitlock's ire.

He blinked, and the memory whirled away. All the color of the room fell to darkness.

Blackness replaced by crystalized blue light. It coated his skin in a blissful cooling sensation. Not enough to soothe his hate. *How'd they find us? Those sigils containing Darla's counter should've kept us unseen by anyone's magic. Even that trash, Enchanter Evergreen.*

He peered through the portal. I shivered. In the back alley, Theodore reached for a dagger, ready to pull me off Dr. Kendall. My hands wrapped around her throat. He was there when I...when I almost killed her.

"Dorian, stop." Milo's voice helped in resisting this twisting hatred.

Theodore squeezed the hilt of the blade, his hate pouring out as *Enchanter Evergreen* approached my slumped-over, nearly unconscious body. Fear kept Theodore locked in place. Finally regaining his composure, he crept back into the portal.

My mind was dragged along as the alley disappeared and a new memory blossomed.

He stood in a dark room, strumming his candy-coated fingertips on flashing buttons. They were sticky, sweet, and oddly intoxicating. "This is the only one they didn't find?"

"Yes. Did you find out where they're keeping the doc…" Ernesto recoiled, his voice distinct but the tone lacking the calm he'd had during his attack. His face was queasy. He had a young face, maybe a few years older than my students.

In the corner of this tiny surveillance room, the source of the scent Theodore savored revealed itself. Themselves. Several broken, bloody corpses. The glint of golden badges poked out of mouths they'd been jammed into. I fought against the memory, disgusted by the relishing pleasure Theodore derived in. Whether too exhausted from the battle occurring outside these memories or Theodore's understanding of telepathic minds, I remained trapped in these fleeting yet cumbersome memories.

"They knew nothing. I have one more lead to pursue on where my Dr. Kendall might be, but if that goes nowhere, we'll need to reevaluate where we go next."

"Next? They found almost every stash in one night. The news said it was flawless, and I mean, I didn't stick around, but it seemed perfectly coordinated. That's because they're aware of Vincent's enchantments. They have the doctor now. It's only a matter of time until…" Ernesto clammed up; Theodore's cold eyes locked on his frightened face. He ran his bloody fingertips across Ernesto's cheeks, resting his index finger on the young man's lips.

"We'll discuss that bridge when we cross it. Or burn it." Theodore chuckled. "Still got options."

Theodore strolled, his hatred hanging onto the hum Dr. Kendall whispered in his mind, giving him the tiniest of smiles. I trembled at the haunting laboratory revealed. Organs in jars. Aquariums filled with tar. Bright white wisps fluttered in smaller tanks, merging together, casting a calming heat that soothed Theodore. A massive lab with hundreds of glowing glass containers housing demonic energy. Yes, demonic energy circulated everywhere, the price of pollution to convenience our day-to-day lives. But with so many guilds actively working to banish it from our plane, it was incredibly disconcerting how someone obtained such large quantities without arousing suspicion.

"Before that, I need to find my Kendall."

Tobias flashed before my eyes, quickly replaced by a hacked-up image that Theodore craved most of all. The truck escorting a shackled Dr. Kendall replaced Tobias. News reports came next. Corpses toppled atop each other in a mountain of death. The Whitlock Banquet. Me. *Me.* Me beside a still Tara. White hot fury ignited everything in sight. "*You're the filthy telepath that attacked my Kendall.*"

I blinked. My eyes adjusted to the overwhelming rage wrapped within steady hatred.

The sun set early as Theodore crept toward my home. Hatred booming, dagger clutched in his hand. I shivered at the searing rage directed at me, a desire so palpable I felt his stabbing. He'd stalked me since meeting me at the party where we'd crossed paths and it wasn't lingering hatred I'd felt from Tara's memories but actually him following me to my home, waiting to gut me until Milo arrived.

He slinked away, memories silenced.

"I considered killing you then," Theodore said, drawing my disjointed telepathy back into an agonizing reality. "But what kind of message would that send? I'd gathered all those fiends. A plentiful, untapped resource." He pressed the blade closer to my throat, stilling the horrific images of his mind. Could he truly control that entire horde of demons? "Revenge alone wasn't enough. Why take out one meddling teacher—and a few current enchanters, depending on my luck—when I can topple the next generation?"

My neck burned. I reached to stop it, but prodding fingers in my shoulder slowed me.

"It's all about choices, and your interference helped make mine. I decided killing your entire class and destroying this academy would incite so much more panic. My fiends may be delayed, but that doesn't mean the fun's gotta end."

I gasped, choking. Theodore kept me in place, fingers digging into my shoulder, his other hand holding a reddened blade. Each breath tunneled my vision.

"Don't worry. It's shallow. You might live long enough to hear all their dying screams."

He released me. I collapsed, struggling to breathe. Each inhale was pure agony, grasping with slippery fingers to plug a flood that poured from me. The dirt pooled with dark red, sticky and warm against my clasped hand. I wheezed. So much blood. Faint screams. Muffled shouting. Quiet whispers. Everything became cold and hazy. I reached out with telepathy, finding nothing. Were they all dead? No. Not them.

    Darkness…

        Silence…

            Painless…

                Me…

Chapter Twenty-Eight

Dread quelled by the utter fucking cliché of death as I stood alone in an empty white room, awaiting fat, little cherubs carrying the attendance to check me in. Not sure I could call it much of a room since there was nothing in there. The slight lines of tile on the floor beneath me were the only sign I didn't float in infinite whitespace.

"How tacky, right? I don't make the rules, though." Finn appeared, a literal breath of fresh air as I inhaled without choking. Twenty-two years old, hands in his jean pockets, shoulders raised with a boyishly coy smile that held a secret.

An expression I'd memorized a million times over. The sparkle in his eyes, unblemished by death. The joyful glint an indicator he craved to divulge something. Normally, I'd glimpse his mind, play dumb and poorly react with feigned surprise or disinterest to whatever he'd come to share. Silly gossip, a new job, a flirty one-liner he'd spent hours on, or a confession of feelings I never gave the proper response to. Now, though, standing in this empty white void, his thoughts rang hollow. Empty. Secretive.

"Thinking you might've drained too much magic?" Finn brushed my bangs away, effortless, comforting.

"Or this isn't real."

"Oh, nice theory." Finn batted his long lashes, unfazed and flirty that I'd considered him a figment. Yep, this definitely wasn't real. "It could be some blissful neurons firing into your synapse, or is that the other way around? I can never remember. Or maybe this is limbo. Some afterlife collision of magics intertwining between planes of reality."

"Like when my magic merged with Milo's." The merger that brought the void vision, continued feeding that desperate desire to fix it, prevent it, and provide just enough clues to get the worst possible outcome. An outcome where all my students' lives were at risk. Per usual, I'd failed before I began, somehow making everything worse. If I hadn't meddled. Maybe…

"We have to run."

My eyes darted about the flickering white room, searching for the kid who said that. Screamed it. Yet, their voice was distant, muffled.

"They blocked the doors." A glimmer of crystalized blue shimmered.

I blinked a few times, piercing the veil between this empty space and the auxiliary gym. It'd faded as quickly as it'd appeared. I gripped my knees, hyperventilating. Finn's kind touch, rubbing the space between my shoulder blades, did nothing to ease this panic.

"Maybe you're breaking death's hold? That's a good sign, right?" Finn's arms hugged my waist, his chest warm against my back. His chin pressed to my injured shoulder, sending a searing reminder of pulsing pain outside this white room of limbo. "Sorry."

"What about Mr. Frost?" Caleb's voice rang clearer than the rest, muddled in mystery. "We can't leave him."

My neck tightened. I pushed Finn away, desperate for whatever air remained in this suffocating void. I couldn't breathe. There was too much pressure.

"Stop. You're blocking his airway. I-I-I've, I've got it."

"You sure, Carter?"

I exhaled, wobbling until my unsteady knees calmed. I might be dying, locked in here, but at least I could reminisce with Finn. His soft embrace. His friendly smile. His consideration.

"I'd say you're still very much fighting, just like them out there."

Fighting? Every fight I put up made things worse. I pushed through the infinite light, searching for a silent space, finding no matter how far I roamed, their voices remained.

"Don't run from this, Dorian," Finn said. "You can't keep running from things."

"I didn't run. I tried. I did so much to prevent that void vision. You have no idea," I snapped, blood spitting from my mouth and staining the white.

Finn brushed my lips, kind, gentle, and keeping me from the verge of tears. Maybe this truly was death. My mind concocted this white room while my body fought to live out there, surrounded by my students who'd soon die if they didn't escape.

"I know you tried," Finn said. "You know you tried. Obsessed, dwelled, regretted—everything."

"And somehow, I screwed everything up. Those warlocks are here because of me. I intervened. I drew their attention. I am going to get all of them killed."

I fled deeper into the white abyss. Their voices chased my every step.

"We need to stop these warlocks."

"No. Move Mr. Frost." "Run." "No. Fight them."

"Where'd they go?" "They disappeared."

"We need to stick together." "They're planning something."

"Fortify this place." "I'll send copies to scout."

Clasping my hands over my ears did little to silence the barrage of voices. The smell of sweat, blood, and dirt made each breath revolting.

"They fled because they're fucking cowards." Kenzo seethed, his angry words casting a filter of red that veiled around me like a giant tarp. "**That warlock isn't getting away from me. I'll rip his goddamn heart out.**"

Even with my body dying, my magic drained, it appeared some part of my telepathy still worked.

"That's not why they left. The doors are already blocked. My guess is he's looking for the wisps the academy keeps in stock." Tara's voice was so soft and sad I almost didn't hear it, but after listening to her somber echo for so long, her voice rang like a pin drop cutting through the static. Each word that left her mouth cast a blue ripple, quelling the red consuming the white, a reminder of her sorrow. How sad death was. How sad life was.

"What's he doing with the wisps?"

"Theo possesses an arcane branch known as demonic resonance. It allows him to commune with fiends."

"Wait, Theo?"   "Who?"

"How do you know that, Tara?"

"Because he's my brother. He's here because of me. Everyone's

lives are in danger because of me."

Water splashed inside this empty void of death. Finn grabbed me. "It's not real. You know this better than anyone. Hold on, remind yourself what a mind can do. Hold on, listen to what a mind can think."

"Who cares?" Kenzo snapped. "I'm not afraid of these warlocks or a few fiends."

"I wouldn't be either with that branch."   "We should hide."

"We can't hide. The fiends will

just sniff out our magic."

"Fight them." "If the warlocks don't get us first."
"What if we just went through the warp portal?"
"Yeah, because that couldn't end badly."
They all spoke quickly, fueled by adrenaline, fear, and rage.

"Wait." Caleb's thoughts boomed. "*I need to account for everyone's magic here. Our homeroom. What roots they're skilled in. What their branches can do. The warlocks. Their abilities. Obstacles keeping us here.*" An intricate maze tunneling dark passageways in search of every possible exit that carried a safe success. "*I had an idea, but Tara's mention of fiends makes things more difficult. That enchantment blocking tech and magical alerts confines us. Mr. Frost's situation complicates things. A ticking clock with too many variables.*" Scattered webs fixated on the precarious situation, held certainties while allowing half-thoughts to fizzle out. "*Focus on what I know. Avoiding them is best, but not completely possible. That means only the best at predicting magic, what someone might use or how, is best. Is that me? Sort of, but Kenny and Tara are better at...*" Students argued, their voices fighting to carry above each other, but not over Caleb's thoughts. "*Katherine can...*" Static and deep wheezing muffled Caleb's mind. "*Carter needs to...*" The white room flickered. "*I think I've got it, maybe. Too many variables. Too many personalities. Too many things I don't know.*"

Caleb plotted, planning, pining for victory to a battle he should have never found himself in.

"I've got a plan." Caleb's certainty quieted their bubbling dread. "But everyone needs to do exactly what I say."

"Fuck that. Any plan you've got will get us all killed."

"Not if you hear me out, Kenny. Most of this hinges on your magic."

Thoughts erupted, surging, muting Caleb's voice. I fell to my knees, willing this false flooring to break, enveloping me deep into silence. What remained of my consciousness would collapse if I continued channeling the little magic I had.

"*Told you it'd be a breeze,*" Milo's young voice called out. I followed it through the bright white, wondering where the real Milo was. "*And you were worried about landing your fledgling permit.*"

"*I wasn't worried.*" My surly, younger voice echoed. "*The most difficult part of those panels is trying not to doze off because of how boring it gets.*"

"*I was hoping for something exciting. A chance to really show off my magics.*"

Why hadn't Milo arrived? Shown up to protect the kids. Protect me. I squeezed my hands against my chest, fighting back so much doubt. Did he lie about having a solution, or had my interference once again somehow screwed everything up? The reverberations of the memory drew me in, something pleasant before it all faded to nothingness.

Whispering voices clawed, students planning, but they became distant like they stood atop a cliff, calling out to a watery quarry I dwelled deep within. I quelled what remained of my telepathy, desiring calm.

"You shouldn't be hiding from their fear because of your own." Finn consoled me, rubbing his hand softly against my back.

"I'm not hiding. I'm already dead; there's no point."

"You're not dead yet. Why don't you reach out and listen?"

"I can't. My body's too injured. My telepathy won't work."

"You sure about that?" Finn had a questioning grin. "Seems there's a few minds you've established close links to this semester that still haven't severed, even in this state."

Caleb. Kenzo. Tara. Each of their minds drew me away from this white room, desperate to know what occurred out there.

"No." I shouted. "It's too much."

"Why not follow those threads?"

"I can't." I covered my face, blocking out Finn's image, this room, awaiting silence to take permanent hold.

"Are you frightened at what you'll see? That it might not be the closure you need?" Finn lifted my chin until I dropped my hands, fully absorbing his soft expression in this bright room.

"There's no such thing as closure." I caressed his face, forever twenty-two in my mind. "You're proof of that."

My mind wandered to when we found Finn's body, his corpse was so quiet when finally retrieved him. No lingering thoughts to unravel, truths to behold. I carried the wonder of his final moments with me the past twelve years.

"Even if I had the magic to follow their minds, I couldn't help them. They're on their own out there."

"Is it worse than never knowing?" He smiled, boyish, sweet, and unaffected by death that'd captured him so long ago.

He was right. I might be lying out there dying, but I couldn't leave this life not knowing.

Chapter Twenty-Nine

Caleb hid behind the bleachers. Of course, my magic found him first. Sought him above all others because everything moved closer and closer to the void vision. To his death. I hovered beside him through the willpower of my telepathy like a silent phantom observing death. Mine. His. All of theirs. Even in this noncorporeal state, I trembled. Sweat coated his face, but not the dread or terror signaling his dying moments. He gulped, staring at the space between rows.

Three fiends trudged together through the fitness equipment. The largest, almost human in size but quadrupedal, scattered machines with its elongated arms. It sniffed for magic with its slender snout. The other two, not bigger than house cats, strutted behind. My heart hurt. Who would take care of Charlie and Carlie when this was over? One of the tiny monsters extended its tongue and lapped at the dirt, tracking magic.

I joined Caleb in a bated breath, each of us too frightened an exhale might release noise. Though I was nothing more than a specter in this state. Caleb analyzed their size, the number of wisps required to conjure each fiend, and hoped Theodore's command didn't enhance their resistance to banishment.

No. Banishing wisps was one thing, but fiends were on an entirely different level. And you can't take three at the same time.

Caleb paused.

I dwelled on his magic. Yes, his roots were strong, but this was a next-level threat. He wasn't ready for that. None of them were.

```
Name: Caleb Huxley
Branch: N/A
```

He looked over his shoulder.

Did he hear me? A telepathic link involved more magic than I mustered. Yet, barely able to manifest myself here as I lay dying elsewhere, I think he heard. I sighed. Good.

"What are you doing here?" he whispered.

So much to say, so much to warn. I scrambled through a thousand missteps, deciding what he needed to know to avoid death.

Katherine crawled under the bleachers. "You can't do this on your own."

Oh. I huffed. I was truly haunted and haunting.

"I'm not. We've all got our parts to play. My job is to handle any straggler fiends that inch too close to your casting. For this to work, everyone has to do their parts. You're the only one smart enough to decipher those sigils jamming the alarms. The sooner they're broken, the sooner help arrives."

I relaxed a bit. They might be stuck here, but they worked together. Now, I just needed Katherine to convince Caleb to join her, wait it out for enchanters to arrive. Why hadn't they? Surely, Milo had some inkling of what'd happened, what could've. The white room called me back. I tensed, a phantom beside them, refusing to leave.

"I can break the brand after I help you."

"No. It's about more than that. You're keeping an eye out for Carter and Jennifer. They can't help." Caleb choked on his words, dread and death haunting him. Mine. "They can't do their part if they're looking over their shoulder."

"Don't be crazy. The only way you can take out three fiends is either all at once, which you can't do." Katherine grimaced, perhaps guilty over pointing out Caleb's weakness. "Or one at a time, but you'd need to maintain distance—which would require magic to create. Then they'd sniff you out and kill you."

My shoulders felt tight, tense alongside Caleb's recoiled body. He took a breath, steadying himself and leaving all the worry with me.

"That thought occurred. But I might know of one way you could help." Caleb nodded to Katherine's grimoire.

```
Name: Katherine Harris
Branch: Enchantment (Spell Craft)
```

She handed over her book. Caleb clutched the leather binding. Carefully, he flipped pages, tracing his fingers along the spells, fascinated by all the spells she'd crafted independently and others she'd made by combining classmates' magics. "How many of our classmates' branches did you make spells of?"

"Just about every first year. And almost everyone in our homeroom. Well, except Tara, Kenzo, and, um…"

"Me," he said, knowing he had nothing unique to offer her spell book but he dulled that thought with belief in how he'd make use of those pages. "Can I take out the ones I need?"

"Tear away. Take as many as you want."

Caleb tore a page. The crisp rip made him cringe. He looked at the fiends. They snapped their jaws at one another, fighting over territory and unaware of Caleb and Katherine. Caleb took a dozen pages and handed back her grimoire. Anyone with magic could use a preprepared spell from an enchantment so long as the witch creating the spell unlocked them. Katherine's fingertips glowed; the sigils reorganized, giving access to Caleb like she'd typed the pin to her phone for him.

"Thank you," he said. "Now, please go help the others."

"I still don't agree with this plan."

"You can yell at me later."

"Fine. Just don't die. It's harder to yell. Plus, I'd like to take you on another date. Obviously, you'd have to ask me out this time after all the yelling, duh."

"*This time?*" Caleb thought. "*Did she mean the Whitlock banquet? She said that was just a chance to meet enchanters, guild masters, like networking. Katherine never said it was a date. Was I not paying attention? No. I explicitly recall the word friends. Right?*"

Fuck, kid. His mind spun in a thousand different directions, overanalyzing their entire night. Focus on your life, Caleb.

Katherine kissed him on the cheek, then snuck off and left him in the clouds. His face turned bright red.

"Focus," I shouted.

He trembled.

"I have to focus," he said, his mind silencing a million desires he'd never experience if he died. He muttered one of Katherine's spells and slipped away from the bleachers. The abandoned page crackled. Flames burned brightly, engulfing the bleachers.

The largest fiend sprinted ahead, unaware of Caleb, and he took full advantage, banishing one of the smaller fiends. Its tarlike body shattered, unveiling a dozen brightly lit wisps. The other cat-sized fiend leapt to gobble its fallen comrade, its back swelling as the tar expanded with more demonic energy. In this state, it grew stronger but also more vulnerable.

Caleb kept a watchful eye on the first fiend. It devoured the magic in the air produced by the flames. Taking a deep breath, Caleb shook away the grogginess brought on by casting banishment and focused on finishing the further fiend as it grew. He managed to strike it, break apart the wispy remnants, and shift his focus to the final fiend. One far too big to take in a single strike. Still, it hadn't realized the fire, while bright, now burned on its own. The magic of Katherine's spell had faded. Caleb aimed his banishment.

Tar ripped from the fiend's back, oozy black droplets sparkled white above it as wisps bounced. Caleb slammed his palms together, channeling his magic to try again. Not fast enough. The fiend's jaw gaped. Its tongue stretched, extending above its head, lapping at the wisps. They clung to the slimy tongue, sliding into the fiend's gullet, its back restored.

Run. Please run. He couldn't banish a fiend in one strike, and if he couldn't do that, it'd keep restoring itself and hunting him.

Caleb released his hands, reaching for another page. The words shimmered as he muttered them. I'd missed too much of the spell he was casting, but it wasn't going to stop the fiend because Katherine's enchantments weren't at that level.

Frost stung Caleb's hands as he unleashed a tiny blizzard, freezing the fiend in place. He took a breath, channeling his banishment. Ice cracked. *"That ice magic from the primal branch isn't nearly as effective as the real thing."*

Of course not. No matter the power of an enchantment, it can only possess a fraction of the power contained.

The fiend lunged for the active magic, tackling Caleb. I shook, the world fuzzy and white. No. This wasn't how he died. Unless… I took a breath, calming myself long enough to watch Caleb roll back and forth with the fiend. It snapped its teeth, but Caleb kept his hands pressed firmly to its chest. The stench of rot was far more disgusting than he'd ever imagined. He winced at the acidic tar, scalding his palms and dripping onto him. But, despite all that horror—he remained calm and collected.

"Gotcha."

A bombardment of banishment flowed, blowing the fiend back. No. Not banishment. Another spell. He managed to recite it before the fiend tackled him. All the lingering black ooze evaporated, creating wisps, circling Caleb in search of magic and each other. Caleb banished them. The page continued assaulting the fiend, blasting sludge apart and giving him the chance to banish bits of demonic energy one at a time.

Smart. He couldn't handle the fiend independently, so he used a branch magic to break it apart and pick off the wisps before the fiend composed itself.

"Not bad, little witch." Vincent's voice chilled Caleb.

He resisted every urge to yelp or shake like a leaf in the wind.

"This is the enchantment warlock who cast that sigil Katherine's decoding. It's too dangerous to fight him." He levitated away. Good. Fall back. You've done enough. Instead of channeling his telekinesis and flying away, Caleb searched through a few spell pages. *"But I can't lead him to the others. That's what Tara's group was for—contingency three."*

How many contingencies did he have?

Flexing his fingers into a tight fist, Vincent snatched Caleb's enchantment pages away with a telekinetic grip. Caleb's fingertips trembled against the ripped edges in his hands. The warlock examined the drifting pages, grinning.

"You plan on using your spell craft against me?" he snickered.

"Oh, your enchantments are pretty pathetic."

"Those aren't mine," Caleb said, his voice weak.

"They wouldn't help you much, anyway." Vincent unbuttoned his shirt, exposing the sigils tattooed on his torso in the form of reddish brown scars he'd branded, which gave him access to easily a dozen other branches. "See, spell craft is a pretty mundane magic from the enchantment branch. One-hit wonders, I say. My brand magic is forever. Unending so long as I can channel."

Caleb reached for pages folded in his back pocket. Vincent traced a glowing green fingertip along the sigil placed on his lower abs. Tiny green flames ate the pages he'd stolen from Caleb. Fear consumed him, and he kept the remaining few tucked away.

"Where are your little friends?"

Caleb didn't respond.

"Okay. I hate the easy way, too." He traced a finger along the sigil opposite his heart, swiping his free hand in the air.

Nothing. No magic.

Caleb gasped, plummeting to the ground. No. Was that the other warlock, Darla's, counter in effect? Surely, Vincent had access to her magic. Caleb stopped midway.

"That was close," he thought. *"That lady's magic was invisible but from a hex branch like Kenny's. I need to figure out how many different magics this guy has access to before leading him anywhere."*

He easily identified the number of sigils and accounted for their convenient placement. I doubted Vincent would have others elsewhere on his body since he needed to make contact to activate them.

Vincent's fingertips strummed a sigil branded opposite his fire brand. Green light whipped through the air. No. It was the air. A strong gust hurled Caleb back, knocking him off his feet. He levitated to steady himself, staying locked in the wind. Why?

"Hexes affect any magic they strike," he thought. *"So long as I stay within his whirlwind, he can't target my root magics with a hex without muting his own brands."*

Caleb took Darla's copied magic into account. Clever. But he forgot one very important aspect: Vincent had two primal magics we knew about. And the pair possessed were incredibly compatible.

The wind ignited, whirling a green inferno toward Caleb.

Caleb crashed to the ground. Embers singeing his clothes. That was close. Had he tried to outrun the flames instead of ceasing his magic, he might've died right there. My heart thumped. Slow, distant, but beating. Each time, agonizing.

I flailed, grasping at anything and everything, resisting the white room. Finn's presence. Death. No. Caleb. I had to know.

He vanished. The entire world disappeared. No Finn. No death's door waiting room. Just the abyss of nothingness awaiting me this time.

Water splashed. Droplets hit my face. I blinked, ignoring the agony. Struggling to move, hands held me in place while others stayed firmly pressed to my throat.

It's too much.   *I can't count all the open wounds.*
     All this blood.   *I shouldn't be here.*
       I wanna go home.   *I'm not ready for this.*
My magic can't stop this.   *If it'd stayed home, I'd be safe.*
     Why won't he stop bleeding?   *It's useless.*

Tears streamed down Carter's face, guilt striking with each drop. I caused this. I didn't know him. His shame was foreign due to my neglect. Ignoring Milo, chasing Caleb's death. Avoiding my other students, failing Caleb in the process. Had I done better, tried harder…

```
Name: Carter Howe
Branch: Rejuvenation (Vitality)
```

My failure left my students alone in their terror, broken. I couldn't even die right.

I want to go home…
I can't fix it. Why won't he stop bleeding?
If he'd stop bleeding…
There shouldn't still be this much blood…
Every time I stop one injury,
his throat opens back up.
FUCK. *I'm useless…*
If I stay, the fiends might come here and kill us…
I don't wanna die.
I can't leave, though. I have a job.
One worthless job…

I grabbed Carter's wrist, trembling, the both of us. I coughed, gurgling, and unable to speak. Pain seized me, but I couldn't release my grip. He had to know it was okay to leave. To run. Abandon me and survive.

"Stop." Jennifer grabbed my hand, delicately freeing Carter's wrist from my grasp. "*There's so much fear and terror floating around. I can't stop it all. It's too much for me, but…*"

Connected to Jennifer, I saw her magic in full force, radiant auras from all the emotions swimming through the auxiliary gym, but with her magic in effect a luminous white swelled within her, consuming everything else in the vicinity.

"*I can take his fear.*"

```
Name: Jennifer Jung
Branch: Psychic (Empathic)
```

Jennifer squared Carter's shoulders; a ghost of magic siphoned the sickly pale yellow which consumed his aura. His fear oozed into the white light, swallowed, and buried deep inside Jennifer's gut.

"What happened?" Carter's voice calmed, and his mind went blank.

"It's a trick I learned from Mr. Frost's channeling packet assignment."

Witches who match each other's frequencies could enhance their root magic when casting together. But Jennifer learned how to harness the emotions of others by studying the frequencies their feelings casted. It'd help her repel or, in this case, absorb emotions.

"Now, walk me through what you're going to do," Jennifer said.

"I have to close the wound on his throat," Carter said.

"How are you going to do that? How's your magic going to do that?"

"My rejuvenation branch stems on vitality. Increasing his flow of magic, muscular system, even speeding up the healing process. But I can't replace his lost blood."

"It sounds like you can do a lot, though." Jennifer's calm voice was soothing, helping Carter relax by asking questions about things she likely already understood.

They worked together, patching my broken body. I took shallow breaths, pain still coursing but easing. I lay there drifting between this blurry space, flickering white death, and Caleb. What happened to him?

Jennifer winced. A sharp pain in her back.

"What's wrong?" Carter asked, shaky hands wrapped over my throat.

"Nothing, just goosebumps."

"Don't do that again."

It wasn't, though. Jennifer quelled terror and pain connected to Caleb, prioritizing Carter and myself. I couldn't do that. My desire propelled me away from this corpse the two of them sought to resurrect, seeking Caleb again, hopeful he was alive. Hopeful all of them were alive when this ended. If it ended.

Caleb lay on the ground, clothes tattered and scorched, face sweating and filled with exhaustion. But no terror. This wasn't good. Observing from beside Caleb, I tried to gain more visuals on Vincent. No notable weapons—no daggers—but as Caleb's thoughts hinted, this guy was a weapon.

"Nowhere left to run," Vincent said. "Maybe try those flimsy spells since you clearly don't have any magic of your own."

Caleb's fingers lingered on the pages tucked in his back pocket. His mind raced over every scenario he'd considered this entire time. His swift heartbeat rang in his ears, pumping hard as he concluded to see a reckless plan through.

"No," I shouted. "Run. Hide. Find the others. Now."

"*Ignore the doubt.*" Caleb ground his teeth. "*This is the only way.*"

"You know, I got in this trying to help branchless witches like you. You need a real enchantment. Real magic, like myself."

"I learned from a friend that sometimes too much magic can hinder a witch." Caleb dug his fingers into the dirt. "Besides, all those borrowed branches you've got aren't as effective as the real thing."

He'd observed each sigil in action, analyzed how Vincent's branch worked, the limitations to his branded magics, and assessed how to defeat him. There was a time for every enchanter to collaborate with others, utilize tools of the trade to create the best possible outcome, but sometimes a witch had to stand on their own feet. Caleb recalled how far he'd come on his own magic.

"You're just a Jack-of-All-Trades." Caleb propelled to his feet and punched Vincent in the gut. Vincent backstepped, sweaty and panting. His fingers traced a sigil. "Go ahead. I already know which knockoff brand you're gonna choose and how to counter it, and honestly, you're not that impressive."

Vincent held out his arms, dragging Caleb toward him with a powerful telekinetic grip. He squeezed Caleb's neck. "Jack-of-All-Trades, huh? What's that make you, branchless brat? A four of clubs?"

Caleb slipped his hands between Vincent's arms, channeling telekinesis in his forearms. When the hell had Caleb learned to focus his roots to specific muscles of his body so precisely? It broke the warlock's hold. Telekinesis funneled down into Caleb's legs. He levitated, spinning with all the force of a whirlwind, and struck Vincent's head against the hard ground. "I'm the wild card."

A gamble, certainly. Baiting Vincent into believing Caleb was falling back to run instead of evaluating his sigils. Dangerous attempts to get close enough to strike him with a telekinetic blow and render the man unconscious. Still, very clever. All of Vincent's sigils worked on distancing himself from others when fighting. He wrote brands but clearly preferred relying on his sigils.

The terror tingling along Caleb's skin hadn't settled. Adrenaline pumped through his veins. He used one of Katherine's spells to release a binding magic that would hold Vincent if he awoke before they escaped.

"Not such useless spell craft magic now, huh?" He secured the golden ropes of Katherine's enchantment around an unconscious Vincent.

Though sweaty and bruised, Caleb smiled with confidence.

Wild Card. I should write that down. Every good enchanter needs a quality catchphrase. Something with public appeal, that's what Enchanter Evergreen would say." Even fighting for his life, Caleb thought about his future, the future I hoped he'd have.

Chapter Thirty

I drifted alongside Caleb as he sprinted through what remained of the fitness section of the auxiliary gym. His eyes darted about, sensory in full use, searching for any approaching fiends.

A spike of guilt drew me away. In a blink, I found myself hovering behind Tara. Her heart pinched. Her thoughts fixated on me. Why?

"I should've used my magic. Should've told someone about Theo. Should've never believed him. Should've protected Mr. Frost. This is all my fault."

But it wasn't. It was mine. I'd meddled to save one student and brought this horror down upon them all.

Tara floated above Jamius. He was surrounded by four fiends, crawling backward. She hesitated, wanting to use her branches, test her skills, but understood this was not the time for that. She had to think of everyone else. Images of my bloody, beaten body flashed in her mind, nearly drawing me back to my dying flesh. Tara couldn't waver this time.

```
Name: Tara Whitlock
Branch: Ward (Sealing)
Branch: Cosmic (Shadows)
Branch: Arcane (Intangibility)
```

A small fiend lunged at Jamius. Yellow teeth snapping. I tensed. Tara banished it entirely. Her strike was poised and precise, nullifying the wispy remnants as well. She appeared effortless in the motion, channeling her roots simultaneously. Sweat dripping down her brow revealed the strain that proficient cast took.

"Heads up." Yaritza flew past Tara, hurling a flurry of flaming pebbles.

```
Name: Yaritza Vargas
Branch: Cosmic (Star Shower)
```

Dread consumed me. The barrage tore through the tarred bodies of the fiends surrounding Jamius, but her reckless throw hit him, too. Tara's annoyance quelled my panic. Jamius' body burst into watery remains.

Oh.

I sighed.

"I told you to stop doing that." Jamius floated behind them, wobbling because he still needed work on his root magics.

"I said heads up," Yaritza said. "It's not my fault your clone didn't listen. Maybe make the next one a better listener."

```
Name: Jamius Watson
Branch: Alteration (Duplication)
```

"I can only make so many clones in a day. We'll lose all our decoys at this rate. How am I supposed to lure out fiends if you keep destroying them?"

Jamius' clones—made purely from liquids and magic—would easily attract fiends. A smart plan that endangered no one and afforded the rest of the coven time to strike the demonic energy from a safe distance.

Tara ignored their bickering, banishing the broken fiends before they regained composure. "He's right, Yaritza. You're only supposed to use your branch if we encounter a warlock."

"Then I can demolish them." Yaritza punched her fist.

"No," Tara sighed. "Let's just keep moving."

Caleb's plan clung to the surface of her mind as she soared ahead. Jamius and Yaritza struggled to keep up with Tara. She used sensory, tracking fiends along the way to the proctoring room and alerting Jamius to entice them out. Their job was to clear the path of any fiends along the way to the proctoring room. With the exits blocked off by warp portals, they needed to break the branded sigils blocking tech, get to the proctoring room, and alert the authorities.

If they encountered any warlocks along the way, Yaritza had one job: scatter enough comets above to signal the others, and then their coven was supposed to withdraw.

Luring fiends didn't fall on her group's to-do list, only eliminating ones along the path, but Tara paused, guilt and fear battling within her. She banished two more fiends. Then three. Then one larger one. Each exploded due to her proficiency. *My jaw was as slack as Jamius' and Yaritza's.*

Gael was out there, dragging too far behind them, and she wanted to clear the path when he caught up.

"*I shouldn't have left him alone.*" Tara doubled back, floating between Jamius and Yaritza.

"What're you doing?" Jamius asked.

"I wanna check on Gael and King Clucks."

"The plan is to go to the proctoring room, alert someone, and survive. He'll catch up."

"Besides, he's the one who chose to "secure the rear."" Yaritza rolled her eyes, clearly quoting Gael's joke.

"Yeah, because of his and King Clucks' sensory and banishment combos," Jamius said.

And his aversion to flight, one I should've forced him and his familiar to overcome this semester. Tara wouldn't have had her decision torn; Gael wouldn't be risking himself on foot.

"We can't do anything until Katherine breaks the enchantment anyway," Tara said.

"Look, we don't wanna be flying around when the power's restored." Yaritza popped her hip. "We need to secure the proctoring room, keep all fiends and warlocks out, then when Katherine's done, call every enchanter ever. Like literally all of them."

Tara looked at the high-vaulted ceilings. The cloudy gray sky was as somber as her every thought. She considered shattering the glass, but concerned the academy might've reinforced it. They hadn't. The enchantments in the auxiliary gym served as our line of defense against magical destruction on the facility, shielding from unsanctioned casting. It also notified admin and the authorities of unregistered magic, but all systems were fallible and the glyphs that brand warlock used blocked everything. Even if she managed to break the glass and whisk everyone through to safety, fear Theo and the others would be alerted made her falter.

"Let's go," she said, leading the way to the proctoring room.

Her magic remained attentive to the nearby demonic energy, each of her roots in use or at the ready. With all the skill Tara possessed in her root magic, it surprised me Caleb would leave her with the job of defending the proctoring room. Not that I wanted any of them running around tracking fiends or warlocks, but Tara excelled in this. Her connection to Theodore also provided a bit of security. Maybe.

When he said he'd come to kill me and all my students, did that include his sister? The one whose trust he betrayed after she saved his life. The one he swore never to abandon yet had time and time again. I suppose that served as my answer.

Tara stopped mid-flight. Tilting her head. Why?

A giggle echoed above. I sucked my teeth instinctively, tense but taking in no breath.

Tara spun, snatching Jamius and Yaritza in with telekinesis and kicking her legs like a swimmer. She pulled them all out of the line of Darla's dagger, which swung an invisible counter meant to hex their magic. Silent as ever, Darla's presence was revealed only by a mischievous laugh.

Yaritza shook in Tara's hold, fumbling for her bag for spelled rocks. With eyes locked on the dangerous masked warlock, all Yaritza's confidence shrank. Tara tightened her grip until Yaritza flung a star shower upward, alerting everyone in the auxiliary gym.

Blazing rocks crossed paths with Darla's swift strike and spiraled back toward my students. Tara's heart lurched up into her throat. Indecision choked her. Did she need to move first? Grab her panicky coven? Keep an eye on Darla? Release a telekinetic burst to block the countered comets? I drowned alongside her in an ocean of hesitation.

Jamius's copies sprang into action. Clones funneling forward, exploding one after another. Each collided with the star shower, protecting the others. His levitation waned, only steadied by Tara's grip. Expelling so much of his branch made his already less trained roots more difficult to control.

"Well, well, well. I was wondering which witch would show up. Teddy said find them all and let the others go play, but left me alone on guard duty." Darla descended, closing the space between them and the proctoring room. She toyed with the tip of the dagger pressed against her fingertip. "Eeny, meeny, miny, moe."

Darla's green eyes darted beneath her fiend mask, eyeing Tara, Jamius, and Yaritza. A powerful force of telekinesis built within Tara. Stop. Darla's counter would repel it, break it, send it hurling back. Too dangerous.

"You have to run," I shouted.

Tara's face calmed, all the tension of sadness consuming her for a brief second gone as the answer revealed itself. She couldn't run, but she wouldn't allow anyone else to be harmed. A quick wave of her hands threw Jamius and Yaritza away. The pair whirled through the air, crashing hard against the ground, tumbling far off, and falling out of sight. Guilt hit Tara, a natural feeling but they were safe, which provided minor relief. A lifejacket when she was already deep beneath her sea of sorrow.

"Look out," I screamed.

Not fast enough. Not loud enough. My voice carried nothing in this moment, and it ate away at me, observing everything but unable to offer assistance.

I lingered at Tara's shoulder as Darla sliced the air. Her dagger hacked wildly. Tara weaved, dodging invisible strikes, studying Darla's movements, hoping to gain insight. She closed the distance and channeled her telekinesis into her fists, preparing to take this woman out in one powerful punch. Her gut hardened. Heavy as a boulder. Darla wiggled her fingers in a playful wave. Shock filled Tara's face.

Darla countered Tara's levitation, sending her plummeting to the ground. Earth cracked; her body dug into the dirt.

"I was gonna start with you anyway, Widdle Whitlock." Darla skipped toward Tara, her feet not touching the ground as she levitated.

I cringed as Tara resisted the hex. It pinned her to the ground. She'd released her levitation root, but it still fought against her. Tara groaned, the pit in her stomach swelling.

"It's a nifty magic, right?" Darla giggled. "I can deflect or destroy magic my counter hex hits, but when I strike the nerves holding that magic while it's in use…well, that creates a whole new level of fun."

Darla brushed Tara's hair, stroking it. "A perfect pretty little princess with a silver spoon. Bet you think you're better than me with all those branches, huh?" She cut off a strand of blonde. "Not that they'll do you much good now."

Tara sank into the ground, her countered magic tunneling into the earth bit by bit with each agonizing second. Tara gritted her teeth, raising a hand.

"Please. I dare you." Darla clapped Tara's open palm.

"*If I cast, she'll counter my telekinesis. I can't use my new technique. It's not ready. I'm not. My magic's too chaotic.*" Darla sliced Tara's cheek. She shouted. The pain of the cut paled in comparison to her back grating against the ground.

"So, why'd you send your classmates away?" Darla asked, lightly cutting Tara's thigh. "To protect them? Or was it so they couldn't leave you? Teddy mentioned everyone leaves you."

"You act like you know him." Tara ground her teeth, biting back her anger and a yelp from the sharp searing pain of Darla's cuts.

"I know Teddy better than you."

Tara's doubt surfaced above all the pain.

"Must be hard having so much, yet no one wants you. Not mommy. Not daddy. Not anyone." Darla dragged the dagger along Tara's waist, her eyes searching for a hint of magic. Her thoughts remained silent, but I knew her cruel cuts meant to force a magical reaction. "I bet they're not coming back, your little witch friends. Probably happy you sent them away. Relieved."

Tara stared off at the distance where she'd tossed Jamius and Yaritza, believing in her short, miserable life, she'd finally done one thing right. If that meant paying the ultimate price, she'd gladly do it again.

My heart ached. My magic boiled. The white room called out, a comforting reprieve from this hellish torture.

"Snap out of it, Tara." I dropped next to her, shouting. "You're not chaos. You're not alone. You're not your past regrets or anyone's poor decisions around you. You're worth so much more than you realize. I need you to fight. Believe in yourself and your magic."

"But I am chaos," Tara whispered.

I fell back. Did she hear me?

"Huh?" Darla slid the knife along Tara's neck.

"I just thought of something." Tara sank into the earth, vanishing entirely.

Darla jumped, floating back but hitting a nearly invisible wall. A slight golden hue revealed the seal in place. It confined her in a tight area. Darla squeezed her dagger, ready to break the wall with her hex.

Shadows sprang out, whipping erratically.

Darla's dagger was knocked from her hand.

She shrieked when her fiend mask was cracked in half by a shadow. Half the mask fell into the ground vanishing from intangibility, the other half locked in a golden-hued seal midair.

Darla's expression shifted from shock to fury. Her brow wrinkled, green eyes scanning.

"Enough of this." She clapped her hands together. Tara rose from the ground, rage in her eyes, shadows striking benches sending them phasing into the ground or sealing them in gold.

"I thought I'd have to wait out your counter on my levitation. Guess you got impatient."

Everything had its limitations, so by casting her intangibility, Tara was able to wait out the physical world, hiding beneath the ground as an untouchable phantom. That said, Darla clearly believed undoing her counter and propelling Tara to the surface was the way to win this.

"Run. Fly away and regroup," I said uselessly because Tara quelled her chaotic branches.

She remained afloat, her arms moving to cast.

"Bold of you to cast," Darla said.

"Bold of you to bluff." Tara widened her eyes, staring at the discarded dagger.

Of course. Darla lost a dagger because of Kenzo's disruption and hadn't countered two-handed since. Clearly, she required support tools to utilize her hex branch counter. It was amazing Tara noticed that. How had I missed that detail? I needed to do better.

"So you've got some crazy branches. I can counter them. You can't seriously think you can beat me on your own." Darla leapt for her blade.

Tara remained silent. Air rippled from her telekinetic force. Darla dodged, silently spinning in an acrobatic flip. Even without her branch, Darla possessed extreme finesse of her root magics, possibly more refined than Tara herself.

"She's not alone." Gael bolted for Darla. "Hex this, motherclucker."

```
Name: Gael Rios-Vega
Branch: Bestial (Familiar)
```

His foot met Darla's face, kicking her to the ground. Though Tara struggled to speak, more shocked than anything, she relaxed. Gael's arrival conjured joy within her that eclipsed the doubt in her heart.

King Clucks pecked Darla in the face. Given the dazed expression and how fast the blows rendered her unconscious, the feathery familiar evidently channeled Gael's telekinesis.

Unconscious and with her hex quelled, Darla dreamt of the girl who wanted guild life, a hopeful girl who never made it through the previously strict academy guidelines. Her envy intertwined with

Theodore's hatred and corrupted her into a warlock bent on countering the system holding her back.

"Bawk."

"Nooooo," Gael said, flailing his arms. "You were supposed to crow."

"Ba-ba-bawk." He flapped his wings, squinting.

"Yeah, I know I was supposed to lead with cock-a-doodle-doo but 'hex this' felt natural. This was the first introduction to our catchphrase, and you ruined it with your weak ass muttering."

Tara blinked, watching Gael and his rooster caw at each other over who ruined their grand entrance. She laughed, genuine and filled with utter relief. She hugged Gael. Happy he was okay. Happy he'd arrived. Happy to have him in her life. Simply happy. His arms tightened around her, though a single eyebrow was raised in confusion. His gentle embrace was a kindness I doubted she'd had in so long.

"That was one powerful kick." Tara released him. "See, your telekinesis is improving."

"Oh, no. Prince-Bawks-A-Lot—yup, I'm still mad at you—was the one channeling our telekinesis. My kick was straight-up rooster strength."

"Well, it was impressive. You were impressive." Tara picked up Gael's familiar. "You were also amazing, King Clucks, Peckfender of the Unhatched Dozen." The rooster crowed.

"Now you do the catchphrase, seriously?"

Tara chuckled, petting the rooster. She side-eyed a giggling Gael. "Go ahead. Make the joke."

"What joke?"

"You've obviously got one."

"No joke. Just surprised you're this happy holding my cock." He wheezed with laughter.

"You're impossible."

I'd often found Gael's obnoxious humor and sexual innuendoes tiresome, but the laughter bubbling within Tara, ready to burst any moment, brought a smile to my face.

King Clucks fluttered free and pecked Gael into submission. "Sorry. It was a bad joke. Yes, I know lives are at stake. I said sorry. No, I won't make any more jokes. Of course, we've got too much going on for crude humor. Stop hitting me."

"No," Tara said. "I like the levity."

For the first time since meeting Tara, she seemed truly at peace. With a half-smile, unforced, she slowly swam to the surface of the ocean drowning her each day. Tara's smile grew as she took a deep breath and freed herself through Gael's pleasant distraction. "*I hope I'm ready for what comes next,*" she thought. "*Grab Jamius and Yaritza, clear the route to the proctoring room of fiends, secure it, and finish this.*"

I hovered nearby, shocked at how clear and confident her thoughts came through. Tara had achieved so much.

Chapter Thirty-One

Sunlight cut through the clouds, casting a glare on the glass ceiling, stinging my eyes. My tongue scraped against the roof of my dry mouth, attempting and failing to produce some type of saliva.

"I think he's awake," Jennifer said.

"Mr. Frost, you're going to be okay. You just need to rest," Carter said, patting my shoulder. Haunting images of my bloody body flashed. I looked ghostlier than ever in my life. *"He had so much blood loss."*

A high-pitched squeal rattled me. I sprang forward, panting as I sat up, magic channeled in my arms.

Katherine bounced in front of the green enchantment. She turned, blinking at her frazzled audience, Carter, Jennifer, and myself.

"So-so-so-so-so, sorry." Katherine clenched her teeth with an apologetic grin, green reflecting off her glasses. "It's just I broke the first sigil to the enchantment. This guy's brand magic is hyper-complex. No way he made something this sophisticated off the fly. Why? Either he's the best of the best when it comes to crafting intricate sigils, or someone gave him a massive blueprint to how the enchantments at Gemini Academy work, plus schematics for like all the software ever. It has adaptive rules in place—basically meaning it'll cause all types of havoc if disarmed incorrectly—so that's mildly irritating."

"Katherine," I forced myself up, "you need to step away from it then. I don't need you…" I tilted backward, shaky and wincing.

"Careful," Carter said. "You need to take it easy. I used my branch to restore your vitality—improving your magic, channeling receptors, muscles—but sort of tweaked it so all that would tie into healing your injuries. It's not an exact science or magic or either, well, kind of both, but I'm not very good. You need to let your body rest, recover."

"Yes." Jennifer took a more direct approach, forcing me to lie back.

Katherine continued talking while she worked. Her quill tapped with a rhythmic pattern, creating a soothing beat that made sleep easy. I ground my teeth, my eyes firmly shut. I couldn't rest. Not yet. If Carter had truly restored my magic, I should be able to interact with the minds of all my students with more ease. My telepathy radiated in waves, stronger than my body.

Frustration spiked, carrying a torch of rage through the forest terrain. I followed, a spirit in the wind.

"*This son of a bitch is mocking me. Thinks he can outrun me. Damn warp magic. I'll eviscerate him. The last two times I closed in, he moved left and reappeared from the right.*"

Kenzo soared between thickets of trees, channeling telekinesis to close the distance between himself and Ernesto, unfazed by the branches nicking his arms. A blue portal opened from the left again and Kenzo's eyes sprang wide as he maneuvered split seconds away, avoiding the trap.

A shot of gray static distorted the doorway to droplets of broken magic.

```
Name: Kenzo Ito
Branch: Hex (Disruption)
```

"*His movements are annoyingly unpredictable.*"

Kenzo's strategic mind did him no credit here. Everything about Ernesto infuriated Kenzo. His evasive strategy. His taunting portals. His swift reaction time. The fact Kenzo couldn't catch him. The fact Kenzo's magic waned. The fact Kenzo had no choice but to rely on his coven. A coven Caleb declared he'd need for this plan. A coven who couldn't keep up. A coven he didn't want harmed.

Kenzo cycled through all these feelings again and again, looping them in tandem with the current strategy, new tactics he wanted to try, a buried past that continued haunting him, and blood gushing out of my throat—which he refused to let anyone else experience. Kenzo couldn't fail again. Wouldn't.

I reached out, desperate to assuage his angry mind that carried a world of regret.

His eyes flitted back and forth, scanning thirteen small portals. None large enough for Ernesto to steal someone away or leap within. Still, they posed a massive problem.

"Move, porcupine!"

Gael's levitation staggered; a silver dagger darted through a blue pocket. Sweat poured down Kenzo's brow. A telekinetic burst wouldn't reach in time. His heart pounded against his furious anxiety. Gael's spikes along his forearms grew, coating him with a makeshift shield, deflecting the sharp blade.

```
Name: Gael Martinez
Branch: Augmentation (Spikes)
```

The dagger bounced along the grass. Kenzo counted the seconds. Thirteen crystalized pocket portals dropped to eight, and a larger portal swallowed the weapon, returning it to the elusive warlock who sprang out, reaching for Gael's back.

My physical body twitched, tugging at me, demanding I return and recover. I latched onto Kenzo, allowing his anger to consume my fear.

"Now!" he shouted.

Gael's forearms and calves erupted with spikes, perfect projectiles forcing Ernesto to pivot back to his portal. Splashing out of the rippling blue, Layla sprang up. Feral and ferocious, she lunged for Ernesto in her gigantic humanoid cougar form.

```
Name: Layla Smythe
Branch: Bestial (Therianthropy)
```

"How the hell d'you—"

"I couldn't track your wild movements, but she sniffed out exactly where you were heading and waited." Kenzo gloated. His muscles flexed with excitement, ready for what came next. More than anything, he relished the takedown.

Just as the stink of fiends wafted through the many portals Ernesto opened to surround the students earlier, his scent trickled through too, which Kenzo knew could be exploited by a member of his coven.

Layla caught Ernesto's scent carried in the air, tracked it to a recently opened portal, and safely jumped through. *What a reckless plan.* She didn't know it'd actually open to Ernesto. Somewhere safe.

She could've ended up dropped into a pit. An ocean. Outer fucking space. He could've felt her presence once she entered, closed it off entirely. My telepathic link intensified the more aggravated I became, syncing to Kenzo's fury.

Ernesto's portals vanished all at once, and he flew to the side, evading Layla—who barely got her legs through in time.

Fucking first-years.

Kenzo grinned, soaring after him. He quickly closed the distance of the slow-moving warlock. The smaller portals didn't hinder Kenzo's movements. He released tiny gray bolts to disrupt them.

It took a moment, but Kenzo's calm calculations simmered beneath his hot-headed pursuit. When Ernesto opened smaller portals, there were easily thirty surrounding me, making it impossible to gauge where Darla's delicate hand would slip from next and strike. However, since blocking the exits to the auxiliary gym with his warp branch, Ernesto's overall number remained at thirteen. Fewer when he opened a larger portal. He'd overextended himself.

Kenzo kept hurling his hex to force Ernesto forward with his weaker root magics. Since Layla carelessly leapt through his portal, he couldn't chance opening one until he pinpointed their final coven member and gained a safe distance. The anxiety of failure consumed Ernesto.

Was I channeling his mind? No. This came from Kenzo. Even with a fiendish mask covering Ernesto's face, Kenzo read the warlock's body language. The toil behind his root magics which he'd avoided for so long while taunting them.

"Where ya going, buddy?" Kenzo asked, propelling himself faster, his muscles ready to buckle at this rate of channeling all his magics.

I gasped, drawn to my body momentarily. No. Not yet. I tugged at the angry tether and remained. This entire time, Kenzo utilized his hex branch to cast disruption. He also relied heavily on levitation and telekinesis in tandem to fly. Sensory blossomed, ready to identify nearby demonic energy. But stirring within him came banishment, prepared to eliminate fiends instantaneously if they approached him or his coven.

"Scorch his ass!"

Dread exploded deep within the forest terrain, followed by an inferno.

```
Name: Melanie Dawson
Branch: Primal (Fire)
```

Though she required a support tool to conjure flames, her amplification and control were on point. Intensifying their heat, reducing their need for oxygen, magnifying their reduction to smothering, and spiraling them ahead like a mighty stampede.

Ernesto halted all his root magics at once, his body quaking. A protective portal emerged, ready to free him, but Kenzo was on his heels, same as the flames licking at his fiend mask. Disruption coiled around the warlock's arms, silencing his branch magic entirely.

"Gotcha." Kenzo slammed Ernesto to the ground.

The blaze singed the hairs on Kenzo's arms. Sweat drenched his face, but he didn't slow. Ignoring the furious fire, Kenzo placed a shocking hand against Ernesto's mask. His palm sparked.

"You don't understand. I had no choice. If I…"

Kenzo pulled his arm back and punched Ernesto, cracking the mask. "I don't give a shit about your sob story."

As the flames settled to embers along the forest terrain, the rest of his coven approached. Kenzo swallowed his pride, almost smiling at their success.

"We did it." Layla bounced with joy.

"I was totally nervous about the plan," Melanie said. "When he said burn it all up, I wasn't sure I was ready."

"You weren't ready," Kenzo muttered, only audible to the ever-listening Gael.

"We totally rocked the most important job." Gael grabbed Kenzo by the shoulders, lifting the smaller boy off the ground and spinning him.

"Put me down, porcupine," Kenzo snapped. Brushing his charred sleeves upon release, he glared. "I could've handled this on my own. It was simply convenient to let you help. After all, I didn't want to overexert myself in case a real threat showed up."

And there was that humility. I scoffed.

His mind weaved within as many twists and turns as Caleb's when it came to plans. Though his thoughts led more directly to an exit. Kenzo believed adamantly what he'd have done had they failed, but I couldn't pinpoint why he needed that certainty. It wasn't for their safety. He had other ideas to ensure that. Many, in fact. More than I'd come up with before failing. No, there was deep-seated hatred shrouding Kenzo's ulterior motives. The type of hatred that stung to touch. The type that enveloped me when Theodore arrived.

"He was totally a real threat. Gran amenaza." Gael smiled at Kenzo.

"Honestly, I don't get it." Melanie shook her head, half exhausted. "He's so fucking annoying."

"Me either. Must be a boy thing. Couldn't see myself going that stir crazy over a guy." Layla eyed Kenzo from head to toe, questioning every angry breath released. "He's not even that cute."

"Gael could do so much better," Melanie loudly whispered.

Goosebumps trailed Kenzo's nape, his sensory whispering danger, ignoring their prattling. He tackled Gael, spikes scratching him. Gael winced, sharklike teeth frowning at the scrapes that trickled blood.

"It's fine." Kenzo pivoted, and the pair spun away from an encroaching fiend.

Its landing shook the earth. The quake was strong enough to knock a nervous Melanie's footing. Layla snatched Melanie's arm, dragging her away from the ten-limbed monster. Its head was a bulbous collection of mouths; jagged teeth snapped. Its muscular torso—the only humanoid quality—connected the four arms to six spiked legs. Tar dripped, scalding the grass.

Kenzo unleashed a storm of gray lightning, breaking apart the toxic magic holding this monstrosity together. Its discombobulated oily flesh fell apart but didn't break down into wisp form. Static coated Kenzo, quelled, as all his magic channeled into a banishment that shattered the fiend to nothingness in a single rapid shot. The strike left Kenzo groggy, eyes heavy.

A scratchy chuckle awakened Kenzo with a spike of rage.

"I'm gonna need my ride back." Theodore hovered between trees.

Scaling the trunks, two grotesque fiends equal in stature to the one Kenzo barely banished without passing out dug their claws into the bark.

Frantic for escape, thoughts of the worst-case scenario circulated through my students. Except Kenzo. With an unblinking scowl and clenched jaw, he obsessed over his target.

Melanie manifested more flames, but they wildly burst, her control too exhausted. Layla's therianthrope form faded, maintained well past her limit. Gael grunted, his spikes receding inward. Gael's augmented spikes appeared as nothing more than nubs lining his flesh. He'd extended himself far beyond his limits, forcing the magic to perform its primary function. Augmentations offered a multitude of offensive and defensive measures, but they also acted as life support for those witches bearing the branch, each base of his spikes connected to his nerve endings and circulatory system.

Kenzo cut his gaze, keeping his peripheral locked on Theodore. He guarded his coven, rolling Ernesto's unconscious body forward with a kick. "You want him back. Take him. But he won't be casting portals anytime soon."

"And how long does that little hex of yours last, exactly?" Theodore asked.

"Why don't you come down here and find out?"

Theodore descended to the charred ground; his fiends slinked down the trunks of the trees.

"Wait, we're not supposed to engage with other warlocks," Gael whispered. "That's the whole point of the plan."

"*Your disruption can take the warp portals out of play. If you use it on a portal blocking the door, there's no stopping him from creating a new one before we get everyone out.*" Caleb's words played in Kenzo's mind. "*Your group needs to handle him, but if you encounter any of the other warlocks, you need to withdraw. Regroup. Especially if it's the one controlling fiends.*"

"Screw the plan. I've got my own." Gray static popped, making it difficult to remain close to Kenzo. His hex pushed against my telepathy. "***I'm gonna kill this guy for everything he's done. Everyone he's hurt. Everyone he's trying to hurt. But first, I have to make sure the others fall back.***"

Kenzo took shallow breaths, the smoke in the forest terrain weighing on his lungs. His magic declined, gray disruption fading. His muscles burned; so much constant channeling left him vulnerable.

"When I make my move, I need you three to run," Kenzo whispered.

"You can't take him and those fiends on your own," Gael said.

"I can." Kenzo kept his gaze locked on Theodore.

Kenzo sprinted for Theodore, conserving his magic. A single

bolt, ready to release once he'd closed the distance between himself and the warlock. I trembled in my restless body, struggling to stay with Kenzo. Not that I offered him any assistance. He was alone in this which he preferred, constantly pushing others away. I couldn't have changed that about Kenzo, but I could've recognized it sooner, acknowledged him as more than a potential threat to Caleb, tried to help him grow. Instead, all I did was lay somewhere in the distance dying, my magic barely latched to Kenzo's mind.

A fiend lunged at Kenzo. The collision caused an explosion of gray lightning and acidic tar which splattered everywhere.

All minds silenced.

I shuddered.

Chapter Thirty-Two

I jolted awake, slumping forward. My bloody shirt stuck to my skin, heavy against my chest. They'd rolled my sleeves and pant legs up, exposing dried, flakey blood along my skin. Bloody fingerprints swirled within the splatters along my pasty flesh, but no cuts. Shaky and lightheaded, I slid my damp sleeves down. I rubbed the caked blood across my neck; it tightened against my skin. My throat was sore. Every muscle ached.

Jennifer's hand pressed against my shoulder. "You shouldn't move. Relax, or I'll make you relax."

Cute. She'd conquered Carter's emotions and believed herself capable of handling mine. I gripped her forceful wrist, shifting rest upon her instead of myself. Psychics were the easiest minds to hack. Less protective, believing they understood the fundamental aspects of our magic. They didn't. I didn't. Jennifer's empathic desire weighed on her, relaxation eased her into a drowsy half-sleep. This wasn't exactly the hammer Dr. Kendall hit me with, but it calmed Jennifer.

I had to prevent Theodore from interfering with fate. Causing fate. Killing Caleb. Killing any of my students.

"Carter, I need you and Katherine to take Jennifer to the exit," I said, a hand pressed to Jennifer's shoulder, keeping her upright. Her eyes were heavy, her mind dazed.

Carter and I helped Jennifer to her feet. "You need to be careful, Mr. Frost. No casting or overexertion because those sealed injuries are tied to the flow of your magic. A quick fix but temporary. You need real treatment."

"I'll be cautious." I walked up to Katherine, mind fixated on sigils and eyes glossed over with green light. "Katherine, it's time to go."

"What? No. I'm this close to cracking the enchantment wide open, then we'll be able to contact—"

"No need. The portal blocking the door is gone. It's time to leave, contact the authorities, and let them remove it." Hopefully, they could secure this place and the students, too.

"After all that work, someone else gets to finish breaking the enchantment? So unfair."

"Leave now. Grab the others on your way past the proctoring room." I walked opposite Katherine.

"Wait. Where are you going?"

I followed the terror trailing through the auxiliary gym. "A few of your classmates are further out."

I needed to find them. Keeping telepathy on where their frantic minds buzzed loudest, I channeled magic and flew.

"I said don't cast, Mr. Frost," Carter shouted.

Tearing through the air, I tracked Gael, Layla, and Melanie's erratic thoughts. No words. No planning. Only fear and survival. Their emotions wailed, and their bodies moved on instinct. Wind stung at a freshly opened cut along my forearm. I winced, ignoring it, and flew faster.

A behemoth fiend chased my students, knocking fitness equipment aside they'd used as a buffer to distance themselves. It didn't work. Using two arms, it raced closer, and another pair of hands reached out, almost snatching them.

Quelling my other magics, I landed ahead of them, focusing everything on banishment. Its jagged teeth snapped, and I hesitated. The fear along my students' faces, their raw emotions stabbed at me, and I shook.

I took a deep breath, releasing all their uncertainty and inhaling what little confidence I could summon.

Tar exploded behind them. White wisps whirled among the sludge. Bright orbs bounced together, catching acidic droplets. Not happening. I clapped my hands together, sending a wave of banishment through the fitness area.

The kids panted, hands pressed to their knees, and gave grateful thoughts to words they were too exhausted to utter.

"You three need to leave now."

"You're okay?" Gael asked through heavy wheezes.

"All better." I ground my teeth to force a smile, ignoring the fresh throb on my calf. Another opened cut from casting. "Get to the exit. Thanks to your teamwork, the portals are gone."

"How'd you know about that?" Layla asked.

"We'll discuss your careless strategy later." I glared, still very aggravated she'd nose-dived through a portal to counterattack a warlock. "Go."

"Wait." Gael's panic bloomed. "Kenzo's still—"

"I'm aware. I'll find him."

Buzzing through the auxiliary gym, most of their minds gathered toward the exit, but Kenzo's mind boomed from the edges of the forest terrain, so loud it made it difficult to hear anything else clearly.

"Another fiend. Too many fiends."

"I've only got a few shots of disruption left in me."

"Less if I keep using my telekinesis and levitation to evade these monsters."

"How's he controlling this many?"

"I don't have enough strength to banish them all."

His thoughts bounced from one end of the terrain to another as Kenzo soared throughout the auxiliary gym toward the rock terrain, perhaps. I couldn't be certain. It was difficult getting a clear picture of his thoughts, his process. I wasn't sure he had a plan beyond survival.

"What the hell is Kenny thinking, fighting that warlock?" Caleb's mind called out, providing clear flashes of the battle he studied. *"If I take Theodore out, that won't remove the fiends from play, just his control. Still, I have to do something."*

Six behemoth fiends chased Kenzo, each guarding and switching places when he managed to damage one, banishing pieces of their tar flesh. Theodore hovered behind them, too distant for Kenzo to strike with well-placed fiends ready to shield the warlock if Kenzo charged.

"Wait, what's she doing here..."

My shoulders curled inward; my chest caved in as I took unsteady breaths. The wounds along my forearms were hacked to ribbons again. Caleb planned to surprise Theodore, force him to stop the fiends, and protect Kenzo. He couldn't handle that, though. Neither of them could.

I pursued them on foot. What magic I had left, Carter linked toward my recovery. A smart double-edged sword. Vitality provided stamina both physical and magical, but vitality didn't heal injuries. Not truly. It was impressive he'd found a way to do such a patch job on me. I'd reserve magic for only the necessities like ensuring all my students got out of here alive. To do that, I'd have to stop Theodore, contain or eliminate the fiends he'd gathered.

A flurry of explosions cracked apart the rock terrain, causing a dust storm. Was that Yaritza's magic? No. Katherine's spell containing it. Good. Caleb used those to provide cover, a diversion. Now I had to get there before he and Kenzo did anything reckless. More reckless.

Ignoring my shaky body, I soared, desperate to reach them in time.

I made it to the destroyed rock terrain. Fiends cornered Kenzo, blocking his movements as the dust cleared. Caleb sprinted through the rubble away from Theodore. Terror in his eyes, dread on his face. I linked my telepathy, struggling to comprehend Caleb's thoughts, oddly only seeing an image flash again and again. Theodore's stunned expression as Caleb leapt behind him, punching him full force across the face, then bolting away before fiends gathered. Each step that carried him further from the warlock brought him one step closer to bringing the void vision to fruition.

I descended, meeting him halfway, and rechanneled magic into the only root that could protect him in this moment.

"*That brat,*" Theodore thought, flying after Caleb. His face was exposed; his fiend mask lay broken on the ground. He clutched a dagger. I shuddered—the dagger, the one which would kill Caleb.

Theodore threw the dagger.

I ran to catch Caleb before the hurled blade found its target, trajectory perfected by a telekinetic pulse. I reached out with my own telekinesis, halting the dagger's pursuit. Caleb continued running, knife aimed at his back.

"Move," I shouted.

A piercing pain struck. My arms trembled. My neck stung. Blood trickled. The healed cut along my neck ripped at the edge like a deep nick, enough for my magic to falter and carry the blade closer to Caleb. No. I didn't endanger everyone's future to protect Caleb, to bring him to this moment through my own arrogance, only to allow him to die, anyway. My knees buckled, gashes along my legs brought a searing pain as I fought Theodore's dagger.

"Mr. Frost, stop. It'll be okay. You'll see," Caleb thought, so distant and faded it echoed or perhaps my telepathy had finally reached its limit.

In a second of hesitation, the blade plunged into Caleb's back.

No.

No.

No.

I crawled on my knees, weak and tired. Caleb stumbled forward, his steps aimless as he collapsed before me.

No Kenzo in sight. No Tara. The only part of this horrible future I'd changed was bringing myself closer to his moment of death and failing to stop it. I slumped over Caleb's still body gasping. My body trembled, ached, and tears welled in my eyes. I couldn't do anything right—ever. I brushed his curly bangs from his cold eyes. His breathing stopped. Instantaneous. But a single memory circulated in his fading mind.

"That star shower gives maybe a minute before those fiends sniff us out. I've got two spells left from Katherine. Vitality, which you need more than anything. He's not gonna let you anywhere near him. Even at full strength, you need a diversion. That's where I come in. But disrupting his magic will only stop his control of the fiends, not remove them. When that happens..."

The memory faded incomplete, like his life. Poor Caleb.

My heart broke, devastation crackled along the slashes on my flesh, amplifying the pain of Caleb's loss.

I failed.

After all I'd done, every life I compromised—I still failed.

Caleb died. I fought back tears. My other students were going to die. This was all my fault. *Everyone always dies because of me.*

Theodore's smug satisfaction drew my attention. Desires to slaughter the other students. Me. Destroy this building and all it represented. I stood, every fiber of my being ready to buckle, but I'd kill him before dying.

Magic stirred within Caleb, radiating. What? If there was even an ounce, then—

Pop.

His body burst, dissolving into a pool of watery liquids. I released a breath, teeth chattering and cheeks wet.

It wasn't Caleb.

It was a copy. Jamius's duplication branch bound within a page of Katherine's grimoire. That was the second spell page he had on him.

But this wasn't at all how the void vision played out. He lay there dead, long enough for Kenzo to approach and Tara to arrive. Had I changed things? Or was he still in danger?

"Now!" Caleb shouted. His voice boomed above.

Mid-flight, he kicked his leg, throwing telekinesis into the strike, sending a rippling wave past the fiends. Dividing them momentarily for a fully restored Kenzo to dart through, lightning in his palm. Theodore's eyes widened. The bolt of disruption coursed through his body. Theodore fell through the air, his magic silenced, and collided with wet gravel where Caleb's copy had perished.

"You lose." Kenzo stomped his foot against Theodore's chest, desire to crush his lungs palpable in the air.

"All you did was break my control," Theodore groaned.

"Kenny." Caleb floated in the distance, fiends clambering toward him.

"You deserve to die." Kenzo ground his teeth. "**But I chose to become a guild witch to save lives.** *Not take them.* **What matters is we stop this so everyone lives.**"

"Have fun handling the chaos." Theodore cackled between heavy wheezes.

I shook, knowing if I continued pushing my magic, I'd collapse. But they needed help.

Fiends roared, shifting between Caleb and Kenzo. These fiends were too much for them. If I casted enough magic next to Theodore, we'd lure the fiends away from the boys. Easy prey. It'd save their lives and I'd do one thing right here.

A hand pressed against my trembling shoulder. "*I've got this, Mr. Frost.*"

Tara stepped forward, her quiet mind revealing her role.

"I've come to learn to handle chaos quite well, Theo." Her hands shifted, channeling magic and spinning it into something spectacular.

She hadn't remained at the proctoring room at all. After dealing with stray fiends, she stumbled onto Caleb moments before he reached Kenzo, and followed a plan the three of them created to end this.

Shadows circled each other, brightening the area surrounding the fiends and drawing all the darkness into one large ball. Shifting shadows sealed the core with a single vortex, sucking fiends into an intangible entryway. She'd created a blackhole from her three magics, perfectly entwined them and bound the demonic threats inside a black sphere. Wind whirled, drawing fiends inward to a chasm they stood no chance against.

The void vision unraveled in this instance completely differently. Had my involvement changed things for the better?

Doubtful.

None of them should've been involved in any of this.

Caleb carried terror within him this entire time, but not how it enveloped him in the void vision. Kenzo carried rage and sadness within his mind, but not with the same venom as the void vision. Tara always carried her guilt and sorrow, but not the drowning ocean she had in the void vision. I created none of this outcome. It was them, united with their classmates. Together. Alone. Each of them was so much more than a vague untold future could ever predict. They defied the hand dealt to them.

"I wonder what will happen when I counter tragic little Tara's branches all at once." Theodore crawled toward his discarded dagger. *"Bet it'll be a splendid sight to behold."*

A sigil glowed along his retrieved blade. Each channeled thread of magic burned, but I forced myself upright, shielding Tara as Theodore sliced the air. The invisible counter struck me. Quelling my magic did nothing to protect my body. Every injury burst open. Blood. Darkness. The vitality which stitched me together now dug deeper into my wounds, attacking my body. I gasped, collapsing.

"**That son of a bitch.**
I'll kill him."

"*No. If I move, it'll break my magical hold.*
The fiends will be unleashed."

"*Hang on, Mr. Frost.*
I'll save you."

No. What I needed was to know they'd be okay. Survive.

Chapter Thirty-Three

The white room brought me back, dulling the agony breaking my body apart with each breath.

"Did it help?" Finn asked, his voice a small relief in this terrifying place.

"I can't tell if my interference brought this about, made it worse, or better. I just wish I knew how it all ended."

"Sort of everyone's big thoughts as it all comes crashing down around them."

Light flickered in and out as Finn spirited his fingers with enthusiasm.

My vision faded from his smile here in the white room and I choked on the ground in the auxiliary gym.

"The children are secure. Enchanter Campbell, banish the fiends," someone shouted.

"There's nowhere to run, Theodore."

"Who's running?"

Milo's mind collided with mine, but I barely held a visual of the world. A tremendous magical burst. Something knocked Theodore Whitlock back to the ground.

"Dorian, hang on," Milo said, his voice a huge relief in this terrifying moment. "*I've got you.*"

"W-wh-wh…" I couldn't form the words because blood blocked my airway, and the white room obscured his remorseful expression.

His clasped hands to my throat brought his mind to life, answering the questions I had. Where was he? Why hadn't he come sooner? What was happening?

Milo paced back and forth in his office, awaiting Enchanter Campbell's arrival. An irritating witch with whom I didn't understand such trust he held in. Yes, they'd worked together frequently. Yes, they'd confided in each other often. Yes, they'd grouped as coven mates regularly. It still annoyed me, stirring in his memory, barely conscious, and latched onto his emotions.

Enchanter Campbell entered his office, reading a piece of parchment. The sigils glowed, releasing a blissful aroma. No, that was her branch magic interacting with them. Milo had laced the enchantment with a message only her specific branch and magical frequency could trigger. Whatever was written, Milo took multiple steps to ensure the intel didn't find its way into anyone else's hands. A rose-colored mist seeped from Enchanter Campbell's pores, crumpling the paper.

"And this is the best outcome you see?"

"The only one where everyone lives." Ice clinked as Milo poured drinks.

"You're certain?"

"I've seen every potential outcome to this. Every inkling that's crossed your mind, I've thoroughly considered. Countless times. I won't insult you with numbers, but if we do nothing, they die."

"Canceling this weekend's school get-together obviously won't work either." Enchanter Campbell sipped her drink. "Warlocks get wind, the whole potential drama gets pushed back or onto something new we have to account for."

"Exactly," Milo said, certainty in his tone.

"What if our guild substituted for the students? Since canceling holds such terrible potential."

"That won't work. One, it could spook them entirely, and they don't show. Two, I'm not completely certain there isn't something compromising the academy which could tip the warlocks off."

"You mean someone within the academy working with the warlocks?"

"Tiniest of variables, but it's there all the same."

"It must be so annoying seeing the spoiler ending to a thousand versions of the same story, most of which you never get to see through."

"You get used to it. Trust me. Plus, a thousand's a good week." Milo finished his drink.

"To clarify, we interfere too soon, the warlocks flee and more die. We show up before containing the fiends, the warlock with demonic resonance summons too many for one guild, and we die. We wait for approval from other guilds, bureaucracy kills the kids."

"Yup. I've been bouncing around ideas for months now. With half the puzzle pieces I gave you, might I add."

Months? The void vision, sure. But the warlocks kept their predictions shrouded with the brands hexing all psychic interference, including Milo's clairvoyance. How long had he been preparing for this future? How many other futures was he balancing at the same time?

"Add it all day, you're still holding back, Milo."

"I've given you everything."

"Unlikely," Enchanter Campbell said. There was a curiosity and craving in her eyes, which Milo avoided by averting his gaze to a bottle of Finn's favorite whiskey. "Let's discuss the big golden shielded elephant in the corporate office. Why not involve Tobias Whitlock? With the right strings pulled, proper pockets filled, I think we'd have several guilds aligned quite quickly. He's expressed immense public desire to mitigate this warlock threat."

"Quietly." Milo licked his lips and smiled, quelling the budding headache of a dozen visions hidden from my telepathy while pressing forward in innuendo and flirtation. "A desire that's made Dr. Kendall all but vanish from the public eye. Someone who terrorized a city for weeks, conspiring for years, yet our attention spans faded in days."

"Please, I hardly remember anything after the weekend." Enchanter Campbell strutted around the bar, reaching for Milo's stash of good wine bottles, unsatisfied with his offering. "Still, it's curious you'd glimpse futures where he'd risk his daughter."

"What if I said he was willing to risk more than his daughter?"

The cork popped, startling each of them. Enchanter Campbell's eyes widened. "Do tell."

"I'll give you everything if you give your word."

"Give a gambling girl a number."

"Better odds than him, with or without you."

"Hmm." Enchanter Campbell passed her wine glass to Milo. "I'll take those odds. Now, what are your conditions?"

"In house only. Obviously. Enchanters. No acolytes. Not even the best of the best. Not one. Any enchanter tempted to bring theirs stays. Non-negotiable. If you can't figure out who they are, who might feel that way, eager and believing in their young witches, then I'm asking the wrong witch."

"Don't insult me. Continue."

"We strike the facility and contain the demonic energy entirely before going to Gemini Academy."

"Fine by me." Enchanter Campbell leaned against the bar. "Question, though. You're worried about acolytes handling themselves against fiends, mostly in containers, yet you're not worried about first-year witches holding their own against warlocks?"

"I'm not depending on the kids here. Though I do believe in this group through and through."

"Save the speeches. The cameras aren't rolling, Enchanter Evergreen."

"You're one to talk." Milo finished her wine glass. Slamming the empty glass and holding the rattling stem as it clashed with the bar surface. "Dorian will ensure they hold and survive until we arrive to contain the situation."

"The teacher?"

"The former enchanter who's dedicated his life to making capable enchanters. He'll keep them alive, unharmed." Milo quivered, settling his mind. I ripped at the seams holding his thoughts in this memory. *"The question isn't if he can keep them safe. It's if I can save him before the best outcome kills him. Any other outcome would drag this out for years, harm more, or break him. But why does the best one have to risk him above everything?"*

I backed away, suppressing Milo's sorrow and his phony persona as he convinced Enchanter Campbell to follow his self-imposed prophecy, one that'd save the kids. That was what should matter, right?

Right?

Right?

Right?

I clutched my shoulders, consoling myself in silence. Sobbing. This really was going to kill me.

Guilt consumed Milo as he held my bloody neck. The memory

merged with the reality of the auxiliary gym and the white room, all of it consuming what remained of my mind. *"You weren't supposed to intervene. You were supposed to hesitate. Pause. Regret it for a minute. A horrible minute until we arrived. We moved too slow. Should've been here sooner. I failed. I failed you. I can't do this again. Anymore. You can't die on me, Dorian."*

Milo's tears splashed against my face, each drop pooling into this void we'd conjured together through false futures. Fake fates. None of it mattered. I'd drown in this sorrow.

Finn hugged me, his arms draped over my shoulders, pulling me into the flickering white abyss and quelling the outside world. "It's time to say goodbye."

My breathing hastened. I lost my composure. The strobe effect of the lights made me dizzy. Blood loss chilled every inhale. This safe hideaway had become a chasm of doubt.

"I don't wanna say goodbye. I-I-I'm not ready to leave. I should've said something. Said something to him. Anything. Should've tried harder, should've—"

Tried anything. Instead, I stood here absorbing Milo's truth. Milo's best outcome. Milo's silent confessional. All without Milo. Alone. But not.

Finn spun me around, his eyes locked with mine. Water pooled around us at our waists. Inch by inch, this place flooded. We'd drown in doubt and sorrow and the feelings of the world that we'd left behind. No. Not the world. One person who meant the world. Milo. But this deceptive world would kill me soon enough. I had to let go. Accept nothingness. Loneliness. I didn't want it, though. I wanted… *I wanted… More.*

"I don't want to leave. I'm not… I can't… Milo can't be alone. He has to know… Has to, has to…" I heaved; my lungs were ready to collapse. Water splashed, ready to destroy everything. I had too much to say as all the light in this room disappeared, suppressing screams best left silent.

"What would you even say to him?" Finn's hand caressed my cheek. I embraced his kind touch, clinging to any warmth left in this devoid realm.

"Apologize. Take back the twelve years I dragged my feet. No. All the years before that, even when you were still here with us. Tell him I love him."

"Sounds like you have a lot to unpack next time you see him."

I blinked, confused by the bright smile on Finn's face.

"It's not Milo you have to say goodbye to, silly." Finn brushed my bangs aside. "I'm not really sure whether I'm a piece of your subconscious working through old wounds, a ghost dragging my soul back from the ether of the afterlife, or a fragment of magic broken off from the source to whisper words of wisdom."

"What?" My hands trembled against his chest.

"You're not the only psychic who can conjure manifestations. Remember, thanks to retrocognition, I'm the past incarnate," Finn said. "Truthfully, I don't believe I'm a manifestation of your making. And we both know you don't buy into the theory of souls. I like to think I tucked away a piece of myself safely in your mind, waiting for when you'd need me most."

"With words of wisdom," I said. It was a beautiful thought and something Finn would completely do.

"Can't say I was ever all that wise," Finn said. "Whatever was holding me here with you, whispering to you, breathing life into my ghost—it's changing. I feel it fading."

"No. I'm here with you. I don't know what I want. I still need to talk to you."

"You need to stop holding onto the past so tightly, Dorian." Finn kissed me, a soft and fleeting sensation. "Enjoy your present. Look toward your future. You've still got a bright one ahead of you. You don't need clairvoyance to see that much."

I held onto Finn until the darkness enveloped me. The water, light, and sensations all vanished. Replaced by an infinite and unforgiving abyss. I could drift in this still, silent space for an eternity. But I didn't want that. Not yet.

Chapter Thirty-Four

I choked on a tube, coughing and fighting wires tangled around me. Everything hurt. The hospital room did little to assist as minds shouted more than my broken body could handle. A collection of doctors worked on me, saying things, asking questions I couldn't hear with so much noise. How'd I get here? When'd I get here?

Sleep took hold.

Sleepless recovery in dark, dreamless days as the world whizzed by.

Milo arrived. His mind reached out to steady me in this whirlwind. Relief. Happiness. Hopeful. *"You're going to be okay, Dorian. I'm so sorry."*

Then total silence. No minds. No bustle. No worries. Just quiet rest.

…

…

…

Sunlight so bright it stung my closed eyelids. I rolled over, half-dazed.

"For someone who's slept the last three days, you really look like shit," Chanelle said, sitting in a chair facing my hospital bed. She licked her fingertip and flipped a page to her magazine.

"What's going on?"

"You're recovering after the attack on the academy. Apparently, you were in rough shape. Though I'm convinced our insurance premium is more likely to kill you than some shady warlocks."

"What happened?" My throat burned, and I reached for the pitcher of water too heavy to lift.

Chanelle waved a hand, tilting the pitcher into a plastic cup and floating it into my grasp. I guzzled it down until I coughed.

"They closed Gemini for the week, allowing authorities to secure the space, yada yada. Honestly, I'd be okay with extending this time away through winter break, but apparently, we're all back at it Monday. Except maybe you. I'd milk this overpriced hospital bed for all it's worth. Which, if not expressly clear, is a lot."

"Chanelle. What happened to my students?"

"Oh, they're fine from what I know. Cerberus Guild showed up, took care of everything. I'm mostly grasping at rumors because the rumor mill is strong, but Milo has dropped by a bit, so that's my insider intel. We're sort of taking shifts since you don't have an emergency contact. Seriously, who does that? Anyway, he says the kids are good. Home in their beds, enjoying their mini vacation."

"Milo…" I wanted to know where he was, what'd happened, why he wasn't here when I woke up. What was he doing to fix the world while fitting me in?

"While you sit here in a hospital bed, alone, when you could be in another man's bed instead, I want you to hold onto this feeling."

"Excuse me?" I gripped my thin blanket a bit too tightly, considering casting some magic I definitely was unprepared for.

"You're basically responsible for every PD on safety precautions we'll receive next year. And to clarify, when I said these Saturdays would be the death of you, I didn't expect you to take my comment so literally."

I eased. That was kind of funny in an annoying way that allowed me to drop my guard and forget my desires. I relaxed if possible. Chanelle stayed with me until visiting hours ended, attempting to coax me into staying, but very much against the doctor's advice, I discharged myself, picked up my prescriptions—including a poultice laced with magic to remedy the scars—and had Chanelle take me home.

By the time I got inside my house, I collapsed on the couch. Charlie and Carlie meowed, demanding food and attention. Carlie's overly affectionate chirps could only mean she was truly starving. I dragged myself forward into the kitchen. Carlie led me to her very overfilled bowl.

"Who?"

Milo. Who else?

When I finally revived my phone with a charger, I half-expected a hundred unread texts from Milo. Nothing. Well, not nothing. Lots of well wishes from everyone I'd ever briefly encountered, some from numbers I had never bothered saving. The incident was trending everywhere.

I hid in my room, composing a text to Milo. Something that conveyed I knew what he'd done, mostly, when it came to resolving the vision, but every word I chose sounded more like I was piecing together a little conspiracy he'd crafted. Maybe that was my paranoia about his intentions. He did this for me, for the kids, for a better future. Right?

It was hard quieting tiny doubts when I only had a fraction of the picture.

> Me: I need to talk about your vision. All of it.

I had to understand the horrors he held back.

Sinking into my bed, I watched the news. The closest I'd gotten to puzzling this mess together and talking with *Enchanter Evergreen* at this point.

"It's just further proof that Illinois' mandate to open the floodgates to everyone with new casting and licensing policies isn't working. When academies held higher standards, the staff could focus on proper safeguards, proper education. Now, suddenly, warlocks can just walk through the front door."

Wrong network to tune into. Change.

After fifteen minutes of distant tragedies, celebrity commentary, and puff pieces, the news cycled back to a report on what'd happened. Shadowy shots of Gemini Academy, making the entire building overcast with gloom—anything to sell the doom of their story.

"After the warlock incursion at Gemini Academy, we can confirm at least one instructor has been hospitalized. No updates on the severity of their injuries or current condition. Several students were targeted during this strike, possibly as a result of the new state mandate, though neither the academy nor Cerberus Guild—the first to respond to the incursion—would comment on the warlocks' motives."

The news cut from the on-scene reporter to the anchors.

"It's fortunate Cerberus Guild acted when they did. While the severity of student injuries is unclear, it's been confirmed the lack of fatalities comes from enchanter intervention as well as Cerberus single-handedly containing a facility with over eight hundred active fiends."

Christ. They were really running with it. I changed the channel, hopeful for an interview with Enchanter Evergreen circulating. There was a way to read the honesty between his staged discussions for those of us who knew what tells to look for.

"Though the case has been handed over to federal law enforcement, Enchanter Evergreen was able to give us some insight on the implications this warlock incursion raises."

Milo appeared on the screen, bright blue eyes bringing life to my dreary bedroom.

"When you only glimpse fragments of futures, it's challenging to know when and how to act. I'm disappointed in myself, the delay in my response, and the information we collected. I had no way of knowing potential links to Whitlock Industries. As always, I'm grateful to Cerberus Guild for knowing when to pursue and when it's appropriate to pass intel to other authorities. I can't give an opinion until the state makes sense of this. Honestly, I've tried to stay clear of it despite everything flying around online. Tobias has been good to the city and many guilds, but whether that's because of care, sound business, or a conscience that needs clearing, I couldn't tell you."

How the hell did Tobias Whitlock get dragged into this? Yes, Theodore was his son. Yes, my invasive delving into Tara's past made his connection to Dr. Kendall evident. But what about this demonic laboratory implicated Whitlock Industries?

I scrolled through my phone, searching through news articles.

> **Tobias Whitlock A Sinking Ship?**

Clickbait in the truest form. All it did was clear up the implications. The facility Cerberus Guild banished the fiends from was evidently an old property of Whitlock Industries, one not on the books any longer. Information retrieved connected emails between Tobias Whitlock and Stephanie Kendall, the pseudo ringleader to the most recent warlock faction. While officials withheld all details during a pending investigation, enough of the emails were leaked online to gain traction.

Whitlock Industries wasn't a sinking ship so much as holding off on public statements and postponing projects. The board of Whitlock Bank wanted to wait for certain real estate deals to smooth out but wouldn't comment if that had to do with the public outroar for Tobias Whitlock or interest rates.

Though, who could be sure if social media garnered enough to tackle a tyrant?

Milo's only tweet was a pinned retweet of a screenshotted picture to an official Cerberus Guild press release.

> The warlock faction attacking the past five months is something we should've worked harder to handle. We're saddened it took this long to resolve an issue that has plagued the hearts and minds of many within the city for months. The time it took to coordinate with other guilds and local authorities cost lives. While the most recent incursion on Gemini Academy didn't lead to fatalities, we can't call it a happy ending. We're deeply regretful for how this turmoil boiled over and affected young, aspiring witches. Moving forward, Cerberus hopes to work more closely with all the academies in the state to build stronger connections, implement better safety protocols, and educate others as well as ourselves. We're hopeful this, in some small way, can begin the process of making amends as we seek a more transparent system with city/state/federal law enforcement as well as the public at large. As much as anyone, we're deeply shocked and disturbed by the implications involving Whitlock Industries.

The retweets on that reached the thousands.

> Emily Real Take Regal @Magic4All
> Shocked? Is that why #TheInevitableFuture kept @CerberusGuild in-house for a covert strike on a facility linked to classified and undocumented research done by @WhitlockIndustries? M'kay.

They dropped a gif with a woman profusely nodding her head with the word "suuuuuurrrreeee" blinking beneath.

> Cami Castle Enchanter at Heart @CastingCowgirl
> Lots of concern about handling academies poorly. How about telling us where the #Warlock more like #UnderfundedWitch connected with @WhitlockIndustries is? #WhereIsKendall?

> Alexander Devroy Sharing What The Magic Media Won't @AlexDevroy
> #WhereIsKendall? You know, the *checks notes* warlock connected to government-sanctioned experiments funded by @WhitlockIndustries?

I scrolled through about a thousand quoted retweets, searching for any commentary by Milo. He remained absent online and from my phone. Bubbles appeared beneath my text, then stopped. Not a quippy comment, apologetic concern, or indifferent response. Just silence.

Using my dulled magics, I slept away the loneliness.

Chapter Thirty-Five

Chanelle was completely right; I should've stayed home, and come back after winter break when things calmed down. The academy buzzed with rumors and curiosity. Even in the parking lot, quelling my telepathy did little to silence the barrage of minds.

Very much against the doctor's recommendation, I lit a cigarette to settle my shaky nerves. Each inhale gave a tiny bit of confidence that I'd come here for the students. I pulled out my phone and reread Headmaster Dower's thoughtfully irritating email.

> My deepest condolences, Mr. Frost. I understand you may need more time away, which I encourage you to take. Unfortunately, I've been in contact with the panel for your homeroom coven, and they believe it's still pertinent to meet with the students and offer them the opportunity to demonstrate their magics.

Her email made it abundantly clear the panel for fledgling permits was still meeting with all the homeroom covens before break. I needed to check on my students, their state of mind, and remind them it was okay to wait. After everything, I didn't know which I feared more when I walked into my classroom. Seeing all their faces or not.

Each step brought them closer, making their thoughts and voices boom over the rest of Gemini Academy. I lingered outside my open classroom door, building the courage to face my students.

"Okay, has anyone else been interviewed?" Gael's sharklike teeth beamed.

"My dad said not to talk to the press," Layla replied.

"Yeah, but it's really cool," Gael said. "We're like local celebrities now."

I clung by the door, my forehead pressed to the cold wall, absorbing snippets of their fast-paced overlapping conversations.

"Try national."

"King Clucks and I've gained hella followers."

"My TikTok's taken off."

"All my stuff is blowing up. In a non-star shower way."

"You think the academy would let me use the footage in one of my vids?"

"No." "Really. Too bad." "Yeah, I'd love to have a clip."

"Didn't Katherine say the enchantment jammed the surveillance?"

"Oh. No recordings, I guess."

"Too bad. I wanted to show people all my badass moves."

"All you did was get your copies smashed a bunch."

"Not true."

"You wanna talk badass moves? You should've seen Kenzo."

Kenzo huffed, glaring at Gael and his other classmates.

They all continued talking over one another, making it difficult to follow, but genuine peace of mind came from each of them. Even Tara, who'd removed herself from the back of the classroom and sat comfortably in the center, nodding to questions and processing the strange sensation that came with participating. I smiled.

Of all the students, I didn't expect such relief to radiate from her. But it did. All that'd happened with Theodore, the implications with her father, rolled off her like shackles unbound.

Katherine and Caleb walked down the hallway, confidence in each as eyes from classmates fell on them. Though, Caleb brushed his hand back and forth along his recently shaved brown hair. A nervous tick and a simple gesture to remind himself not to overthink the looks; however, Katherine ran her fingers through her long-straightened hair. Bright green and almost as flashy a sight as Gael's monthly hairdos. Inspiration loomed along her surface thoughts. She'd found the emerald radiance from the sigils quite complementary to her light brown complexion and wanted something to remember the event.

They truly were unfazed by such a horrific encounter. Each of them bounced back better than me, compartmentalizing and proving increasingly resilient.

"Are your grandparents still giving you a hard time about coming back to the academy?" she asked.

Caleb paused, torn between his love for them and all they'd done in his life while equally resentful that their concern threatened his dreams. "They're not the happiest, but as of now, Gemini's still a go next semester."

Katherine leaned against the lockers with Caleb. The pair was a few feet away from me and the classroom, yet completely lost in their own universe. I crossed my arms, curious when either would notice my presence.

"Maybe you should have Enchanter Evergreen talk to them," Katherine said.

I jolted. What?

"Wait. Did he stop at your place, too?" Caleb asked.

What? My jaw was very much not on the floor. But what actual hell were they talking about?

"Yep. And I think it went well because my folks decided not to lock me in my room behind a billion protective sigils until my hundredth birthday. Guessing everyone had a similar experience."

Had Milo gone and spoken to every family involved? I had so many questions for him.

"It was totally the most amazingly spectacular visit of my life. One I missed because my grams forced my aunt to take me to another follow-up with the doctor. Apparently, I coughed suspiciously in my sleep, and they were concerned I'd gotten a lung infection or had my breathing hexed."

"Oh, that's so sweet. And completely inaccurate, but adorable." Katherine rubbed Caleb's shoulder. Each of their minds shuddered, filled with insecurity and confusion.

"More like overbearing and—" Caleb froze, his eyes rattling like a snake, locked onto me. "You're back."

"It's only been a few days," I said, biting back all the concern that exploded from them. If I let even a fraction in, I'd collapse. "You'd be amazed by the doctors and nurses at Chicago Med. Those with and without rejuvenation at their disposal."

Caleb's eyes swelled. He smiled, cheeks raised high to contain all his bursting emotions. Every doubt and fear and regret he'd had for that day bombarded my mind, a thousand feelings of failure, like he'd somehow messed up by not predicting the ending. He carried more guilt for my injuries than I did for his void vision, which I'd finally buried.

"It was practically a vacation." I suppressed his emotions, grinning like a fool. My contorted face felt foreign, so I scowled. "Now, if you don't mind, you two are already late."

"Sorry." They scuttled into the classroom.

I stepped in behind them, stunned by Jennifer and Carter's teary eyes when I entered. The entire classroom became silent—even their thoughts were cautious yet quietly curious. They'd all seen what had happened, the extent of my injuries, but it was Carter and Jennifer who worked to stitch me back together during the attack on the auxiliary gym.

"Remember, think softly," Gael Martinez whispered. *"How loud are my thoughts right now?"*

"Quiet thoughts. Easy."

"Stop thinking."   *"I hope Mr. Frost is okay."*

"He looks better."   *"His neck, it's..."*

"No, you're thinking too loudly, King Clucks. Stop it. You're distracting me."

"Everyone stop thinking so loudly," Jennifer snapped, likely wanting to add a note they not feel so much, too.

"You're all fine. I'm fine. I wouldn't be here if I wasn't."

"**Of course, he's fine. If he were that bad off, he'd still be in the hospital.**" Kenzo ground his teeth, and his glare softened. "**He's totally fine.** *Probably.*"

"You all probably assumed you wouldn't see me until the start of new year. But it'll take more than a couple warlocks, a few fiends, and some scratches for me to leave you with a sub this long. This last week before vacation isn't a break. Quite the opposite. In fact, some of you still have essays that need to be polished." I eyed a few students who gulped. They'd assumed their ordeal would give them some leeway, something I wanted very much to offer. "And everyone here has to make a big decision today."

Lots of sighs, scrunched faces, and a couple furrowed brows. Almost like a normal day.

"It's been brought to my attention that the panel which determines which first-years receive their fledgling permits will still commence."

"Wait, seriously?" Gael Rios-Vega raised his brows, flabbergasted frustration fluttered in his mind, an annoyance I shared in equal measure after reading the headmaster's email. "They should just give us our permits because of how awesome we were. Mostly me, but other people did okay, too."

"Why stop there?" I asked. "They should issue you each your very own license, too."

"Hell yeah," Gael said. "We're clearly enchanter material."

I smirked. Sarcasm soared over his head where his mind danced in clouds.

"You know, I bet I could start an online petition for it." Gael reached for his phone, typing away.

"Ba-bawk," King Clucks said.

"You're right. We should use your account."

I strolled toward Gael, placing a hand over his phone, eyeing him.

"What? King Clucks has a major fanbase. What can I say? Everyone wants my cock."

My ribs ached, stifling a chuckle. So damn irritating. "Jokes aside, the panel will be reviewing your essays over break and expecting to evaluate your magic at the end of this week. It's completely understandable if anyone would prefer to postpone until after the break."

"But I thought you said the next panel would be months away," Caleb said with a raised hand.

"Under normal circumstances, certainly. Nothing about what

happened was normal. The panel will be completely open to assembling again after the new year." I'd make certain of it. I'd hunt each member of the board down over the break and make them see reason, something clearly the headmaster couldn't handle. The kids didn't need to know it wasn't a sure thing. They needed to make this decision without the pressure of failure. And there wouldn't be any. I'd ensure it.

"Who are these panel people anyway?" Gael Martinez asked.

"A bunch of worthless nobodies who've got nothing better to do with their time, so they sit around deciding who gets to use their magic when," Kenzo said.

"Never considered myself the most renowned witch out there, but thought I was a sliver above a worthless nobody." Milo waltzed into my classroom wearing a bright smile, stunning gray suit, and flashy pink tie.

I masked my surprise at his sudden arrival. There'd been so much distance between us since the warlock incursion, since the void vision finally concluded. Milo had avoided me, likely uncertain how the conversation would go. Or perhaps glimpsed something suggesting it would go poorly. His mind was unguarded, his smile inviting, but the students made it difficult to read anything.

"Enchanter Evergreen."   *"He's so cool."*
"What's he doing here?"
"I'm gonna ask how his guild unraveled the last layer of sigils."
"I wonder if he has news on Theo."
"This is probably a better time to ask for an autograph. Less blood and carnage."

Caleb's mind whirled above the others, stitching together all the news reports he'd followed since the attack.

"All the reports said while the warlocks attacked, Enchanter Evergreen fought hundreds of fiends. Fiends that would've otherwise

gotten into the academy when that warp portal warlock opened all those doorways. Fiends that would've killed us. He also did it with limited use of his clairvoyance because of the hexed enchantments the warlock faction used to hide their intentions. He'd been tracking them down for months, using the faintest of clues. I wonder how he managed that. Guess we're lucky."

"**That loser just walked in like he owns the place.**" Kenzo crossed his arms and scoffed.

I cleared my throat, running a hand along the faint red line which remained a reminder of the warlock incursion at Gemini Academy. The gesture silenced the classroom. Each of them stared at the scar, a scar I'd hope to remove once my body required fewer antibiotics and healing treatments. No matter the rejuvenation branch, a witch could only handle so much healing in close succession.

"To answer the question on the panel, they're comprised of currently licensed and active guild enchanters. It's how academies have always given early glimpses to potential recruits."

"And I'm basically running your panel this year," Milo said, stealing their attention with enthusiasm. "I was absolutely honored by the privilege of observing your magics in action."

"I'm suddenly super pumped for Friday," Gael shouted with raised arms and inflated spikes.

"Watch it, porcupine."

"About Friday." Milo tapped his chin, appearing inquisitive, but his mind remained quiet. "The panel would actually like to speak with you all today."

"They have until the end of the week to decide. You can't just spring this on them today." On me. All while avoiding me. And every message I'd sent.

"Yes, of course, but it's just." Milo fought a frown. "Come on. It's a totally good thing."

"Fine." I ushered the students into the hallway.

Both Gaels led the class to the auditorium. One with far too much enthusiasm, the other ready to give the panel a piece of his mind with a cocky familiar at the ready.

"This is highly unorthodox, Enchanter Evergreen," I said.

"You're so formal," he whispered. "It's hot."

Kenzo strolled close to Milo, hands stuffed in his pockets. "Just to be clear, I had everything under control without you. You showing up at the last minute was unnecessary and clearly an attention grab."

Milo laughed. Kenzo's scowl didn't lessen. Milo turned back, eyeing me, then Kenzo's angry frown, then back to me. *"He's like an angrier version of you."*

"You have no idea," I said.

"You know, I think you're absolutely correct," Milo said. "Kenzo, right? I'll remember that name. The first-year student with an impressive hex branch and all that control over his roots. You're way better than I was when I joined Gemini Academy. Bet you're gonna be a hell of an enchanter one day."

Kenzo's scowl fell, his face a bit flushed. "Whatever. That's because you were probably an even bigger loser back then than you are now."

He stormed ahead, walking with both Gaels. Curiosity and excitement boomed from my students. Milo hummed a tune on loop in his mind. The academy was quiet as I stepped through the hallway. Classrooms closed off, but their minds, too. Strange. I'd figured my telepathy had recovered at this point.

We arrived at the auditorium, but it wasn't a simple panel of a half dozen enchanters. It was the entire academy. Chanelle stood by the door, removing an enchantment that brought everyone's bustling minds to life.

"I've wanted to pull one over on you with this enchantment for years now," she thought.

Cerberus Guild members lined the brick walls, none sitting, admiration in their eyes, and pride floating on the surface of their minds. Not pride in how they'd handled the fiends or in their great guild but for my homeroom coven.

"Whoa," Caleb said. His mind zipped through the full roster of enchanters in attendance in more thorough detail than I'd ever managed. Cheering classmates made him clam up, hiding behind Katherine, who smiled at the crowd.

Milo hovered past the audience to the stage, ever the showman, and walked to a podium off to the far right. What was he doing?

"When it came to my attention that the academy intended to delay your fledgling permits, I gathered the panel and recommended something different. While our guild worked tirelessly to remove the demonic threat in the distance, we did not move quickly enough to assist this passionate group in their time of need." He eyed my students. "You did that. Each of you possessed swift actions, skillful collaboration, and a true understanding of what it means to be a part of a guild."

I wandered behind the students, each hesitantly creeping forward. Enchanter Campbell urged them ahead, gesturing toward the front rows.

"Asking your homeroom coven to demonstrate your magics would be an oversight. These permits are issued based on evaluations to ensure young witches are safe and capable of casting their magics. You've all shown this." Milo grabbed a folder, withdrawing paperwork. "The most amazing aspect behind all you young witches' accomplishments comes in your humility. Reviewing the statements each of you made on the accounts of the warlock incursion on Gemini Academy, not one of you boasted your greatness. Instead, each of you detailed the successes of your classmates, sharing your pride in them, your belief they made a difference that day. I'm here to say each of you made that day a success."

Enchanter Campbell swayed to the stage, joining Milo with a large wooden box. Milo opened it, withdrawing a single fledgling permit and a pin of Cerberus' emblem.

"We'd like to show our appreciation for your homeroom coven by issuing you each your fledgling permits today and a tiny token of our gratitude with these honorary Cerberus Guild Member emblems."

"Wait, so that means no display of our magic?" Gael Rios-Vega asked, hands clutched to the back of Melanie's seat.

"I believe each of you has done a splendid job at that already," Milo answered.

The statement thrilled my homeroom.

A few first-year classmates resented they'd have to wait until break for theirs, but enthusiasm and support quelled overall envy.

Gael leaned in close to his familiar.

"This means we don't have to finish that damn essay." He snickered under his breath, recoiling when he caught me staring. *"Which is a total shame because I was so excited to finally review all of Mr. Frosty's amazingly helpful and not at all annoying or excessive notes."*

"Would Carter Howe please come up to the stage?" Milo asked.

```
Name: Carter Howe
Branch: Rejuvenation (Vitality)
```

Nervously, Carter walked up to the stage. His usual delight in the spotlight was replaced with a shyness of the audience.

"Your magic saved a life. Your resourcefulness kept your teacher alive." Milo handed Carter his permit and pin.

My eyes watered. I rolled them up to the ceiling, composing myself. Pretty certain it was all the kids' minds getting to me. Still, I joined everyone in the auditorium applauding his valiance.

"I knew you were a big softie under all that gruff emo angst,"

Chanelle's thoughts carried through the crowd.

Emo? As if.

"Jennifer Jung," Milo said, awaiting her to make her way up to the stage.

She hid behind her hair, quelling everyone's cheer because the big smile on her face felt unnatural. I sympathized, frowning in support of her desires.

```
Name: Jennifer Jung
Branch: Psychic (Empathic)
```

"Your magic kept your coven mate calm and composed. The life saved is as much because of you as anyone." Milo handed Jennifer a permit and pin.

Applause followed Jennifer all the way back to her seat.

"Katherine Harris," Milo called.

```
Name: Katherine Harris
Branch: Enchantment (Spell Craft)
```

Unlike the first two, Katherine didn't hesitate when strutting to the stage, waving to her classmates, giddy and eager for each of them to cross the stage and receive their permits, too.

"Your skill in not only deciphering sigils but in crafting spells kept fellow students safe and unharmed. The connections and magics you've harnessed this year will take you far in the future." Milo handed Katherine a permit and pin.

Each of them held such joy for the other, excited and nervous about their turn. I continued joining them in applause, hopeful of holding onto this happiness for the entire day.

"Jamius Watson," Milo called.

```
Name: Jamius Watson
Branch: Alteration (Duplication)
```

Unwilling to walk up alone, two copies dragged the anxious original onto the stage.

"Your wonderful magic helped divert many fiends from your classmates. It's with no uncertainty I can say that you made a vital difference." Milo handed Jamius a permit and pin.

I clapped, realizing how each of them had such an intricate role during the warlock incursion. Each of them made today happen.

"Yaritza Vargas," Milo called.

```
Name: Yaritza Vargas
Branch: Cosmic (Star Shower)
```

Bursting with delight, Yaritza squealed and flew onto the stage. I tensed, only mildly concerned at her desire to unleash a small celebratory flurry of comets.

"Your very unique magic not only assisted you in eliminating fiends but provided your classmates with a power they needed in the right moment. You should be incredibly proud of your gift." Milo handed Yaritza a permit and pin.

I applauded her, more impressed she'd resisted her urge to show off in front of all the enchanters.

"Layla Smythe," Milo called.

```
Name: Layla Smythe
Branch: Bestial (Therianthropy)
```

"No, you gotta walk up full-on cougar!" Gael shouted, and his familiar clucked at the suggestion.

Layla cracked her middle finger against her chin, smirking and not so subtly flipping Gael off.

"Your bravery and belief in your coven mate's plan ensured a safe detainment of a very dangerous and elusive warlock." Milo handed Layla a permit and pin.

She walked off stage, growling at Gael, which the applause helped mask.

"Melanie Dawson," Milo called.

```
Name: Melanie Dawson
Branch: Primal (Fire)
```

"It wasn't the power of your flames which made a difference, but your control of them." Milo handed Melanie a permit and pin.

I honed-in on Milo's mind above the others and the applause.

"Gael Martinez," Milo called.

```
Name: Gael Martinez
Branch: Augmentation (Spikes)
```

Sheepishly, Gael fixed his spiky snowflake blue-white hair, emulating Milo's spiky blond hair. He waved to everyone as he waltzed onto the stage.

"I can see you possess a lot of pizazz and charisma that'll take you far in this industry. It's also impressive how well you understand your branch. It was your swift thinking and collaboration with a classmate that shielded your instructor in his time of need." Milo handed Gael a permit and pin. "Thank you."

Milo's mind stirred with the memory of witness statements he'd read a hundred times over but also with the literal actions of Gael lunging flaming spikes, which intercepted a counter that would've taken me out full force. This was a potential future he'd seen—no longer potential, but a cemented memory Milo carried. He'd believed in me, in my students, so much so that it blossomed brightly along his surface thoughts.

"Gael Rios-Vega and King Clucks, Peckfender of the Unhatched Dozen," Milo called.

```
Name: Gael Rios-Vega
Branch: Bestial (Familiar)
```

Gael kept his familiar perched on his shoulder as he walked onto the stage. He remained quiet and formal with each step. I squinted, trying to glean his scheme, but his mind was simply in awe of Enchanter Evergreen.

"You and your familiar possess quite a powerful bond, one that allowed for a tremendous combo, saving a fellow classmate."

"Woo," Tara shouted, before crouching low in her seat, cheeks bright red.

Milo handed Gael a permit and two pins. Gael slung an arm around Milo's shoulder and snapped a selfie on his phone. Gael and King Clucks crowed in unison as the camera light flashed. Everyone applauded and giggled as Gael and his rooster strutted off stage and back to their seats.

"Tara Whitlock," Milo called.

```
Name: Tara Whitlock
Branch: Ward (Sealing)
Branch: Cosmic (Shadows)
Branch: Arcane (Intangibility)
```

"You possess incredible control over your root magics, which helped so many. But it was your powerful branch magics which you showed such mastery for that helped contain dangerous fiends." Milo handed Tara a permit and pin.

"*Maybe I'm not useless. I do belong here.*" Tara swelled with pride for the first time in her branch magics. I clapped for Tara quite possibly longer than anyone else, amazed by how much she'd accomplished on her own.

"Kenzo Ito," Milo called.

```
Name: Kenzo Ito
Branch: Hex (Disruption)
```

"I heard you were a bit rattled when the warlocks arrived, something even I still struggle with each time I start a new mission. It's commendable that whatever personal emotions were going through your mind, you didn't allow them to consume you." Milo was aware of Kenzo's history, carefully talking around it in the auditorium. "Maintaining composure, pushing through the exhaustion of casting, and balancing the needs of those around you above yours are all traits that take many guild witches time to learn. Based on the admiration from your coven, it's clear you'll make a fine enchanter one day."

Milo handed Kenzo a permit and pin, leaning close and whispering something. Kenzo stepped back, eyes wide. His entire body stilled. Everyone stared, waiting for something from either of them. Kenzo nodded, and Milo gave him a half smile.

"**Say it. Just say it.**" Kenzo squeezed the pin tightly, his fury not quelled but pieces broken off, released into the ether. His gaze met Milo's and expressed what he couldn't say. "*Thank you.*"

He rushed back to his seat and sat between both Gaels.

"Whoa, dude. What'd Enchanter Evergreen say to you?" Gael asked.

"None of your fucking business, bird brain," Kenzo snapped.

Okay, not all his rage.

"Caleb Huxley," Milo called.

```
Name: Caleb Huxley
Branch: N/A
```

Caleb's mind whirled with a thousand confident reactions he needed to display in this moment, his first opportunity to show he'd earned his place at Gemini Academy and would one day be a guild witch. All that planning melted away when Milo patted his shoulder, and the boy trembled with a frazzled expression. Stage fright was something we'd have to work on next semester because there'd be a next semester for all of us.

"Everyone in your homeroom noted it was your swift thinking which provided the direction they required during a highly stressful situation. Your resourcefulness, bravery, thorough attention to detail, and a thousand other factors I'm sure I've overlooked helped make this happen." Milo handed Caleb a permit and pin. "You're going to make an incredible enchanter and leader one day."

Everyone applauded Caleb while I fixated on the future Milo gleaned. I couldn't see it, wrapped in the magic of his visions, but the joy and certainty radiating from Milo eased the weight I'd carried this semester. Our roles might've been small and secretive, but whatever bright future Milo saw for Caleb Huxley, we made happen. All of us. Caleb himself. His classmates. Milo. Even me.

The auditorium became silent, and I waited for the headmaster to dismiss us or Enchanter Evergreen to spout off some speech about how every kid in here helped make a better world.

"Would Mr. Frost please join me on stage?" he asked.

Silencing the thoughts of the auditorium didn't remove any anxiety. Everyone's eyes locked onto me, but I fixated on Milo's, hopeful it'd ease my tension. I'd wanted a moment alone with Milo since waking at the hospital. Now, I literally had a room full of people watching our every word.

"I actually attended this very academy alongside your teacher. Back then, I knew him as Dorian. Eventually, we both joined Cerberus, where he had a stage name almost as cool as The Inevitable Future." Milo winked, using it to pause, composing the fear he'd kept buried this entire time. But in the silence, I caught a whiff of it. "I'd like to believe every instructor would demonstrate the devotion and selflessness you did during the warlock incursion. Your students mentioned your bravery, how hard you fought, the strength of your magics, and I am honored to know you, Dorian Frost."

He grabbed a plaque with a golden etched inscription from Enchanter Campbell.

>   Dorian Frost
>   The Ubiquitous Present
>   Thank you for always keeping a watchful eye on
>   your students

I let the audience's kindness and excitement envelop me, thankful to Finn for teaching me to embrace the present, and grateful to Milo for helping create a future I could be happy in.

Chapter Thirty-Six

I awaited the ceremony's ending and found Enchanter Evergreen backstage. My homeroom coven was content "chilling" in the auditorium or pestering Cerberus Guild Enchanters with questions.

"You've been avoiding me," I said.

"I haven't." Milo smiled, his cheeks shaky. "Since the warlock incursion on Gemini, the fallout's been… hmm… catastrophic isn't the right word. It hasn't been bad, but not good either. Potentially hopeful so long as it assuaged the right minds, the proper hearts eased, and the well-positioned egos are stroked."

"Egos like Enchanter Campbell?"

"She's wanted to run Cerberus for years, so when presented with an opportunity to jump over the throne and onto the board where real power and connections lie, she couldn't pass it up. Of all the witches I know, she's not one easily deterred in the future I've glimpsed." Milo chuckled. "I felt you, you know. When you were—when I thought I'd made the wrong choice. I felt you in my mind touching my soul."

With careful steps, I slowly closed the distance between us. Each step made my knees weak, my hands clammy, heart bursting. "All this was to expose Tobias? Whitlock Industries?"

"No. That's a man and company that have weathered many storms. He won't so easily be contained, but this future, present, offers one benefit on his outcome. For the first time in a long time, the right eyes are watching him, observing everything he's done, doing, or will do. Something I've been good at."

"And that's because of the intel gathered at the warlock facility, that laboratory?" I shuddered at the lingering memories from Theodore revealing that dank, dark place.

"Yup."

"So releasing that information to the public helped ensure this present?"

"I didn't release anything. Didn't touch the intel at any point of the investigation. And I can honestly say I have no idea how this leak occurred, no matter who asks or what magics they ask with." Milo's mind opened, inviting me. There'd be a lengthy investigation of all the events that occurred and the implications made. The dots connecting Milo's memories held gaps because his only involvement came from unreadable, hidden potential futures.

"Clever," I said. "But that still doesn't answer why this future. Why this plan?"

"I'm so sorry, Dorian. I never meant for it to be this, this…" Milo's breathing hastened, and his entire body shook, a trembling leaf ready to be carried off in the wind, never to be seen again.

"I understand why you kept it from me. If I'd known leading my students into this, relying on them, trusting them to protect themselves, each other, and me, I would've shut it down," I said softly. "What I want to understand is why this future meant so much to you. Why you gambled so much."

"It wasn't for you. Not entirely. Although yes, in every future I glimpse, I make sure there's some potential for your happiness."

"Our happiness." I steadied his shaky shoulders. With a soulful, compassionate gaze, I wanted him to understand I didn't resent him for his choice. "I'm not mad. I don't require an apology because there's nothing to forgive. Simply understanding."

"Every vision's different. Some are binge-watching an entire series in a matter of seconds. Others, a final episode with no context or snippets highlighting the best of moments. I can't say what potentials outweigh the others, but before our kiss, the merger of magics, the glimpse of that void vision, I'd seen your students. A few. A branchless boy trying to be a hero without the support or heart he required. An angry kid pursuing forces no amount of rage could overcome. A girl lost in despair as feuding tyrants devastated the city."

"Fuck." So much of their potential futures concerned me, and while nothing I did would prevent them from any choices they made in their lives, I didn't want those potential outcomes for those three or any of my kids. I'd push myself further than before, ensuring they had as many opportunities as possible. I casually nodded to the side exit. Bracing for the frigid outside, I reached for my smokes. "Care to join me?"

Milo's somber blue eyes gave me pause. I'd started and stopped smoking a dozen times in my life, unwilling to surrender an addictive habit that made this unbearable world a little easier. Always wondering, though, which would be roulette. The doctor's speech on my immune system requiring all its strength for the coming weeks rang in my mind. I tucked the pack away. Not forever, but until Milo's expression didn't contain such concern.

"What happens next, Enchanter Evergreen?"

"Not sure. Guess it's up to you. I've sort of been afraid to look since your near-death experience after I betrayed your trust and confidence for a future I hope was the correct path."

"You didn't," I said.

Milo's shyness bloomed, his anxious youthfulness reemerging after years spent burying that panicked side of himself. My mind stirred up memories of Finn dragging Milo out of that shell, tapping on mine despite furious protesting. He never allowed us to accept our futures were anything other than three meant to be together, successful, and happy.

I smiled, thinking about Finn. For the first time since his death, I didn't bury the regrets which still rang from that day, the doubts which always lingered, or the happiness which I'd spent so much time resisting. I sat in those emotions, content to move forward.

"Well, whatever potential future there is, it better get us on that happiest happy ending that ever happened," I said. "God knows, you've been spouting it for so long, I'd be a bit disappointed."

"Just a bit?" Milo's mind calmed, confidence returning, joy taking root where it belonged. "There is one thing I saw, which could potentially—though never certain—be a good sign for the future."

"And what's that?"

"Cerberus is throwing this party over the holidays. Sort of a holly jolly, let's make sure the clients forget all the recent news and get them hammered on eggnog."

I brushed Milo's hand, an image of my younger self in an ugly sweater, frowning between a jovial Finn and Milo flashed.

"It could be fun," he said.

"It won't be. It's not how I spend my breaks."

"It's one night."

One I'd give. Because it'd make Milo happy, and that made me happy. "I hate that I love you."

"What don't you hate?"

Milo ran his hand along the small of my back, pulling me into a soft embrace. A gentle kiss quelled all outside thoughts. His easy temperament revealed the potential futures constantly playing had paused. In this brief moment, the world vanished, our minds resonating on a memory of a ridiculous holiday party, one Milo and Finn had dragged me to for prospective clients at Cerberus. I couldn't hold the three of us forever, but I was happy moving forward with Milo.

I'd use this time together, this winter break, to build something with Milo. I'd repair what I had kept severing for years. Then I'd return to the academy after the new year, hopeful and ready to invest my heart in more than my students. In myself, too.

THE END

...until second semester.

Acknowledgments

I would like to thank all the readers who took a chance on Three Meant To Be! I truly hope you enjoyed the journey of Dorian and his first-year homeroom coven. One of my favorite things about this story was working to bring the students to life. Exploring their personal journeys alongside Dorian's was the most cathartic experience of my life and I really hope some of the characters stick with you like they have with me. And, if you're curious to see where Dorian and Milo's next step leads, please know I'll be sharing book two soon. There are plenty of adventures left to share from the staff and students running through the halls of Gemini Academy.

If you enjoyed the story (or even if you didn't) please consider leaving a rating and/or review on your thoughts. It means the world to me that you gave my story a chance and every rating/review really helps boost a book's visibility for other readers. No pressure though because I'm already grateful you picked up this book to begin with.

I'd like to give a huge shoutout to my wonderful editor, Charlie Knight. They are the greatest champion I could ask for when strengthening my stories and helping make them the best version. It's been a fantastic experience working with them and their notes on shaping all the stories I want to put out to the world.

For those of you who enjoyed this adult fantasy with some teenage angst, keep in mind I also have a delightful young adult paranormal fantasy. Crescentville Haunting is equal parts snarky and scary. There's also another adult project planned for 2023, so if you're interested in learning more, consider checking out my author website (mnbennet.com). Feel free to subscribe to my newsletter where I offer monthly updates and some sneak peeks.

Author Bio

MN Bennet is a high school teacher, writer, and reader. He lives in the Midwest, still adjusting to the cold after being born and raised in the South.

He enjoys writing paranormal and fantasy stories with huge worlds (sometimes too big), loveable romances (with so much angst and banter), and Happily Ever Afters (once he's dragged his characters through some emotional turmoil).

When he's not balancing classes, writing, or reading, he can be found binge watching anime or replaying Dragon Age II for the millionth time.

Author website:

https://www.mnbennet.com

Amazon page:

https://www.amazon.com/stores/MN-Bennet/author/B0BLJJK5NF

Goodreads page

https://www.goodreads.com/author/show/23017668.M_N_Bennet